The Pennymores

The Pennymores

and the Curse of the Invisible Quill

Eric Koester

New Degree Press

The Pennymores
and the Curse of the Invisible Quill

ISBN   979-8-88504-053-2 *Paperback*
          979-8-88504-054-9 *Kindle Ebook*
          979-8-88504-056-3 *Ebook*

To Quinn, Parker & Aven,

We imagined this story together and its heart, magic, and sparkle come from each of you. I was honored to be the scribe who tried to bring your imaginations to life on the pages of this book. Please don't forget this when you're teenagers and think much less fondly of your dad.

All Writing Is Magic.

Contents

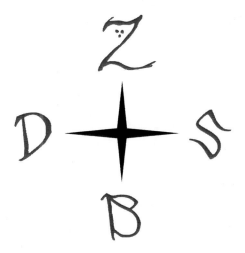

Chapter One

The Match Was Struck

"Start with *once upon a time*, okay," the elderly woman offered gently, "and you just go on from there."

The young girl standing in front of the woman nodded and took a deep breath.

"Once—once upon a time," said Parker Pennymore. Both her sisters and her brother stared at her, waiting for the nightly ritual of a bedtime story to begin. Parker paused and bit her lower lip.

"You've heard this like a bazillion times," her older sister Quinn offered. "It's totally easy."

Lady Julie Windhorn glanced at Quinn, narrowing her eyes slightly before turning back to the middle sister. "Parker, just recite the story however you remember it. You're a beautiful storyteller. I know that."

"Okay," Parker said, her fingers fiddling with the edges of her nightgown. "So, once upon a time... once... there—there was..."

Quinn shifted around in her bed while her younger sister Aven and brother Riley made faces at one another. But no words came from Parker's mouth. All she could see were the words jumbling in her brain like they always did, her heart beating so strongly she could feel each *thump-thump,*

thump-thump into the tips of her fingers. Faster and faster, she felt the beats. *Thump-thump, thump-thump.*

"Do you just want me to do it?" Quinn whispered to Lady Julie, who shook her head.

Thump-thump, thump-thump.

"Once upon—" Lady Julie repeated.

"No, no, no! I hate this—all of this!" Parker yelled, running to her bed, her face red and flushed.

"See?" Quinn said. "I could've just done it."

"No! It's not fair. None of it," Parker said through her rapid breaths. "Why do you make us stand and say these stupid stories over and over and over again?"

Lady Julie walked over to the girl and sat on her bed, patting her forearm. Then she leaned down to meet Parker's gaze. "We recite our stories so we never forget. It's how we all remember. All stories are magic."

"Hmmmmmffff," Parker responded.

"You know she doesn't even care if you get it wrong, Parker," Quinn said. "So, you just try. That's what I do."

Parker rolled her eyes at her older sister. Julie brushed a strand of her gray and black hair over her ear and turned back toward the eldest sister. "Quinn Pennymore," she said, shaking her head as she spoke, "you are just like your father. You'll always try to fix everything, even a younger sister's hurt feelings. This will certainly serve you well, my dear—just not right at *this* moment."

Then she turned back to Parker, the girl's eyes closed and lips pursed as she stewed over her embarrassing recitation performance. "But you, my love, remind me every day of your grandmother, one of the most amazing people I've ever known. Her spirit fills you. And one day soon, you'll understand why you must recite these stories so that you can be like her." She leaned in close and whispered with a mischievous smile, "It's your destiny, Parker Pennymore."

The children's bedroom was tidy but littered with patterned rugs, colorful cushions, and the children's toys, including well-worn dolls, a yellow dollhouse, and a pile of adult clothing they'd wear in their imaginary parties and events for the youngest children. Each of the four beds had its designated bright color, complete with matching quilts and shams. The children's parents stood in the doorway to their room, admiring this happy evening ritual.

The eldest sister, Quinn, almost a teenager now, begged for her own room away from "the littles," as she often called them. But their parents resisted, hoping to keep their children together in the room as long as they could.

"Tonight, you will hear this story; an important story; *your* story," Lady Julie, their caretaker, said as she brought a small stool in front of the four beds and lowered herself down. Her kind eyes locked with each of the Pennymore children now tucked in for the evening.

"In the beginning, there was only water."

The sound of a towering wave echoed through the room, but the walls and bedding remained dry.

"Until mountains and land rose from the seas."

The candles lighting the bedroom cast eerie shadows as the flames rose and danced in oranges, reds, and yellows. The resulting smoke twisted, creeping upward to fill the ceiling.

"And a new world emerged—Fonde."

Quinn groaned. "Not this story again. Can't you tell us an adventure story? Maybe about a girl who builds a flying carriage to escape and go on quests around the entire world? You know what, it's okay; I can tell it."

She squirmed into the pillows propped behind her, adjusting her goggles atop her head. She insisted upon wearing them even at bedtime. As the eldest, she staked her claim on the bed nearest the door, and no matter how much her siblings begged, she would not move.

"Noooooo, we *always* do inventions and exploring—always, always. Tonight, let's do one about the hidden magic libraries, the literati," Parker said from the next bed.

The third and youngest sister, Aven, threw her head back and howled. *"Arrrruuuuu!* Wolves, we have to do wolves tonight. My brother and sisters get to hear their stories every day."

"Sea. Creatures. Sea. Creatures," chanted Riley with a slight slur of his R's as young children often do. He was the youngest of the siblings and the only boy, which meant his sisters stuck him in the bed nearest the window. "Come on. It's my turn."

Lady Julie outstretched her hand, slowly lowering it to her lap until the children settled. She inhaled deeply.

"Fonde, the motherland, was a perfect home, and deep inside her was a great power, the greatest ever known—magic to bend mind, heart, and body. And soon, all of Fonde was teeming with life: men, animals, birds, dwarfs, elves, giants, fairies, wolves, sea creatures, flowers, treetops, great and small, and so many others flourished in harmony and peace."

Another sigh. "But everyone already knows *this* story," said Quinn with a grimace. "We've heard it like a *thousand* times."

Parker furrowed her brow, furiously nodding in agreement.

Their mother brought a finger to her lips, encouraging her children to listen. Their father touched his wife's arm and motioned to the hallway, where they spoke in hushed tones while Lady Julie continued her story.

"Fonde was generous with her power and would gift some creatures with capabilities, which would let them harness her magic. These remarkable individuals would come to be known as the Serifs. They were the magic writers, and through their writing of ancient letters, they were able to heal the sick and make cities and entire mystical worlds rise. They could also soar with the birds and swim underwater with the fish, feed the hungry with bountiful harvests, explore the highest peaks and deepest caves, and bring all of Fonde's creatures into a golden age."

"So cool," Aven whispered.

"You guys wouldn't believe the engineering that went into building a place like that," Quinn said.

Lady Julie smiled. "Oh, it was the most spectacular thing I've ever seen. Magic can be so stunning." She lowered her head and continued, "Alas, danger, destruction, and death lay in the magic too. And as so many awed at its beauty, others fixated on the darkness within it. Some began to use Fonde's powers, especially its magic writing, to destroy, imprison, and kill. Evil magic writers terrorized the lands, wiping entire villages away and raining darkness that killed the crops and livestock with a stroke of their dark quills that bore the evil eye."

She paused to let the words sink in.

"Anyone who stood up to them would vanish," she continued. "And so, this dark magic grew stronger and stronger, causing fear, anger, and chaos. Soon a great war broke out among all the creatures of Fonde. The Serifs' bravest warriors battled the Ravagers, and magic Serif writers saved Fonde from evil. Many were lost in the battle."

"Oh no, were they okay?" Riley asked, shaking his head.

Lady Julie gasped.

For the briefest moment, Parker saw a glowing red aura circling Riley. She blinked, and it was gone.

"Then what?" Aven asked.

"Then, one day, high in the Grootten Mountains," she continued, "one brave Serif writer summoned the ancient power of goodness and light and pushed back the evil forces from the brink. That act defeated the leader of the evil magic writers, snapping his dark-eyed writing quill. Through this sacrifice, his powers were destroyed, and his forces scattered to the four corners, never to return."

As the woman emphasized the words *snapping*, *destroyed*, and *scattered*, the candle flames seemed to dance in unison, causing the two youngest children to flinch in their beds.

"And after this brave victory, the Ancients would forever forbid all magic writing to keep Fonde safe from the evil dark forces that once invaded the land. Never again were magic writers to return."

She glanced at the children's parents, who still quarreled in whispers outside the bedroom. Then she leaned toward the children.

"But they *did* return," she said in a hushed voice. "The Ravagers, the evil magic writers, they returned to *this* world."

"Wait, what?" Quinn exclaimed, leaning forward.

Quinn and Parker looked at one another, their eyes wide. "Ravagers— evil magic writers—have returned to this world?" Parker asked.

"A few short years ago, before any of you were born, a young writer, a poet named Dagamar, became filled with rage, greed, hatred, and vengeance. He found a way to harness dark magical writing once again, controlling powers deep within Fonde, and the attacks began again. The silent darkness."

"Silent darkness?" Parker asked.

"Yes," Julie said, taking a deep breath. "His is a power to inflict a permanent silence on his enemies. That is the silent darkness. Silence *forever*. His attacks left many without words, wandering aimlessly and unable to speak or communicate. This darkness silences your tongue for *eternity*."

The children shifted in their beds, transfixed on her story.

"Dagamar and his army of Ravagers gave birth to this terrible darkness, and from it, the silent darkness afflicted all those who dared confront him. The grim, heavy smog of evil rose from the heart of the Grootten Mountains once again."

"Dagamar?" Quinn asked. "He can steal your voice and stop you from ever speaking?"

From outside the doorway, the parents silenced. They turned their gazes to Lady Julie. But Julie didn't stop.

"Yes. Forever. But thankfully, a brave magic writer—a Serif—once again stopped him," Lady Julie said. "*But,* this time, the writer could not snap the dark quill. They left Dagamar wounded and scarred on the left side of his body."

Her fingers slowly traced down from her left shoulder to her left hand.

"He's been in hiding ever since, healing and regaining power at every chance possible," Lady Julie said. "We see the voiceless again... more struck by the dark quills, the evil eyes. The Ravagers leave a black inscription when they do. I've seen them. This darkness is rising again and will continue to spread, forcing creature after creature into hiding, destroying our homes, muting children and anyone who dares stand up, and draining the life from Fonde..."

Father rushed into the room and motioned her to stop. "Thank you, Lady Julie," he said with a forced smile and awkward chuckle. "That's enough stories for tonight. Let's not put such wicked thoughts in the children's heads before bedtime."

"We *must* destroy his dark quill," she continued speaking over him louder than before with her eyes closed. "Otherwise, the silent darkness will *devour* us all."

A dark shadow moved across the wall behind her, consuming shadow figures in its wake.

The youngest sister screamed.

"That's enough!" Father shouted, stomping toward the center of the room. He calmed his voice before saying, "There are no Serifs or silent darkness or dark quills. We're safe. Dagamar is a bedtime story villain. That's all."

"There are *real* magic writers?" Parker asked Lady Julie, completely ignoring her father and standing on the bed waving an imaginary feather quill in the air at her younger sister and brother. "Poof! Poof! Zap!"

Her siblings squealed and ducked under their covers.

"No. Stop," answered their father with a tense smile. "Nothing lies beyond Everly but fields, streams, and mountains. As long as we stay in our very safe home, we'll be fine."

"You know the legends are true," said Lady Julie, standing to face their parents. "They should know the truth. I see her in them."

Mother looked at their father and shook her head. "It's not their time."

"His power is growing," Lady Julie continued. "They will have to destroy him. They will have to stop the silent darkness again."

"They?" Quinn asked, clutching her bedsheets. "They who?"

"Wait! I think she means *us*," Parker exclaimed, pointing to herself and jumping up and down. "You mean *we* are the *they*? She means *we* are the *they*!"

The two youngest siblings stood on their beds and joined in, jumping up and down, chanting: "We are the they! We are the they!"

A smile crept across Lady Julie's face.

"I said *enough*," their father repeated, his arms folded across his chest.

"How come you never told us this before?" Quinn said, still huddled in her blankets. "Is this true? Magic writers returned? Dagamar and the Ravagers could bring silent darkness *here*?" She looked at the adults and waited for an answer.

Mother solemnly stared at the floor.

"You can go," said Father, motioning Lady Julie to the door. "Good night."

She nodded, her expression unchanged as she walked through the door, closing it behind her.

***

It was quiet in the tunnel-like hallway, save for the muted voices of the parents and their children through the closed door. A long breath escaped her lungs as Lady Julie stood outside the bedroom in the tower of Garamond Castle.

Then she smirked and slowly shook her head. This wasn't quite how she'd imagined the four most important children in both the magical and non-magical world would learn of their fate.

"*We are the they*," did have a nice ring to it, she thought. They were only children, and being responsible for stopping the most powerful magic writer in history wasn't something she wished on anyone. She hoped her actions tonight would be enough.

Forces far beyond what their parents wanted the children to know were at play. The Ravagers had become bolder and brasher in their use of magic writing, leaving their black etchings in the fabric of the non-magical world again. The Illiterates hunted the non-magical and magical writers without distinction now, threatening anyone with a quill. Since the great war, these anti-writing zealots took it upon themselves to enforce the rules from the Ancients, who first forbade only the Serifs from magic writing. Fear had a powerful way of warping reasonable ideas into wickedness and retribution—even if the intention had been to prevent another war.

The zeal of the Illiterates moved beyond the rules against magic writing into the writing of any kind—letters, books, news, any symbols, and all teachings that could lead a child to learn to read or write. Soon, the people of Fonde feared the written word far beyond the Ancients' decree.

The kingdom was teetering on edge. It had become a powder keg.

Outside the children's room stood the small, wooden chair Lady Julie sat in each night until she was sure all four children were asleep. As she'd done every night, she lowered herself into the chair and closed her eyes. Tonight, she slumped over, rubbing her temples as though she had a headache.

The bedroom door opened, and the parents rushed past her without a glance.

Everything was in motion.

Lady Julie opened her eyes and stood with a deep, cleansing breath. She traced the staircase's iron railings with her fingertips and admired the sconces she'd lit many times. She'd climbed these stairs and chased the giggling children for more than a dozen years since Quinn was only a tiny baby. Tiptoeing toward the door, she avoided the planks of wood that would groan under her weight. She felt she belonged in that room with these children who showed her love, compassion, and happiness for many years. Inside the bedroom, the horrors of her youth blew away like smoke.

The time had come.

Lady Julie adjusted her gray cloak, tucked her long hair at the nape of her neck, and pulled the hood over her head.

Her hands shook as she twisted the doorknob to the bedroom door. Nothing had changed—Quinn's leather riding boots, Parker's sewing needles, Aven's yellow dollhouse, Riley's worn wooden toys, and the familiar and comforting musk of sweat from long summer days outdoors.

As she stepped inside and closed the door, she squinted, trying to highlight any source of light as a guide, but only found an eerie glow from the full moon peeking through the curtains. It made everything, even a pile of dresses heaped in a corner, look like a shadow man. Unsettling voices echoed in her head.

Lady Julie reached inside her dark cloak and removed a gray and white feather quill, gripping it between her fingertips. Her lips moved without a sound, and the tip of the quill began to glow a deep red-orange color.

Sparks exploded into the air around her as she pressed the glowing tip of the quill into the stone wall next to the door. Their hot glow lit her smile, extinguishing on her shoulders as she wrote.

Energy flared through her fingertips, tingling along her limbs with each stroke of her quill. For so long, she had slapped her hand to stop the urge to write. She felt younger in the glow of magic, the powerful jolt of energy pulsing through her body as each stroke of her quill left an inscription burned into the stone.

With the last stroke on the stone, the clouds framed by the window formed into animal-like figures, galloping across the horizon and sucking away the light from the moon and every star as though inhaling them. The owls, crickets, and frogs fell silent. Not even the wind dared make a sound.

Writing these simple words was punishable by death. There was, however, no turning back.

Lady Julie paused to let her eyes adjust before gliding the gray quill over the stone wall again, a glimmering cloud of illuminating dust spread from its tip across the room.

"Stardust," she imagined the children would say if they saw. It hovered over each bed and then settled across the four sleeping children.

The windows flew open.

Be quick about it.

Lady Julie snuck toward the sleeping girls on her tiptoes and held her breath. As she approached each, she steadied herself on the bedposts at the foot of the bed, pausing at each sleeping child, staring for a few seconds before finally settling beside the last bed near the open window.

"Witch," the townspeople would say. "The dark witch will kill our children."

She never meant to hurt any of them.

This was the only way.

She retrieved a small, tattered cloth from her pocket, drew back the hood of her cloak, and knelt beside the bed where Riley soundly slept.

Hands shaking and heart thudding, she touched her quill's tip to the bedpost. Silver dust whirled and sparkled around the bed, lifting and pulling back the covers, revealing the petite child, only a few years old, wearing his favorite King Arthur pajamas. She gently placed the fabric on the sleeping boy, covering Arthur's smiling face.

He tossed and turned, and his eyebrows furrowed.

Lady Julie rolled the quill between her fingers, anxious the cloth would fail her. She touched the quill to the tattered cloth, stroking a single letter. When she'd finished, the fabric gleamed a soft lavender before stretching like taffy and covering the boy's entire body until only his face remained exposed. A smile crept across the boy's face.

Bang.

Startled, Lady Julie used the bed as cover and stared back at the door.

Bang-Bang.

Riley stirred again.

She tucked her arms under the boy, pulled him from his bed, and hurried to the window.

Bang. Bang.

The sound was closer.

With the boy in her arms, she climbed onto the windowsill.

What if there is another way?

She shook her head, remembering the reddish aura she'd seen surrounding the boy. One life for three lives was the bargain.

Cupping the boy's neck under her right forearm, Lady Julie reached into the pocket of her cloak and removed the quill. She raised it to the top of the window and inscribed a series of words on the wooden frame, which pulsed red and orange, spilling bright sparks upon them both, enveloping them.

"Be safe, my children," she whispered, pulling her hood up. She nestled the small child close to her chest and jumped.

***

A flash of silvers, golds, oranges, and reds exploded over the town of Everly, and anyone watching the night sky throughout Fonde would have seen bright, vivid, beautiful colored shooting stars racing across the night sky as if streaking to every corner of the world.

The unusual cloud creatures evaporated from the sky, and the lights of the moon and stars and sounds of a summer night returned. Above that window, three words remained singed into the wooden window frame.

The bedroom was quiet. Hidden by the back leg of the bedside table was a tiny red-orange stone. It glowed ever so slightly and then burned out.

Magic writers had returned.

The match was struck.

Chapter Two

The Secret Writing Society

Look, no eleven-year-old sets out to start a rebel alliance, but as the leader of the Plumes, the largest secret writing society in all of Everly, it's my duty. Isn't it? Parker Pennymore thought.

A war is coming; I know it is. So we built a secret society because no one else was doing anything about it. And yeah, we're just a bunch of misfits, outcasts, and nobodies, but when the punishment for writing was... well, death, who else was going to join us? It's not like the royal kids are trading in their comfy lives for death sentences.

Nope.

Does that make me some kind of troublemaker?

I guess if that all counts as trouble, then yeah, you can call me a troublemaker. Turns out, someone needs to be.

A full year had passed since the Pennymore sisters had discovered Riley's empty bed and read the charred inscription above their bedroom window. Things had been challenging for them all, but Parker found herself at odds with nearly everyone. She'd been expelled twice, had four tutors quit, and had made at least three of them cry. She knew one thing for sure: Today was the day her parents had finally had enough.

She honestly tried to be good, do what she's told, and follow the rules. No one understood her. Everyone said she misbehaved, needed to try harder, or had stage fright.

Today her tutor, Frau Dagogus, had given her a paragraph to memorize. One single paragraph. Four sentences. They'd practiced it at least a hundred times. It was in her head, and she could do it. Then, her tutor had her parents come to listen to her recite what she'd memorized at the end of the day.

"Okay, now like we practiced. Recite the words back to me," Frau instructed in her annoying, singsongy voice. "I know you can do it."

Standing in front of her tutor and her parents, Parker felt it—her heart racing uncontrollably and each beat pounding in the tips of her fingers. *Thump-thump, thump-thump.* She felt hot, her eyes became hazy with purple streaks, and she ground her teeth as the words and sentences and letters began to jumble and twist in her brain.

It was going to happen again.

"You're doing great, Parker," Frau offered. "Just breathe."

She wasn't doing great, and she knew it. *The pounding. The pounding.* Standing in front of the class to recite something was her absolute worst nightmare. That's why kids started calling her Freeze Pop. And why punching her bully, Frederick Chickory, in the nose had felt so good. Totally worth the second expulsion.

"You're doing great," Frau Dagogus singsonged.

Heart thudding in her fingertips was the opposite of great. Her parents watched from afar and nodded her on, but brain freeze shot through her temples worse than any ice cream headache.

The brain fog cleared, leaving her mind blank. She opened her eyes, looked straight at Frau Dagogus, and blurted, "Detestable Dagogus! You're as disgusting a person as the world has ever seen! Plus, your singy-sounding voice is like knives in my ears. You are *de-test-able* and the worst tutor I've had yet!"

Yep, *exactly* not what she'd spent all day memorizing. *Freeze... popped.*

A pitcher of purple juice floated off the table, flew above Frau Dagogus's head, and dumped the sticky liquid, drenching her from head to toe. Vases of flowers followed, tossing an endless river of roses and daisies and lilies from all angles. It turned her teacher into a human-sized abominable flower woman.

Okay, that juice and abominable flower woman part didn't happen, although Parker definitely imagined it. She smirked, wishing it had.

Mother and Father's smiles turned to frowns, and they ducked their heads to not look at Parker. They'd seen enough, and her tutor excused herself from the room.

As Frau Dagogus left, Parker saw she was crying.

Make it four for four, Parker thought.

Her heart was no longer pounding in her fingertips. The three of them sat silently in the room now. Parker looked to be sure Frau was gone before she spoke.

"I don't know why I can't just write."

"No," her father sternly replied.

"You know it's not allowed," her mother said. "Writing is forbidden for a reason. You know that."

"But you let me write before—"

"That was *before*," her mother said, cutting her off. "Before. Okay? Before we lost him... your brother. We do *not* talk about this, Parker."

Silence hung in the air for several minutes before her father spoke.

"You haven't heard from your younger sister?" he asked his wife.

Parker stared at her mother, half expecting her to look offended or annoyed or storm out of the room. Their parents rarely argued, but it nearly always had to do with Mother's family when they did. There wasn't even a single shred of evidence that their mother even had a sister visible in the castle. What would possess her father to bring up their aunt? Did he want to start a fight with her? Was he looking to make Mom furious?

"No," she snapped. "Why?"

"Well, it's just with everything like those strange reports from the Shadow Territories," Father muttered, "those etchings, the attacks on that child, and this…"

"This?" Mother said, tilting her head.

"It's just—that, maybe, your sister… with all this. All this is part of your sister's… well, *her* work."

Her work?

Parker waited for her mother to explode as she stood there staring off in the distance, rapidly tapping her foot as she often did when she was upset.

Her father awkwardly shifted, trying to find a way to change the subject. "She's a teacher—right?" her father asked.

"That's right," Mother said after a pause. "A teacher *of sorts.*"

"And your nephew would be in her grade, Parker's cousin?"

"Probably."

"Then maybe that's best… for Parker," her father quietly said.

Her mother's foot instantly stopped tapping.

"You," her mother snapped, looking at Parker, "stay *here*. Let's discuss this outside. Now," she ordered Father as she stepped out of the room. He followed close behind and slammed the door shut.

What did he mean about my aunt and her work? I mean, I've never even met my aunt, and now suddenly he tells me I have a cousin who's my age too? I mean, what other surprises do they have up their sleeves?

The slammed door startled something now scurrying in the yard.

Parker craned her neck to peer through the window. She stood to get a closer look and saw a grayish color. One of the animals must have gotten out of its pen and wandered onto the castle grounds.

What did he mean about attacks on a child? I'd never heard them even mention the Shadow Territories. That place was supposed to be sketchy.

Their voices were raised outside the door, but Parker could only make out a few muffled words. As she walked nearer to the window, she heard her mother say something through the door. Parker listened closely, and she heard her mother repeat it. That couldn't be, but she swore she heard it. Her mother had just said something Parker could never imagine:

"Send her away."

"Wait, they want to send *me* away," she whispered to herself, shaking her head as she did.

They'd never do this to Quinn. Never. But for me, of course, they just send me away when I can't memorize something. I just see them all staring, judging, mocking—the kids, the teachers, parents, everyone. Do they think I'm doing this on purpose, causing this trouble and mischief, and don't want to learn?

No one gets me.

Parker's eyes followed the escaped animal as it moved along the grounds. She was pretty sure now it must be one of the goats, as she squinted to make out its shape and the curved horns on its head. The goat stopped to eat some clovers before something startled it. It hopped in a circle, kicking its back legs as it did.

"You're quite the lucky goat, out there on your own and free," she said to no one in particular. But as she did, the goat appeared to stop, turn, and look back at her, nodding as if it understood. "Did you *hear* what I just said?"

She took a step forward toward the window as the goat turned and continued munching on clovers.

"Well, anyway, mister goat, it'd be a lot easier for me too if I could just escape the barn and be free to explore and wander and avoid all this. No one wants to be trapped, as I'm sure you understand. Maybe it would be for the best for everyone if I just wasn't here anymore."

The goat turned back to her and appeared to smile, if a goat could even do that. *That's so strange. I swear that goat just winked at me.*

The goat continued toward a large oak tree and then disappeared from view, oddly never appearing on the other side of the tree. Strange. Parker took another step toward the window, trying to see where it had gone. Strange.

The door burst open, and her mother and father stepped inside.

"We're sending you to live with your aunt," said her mother. "We are sending you away from here for a bit."

"You'll be safe with her," her father added.

Parker began to argue, but her mother interrupted her.

"*And* we think it will help you," her mother continued, glaring at her husband as she did.

Help me? She must be kidding, sending me to live with someone I've never even met to help me.

Parker exhaled sharply, drawing one of those looks she'd grown accustomed to from her mother.

Parker's parents went on and on about this being temporary, the family missing her kidnapped brother Riley, trying to behave more like her older sister Quinn, having trouble expressing her feelings, being part of the royal family, and a million other things she tuned out. *Blah-blah-blah.* Her father awkwardly tried to say something about her body changing and becoming a woman. *Eye roll.* They'd had the nerve to tell her Monty, her best friend and her co-leader of the Plumes, was a bad influence.

Honestly, I don't think they have a clue how bad things are getting out there. They don't even realize Monty and I are running a covert group teaching kids how to write. They'd understand who the bad influence is here if they did.

I'm not sure anyone does.

"Your father and I think your aunt is the good influence you need right now," said her mother.

No way I let them send me off to rot in some basement dungeon with a stranger. This is how these sorts of stories always go. I end up living with some evil aunt as my stepmother, have to eat cold porridge for every meal, and wind up crazy... singing songs with the birds or mice or squirrels.

Nope. No, thank you. Plus, I'm allergic to porridge... I think.

And that was it. Parker had run to her room as the tears poured down her cheeks.

Parker wiped the tears with her sleeve. She sat and looked around at the bedroom she'd grown up in and shared with her sisters now. *Why were they doing this? Where had everything gone wrong?*

And now, her parents had decided just to send her away.

***

"Stop, Owen! Owen!"

The undertow seized the boy, dragging him further out to sea. He thrashed his arms, struggling to keep his head above the rampaging dark water. He cried for help, but it was like a creature hidden beneath had grabbed him. It left him thrashing and fighting, unable to escape the predator's jaws.

The boy vanished under the stormy water—snatched away by some fearsome creature.

"Please! Someone! Anyone! Help him!" Owen's mother screamed. *"Please!"*

Parker jolted upright in her bed. She looked around, her heart racing and beads of sweat dotting her forehead.

Breathe. It was just a dream—another nightmare. Breathe.

The clock in her room read two in the morning.

Looks like there's no point in trying to fall back asleep now.

Owen Wickerland—she always dreamed of Owen Wickerland. He was a boy in her class she had barely known. His birthday was one day earlier than hers. The children at school always sang "Happy Birthday" to them on the same day. But that was it. Now every night, she sees his freckled, round face, his chestnut hair, and his terrified dark eyes calling for her help. Parker just couldn't stop seeing those eyes stare back at her.

It had been exactly one month ago. She'd stood right next to Owen with Aven, Quinn, Monty, and the rest of the school children gathered on the seashore to celebrate as they'd done every month.

Drain Day was a celebration, a tribute, a ritual, and a display of power.

Each month, thousands gathered in the Everly amphitheater to watch the majesty of the spectacle. The children's lantern boats signaled the start of the display. Everly was an island, isolated from the rest of Fonde thanks to a protective sea created with powerful magic. Yet for this one brief day each month, that ancient, forbidden magic would be used to vanish the seawater and reunite Everly with the surrounding lands.

That day became known as Drain Day, a day when a magic inscription would suck the seawater away into a powerful, swirling vortex in mere minutes.

And the festival always began with children releasing burning boats into the sea to be drained away with the water.

But Owen had changed his mind about burning his boat and chased it out into the water to recapture it. With the crowd's noise gathered and dozens and dozens of children to monitor, the boy was up to his waist in the water before his mother spotted him.

She cried out for him to stop.

The thunderous chants of the festival goers drowned out her voice. The sky darkened, making it difficult to see the small boy caught in the waves. A boy raced after Owen. Their hands touched for a mere moment before Owen was jerked away by the seawater, sucked into the enchanted vortex. The guards ran in to pull back the boy who'd tried to save him. Owen's mother thrashed her way through the crowd. An eerie calm fell over the crowd. The painful scream from Owen's mother echoed off the stone walls of the seaside's new amphitheater. "Owen, stop!" she bellowed. "My son!"

Wind rushed through the kingdom, a cold surge unleashed from the mountains. Panic filled Owen's face.

Owen's mother wailed as he disappeared beneath the surface. The violent water held him in its grasp, like a cat capturing its prey.

"Please! Someone! Help him!" his mother begged.

It was too late. Owen's bobbing head and flailing arms were gone.

Night after night, Parker saw Owen thrash in the dark waves, vanishing with the water of that vast, enchanted sea.

The clock read four minutes after two. She closed her eyes and inhaled, trying to shake the nightmare and the visions from her head.

She knew it would be impossible to fall back asleep. She stood, tied her thick, wild light brown hair in a braid, and gathered her belongings.

It was time to go.

Chapter Three

The Hidden Library

Whatever "going to live with your aunt" actually meant, Parker wasn't just going to wait to be locked in some terrible, secluded dungeon basement with only a bedpan, chores, and a straw bed.

Rebels and troublemakers don't get themselves locked away in some tower prison until the end of time; they grow out their hair and climb out the window.

But she didn't have the patience to wait for her hair to become an escape ladder, so Parker came up with her own plan.

First, one last epic heist to retrieve a few items her parents had confiscated and forbidden her from ever using again. Then make a break for it.

It's not stealing if it was yours to begin with. Right?

She only needed to sneak out of her bedroom and past a dozen castle guards in the middle of the night, scale the tower steps, pick a lock on an ancient door, break into a hidden and boarded-up room, find the items, and get back before being spotted.

This was the stakeout phase of the heist. Crouched behind a potted plant, Parker barely felt her legs as she nervously peered between the leaves, watching for any movement through her cupped hands as if they were imaginary binoculars. She'd hid behind that potted plant for almost an hour, staring at the grandfather clock with its incessant ticking while trying to determine the exact schedule for the night guards.

Twinkle, twinkle little star, she hummed, trying to calm her nerves.

Maybe I should have spent a little more time devising this plan for thievery before sneaking out of my room.

According to her meticulous calculations, she would have exactly four minutes and seventeen seconds to sprint from the planter, pick the lock, bust through the boards, and squeeze herself into the hidden room without being detected.

This hallway led directly to the Hall of Resplendence, the king and queen's massive, open room for entertaining, serving state dinners, and hosting royal affairs. Outside the Hall of Resplendence was a bronze, antique chandelier that took the guards almost an hour to light every candle in the evenings.

A Hall of Resplendence? Why couldn't we just call it a Great Hall like every other castle? What's resplendent anyway? My dad has always had this thing for his big, dramatic, hard to pronounce words.

Parker puffed out her chest and murmured in a faux grand voice, "I am Parker the Resplendent." *That's not bad.*

Tik-tok. Tik-tok. Tik-tok.

"What are you wearing?"

Parker jumped and wheeled around, almost tumbling into the plant.

"Aven!" Parker hissed at her younger sister. "A little warning next time."

Her thievery skills were a bit rusty—a terrible way to start a heist.

"Did you dress in the dark?" Aven asked, examining Parker's all-black attire, with a winter hat and dark towel draped over her shoulders like a cape. Aven was three years younger but refused to let her older sisters exclude her from anything they were doing.

"They're pajamas. *New* pajamas."

"They are ugly," Aven said with a straight face. "Really ugly. I probably wouldn't leave the bedroom wearing them again. Ever. Unless that's what you were aiming for." Aven sarcastically flashed her sister two thumbs-up.

"Thanks for the fashion tips, especially from the girl who never takes off those funny wolf ears you're always wearing," Parker said, shaking her head.

"Hey," Aven said, narrowing her eyes at Parker, her hands reaching up to touch the gray, sewn ears she had clipped into her blond hair. "That's rude."

"I'm sorry. Now, did you bring it?"

A smile flashed across her younger sister's face. Reaching behind her, she pulled out a three-foot-long black crowbar and handed it to her sister.

"Why do we need a crowbar again?" Aven asked.

"*We* don't need a crowbar," Parker corrected. "I need it. You can go back to bed. I've got this."

"*You* need *my* crowbar," Aven said, placing her hand back on the black metal bar. "I found it. I brought it. So, *I'm* coming. What are we breaking?"

Parker sighed, pointing down the hall from their hiding spot at the bottom of the tower steps.

"See the tapestry?" Parker asked.

She stood up from behind the plant, pulling her sister up by the arm while scanning for any of the patrolling guards. They'd need to go down the hallway, past the portraits hanging on the wall, to that solitary tapestry. Looking closely, it would seem out of place… because it was. A year ago, her parents had hastily hung the rug hoping everyone would forget what had been there. Most people probably had.

"A rug?" Aven whispered. "We are taking a rug?"

"No, we are not taking a rug," Parker replied. "It's what's *behind* the rug."

"What's back there?" Aven asked her sister as they ducked back down and squinted at the tapestry again through the plant's leaves.

"A door," she answered. "But it's boarded shut."

"A door to what?" Aven asked. She had been too young to remember the door, and her parents had only ever allowed their elder daughters inside.

If I don't tell her, I don't get my stuff back. I get an evil stepmother and a bedpan if I don't have my things back.

"It's a library," Parker said.

"A what?"

"A library," Parker repeated, "with stacks of books in there and a writing room."

Aven's eyes widened. "*Writing?* But… that's not allowed. Do Mom and Dad know?"

Parker smirked at her little sister and said, "Of course they know. They're the ones who nailed it up in the first place. They took something from me, and I'm going to get it back."

Aven wrinkled her nose. "Can I go inside?"

"Only if you promise to keep this a secret," Parker said. "I need you to cross your heart." She motioned across her own heart with her fingers.

"Cross my heart," Aven replied, moving her finger across her chest. "Now what?"

Tik-tok. Tik-tok. Tik-tok.

"This is what we call a heist," Parker said. "Any great heist story needs a team, something worth stealing, and some rules to break."

"Looks like you're my team," Parker whispered. Just then, a castle guard stepped into the far end of the hallway. "And here comes our *rules.*"

Spending the night alone and wandering empty halls while the others passed the time joking with one another outside was punishment, meaning the night guard was always the person who had done something wrong.

"He should be gone in thirty seconds, and then we go," she continued. "You remember the plan?"

Aven nodded, giving her the double thumbs-up again.

"I forgot to ask," Aven whispered. "What are we trying to steal?"

Parker raised her eyebrows and shot her a mischievous smile. "A feather. Just one feather."

"A feather?" Aven hissed. "All this for a feather? That isn't something *worth stealing.* I can get you fistfuls of them from the chicken coop!"

Parker pulled her sister's hand as the guard disappeared from view. They crouched down and crept across the hallway past the portraits until they were in front of the maroon and gold tapestry.

Tik-tok. Tik-tok. Tik-tok.

Parker pressed her back against the wall, scanning for anyone who might have seen them. It was exhilarating to be there, ready to pull off this first part of her plan. She knelt, listening for any sound. Reaching for the bottom corner, she pulled up the tapestry and peered at the old door with wood planks nailed in place, sealing it from entry. She reached through a crack in the planks, grabbed the door handle, and twisted.

Parker looked back at Aven, "It turns," she whispered. "This means we don't need to figure out how to pick the lock, which is an excellent development since I have had no idea how to pick a lock."

"Good thing I brought the crowbar," Aven said.

Parker nodded. "And it's not *just* a feather," she said to her sister, her breathing labored as she felt around the boards hidden behind the tapestry. "It's a quill—a writing quill. An *important* quill, and my writing journal."

Her sister eyed her suspiciously. "You're stealing a quill? But what if the Illiterates found out? They... they'd..." she trailed off, unable to say what they both knew.

The Illiterates were the worst.

The. Worst.

You didn't want to test your luck with Illiterates.

Their numbers were growing, and attacks on writers were no longer fiction. They even hunted children now, teaching others to fear those who wrote no matter the subject or the reason. Everly's educated citizens had become a roving mob with a taste for retribution. On the whisper of a rumor, they'd break into the home of a suspected writer. If they found paper, a quill, an inkwell, any books—even planted by one of their members, they'd drag the person from their home and—

Parker shuddered.

Aven was right. Being a writer was dangerous now. Parker worried about the other kids she'd recruited to join the Plumes, her secret writing society.

"I know," Parker said. "It'll be fine. I'll be fine. No big deal."

She let out a breath.

"Okay, you hold back the tapestry," Parker instructed her sister. She removed the three-foot-long black iron bar hidden under her towel cape and pushed her sister against the wall with her free hand.

Aven pulled back the tapestry enough for her sister to sneak behind it.

"Good thing you brought this bar," came Parker's muffled voice from behind the rug. "There's a small crack we can pry open and crawl through."

Aven bent down and whispered, "Someone's coming. Freeze."

Another castle guard rounded the corner with a big grin holding an armful of Aven's favorite cinnamon pulls he'd taken from the kitchen. He spied Aven, eyes widening and face paling as he realized the king's daughter caught him stealing food.

Aven eyed the cinnamon pulls and then looked up to his face with a smile. Theatrically, she pointed to the lump behind the tapestry, brought her finger to her lips, and mouthed the words, "Hide and Seek."

The guard smiled back, nodded, and brought his finger to his lips, careful not to drop the pastries. His sleeve slid down his arm, revealing four black dots on the back of his hand arranged in a perfect square.

A chill ran through Aven's entire body.

She stared at his hand as her body froze, now certain of what she'd seen.

The guard had been branded with the Illiterates mark. Aven's heart raced, aware of what this meant for her and her sister. The Illiterates were inside their home, the castle itself. Aven gulped, trying to make sure he couldn't see her shaking.

They were no longer safe here.

The guard lingered, an awkward smile plastered on his face. After what seemed like an eternity, he gave Aven a wink and snuck past her on his tiptoes in an exaggerated manner.

Her heart pounded as she watched him slink out of the hall. When he was out of earshot, Aven ripped the tapestry open.

"Parker," Aven urgently said, "that guard found us." She stammered as she tried to get out the words.

"You did great," Parker reassured.

"No. You don't get it. He's... he's an Illiterate," Aven said.

"What?"

"He had the mark on the back of his hand," Aven said. "The four dots. What do we do?"

***

How had the Illiterates infiltrated their home?

Parker turned from her work to see Aven's scared face peering from behind the tapestry. She understood her sister's concern. It wasn't only that someone had caught them, but *who* had found them and what he could do.

Working quickly before the guard made his next round, she dug the crowbar into the gap between the door and the nailed plank and pulled.

"We've got to hurry," Aven urged.

"I'm going as fast as I can—but I can be quiet and slow or fast and loud," Parker answered. "Your choice."

"Fast and loud."

Creeeeeak. Crash.

"We're in," Parker's voice echoed. "Get in here, quick."

The sisters squeezed themselves through the small gap she'd made in the boards and entered the hidden library. The familiar smell of old books wafted into Parker's nostrils.

Caw-caw. Caw-caw.

Why are bird noises coming from inside the library?

Parker stood. The once-hidden room was a massive space with thirty-foot high ceilings and dark wood paneling lining the outer walls. But this wasn't how she'd remembered it.

"Uh, Aven," Parker said to her sister, who was still on her knees after making her way through the gap. "You. Have. Got. To. See. This."

"What is it?" Aven replied as she crawled behind her sister.

"The books... the books are flying."

Bookshelves, dusty books, writing tables, chairs, and illuminating torches used to fill the room. Now books flew around the airy space, organizing themselves in color, shape, and size patterns, flapping their pages like wings. They fluttered, swooped, and squawked, nesting on chairs and making the room feel like a jungle canopy.

"This room's alive," Aven uttered. "This is a library?"

Scrolls of paper slithered across the floors like snakes, moving in and out of view. Bookshelves slid and twisted at the center of the room, rearranging themselves into new mazes. The flames of the torches leaped from torch to torch—like frogs hopping from lily pad to lily pad, their tongues catching embers like flies.

To her left had sat rows and rows of inkwells filled with the dark ink Parker and Quinn had used to practice writing. But now, they arranged themselves in a series of rows and stacks like a pipe organ. And in front of the hundreds of inkwells, moving wildly on the makeshift stage, was a large, rainbow-colored inkwell waving a long stick like a conductor's baton.

The rainbow inkwell tapped its baton, and beautiful music played, with colorful sparks and magical dust shooting out of the top of the inkwells like fireworks. The bright dust formed into a fox, a horse, a raven, and a red bird, moving gracefully through the inkwell orchestra. Books flew by the performance and clapped in rhythm by quickly closing and opening.

A massive mirror still hung in the library near the inkwell orchestra. It had the ornately carved word "Scott" at the bottom, her mother's given family name before she'd changed it to be a Pennymore. All around the outside of the mirror frame were what looked to be hundreds of miniature carvings, paintings, gems, and tiles inside the frame.

Parker had a love-hate relationship with the mirror. When she was doing writing exercises, she often saw Lady Julie watching her through the reflection, making it impossible for her to daydream or doodle. But she figured out a trick, learning to position herself in just the right spot in the room to make it more difficult for Julie to spot her when she wasn't writing her lines.

The mirror was different than the other mirrors in the castle due to the rainbow-like glimmer it had when you looked at your reflection.

Parker's eye spotted something surprising in the reflection: there were shelves filled with books on the ceiling. She pointed up to the bookshelves that now hung like bats in a cave.

"How in the world would you get a book from those?" Aven asked.

"Maybe a massive book ladder," Parker said with a shrug. "Or you hope the book flies down on its own. No wonder our parents didn't want us in here. The room… it's enchanted."

"Enchanted? What's that?" Aven asked.

"Magical. This is magic, I guess, but—" Parker paused as a group of picture books hopped in front of them.

Aven bent down to get a closer look at the little book struggling to keep up with the others. The book had a wolf drawing on it, and Aven loved nothing more than a story about wolves.

"Can I?" she asked her older sister, holding the book in front of her. "I think it's a baby wolf."

Parker shrugged. Aven reached out, picked up the book, and slowly opened it. A howl bellowed out. She slammed the book shut, and it fell to the ground. The book shook itself and hopped away, scrambling to catch up with the others.

The two sisters looked at one another and laughed hysterically.

"I thought it—this—was just in stories, but this looks pretty real to me," Parker said, motioning to the howling book Aven had dropped on the floor.

"This is what you were doing when *you* learned to write?" Aven asked her innocently.

"Oh no," Parker said with surprise. "My words didn't howl back at me. We learned how to write letters and words to tell stories, create poems, send messages, or remember. I'm... I'm a writer, Aven, and it's the most wonderful feeling in the world... to write and put words on the page. Like nothing I've ever felt before. Writing makes me feel alive."

Parker was nine years old when her parents had first brought her to this library. Her father had taken a long brass key from his pocket, opened the door, and let her and her older sister inside. He'd made sure no one saw them enter or exit, not even his closest advisers.

Writing was banned, but her parents told her writing was critical for her future and instructed Parker and her older sister Quinn to come to the writing room each day for lessons in the forbidden art of writing. Their parents had laughed when they read her stories, cried at her poems, and told her she had a gift. They even gave her a teacher to help her improve.

Those moments in this room were the first time in her life Parker hadn't been embarrassed, her brain hadn't frozen, no one had laughed at her, and she had loved to learn. She could express herself. They were finally proud of her.

In this room, her brain thrived as she worked through arcs and characters, tension and spectacle, plot twists, dramatic irony, triumph, and tragedy. It was as if she processed the world around her through its stories. She knew writing was her destiny.

"Can you teach me?" Aven said, smiling back at her sister. "Can I write like you?"

Parker put her hand on Aven's shoulder. "Absolutely. I—I've been teaching some of the other kids… Monty and the Plumes… a little bit, and they love it too. The Plumes are this secret writing society we have. We all believe writing shouldn't be scary. We all should be able to write. The Ancients never wanted to ban all writing, just those who wrote evil and dark magic. So we write together, in secret. Writing might be important someday… to keep us safe, as Lady Julie said. Writing is just something everyone should get to do. You too. We'll start…"

She paused as a knot formed in her stomach, realizing after she ran away from Everly she wouldn't be able to teach her younger sister to write.

"You'll learn too," Parker continued, a forced smile forming on her face. "When we first came here, Quinn and I learned not to be afraid of writing. It isn't something to be feared. Writing is how we connect. But people were afraid, and they thought if they stopped us from writing, they'd stop feeling that way. The Illiterates were just afraid, that's all."

Parker saw Aven wince at the mention of the Illiterates.

"We'll be fine," Parker said. "We will."

A year ago, her younger brother Riley and her writing teacher had vanished in the middle of the night. Her parents called it a kidnapping, but she wasn't so sure. Her parents had taken her quill, journal, inkwell, and books. They forbade her from writing, locking the library and hiding it behind the solitary tapestry. But it didn't matter what you called it. That night took away nearly everything Parker loved.

They stopped being proud of her.

A part of her understood why her parents did it. The Illiterates were becoming more vocal and more emboldened. They had even infiltrated her father's guards. Last week one of the teachers at the school had mysteriously disappeared under the rumor one of her students identified her to the Illiterates after receiving poor marks. Some kids at school drew the Illiterate's mark on the back of their wrists. Most of her old friends had joined them already.

You were pretty much a misfit, an outsider, or a nobody if you didn't.

She just missed being herself, and this room was one of the only places where she still felt that way.

Aven eyed her sister.

"Trust me, our writing was never like any of this," Parker said, motioning to the room of flying books. "It's not magical or scary or something to be afraid of. It's just how you connect and feel, and it's sorta the only way my brain can make sense of everything—to write it."

A wad of paper about the size of a peanut flew past Parker's face and hit Aven in the nose.

"Hey!" she called out, her eyes tracking to the stacks of paper that were folding and unfolding themselves into recognizable shapes on the writing desks on the opposite side of the room.

Aven pointed to the paper. "Is that a sailboat?"

"I think that was more like a pirate ship," Parker said. "And I think you just got shot by a wayward cannonball."

Sure enough, the stacks of papers had transformed into a fleet of boats and sailed over waves of paper while another smaller set of paper boats raced to attack the fleet, their cannons firing paper cannonballs at the larger ships. The papers staged the story of a family of rabbits and a little boy on the next desk

"Why didn't you guys bring me here before?" Aven asked, transfixed by the paper stories.

"It wasn't like this the last time; it was just a room, I guess. It was only books and shelves. Now, the books think they are animals, and the paper fires spitballs!"

A frog-like flame leaped overhead and barely missed landing on the paper sea monster rising from the desk to devour the pirate boats closing in on the fleet.

"Look over there," Parker pointed to two rows of bookshelves arranging themselves into a doorway entrance. "It looks like the quills want us to go inside."

The entrance was beautiful, with multicolored quills floating above in a half-circle across the two shelves, as if a peacock had spread her tail feathers to form an archway.

"You want us to go in *there*?" Aven asked.

"I came here to find my writing journal," Parker answered. "Maybe the shelves know where it is."

Aven shrugged. "Watch out for flying books; some of those big ones could hurt!"

"Let's hurry before the guard comes back or Quinn realizes we aren't in our beds," Parker said, taking her sister's hand and guiding her toward the archway.

The sisters raced down the first narrow corridor of bookshelves, the books on the shelves dancing and jumping when they ran by. The pair continued moving through the shelves, following the path ahead of them: a left, a right, another left.

Parker stopped at a dead end.

She grabbed Aven's arm and pointed to the dead-end a few feet from them. Then she motioned to the shelf on her left, where a set of particularly excited brightly colored books bounced and reordered themselves.

"Maybe those books are trying to give us a clue," Parker said.

Aven recoiled as Parker cautiously reached out and touched the shelf in front of them with her index finger.

The shelf glowed and then gave a loud creaking noise as it arced open to reveal a new passageway. The sisters walked forward. Parker touched more shelves, and each creaked, the heavy wooden bases scraping against the stone floor as they moved and glided to reveal a new route.

It's like these shelves know why we're here.

After a few minutes of walking, they stood at another dead end.

"Did we take a wrong turn?" Aven asked.

"I guess," Parker replied. She reached out to touch all the shelves, hoping one would swing open like before. "Wait, look."

On the bookcase in front of them a small stack of notecards hopped up and down. She looked closer and realized the cards were folding themselves into two shapes remarkably similar to the Pennymore sisters. The paper figures smiled and waved and then motioned to the sisters to look down at the lowest shelf.

There was a small, leather-bound book on the bottom shelf with a thin brown leather cord wrapped around it. The purple cover had an eight-point compass etched into it.

Aven gave the notecard figures a thumbs up, and Parker smiled to show her appreciation as she knelt. The paper figures waved back to her before folding themselves into a paper swan and leaping off the shelf, soaring through the room.

"It's my journal," Parker said to Aven, removing the book from the shelf and handing it to her sister. "I learned how to write in this."

"Will it howl?" Aven replied, concern in her voice.

"No. I don't know how to write magic. Look, these are just letters, and together the letters become words," Parker pointed to the pages inside the journal. "Our parents wanted us to learn to create these letters and words to tell stories and poems and messages. They said we needed to learn to write—Mom called it our destiny, I think. So, Quinn and I learned to write, and we thought you would learn one day. Until—"

A dozen paper cannonballs pelted Parker, who realized the folded paper pirate ships from before were aiming at them. Then the bookshelves creaked and groaned as they chaotically slid around the floor. The shelf that had held the journal swung open, revealing a long passageway.

"We should go. Something isn't right," Parker said, looking up as a flock of small, red-covered books flew overhead. The books dove in front of them, skimming their heads and causing the sisters to duck. The bird squawks became more agitated.

The pair ran down the bookshelf corridor as loud caws and whistles came from the books now circling overhead.

"Did *we* do something wrong?" Aven said to her sister.

"Maybe it's the journal. We took something, and I think we might have ticked off the library," Parker said. "The books seem to think we are intruders now."

"Yeah, let's get out of here," Aven agreed.

The shelf-maze guided the pair back to the doorway where they'd first entered the enchanted library.

"I think it's telling us to leave," Parker said, looking over her shoulder as the shelves shut behind them. The books on that shelf flipped around, and they turned their spines to face away from them.

"Do you hear that?" Aven asked, looking for the source of a loud rumble. "It's coming from over there." She pointed to the far side of the room.

"I heard it too," Parker replied. "It's coming from the bookbindery—the place where you take papers and turn them into a book with a cover. It sounds like a giant is snoring." She craned her neck, hoping to see the source of the noise.

Aven grabbed her sister's arm and pulled her behind one of the shelves. "Look," she said.

Parker surveyed the area above the boarded-up door they'd broken through. She hadn't seen it since they'd been focused on the library turned aviary, but visible above the door was a glowing, teal inscription:

ꓔꓤꓴꓔꓗ ꓲꓠꓢꓲꓓꓰ

"It's like in our room," Aven said.

"I know," Parker said.

Aven lowered her eyes. "Do you think she left it... I mean, wrote it... before she took him? Lady Julie?"

The words looked eerily familiar. Parker didn't know what they meant, but it was the same script they'd found above their window last year. Unlike this inscription, the writing above their window didn't glow. Was this why their parents had hidden this room and refused to speak of it?

Parker sighed. "We don't have time right now."

The books circled them, flying closer and closer overhead.

"We need to catch my quill before we can go," Parker said, pointing to the feather quills forming the archway.

"Catch one?" Aven replied. "Are you crazy?"

The quills each darted like hummingbirds, hovering before making sharp turns in a shared pattern, forming symbols and shapes as they soared through the room.

"How would you catch one?" Aven asked.

"I've got an idea. I'll need you to go grab one of those musical inkwells."

"Me? Really? But how do I know which one?"

"I don't know either. Just figure it out," Parker replied. "You don't always need me to do everything for you."

Parker looked over the inkwell orchestra and saw they must be nearing the crescendo—the big, loud dramatic part—as bigger and bigger sparks flew out of some of the inkwells at the end of the row.

"Oh, great," Aven said, shaking her head. "Just go over and try to pick out a flute or an oboe or something that won't burn me from the flaming ink show."

"Yep, and avoid the tubas," Parker said with a wink.

Parker walked to the writing desks and looked around to see what she could find to help her while causing the least disruption to the unfolding paper-story scenes. One of the delicate pink pieces of story paper was not folding and unfolding into a ship, rabbit, or flower. She grabbed it, but the paper wiggled and tried to escape like she'd caught a fish.

"It's going to be all right," she whispered to the shivering paper as though she spoke to her pet cat Boots.

Taking the paper, she held it up between her hands and waved it around, hoping to attract the attention of the quills.

"Write. Write," Parker called to the flock of quills.

The swarm of quills moved in jerky, sporadic bursts toward the paper she held above her head. She trembled, unsure what would happen as the quills with their sharp tips raced closer. She glanced at Aven, who nervously wrung her hands in front of her, having returned to observe the scene.

As gently as a butterfly approaching a flower, the swarm hovered and landed one by one on the trembling paper. It was beautiful, as if the quills formed a feather meadow on the small sheet of paper with their various colors, shapes, and sizes perfectly aligned.

It worked.

Parker let out a sharp breath and smiled at Aven.

She delicately moved the paper covered with hundreds of quills and placed it on the empty writing desk. Looking at the quills moving ever so slightly, a small, speckled feather with a reddish tip on the end drew her in.

My quill.

Parker reached down, but the red-and-white quill lifted itself from the paper before her fingers could touch it. She grabbed the pointed end she'd held to practice her letters, excitement pulsing through her. She turned to Aven, whose mouth was agape.

Parker shrugged and then smiled at her younger sister, taking a few confident steps toward Aven with her chest puffed out like the victor returning from battle with her journal under her arm and the quill in her hand.

Aven's face contorted. "Run!"

Hundreds of quills hovered above the desk, buzzing in agitation, all of them pointing straight at her.

She looked down at the red-and-white quill and saw the tip was glowing.

"Run!" Aven called out again.

The sisters raced to the door. Aven scrambled through first. As Parker pulled her leg through the small gap, the quills pricked her calf with their sharp points.

"Close it," she instructed her sister.

Aven pulled the ancient door shut and jammed the wooden plank over the gap. Parker limped from behind the tapestry as the rug fell back over the once-again-hidden door.

Thump. Thump. Thump. Thump.

Those quills are peppering the door as if it were a dartboard.

"Whoa," Parker said breathlessly, patting Aven on the shoulder as the pair sat on the floor.

"Are you okay?" Aven asked, staring at Parker's leg. Several small dots of blood speckled her calf where the quills had attacked.

"Whoa, yeah," Parker said. "That was intense. I'm good, really."

She placed the journal on the floor in front of her. The quill in her hand was no longer glowing.

"Did you get the inkwell?" she asked.

Aven held up the large, rainbow-colored inkwell that had been conducting the orchestra. A grin crept across her face.

"Of course you picked the biggest and wildest one," Parker teased.

"I'm smart," Aven replied. "The rest of them were shooting out sparks. This one was only wildly waving a baton. Batons don't seem quite as dangerous as flaming, sparking music. Let's go back again tomorrow and get stuff for *me* to write!"

"Are you kidding me? Those quills are not going to be excited to see us for a while."

"Then can you start teaching me to write instead?" Aven asked.

Guilt rushed over Parker.

"Maybe not tomorrow," Parker said, motioning to her calf. "We probably ought to give it a few days for the angry swarm of quills to calm down. But soon, definitely soon. Promise."

Whistling.

The guard.

She grabbed Aven's arm, jerked her to the wall beside the tapestry, and held a finger to her lips.

Backs pressed against the wall, they hoped he wouldn't come this way. Parker felt Aven squeeze her upper arm and point to the center of the hallway.

She'd left her journal open on the carpet.

"Who's there?" the guard called down the dimly lit hall.

Parker crawled toward the open journal on her stomach, hoping her dark-colored attire would keep her out of sight. With her hand still holding the quill, she reached out to grab the journal.

The moment the quill's tip touched the journal, a bright red-orange glow burst from the quill and illuminated the hallway.

"Shhhhh," Parker whispered, trying to cover the glow with her other hand. A picture of the massive, ancient bronze chandelier hanging in the hallway flashed through her mind.

"Whoa," Aven uttered as bright silver and gold dust began to spark from the book and float across the hallway like stardust.

As the dust filled the hallway, the flames on the candles began to crackle before burning an eerie black, plunging the hallway into darkness. Another flash lit the room as a massive, silver lightning bolt exploded from the book and spiraled down the hall toward the guard.

Crack. Crack. Crack.

The electricity in the bolt fractured and spread out across each surface in the hallway until a massive, bright silver and blue blast filled the hall.

Boom! Crash! Crash-Boom!

"Aaaaaaahhhhhh," the guard screamed.

A thud echoed down the hallway as sounds of broken glass and metal reverberated through the room. Then the guard screamed again, louder this time.

"Go-go-go! Let's go," Parker hissed, picking up the book and the other items before reaching for her sister's hand. "Hurry!"

The pair raced back to the potted plant, Parker breathing fast as she counted the steps in her head until they reached the bottom step of the stairs to climb up to their room. They raced up the stairs, trying not to make a sound.

"What was that?" Aven asked as they stood outside their bedroom door at the top of the tower.

"I don't know," she said, her heart thudding in her chest.

"Do you think he's okay?" Aven asked.

"Yeah, I'm sure he's fine," Parker said, knowing they'd both heard his frantic scream and seen the powerful electricity fill the hall. "I'm sure other guards are around who heard the crash to help, and… well, at least we didn't get caught. Can you imagine if that guard had seen the book?"

"Or the silver magic lightning bolt," Aven replied.

Parker nodded, clutching the things she'd taken from the enchanted library. She exhaled. "Silver lightning bolts from a book are not what I expected tonight, either. I see why the Ancients banned magic writing. That was way scarier than writing a couple of poems."

"You think?" Aven replied.

They crept back into their room, sneaking past Quinn's bed and getting into their own. As she sat in her bed, Parker carefully hid her purple journal, the rainbow inkwell, and her red-and-white quill in a crack in the stones beside her bed.

Something extraordinary happened, weirder than even the enchantments in the library. Her quill glowed when it touched the journal. Her mind had formed a perfect picture of the chandelier—an image as if she was looking right at it up close. Then the candle flames went black, and everything went dark before that bright flash, the bolt… and then the crashing sound. It was unlike anything she'd experienced before, the power, the calm, the stillness.

It all felt *good*.

Parker shook her head and sat up in bed for a moment. The heist had been a success, save a few minor hiccups on the way—all part of a great heist story.

Tomorrow would be the real test. She'd need to leave Everly and her family… probably for a while. She had to be careful. The Illiterates were lurking even inside the castle now, so nowhere seemed safe anymore. What did she expect after what she saw in the library? Just another reason to get off the island.

All heroes in her stories had to leave like this. That was their destiny and made them heroes. They had to go on their voyage, their adventure, but they came back. And they didn't just come back; they came back *better* than before—with new answers or new powers or even knew friends. She would too.

She would find a way to make her parents proud again. She would figure out what had happened to her brother, her teacher, and why that night had changed everything. She'd find answers.

Parker thought about the inscription again.

Truth inside.

It was an unusual message. It was simple, but at the same time, so complex. *What truth was Lady Julie referring to? Inside of what? Who was the message left for?*

There would be plenty of time to figure out the answers to these questions, and now she'd have the entire world at her fingertips to help. Parker smiled, closed her eyes, and laid her head on her pillow. She had what she needed. It all felt *good*.

One thing was for sure. From the looks of the library, Lady Julie was right. Magic writers had undoubtedly returned.

Time to get off this island before things got any worse.

Chapter Four

Lazlo Grott

Sunlight poured in through the cracks in the curtains.

Parker opened her eyes, groggy from way too little sleep last night.

Did I seriously get chased by an angry swarm of killer writing instruments?

Her mind spun through the moments of flapping books, the mazes of shelves, and the hummingbird quills. She rubbed her calf, still sore from the angry quill attack.

She sat up in bed and looked around the room, seeing the outline of Aven's body in her bed and a pile of sheets and blankets on Quinn's.

She rolled over and ran her hand against the cool stones until she felt her hiding place in the crack in the wall beside her bed and reclaimed her journal, the red-and-white feather quill, and the colorful inkwell.

Crazy, but not a dream. Makes sense why they closed off that room.

She moved to the edge of her bed, holding the quill in her hand, gently rolling it between her thumb and forefinger while examining each streak and color. Last night it flew like a hummingbird. *How did it do that?*

She looked around again to make sure no one was watching.

Parker held the feather over her head and dropped it, hoping the quill might catch itself and hover as she'd seen in the library. But it floated down before resting on the floor in front of her.

Oh well, it was worth a try.

She picked the quill up, set it on her bed, and then grabbed her purple writing journal. She hadn't examined her writing journal since it had first appeared in the bookshelf maze, and she now squeezed it between her hands as if she expected something to happen again when she did.

Did I somehow conjure a lightning bolt with this book? I swore I could perfectly see the chandelier in my head, and then... Maybe it was just my imagination.

Parker realized she had squeezed the book so tightly her hands turned red.

Deep breath. This is why you've got to leave Everly. Hidden rooms, foreboding inscriptions, too many secrets. I've waited long enough for answers; time to find them for myself.

The blue dress her mother picked out hung over the chair near the window. She needed to prepare for the Drain Day festivities and focus on the next phase of her escape plan. Before she'd snuck out last night, she'd carefully sewn several small, hidden pockets inside her dress where she'd tuck the quill, the inkwell, and her journal, as well as any other items she'd need to bring with her.

Parker set the journal on her bed next to the quill, picked up the inkwell Aven had stolen, and began to examine it closely. It was beautiful with a unique pattern of colored stones arranged in a flowing rainbow shape. Aven certainly got her an inkwell people would notice. It was almost too big to fit into one of her hidden pockets.

She looked at it once more and then set it on top of the journal. The inkwell began to glow.

Whoa.

Quickly lifting the inkwell off the book, eyes darting between the two items, she gently placed the inkwell back on her writing journal. A light, yellowish hue pulsed from the ink.

I mean, this is a sign. Right? If you see a glowing inkwell and you have a quill... yep, I'd be silly not to try this.

Parker gripped her quill in her fingertips and looked around to make sure the light hadn't woken her sisters, then uncorked the ink. Then she held the quill over the inkwell and carefully dipped its tip into the top of the glowing bottle.

The ink turned black, and then a rainbow of color whirled around. Blues, reds, greens, and oranges all spun faster and faster, mirroring the colors played by the library orchestra.

The colors faded, purple streaks filling the inkwell. She leaned in. The purple streaks reminded her of the flashes she saw when her brain would freeze—but there were also streaks of red and orange.

She reached down and touched the silver chain of her red-orange carnelian gemstone necklace. She had found the stone hidden behind Riley's nightstand a year ago, and it reminded her of the one Lady Julie had worn on a bracelet.

Holding her necklace next to the inkwell, she compared the unique colors.

Weird. It's almost a perfect match.

"Are you awake?" Aven called out in a muffled voice.

"Uh, yeah, yes," she replied, her heart racing as she jerked the quill out of the inkwell, covering everything with her pillow. The colors disappeared, and she looked over at Aven's bed to see she still had the covers pulled up over her head. "I'm just gathering up a few things," she said, turning away from her sister to hide her writing items quickly.

Why am I nervous? She already saw the flying books and the lightning bolt in the hallway.

"We should get going. Right?" Aven called, stretching and pulling back her covers.

"Going?" Parker said.

"Yeah, breakfast, Drain Day, and everything. Big party, remember? No one can count how many cinnamon pulls I eat today, so time to start eating."

Aven rushed out of bed to the window in a blur, her hands on the ledge.

"Parker, Parker. The Drain Day kites. Get over here. The kites are out. Come see!"

Hundreds of colorful kites of all shapes and sizes with long trains and streamers behind weaved and bobbed. They danced in the sky, creating a bright, festive backdrop against the dark, churning waters surrounding their island. Water that would soon vanish when the terrifying whirlpool vortex was scripted into being and the Drain Day festival began.

The villagers gathered near the water's edge with stalls of delicious treats, pastries, and savory foods, booths of carnival games, and tents to listen to performers entertain with their mystical tales of faraway lands and creatures.

Parker looked to the top of the window frame where the three charred words were still visible:

iꞇ was wriꞇꞇen

Aven turned from the window to Parker.

"Why do you think Lady Julie wrote that?" Aven said.

"Shhh," Parker whispered. "We don't want to discuss her in front of Quinn. You know how she gets."

"Quinn isn't here," Aven said. "She left early before the sun was up. Maybe she was getting ready for the festival?"

Parker surveyed the room to ensure she was gone. "Either way, don't mention last night to Quinn, especially not today."

Aven shook her head.

Part of her wished Quinn had been in on it with her and Aven. But her oldest sister left early and returned late, barely talking with her siblings anymore, and was always cranky.

"It looks just like what we saw in the library," Aven said. "What does it mean?"

"I—I don't know," Parker responded. "When we woke up, the window had been open, and letters were there, in the wood of the window frame and on the stone wall. And Riley and Lady Julie were gone."

Her parents had tried everything to remove those words over the last year—chisels, paint, flames, but the words remained. Her mother had tried to hang a curtain over them, but each time, the wind would blow the curtains off. So, the inscription stayed.

"Is it a clue?" she asked.

"I guess," Parker said. "This and the words in the library are probably both clues, but clues to what?"

These words had led Parker to the library last night to retrieve her journal, quill, and the inkwell before she left. The words had convinced her she needed to write again. The story and the seriousness of Lady Julie's voice that last night told her something was in the room where she'd first learned to write.

Lady Julie was leaving them a message; she was sure of it.

But those exact three words—It Was Written—had led her parents to conclude something entirely different.

The words convinced her parents Lady Julie had kidnapped Riley. Lady Julie *must* be a Ravager. She had broken the sacred, ancient rule. Every man, woman, and child in Everly knew the old stories—how it had been the Ravagers who had used magic writing to destroy, imprison, kill, and kidnap. They left dark etchings with their quills. Ravagers had started the Great War that had led the Ancients to ban all magic writing,

These three words in their bedroom became a new dark etching. A warning. A reason for fear.

That inscription plunged the kingdom into the chaos now bubbling beneath the surface. Magic writing had returned, and her father had accelerated the fear by introducing the magic of Drain Day. This further encouraged the Illiterates to hunt and punish writers. People were afraid.

"You don't think Lady Julie is evil?" Aven asked.

"No, I know she's not," Parker said. "Before she left, in our last writing lesson, Lady Julie told me I was to be a storyteller."

"Like you tell bedtime stories kinda storyteller?"

"No, it's kinda like my job or my place or something. I don't exactly know, but it's sorta what I'm *supposed* to do," Parker said as she shrugged her shoulders. "Lady Julie told me I'm supposed to find answers to things—to figure out the truth—even when people think something else. I'm sure she wanted me to show the truth about what happened to Riley."

"But everyone says she's evil, she's a Ravager, and she kidnapped him," Aven said.

"I know, and that's why those words we found in the library matter," Parker said. "Truth Inside. It means what we found last night is something she wanted us to know. The truth."

Aven wrinkled her nose as she listened.

"I guess I don't know what it means, but you don't need to worry about it," Parker said. "I guess it's nothing we need to worry about today. It's Drain Day, right? Today is supposed to be fun."

Knock. Knock.

The girls froze and looked at one another.

"It's Lazlo," the voice called through the door. "Lazlo Grott. Your father sent me. I have an important message."

"Lazlo? Why would he come here? He's only ever come to our room once," Parker whispered to Aven.

"Shouldn't he be preparing for Drain Day? He's got to, like, vanish an ocean, right?"

"I don't know, but I'm pretty sure he despises me," Parker said. "No, fix that—I know he despises me."

"Why?"

"The last time he came here, I may have accidentally gotten him locked in the castle prison for a few weeks."

"A few weeks? You got *the* royal wizard magic writer guy—the guy who can vanish an entire ocean with a quill—locked in prison? I mean, no wonder he hates you."

"Yea, he refused to tutor me," Parker said. "Refused our dad, the king. I heard him tell our parents I was stubborn, strong-willed, and obstinate, which I figured out meant won't listen to anyone in charge."

"He's not wrong," Aven said with a shrug.

Knock. Knock.

"I know you're in there," Lazlo's muffled voice said. "Aven? Parker? This is Lazlo. I'll wait until you've dressed. It's *imperative*."

"What happened the last time he came here?" Aven asked.

Parker sighed. "It was right after Riley had… disappeared, about a year ago. I don't know if you even remember, but Lazlo came here to Everly and offered to help in the search. Everyone did. He was odd, always quiet in the back of the room, and when I asked him where he'd come from, he didn't answer. He just said something about a small village beyond the Grootten Mountains."

"He's still odd, Parker."

"I know. But you probably don't even remember this, but he offered to tell us a story before bedtime one night. You and Quinn fell asleep before he finished. I let him keep talking. It was nice to have someone to talk to. But then he said something odd."

"What?"

"He told me that his mother would tell him bedtime stories before she died."

"Oh, that's sad."

"No," Parker continued. "It wasn't that. He said his mother told him bedtime stories about her mother. But the stories were about how his grandmother could write *magic*."

"He told you that?"

"I know," Parker said, her face focused as she recounted the details of that night. "But that wasn't all. He told me after his mother died, he lived with her, his grandmother, and he told me how she showed him how to hold a quill and the ancient letters."

"That's how you found out he could write magic?"

"He told me his grandmother showed him the ancient letters and gave him a quill before she died to keep him safe. We talked for the rest of the night, and I told him about Lady Julie and how she taught me to write in that hidden library, but that I wasn't a magic writer. I just knew how to write normal stuff. The next morning, I raced to tell Father that Lazlo was a writer, and he could teach me again like Lady Julie had. And that he was a Serif, and if what Lady Julie had said before she left was true, maybe he could keep us safe from the Ravagers."

Parker paused.

"He just sat there in silence. Then he exploded, telling me to stay away from Lazlo and that he was a danger to us all. Later that day, I saw Lazlo in chains, the guards leading him to the dungeon. He looked so sad and hurt. He saw me, Lazlo did, and he knew. He knew it was me. I still can't forget how he looked at me."

"Could Lazlo know?" Aven asked. "Could he know about the magic library or the silver bolt thing you did?"

"I—I don't know. Maybe."

"Well, we should find out then, right?" Aven said to Parker. "Come in!" she called.

"What are you doing?" Parker hissed.

Lazlo entered the room and stood at the doorway. He was tall and thin, with dark, unkempt hair and a wispy beard. Lazlo wore round wireframe glasses and a brown jacket that was too large for his angular frame as if he were wearing something from a parent. He was just twenty years old, but the last year seemed to age him as if the shy, reserved boy with green eyes who had first come to help their distraught parents had vanished, and this curt and sullen man remained.

He nodded slightly to them.

"Tidings for Drain Day," he said as if searching for a greeting.

"You said you had a message?" Parker asked.

"Ah, right. Your father asked me to speak to you about the water. The water's edge... for today."

"You mean like the whole vanishing an ocean trick you do?" Aven asked.

"Well, not entirely. And it's not a trick; it's a magical inscription I write to vanish the water. But after the incident with Mister Wickerland, the boy who was in the water and... was taken, your father wanted to warn you personally of the power of the water. The enchantment is... uncontrollable."

Parker let out an audible sigh and rolled her eyes.

"Something you'd like to say, Miss Pennymore?"

"You came here to tell us that?" Parker asked. "To warn us or something?"

"At your father's request. King Domn asked me to remind *you*," he said, his eyes narrowing on Parker. Parker's father, Domnall, had always preferred to be called Domn since it was a much more friendly and approachable name for the King of Everly.

"It's Domnall," Parker corrected, narrowing her eyes at him. "It's King Domn-All. The whole thing; that's his name. *My* father."

An awkward silence hung in the air. Aven looked from her sister to Lazlo and back before finally clearing her throat. "So, yeah, Laz. That blue fireball thingy. The whole thing you do that vanishes the water and all. You know, the fireball in your hand. Can you do it?"

"Excuse me?" Lazlo replied.

"Yeah, the fireball thing," she said as she mimicked writing with a quill on her open palm. "I've never like seen it up close, er, *we've* never seen it up close. Could you do it now?"

"Magic is for protection," he mumbled.

"Do you *need* your quill?" Parker asked. "Do you have to have it to write?"

He eyed her suspiciously. "Of course. You script magic *with* a quill. That's how magic is written."

"But in some of the stories we've heard, there are rumors of Serifs—usually only the most powerful ones—who don't even *need* a quill to perform magic," Parker said, pressing him. "Have *you* ever written magic without your quill?"

Lazlo's eyes darted around the room. "Yes. I—I have," he said. "Not much, but... yes, I can. I can."

"Really?" Parker asked. "I thought it might only be a story, but..."

"It's different," he continued. "And difficult, much more difficult—"

"Can we see? See you do it without a quill?" Aven said. "We won't tell. I *promise*. And blue is my favorite color, ya know, for the fireball thing."

"I—I suppose I could show you... writing without a quill, just for a few seconds," he said as he squeezed his fists and inhaled deeply. Then he began to rub his thumb and forefinger together on each hand slowly.

"This is so cool of you. Thank you for this, really," Aven said as they watched Lazlo close his eyes, his lips moving as his finger and thumb now moved in what looked to be an intentional pattern.

Blue dust began to swirl around him, racing to his fingertips, as he opened his palm, and the dust formed a perfectly blue orb, with blue embers rising from it as if it were a flame.

"That's wicked," Aven said as she leaned forward to get a closer look. "Is it hot?"

"It's... nothing really," he replied. "Just the magic from the inscription."

"But no quill," Parker said. "That's not nothing."

"Yeah, it's so mysterious looking up close too," Aven said, reaching out her hand to try and touch it. Lazlo pulled his hand away quickly, shaking his head at her as he did. "Fine, fine. I won't touch it," she continued. "So you know that day, the day when you first brought the water in the amphitheater, the very first Drain Day. How did you know you could? Like, had you ever done that before?"

Lazlo shifted awkwardly from foot to foot, his fingers seeming to spin the glowing orb, as he gazed out the window watching the kites dance in the sky while the rest of Everly was readying itself for the day's festivities.

"I didn't," he said meekly. "I didn't know what would happen."

"That was the first time you did it?" Aven said. "Wow."

"Yes, he gave me a book with the letters, but I didn't... Your father gave me a choice, not really a choice. I was in the dungeon, a prisoner, and he told me I could go, I could leave..." He paused and looked at Parker, a sadness in his eyes. "If I could bring the water to protect his kingdom, to protect its children, then I would be free."

***

The Pennymore sisters sat in the amphitheater on Drain Day a year ago, the first time they'd gathered in public after Riley's disappearance. Perched high above the lush valley, the amphitheater provided a sweeping view for all those in attendance. The Kingdom was ready for this new celebration by their father, but Parker sensed awkwardness.

"Citizens of Everly," King Domnall called to the gathered people crammed in the amphitheater. "I welcome you to a day of celebration to honor our returning soldiers."

The crowd buzzed with anticipation. Rumors and whispers had passed throughout the kingdom following Riley's disappearance. *Has Riley been found? Do they have news from other parts of Fonde? Have they captured the kidnapper?*

As the first public appearance by the king since Riley's kidnapping and their caretaker Lady Julie's disappearance, his kingdom was on edge.

The crowd cheered his words as their husbands, fathers, and brothers who had returned from their searches for the king's son stood on the amphitheater stage with their arms waving to the crowd. Most had been gone for a month, and few had shared any news of their travels. A celebration was normally reserved for good news.

"And I bring you news," the king announced. "There are troubling forces at work in Fonde. These evil forces have begun to assemble, to build in strength and number. Our kingdom must prepare. We must be ready."

Murmurs poured out of the crowd. Many had suspected something after Riley vanished, but now the king was leaving no doubt.

Their father waved his hand, motioning to his guards, who brought forth a figure wearing his royal advisers' odd fitting, formal attire.

It was Lazlo.

This was the first time Parker saw him since they led him to the dungeon in chains. His green eyes nervously darted, surveying the crowd, their hushed voices wondering who he might be and why the king had brought him there.

"We've been tricked!" the king called out in his booming voice.

Boos rang out across the amphitheater. Lazlo shrank and recoiled as they did.

"A witch tricked us—she tricked all of us—and she has kidnapped my only son!"

More boos rained down.

"This boy. This boy, Lazlo, discovered the truth of her plans," the king said as he gestured to where Lazlo stood on the amphitheater floor. "He found evidence of her plot, proof of her deeds to harm my family, to try and destroy our kingdom hidden inside the castle, in the room she once lived in."

More boos. Then the voices in the crowd quieted.

"The Ravagers have *returned*!" he continued, pausing for this to sink in. "Her black etching was left as a message to me, to my family, to Everly!"

A hush fell over the crowd.

"We must be vigilant. We must be strong. We must be ready!"

The guards roughly dragged Lazlo to the newly built stone pedestal in the middle of the amphitheater. Parker couldn't tell if he was resisting or was simply being hurried along.

"We must protect our kingdom!" the king announced with a clap of his hands. "I do this now with great trepidation!"

Lazlo glanced at Parker, his sad green eyes connecting with hers before he looked back to her father. Parker followed Lazlo's gaze to her father and saw him nod to the boy.

Although the sky had been clear, thunder roared in the distance. Parker looked down at Lazlo as he reached into his cloak and grabbed a quill, holding it between his fingers.

The boy's lips began to move, and dark clouds filled the sky. A blue glow pulsed in the tip of the quill as a cool wind began to blow.

He's going to write magic.

"We must protect our kingdom!" the king repeated.

Lazlo pushed the glowing quill down onto the stone pedestal on his instruction. Sparks exploded from the stone, and pulsing turquoise and blue dust swirled around him, gaining speed as he continued to write. Confused murmurs emanated from those seated in the amphitheater at the magic not seen publicly for centuries.

Lazlo turned his left palm upward. The glowing dust raced to his palm, forming the blue flaming ball. He lowered his hand, then threw the flaming magical ball into the air, streaking like a comet across the darkened sky, a trail of dust behind it.

Gasps and screams poured from those still seated in the theater.

The flaming orb arched away from Everly before crashing into the lush valley below the amphitheater, an explosion of colors filling the sky like fireworks.

Then the midday sun darkened as the explosions of glowing dust pulled more, dark, ominous clouds into the sky. A blast of wind pounded the onlookers. Rivers of water rushed into the valley beyond the amphitheater stage, an ocean full of water pouring into the land surrounding Everly.

Lazlo was flooding the kingdom!

Birds scattered from their perches in the valley as the trees snapped like toothpicks, the rushing water crushing everything in its path. Forty-foot-tall waves crashed and exploded into one another.

Parker couldn't take her eyes off Lazlo as he scripted letter after letter with his pulsating quill on the glowing stone tablets. Then, for a brief moment, he looked at her, the ominous smile stretched across his face illuminated by the blue glow of the quill and the stone book.

Onlookers could only huddle with their loved ones, stunned as a sea formed around them, terrified, wondering when the rising water would stop.

As quickly as Lazlo had summoned the water, it simply stopped rising. In mere minutes, Everly had become an island. Dark, churning water flowed around it and completely isolated it from the rest of Fonde.

Magic writing, banned for centuries by the Ancients, was returned to Everly by their father in that instant.

Lazlo collapsed, his limp body falling to the ground near the pedestal. Guards raced over and picked him up, dragging him out of view.

"We are now safe!" the king said. A few isolated cheers went up, which seemed to be coming primarily out of fear of their father and the powerful new Serif by his side.

Crack!

The crowd's stunned, silent calm would not last long as a vast crack caused by the pressure of the seawater formed on the performance floor of the amphitheater. The gap raced across the stage floor as if the seawater was tearing a piece of paper, exactly where acrobats, musicians, and actors from across Fonde had performed.

Screams tore through the crowd as soldiers and officials who had been seated on the floor scrambled up the amphitheater steps. The crack spread, ripping through the ancient marble tiles.

Crack. Crack. Splash.

The floor crumbled under the power of the water. The amphitheater stage, designed for an audience to witness majesty and artistry, was sacrificed to the water.

The sea had taken its place as the leading actor, now drawing them monthly for her magnificent performance.

***

Lazlo closed his palm, and the blue, glowing orb extinguished itself, the flecks of brilliant teal and turquoise floating to the ceiling.

"Your father asked me to warn you of the power of the water," Lazlo repeated. "To be *certain* you received his message." He squeezed his fists tightly again.

"Why won't you fix it, the stage floor?" Aven asked, pointing out the window to the crumbled edges of the amphitheater. Its craggy, broken shore stood in sharp contrast to the crisp amphitheater seats.

Lazlo looked at her curiously.

"Couldn't our father at least remove the broken pillars and tiles?" Aven said. "The rest of the amphitheater looks like it'll tumble into the water too."

"Because he's stubborn," Parker said without thinking. Lazlo fixed his eyes on her.

"Your father is pragmatic. He says the water is too strong," Lazlo said. "He is wise and clever. Few could become a king without royal blood. You should heed his word. There will always be a crack. As I said, the water is *powerful*."

"The Illiterates, they see this—this performance, this celebration as breaking the Ancient's rules," Parker interrupted. "You're not keeping anyone safe."

"You should silence your tongue," Lazlo snapped, glaring at her.

"Silence your tongue," Parker repeated, the use of the odd phrase reminding her of the silent darkness Lady Julie had spoken of.

"I—I said watch your tongue. You could learn something from your older sister. *Watch* your tongue."

But he didn't say watch. He said silence. Why did he use that specific phrase? Why would he suddenly lie about what he'd said?

"Now be careful today," Lazlo said. "We wouldn't want to lose *another* child to the drain." His gaze lingered on Parker before he turned and rushed out the door, slamming it behind him.

Parker looked at Aven. "Did he just *threaten* us?"

"No, he threatened *you*," Aven said, shaking her head. "And why was that all necessary anyway?"

"He promised—Father promised he was not permitting writing again. He'd only enlisted Lazlo to keep the kingdom and its children safe. He'd told us this was just to protect us. But we aren't any safer. The Illiterates are hunting anyone who... anyone who disagrees."

"But that's not Lazlo's fault," Aven said.

"Fine, then I just don't get a good feeling from Lazlo. You saw how quick he was to show off his power. That was all it took to get him to do that. He's reckless, and I still can't believe he'd threaten me. *Me*."

"I dunno," Aven said. "I think you see things. I thought it was nice he showed us that."

Parker shook her head. She still couldn't get over how quickly he'd revealed this aspect of his magic abilities... and the way he spoke to her dripping with disdain. He was warning her about something, something beyond the risks of the water's edge. And she had no intention to stick around long enough to find out if he'd back up the threat. Parker knew she had to go. Between Lazlo, the guards, her parents, and the library. *It had to be today.*

It's a good thing he refused to tutor me. That guy makes my other tutors look faultless.

"Then is Drain Day still safe for us?" Aven asked, turning to watch the rough seas outside their bedroom window and the dancing kites above.

"It'll be fine," Parker reassured her sister. "People are scared right now."

Aven nodded. "But what if the Illiterates find the library, then… then what would they do to us?" she asked.

Parker gently placed her hands on the back of Aven's shoulders and gave her a gentle squeeze. "They won't. Now let's hurry. Being in this room after… whatever that was is giving me the creeps."

Parker took the blue dress with the hidden pockets and stowed the quill, inkwell, and journal inside, ensuring her sister didn't see.

There were already too many opportunities for something to go wrong, and her sister's big mouth was a chance she'd rather not take.

The Illiterates and those four dots were eyes inside the castle, watching everything.

And she was afraid of what they might see.

Chapter Five

The Exploded Chandelier

"Would you just hurry up," Parker said, holding the small wooden lantern boat she'd made for the Drain Day festival.

"Last one down has to *eat* a rotten egg," Aven called out as she burst from their bedroom.

"You seriously think you can beat *me* down while *you* hold your lantern boat for the festival?" Parker asked. "I'm the champ, ya chump."

"You're gonna eat *two* rotten eggs," Aven called back as she tipped her head up, howled, and leaped off the first step, her wolf-shaped lantern boat under her arm.

Parker shook her head. Aven was going through a "phase"—at least that's what her parents and others said—where she believed she was a wolf. In the past year, she had become obsessed with wolf behavior. This included incessant, ear-piercing howls, chasing the castle staff up and down the corridors, wearing sewn wolf ears in her hair, growling on all fours, drinking water from a bowl, and occasionally chasing a terrified chicken or other farm animals across the yard.

Aven's fascination with wolves first began after the girls' father told them the story of *Little Red Riding Hood*. Aven had missed the "big bad" part of her favorite character's infamous title, instead becoming fixated on the idea of a wolf dressed as a grandmother in a nightgown.

Since then, the wolves in stories like the *Three Little Pigs* or *The Boy Who Cried Wolf* could do no wrong, no matter how sharp their teeth or cunning their tricks. And Aven would tell anyone who would listen she would be a wolf when she grew up. So, it wasn't surprising that her lantern boat design of choice was a gray wolf with a fluffy tail, pointed ears, and a mouth she'd made by cutting ridges into small pieces of wood to resemble teeth.

Parker let her still-howling little sister get down the first few steps to give Aven a chance at a decent early lead. Parker had mastered the railing slide and could slide her way down at least forty of the steps before gliding off and running down the remainder. She counted in her head to fifteen, knowing it would be enough of a head start. Then she planned to career down and race in front just before her sister reached the next landing. She boosted herself onto the railing.

"Here I *coooommme*," Parker called down.

And whoosh, she was flying. She wobbled and had to brace herself on the wall. Parker realized the railing slide was faster—much faster—than expected, probably because the railing had recently received a coat of polish. She held her free arm out to keep her balance, slamming her shoulder into the stone wall.

Finally, she saw her sister in her sights as she whizzed down and executed a perfect dismount, sliding off in stride and breezing past her sister.

"Hey! No fair," Aven called out.

Parker purposely let herself crash and tumble down several stairs. "Don't worry," she said, turning back to her sister with a wry grin, "you'll catch up in the next paarr..." She let her hands flail for extra dramatic effect while making sure the tumble wasn't too noticeable.

I am so good at this big sister stuff.

Parker knew what it was like to be a little sister and wanted Aven to feel like she'd won their race fair and square.

"Serves you right," her younger sister called as she zoomed past and made her way to the bottom of the stairwell.

Aven scrunched up her face playfully at the bottom of the stairs waiting for her big sister. The pair performed their elaborately choreographed routine involving each of them bumping one fist, spinning around backward twice with an arm flap and butt-shake in between, before finishing the spin with a bump of their other fists. They looked at each other and laughed before Aven took off with her lantern boat down the hallway.

Parker lingered at the base of the steps for a moment. Their mother despised these races. At least once a month, she'd have to replace a fallen ornate picture frame featuring some painting, all of whom were "at least a hundred years old," Aven would say. Parker knew why her mother was upset when the frames were broken —whoever made them added the same carvings, gems, tiles, and miniature painting inside squares and circles built into the frame she'd seen in the mirror inside the hidden library. These paintings were one piece of art in addition to all the embedded art in the frames.

"Well, goodbye, for now, Mister Old Guy with a doggie," Parker said in a deep falsetto voice as she straightened one of the askew paintings that had about a dozen different carvings of shells, fish, and items you'd find at a beach in the frame-art. "Hope to see you when I return," she whispered.

Parker looked back down the hall, seeing Aven standing still in the middle of the hallway. Then her younger sister turned to look at Parker, looking as if she'd seen a ghost.

The chandelier! I totally forgot about it after Lazlo's surprise visit. The bolt. The shriek from the guard last night. Oh no.

Parker raced toward her sister, seeing the magnificent, ancient chandelier now lying in a broken heap at the end of the hallway. Glass, wood, and metal shards littered the hallway.

"You think anyone will notice?" Aven asked.

Parker turned to her sister, widening her eyes at the ridiculousness of that suggestion.

That was why the guard screamed. The chandelier didn't just fall. It exploded. Did it fall onto the guard? Oh, wow, wow, wow. This is way worse than I thought... like way, way. And what caused the exploding chandelier is hiding inside my dress pockets. This was a terrible idea.

Parker looked across the hallway at the tapestry hiding the door they'd broken into last night. Nothing out of place there.

Maybe this is explainable. Perhaps this isn't so bad.

Pop. Pop. Pop. Pop. Pop. Pop.

What was that noise?

A rapid-fire sound rang out from the Hall of Resplendence, followed by screams. Parker looked down at her dress where the book was hiding, gently patting it to make sure it hadn't decided to fire off blue lightning bolts by itself.

"*Quinndaline!*" a familiar voice screamed.

The two girls smiled, relieved for once it hadn't been them. The pair raced to the door of the hall, eager to leave the scene of the chandelier explosion to see why their older sister Quinn was in a heap of trouble.

A sweet aroma met them as they opened the doors, followed by another wave of the same sounds.

Pop. Pop. Pop. Pop. Pop. Pop.

"Quinn Penny*more!*" their mother's voice bellowed out. "Stop your machine this instant. *Now!*"

Quinn crouched near the wall next to a contraption of tubes, coils, bubbling tan liquids, and wafts of steam. A large circular pipe came out of the gadget, and right on cue, a rapid-fire barrage of golden-brown circles flew across the room, splattering on the walls, the ceiling, the floors, and the clothing of the people gathered to help prepare for Drain Day.

Quinn stood and raised her goggles to the top of her head; black soot formed a perfect raccoon-mask ring where her goggles had been. She waved to the entire room, who stared back at her.

"Uh, yeah, about that... So, it's not quite working *yet*." Quinn gestured to the device she'd been fixing. "I was planning to bring it to Drain Day. Who wouldn't love a doughnut while they watch the whole ocean disappear?"

Quinn didn't apologize and didn't do anything on accident. Today Quinn had a new bright pink streak in her hair, a strand Parker was sure Quinn had chosen, so it fell over her eyes and would need to be pulled behind her ear constantly. This was why she was both the coolest girl in the entire kingdom and, at the same time, the most infuriating.

"What in the world is *this*?" their mother shouted.

The Hall of Resplendence had hosted visitors from faraway lands and festivals to celebrate important moments in Everly. Any visitor would gasp when they set foot in the room, given the blend of colors, scents, and lights that blanketed the massive space. At this time of day, the room was awash in pinks, oranges, and reds from the stained glass windows that covered the walls and ceiling. Massive columns held the glass roof that supported the overhead canopy of intricate shapes and patterns designed to let light dance and move with the sun's rays. But the room was not only an architectural wonder. A team of more than ten gardeners and arborists worked every day to keep the hall filled with seasonal plants and flowers always in full bloom. The use of windows and stained glass enabled their father to fill the space with bushes, trees, flowers, and plants from across Fonde of all shapes, sizes, and colors, creating a feeling of being outdoors in the most lavish gardens on earth.

The hisses, hums, and bangs of the machine contrasted the natural scenery unique to this space in the heart of the Garamond Castle.

This morning, Quinn's invention had splattered dozens of golden-brown globs on the glass walls, forming streaks and blobs that radiated outward like a series of doughy suns. One of the doughnut-suns fell with a plop to the ground.

"It's my doughnut delivery device," Quinn said with a shrug. "I was going to call it the triple D... and I guess it's still kinda a prototype. But I swear it was working perfectly last night, and now—"

She gestured to the wall, her face filling with embarrassment. Parker grinned, hoping her mother would miss her.

Quinn was the family's golden child and their father's favorite because she liked to tinker just like he did. Quinn could pretty much fix anything—though not always on the *first* try. After a bit of tweaking, she'd find a way to make perfectly prepared pastries fly through the air and gently land on the plate. But moments like this when something didn't work, or she didn't get it right, or she didn't win, a whole other side of Quinn came out.

"Just work!" she banged on the tubes with a wrench. "Ahhh! You stupid thing. I should call you triple F for failure. I—I swear it just worked, and ahhhh—" Quinn pulled her inventing goggles down on her face and turned back to the device, her way to escape from the rest of the world.

To make matters worse, Quinn had not arrived in the formal attire her mother had laid out. Instead, she wore pants with pockets she'd filled with tools and trinkets she needed for the day, her inventing goggles perched on her head, and with a brand-new streak of pink in her hair. And it was bright pink, clearly not subtle.

Rebellion is one of the only things we still have in common.

"At least it's not us this time," Parker whispered to Aven.

"What's on her fingernails?" Aven asked.

Parker saw the glints of her fingernails etched in patterns of silver and gold shapes she hadn't seen before. They were intricate and subtle, but the explosions of light when the sunlight caught them were unmistakable.

Where did she get those? Just another perk of being the oldest and the favorite. Maybe that's where she's been sneaking off to. Pink hair and now etching her fingernails with gold and silver, and they think I'm the bad apple they need to send away. Puh-lease.

"Your hair and these inventions," her mother stammered. "Quinn Pennymore, you simply had to pick today of all days to make a mess of your hair and my walls!"

Pop. Pop. Pop. Pop. Pop. Pop…

More doughnuts rocketed from the pipe, now darker in color as a burning scent wafted through the room.

Quinn put a hand on her forehead and began banging on the device again with a wrench. "It was *just* working…"

Their mother sighed and walked toward the entrance where her younger daughters stood.

"Good morning, Aven," Mother said politely. "I—"

Before her mother could say another word, Aven let out an ear-splitting howl jolting everyone who wasn't already cautiously watching the doughnut delivery device.

"Awooooooo!"

She howled again—louder this time—before she could be reprimanded and then raced around the table to show her lantern boat to Quinn.

Aven's eyes sparkled as she lifted her wolf-boat up and down like it was chasing an imaginary sheep or a little girl in a red hood. She raced over to her big sister and threw her arms around Quinn.

"Aven Pennymore!" her mother called out.

As her mother stood beside Parker surveying the Hall of Resplendence, she absentmindedly muttered, wondering how on earth she'd get this all cleaned before dinner.

"They drive me crazy, but I do love them to pieces," Mother said as she exhaled.

Them? Just them?

Parker nodded, unsure what to say.

"How's my girl?" Parker's mother asked.

"I'm fine. I'm good," Parker answered, the first they'd spoken since their fight yesterday and her mother's decision to send her to her aunt's.

"And the hallway?" her mother said quickly. "You saw, yes?"

How could I not see? A chandelier exploded from a magical bolt from my writing journal! Is she saying she knows it was me? Did the guard tell her? Did he see the book and whatever happened? He must have recognized the black towel cape and told her everything… I knew I shouldn't have used one without my initials sewn into it. Stupid Parker. Just play it cool. Play it cool, Parker.

"You mean the chandelier?" Parker asked, trying to sound as carefree as possible. "Yeah, we saw. What happened to it?"

Her mother began to shake her head and bit her lip. Then she faced Parker.

"Disfigured, slashed, will never recover. I couldn't look. I'm just devastated."

"Who? Who won't recover?" Parker asked.

"It's—it's part of living in these old, ancient buildings, I suppose," her mother said, ignoring her question. "The guard thought it was a bolt."

The silver lightning bolt from my book. Oh no. The guard must have seen everything.

"A bolt? Was the guard hurt?" Parker asked, the visual of last night rushing into her mind.

"Oh, heaven's no," her mother said, shaking her head. "The hallway was empty when it crashed, not a soul around. One of the bolts holding it to the ceiling just snapped, we think."

That can't be. I was there last night. Someone had to be there. I heard the guard ask who was there. I heard him call out, then the crash, then his scream when the lightning exploded from my book. Did something else happen last night?

"Well, after the crash, one of the night guards went in and saw the mess," her mother said. "We were lucky it happened in the middle of the night, or certainly someone could have gotten hurt."

"Well, that's good, I guess," Parker said.

An awkward silence hung in the air.

"About yesterday—" her mother said.

"I don't want to talk about it," Parker said.

"Then we won't." Her mother patted her daughter on her forearm. "But I've sent word to your aunt, and we'll arrange everything with her. Your father and I think it'll be good for you."

Good for me?

Her mother hadn't changed her mind. Parker's chest tightened, and her hand clenched the lantern boat tighter, feeling it begin to creak and crack from the pressure. She shifted from foot to foot, seething.

She has no idea what's good for me. She has no idea what's good for any of us, and now they are hiding things like the enchanted library—all the secrets and lies.

Her anger was quickly replaced with a tinge of sadness, knowing this was going to be a goodbye, even if her mother didn't.

I haven't thought about how to even say goodbye. Maybe I'll just do something more casual. Do I hug? Would that be weird?

Parker patted Mother's shoulder. She hadn't planned it, and it turned out more like how you'd pat the top of a dog's head.

That turned out less casual and more awkward than I'd intended. Maybe she won't notice.

Her mother twisted her head to look at Parker's hand, scrunching her face a bit as she did.

"Well, looks like you've got your hands full," Parker said to her mother, gesturing to the splattered wall. "So we're off now, Pip!" She wasn't sure why she'd done it, but using her mother's first name felt good, a little daring.

Pip, and her given name Piper, wasn't a very royal-sounding name for a queen, but she'd gone by Pip since she was young and refused to change it just to appease one of her husband's snobby advisers. She wasn't of royal blood, either; Mother often liked to remind the siblings that royalty came from your actions, not your parentage.

"Eh-hem. My friends call me Pip," she called to her daughter with a disapproving head shake. "And we are *not* friends, miss."

Quinn's doughnut device let out a noisy screech and then fell silent. Even Quinn took a moment to raise her goggles and turn away from her invention to listen.

"And we aren't through, young lady," Mother said sternly to Quinn, getting a sarcastic salute from her eldest daughter when her mother was no longer looking. "Now, just a moment, you two," she called out to Parker and Aven.

Parker should have expected this. She sucked in her stomach a bit to make sure the hidden pocket she'd made in the dress containing her forbidden quill, inkwell, and journal wouldn't be visible.

Quinn had taught the younger girls the word "overbearing," a term she'd said meant their parents were so concerned with their well-being they would check their finished dinner plates to make sure they hadn't hidden lima beans under the mashed potatoes.

"Now, girls, I wanted to introduce you to a nice man who'll be your chaperone," Mother said, motioning to the guards who were standing at the far end of the room.

"My chaper-what?" Aven asked.

"It's the guard who makes sure we don't get into trouble," Parker whispered to her sister.

"This is Major Cappa," she said as one of the guards stood at attention in front of their mother. "He's one of the best—been with us for, how long?"

"Must be at least since your daughter Quinn was a baby, ma'am," Major Cappa said. "It's good to see you both again." He looked at Aven, bringing his finger to his lips exactly as the guard had done last night.

"Now," Mother continued. "When the water is gone, we do not want you to be alone. It's simply not safe, and so the Major will be at the amphitheater, and you'll find him the instant the festival is over, and he'll return with you here. You're not to be alone outside the castle until the water returns. Do you understand?"

Parker nodded and looked over at Aven, nervously staring at the man.

"Wait here a moment, girls. Major, a word?" their mother said, walking with him a few feet away and continuing to speak to the Major as the girls looked on.

"How annoying," Parker whispered, leaning over to Aven. "What next? A leash?"

"That's him," Aven hissed. "From last night." Aven held up her hand and touched four dots on the back of her hand, the sign of the Illiterates.

"Are you sure?" Parker whispered, trying to avoid them from hearing. "The one outside the tapestry?"

"It's him. I would remember him anywhere. And he looked at me like he remembered."

Parker stared at them, trying to see if she could see the four dots on his hand. The two adults walked back to the sisters.

"Thank you, Major," she said, as the man nodded to their mother and smiled at the sisters before returning to stand with the other guards.

"The two of you are under no circumstances to touch the water, either of you." She looked at Parker. "And you keep your eyes on your sister, and once the torchbearer lights the lantern boats and the water has receded, you're both to return—"

"—for dinner with father," Parker answered. "We know. We know. We'll be fine."

Parker looked back to Major Cappa, who continued to stare intensely at them.

"Do you think you'll see your friend, Cassandra Waddle, at the festival?" her mother asked. "I always liked Cassandra when she came around."

"We aren't friends anymore," Parker answered. "She's... changed."

"That's too bad," Mother said. "Maybe you'll reconnect soon, and things will be like before."

"Maybe, but sometimes things change... for the best. Anyway, we'd better get going. Right, Aven?" Parker asked as her sister nodded nervously, still looking over at the Major.

"And where are you two off to this early?" Mother asked. "Plenty of work needing done here, and we could use extra hands to help—especially with the mess in the hall and your sister doing her best to create more work for us all. Plus, you know the amphitheater shore can be quite... dangerous."

Parker knew her mother was referring to Owen. The drowning had been bad enough, but Owen's parents had been particularly critical of her father's decision to use magic writing to protect the kingdom, making it even more of a problem.

"We're going to see the other boats," Parker answered. "We don't get to see them long before they get put into the water."

"And burned," Aven added. "You know they burn them. Right?"

"I'm pretty sure she knows," Parker said, and then she paused briefly before continuing. "And I have a good feeling something might happen today to make for an excellent story."

Parker's voice cracked as she said "sto-RY," and she hoped her mother mistook the crack for excitement for the festival rather than nerves about successfully pulling off her plan. Her mother's glare lingered.

"Now, Parker, remember. We don't want *excellent* stories. I'd prefer no stories, none at all. You two must be at the amphitheater on time—before noon when it begins—and you stay clear of the water. Major Cappa will be waiting to escort you back here immediately after the festival."

An excellent story. What are you thinking?

Pop. Pop. Pop.

The machine was firing a spray of raw dough now. Quinn began banging on her device as their mother shook her head and quickly walked over to her.

"Quinn Penny*more!*"

"Come on, Aven," Parker said, realizing now was their chance.

Maybe for once, Quinn will finally get in some real trouble for this… but I seriously doubt that.

"We should go… *now*," she whispered as Parker caught Major Cappa still staring at them.

More eyes seemed to be watching everything.

Chapter Six

The Plumes

"Check your straps," Parker said.

"I *already* did. I checked, like, twice now," Aven responded.

Parker sighed, unbuckled her own straps in the modified spring-powered wine-cask-carriage, and turned around to check that Aven's were fastened right.

Younger sisters. Always have to argue about everything... which I suppose is a little funny given I'm also a younger sister who loves to argue with my older sister. But that's different. Quinn's bossier than I'll ever be.

Parker had already checked to be sure their underground cask-carriage was properly fastened to the metal rails running the length of this tunnel. She tugged on the straps holding her younger sister into the seat inside the wine cask before facing forward. Then she refastened herself, triple-checking her own straps. She had seen what happened when these wine casks didn't quite complete this trip.

The ancient tunnels beneath the castle had once been a way to protect the royal family in the event of an attack, but they'd sat empty for years until Quinn had discovered the entrance while hunting for one of her sisters during a game.

This particular tunnel led all the way to Everly, and if you didn't mind the darkness, the feeling like someone could be hiding in any corner, or the horrid smell, it was a decent way to get away from normal castle life.

This cask-carriage had been one of Quinn's best and most practical of her inventions. After her eleventh tardy of the semester and being tired of the fifteen-minute walk from the castle to the town, Parker needed to find a way to speed up the trip.

A girl needs her beauty rest. Am I right?

The sisters had dreamed up a million ideas to cut the trip time, including running a rope to create a zipline from their bedroom (too dangerous and only took them one way), a canal and a boat (too much digging), and a pair of handmade wings (something they could never quite get to work).

They settled on this spring-powered wine cask-carriage.

Quinn had first set out to develop the spring providing thrust to propel them from this end of the tunnel to Everly and then back. The carriage required some serious launching power. Because the tunnels had curves and bends throughout, the thrust needed to carry them over a long distance through some turns and twists that made their stomachs drop.

Parker's older sister had spent hours researching the hidden library until she found an old book of their father's. After a few designs, the spring Quinn developed had proven so powerful they had turned a fifteen-minute walk into a ninety-second blur that took their breaths away.

Parker and Quinn had then taken an old wine cask, cut a hole in the side where they could climb inside, and built two cushioned seats. The pair had tried lots of different approaches to get it to work. Eventually, Quinn figured out an elegant solution, raising the metal rails off the ground about three feet up and placing wheels on the side of the cask-carriage on both the top and the bottom of the rail. This allowed the carriage to go as fast as the spring would propel it and avoided careening off when they took a tight turn.

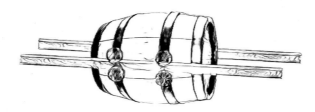

The other benefit was it allowed the pair to create a few places where the carriage would barrel roll in a corkscrew, unnecessary for the trip but worth it for the rider. Fun was a big part of the cask-carriage ride once you were strapped correctly in the seats. The girls had learned the hard way to avoid a heavy breakfast before the trip by cask-carriage.

As Quinn was fond of telling her sister, she put the *fun* in functional.

Quinn had let Parker do the painting and decorating of their invention, and she'd colored the carriage a dark blue with streaks of yellows to make it look like a comet. Then as soon as she released the lever, the spring-loaded comet would slingshot through the twisting tunnels crisscrossing the space beneath the castle.

I still can't believe Quinn didn't tell me about the pink streak or the etched nails. That's rule-breaking we used to do together.

The sisters had only built this section to take them from the castle to Everly and avoid more tardy slips, but they'd had grand plans to expand this to let them travel throughout the entire kingdom eventually.

"Seriously. You didn't mess with the straps. Right?" Parker asked again.

"Just go," Aven said.

Parker checked her straps a fourth time for good measure and looked out the small window in front to be sure no obstacles were in the way. Once, they'd almost taken out a family of storks that had decided to build their nest in the tunnels.

"Three!" Parker called out, gripping the lever in front of her.

"Two!" Aven called back.

"*One!*" the sisters yelled in unison.

Parker took a deep breath and gritted her teeth as she pulled the handle. *Whooooooooosh!*

***

"Drain Day. Drain Day! Still no sign of Owen Wickerland," the boy about Parker's age called out near the entrance of the street. "Parents call for the end of the drain!"

"Hiya, Monty," Parker said.

Montgomery Volmer, who went by Monty and had curly dark hair cut short, wore a bright blue tunic. He had this infectious curiosity and enthusiasm that drew people in and made him the ideal partner to co-lead the Plumes with Parker. Monty had recently become a news shouter because he needed to earn money for his family. They'd been traders, but ever since

Everly had become an isolated island, trading had become much more difficult and made it tough for them to make ends meet.

"Hey, how did *you* get here?" he asked as he uncupped his hands, clearly surprised to see Parker and Aven pop up from nowhere.

"The tunnels underneath the castle," Parker replied with a shrug.

"Underground tunnels?" he asked, his eyes widening at the idea.

"Quinn found them," Aven said.

"And then we built... well, basically she built an underground, spring-powered carriage to get you from the castle to Everly in about a minute," Parker said. "It's pretty amazing."

"Whoa. Your sister built an underground roller coaster," Monty shot back. "She's more epic than I thought. Think you could ask her if I can ride it?"

"Sure, we've got an extra helmet," Parker replied.

Aven shot Monty a skeptical look. "You don't get motion sickness. Right? It's a pretty wild ride—not sure you can handle it. And you know, it'd be pretty embarrassing if you puked all over Quinn's famous invention."

Monty shook his head and smiled awkwardly.

"Wait, are you afraid you might toss your cookies in front of our *big* sister?" Aven said, cocking her head.

"Come on. Leave Monty alone, Aven," Parker said. "Now, I need you to take our lantern boats and head down to the festival." She motioned to an empty alley ahead of them. "I have to talk to Monty."

"About what?" Aven asked.

"Just stuff," Parker said as she handed her boat to Aven.

"But I don't want to go," Aven said, refusing to take the boat.

"Why are you so annoying sometimes?" Parker snapped. "You're not a baby, Aven. You can do things like this and go places and be brave."

Aven glanced at Monty, who looked away from the conflict between the sisters, then looked at Parker.

"I'm—I'm sorry," Parker said, leaning down to her sister. "It's just, I'm not always going to be around or be there to take you places. You're not just some kid. You're a Pennymore."

"Okay, I'll try," Aven said, taking the boat from Parker, her eyes still on Monty. "I will. No, I will."

"Be careful. Stay out of the alleys and stay in the busy parts—"

Before Parker could finish, Aven raced off carrying the lantern boats.

Aven slowed for a second as she exited the street and looked back at them, faintly smiling. "Bye, Monty!"

Parker let out a deep breath. Now that Aven was gone, things felt real and heavy, much like they had with her mother. She was here to say goodbye to her closest friend before she left, without actually saying those words.

"That was a little harsh. Don't ya think?" Monty replied.

"You and I, we needed to talk. *Alone*. And she's—she's just gotta grow up a bit."

"I guess," he replied.

Monty had a way of calming her down when her frustrations got the best of her. One of the few children to befriend Parker after her brother's kidnapping, he wasn't from one of the royal families that her parents knew. She suspected that was one of the main reasons her parents blamed him and her other new friends for her recent issues.

She scanned around them, then leaned in to whisper into Monty's ear.

"I found my quill," she whispered. "The real one, with the red tip on the feather. The one I told you about."

"You what?"

Parker nodded. Monty had been the first person she trusted enough to share her secret: She could write. The boy's eyes had lit up.

He'd admitted he had found scraps of paper in the forest with letters on them he didn't understand. He'd pour dirt and sand on the floor of his room and try to match the shapes on his scraps. That rebellious streak had drawn Parker to him and bonded the pair. When he'd learned she knew how to write, he begged her to help him learn. It had made her nervous, but seeing him feel the joy she had felt allowed her to ignore her nerves. As he'd brought others into their group, she'd seen the new members inspired and changed.

"Where?" Monty asked in a low voice.

Parker motioned behind her shoulder to the castle.

"Wow. There must be hidden things and secrets everywhere. I sometimes can't believe you live there," Monty replied, his eyes scanning the towering castle over Parker's shoulders. "What's it like to live in an enchanted castle?"

Parker recoiled slightly.

Why did he say enchanted? He can't know what we saw last night inside our magical library. Right?

She shrugged, uncomfortable talking about it. "It's like being trapped in a prison where everyone is always trying to make sure you don't mess something up. Any news on Owen?" Parker asked, changing the subject. Owen's story had dominated the news for the last month, much like it had dominated her dreams.

"Nothing," he said, his smile vanishing. "He disappeared without a trace, no body, no nothing. There's not a news shouter in the kingdom I haven't talked to about it, and nobody has told me a thing. Drain's got him now."

Drain's got him now.

News shouters like Monty were how information spread. The web of stories, rumors, and whispers was passed around like a game between teenage boys and girls. Monty knew better than anyone how to get someone to buy a personal telling of the most significant happenings of the day, reeling passersby in with catchy "voice lines" and questions.

"Owen's disappearance last Drain Day has gotten the Illiterates spooked," Monty continued. "I'm hearing rumors about something big... today. I heard they took a fourth suspected writer this month. They just showed up and took the woman right in front of her children—ripped her kids straight out of her arms."

The vision of a mother ripped away from her family jolted Parker, reminding her of the moment that powerful force had dragged Owen underwater.

"It's not right," Parker replied. "None of it is. Words, ink, and paper are not something to be afraid of."

"I agree, but Owen's father is the leader of the Illiterate group hunting writers. They are looking for a fight. And Owen's disappearance has only made them more committed to their cause. Now your father is enemy number one for the Illiterates. We're hearing they are planning something, maybe related to Drain Day. No one quite knows what, and I have spoken to all the other news callers. Not a leak of what to expect, so just... just be careful."

Already angry at her father for letting Lazlo use magic on Drain Day, the Illiterates now had Owen Wickerland as a martyr for their cause.

But why now? Why today? Has the guard told them about the hidden library?

"You think someone knows something?" Parker asked. "Something about the Plumes?"

"No," he replied. "We've been careful, cautious."

"Sure," she said. "But maybe we're pushing this too much. This whole army of writers thing is… it's a lot."

"Listen, don't get cold feet on me now, Pennymore," Monty said.

"It's not your problem," she replied. "It's mine, and I didn't want to drag you into my stuff. I—I shouldn't have gotten you in this mess."

"It's not your mess, Parker," he said, shaking his head. "It's ours, all of ours. Remember, you were the one who told me what Lady Julie said about Dagamar, his power to attack with the silent darkness, and him rebuilding some army. You're the one who told me about the clues she'd left to be ready for what may soon come. That's not a Parker problem. That's an all of us problem."

"I know. I know."

"And if she was right that night, it was a Serif—someone who knew how to write magic—that stopped Dagamar once. If no one else is stepping up to do it, it had better be us. *You* said that."

"But teaching some kids from our class to write letters with a bag of white sand is different from trying to be ready for some magic war. You're pushing for an army…"

Parker stopped and turned away, staring at the castle. Garamond Castle wasn't a giant castle, but her father had helped redesign it to be the most unique and recognizable structure in all of Fonde.

He had an eye for angles, and the fourteen perfectly arranged buildings looked as if the castle were the Amaryllis flower, a flower he'd first seen when he and their mother hiked together as teenagers. He'd built a series of natural tubes and cuts on the castle walls to capture all the rainwater that looked like multi-colored stems weaving up the towers. Then, during his travels as a young boy, Father found a unique, shimmery layer inside a seashell. When he applied the coating to the roof and stone walls, it changed color patterns so that when the sun hit the castle just right at this time of the morning or early evening, it shimmered as if engulfed in pink fire.

A Flower on Fire.

The Flower on Fire began to glow as the light reflected off its towers. What was inside was troubling her. She'd felt torn this morning, leaving her home when she'd learned more secrets, but knew there wasn't a choice; if she didn't go on her own, they were sending her away.

Monty sighed. "You found more than your quill. Didn't you?"

She nodded. "I did. I found another inscription too. And I'm sure it's a clue from her."

"See," Monty said. "I knew it."

"No," Parker said. "This is real, Monty. Aven and I found an enchanted room, a library hidden in the castle."

"Enchanted?"

"Like, books flying around and magic lightning destroying things kind of enchanted," Parker said.

Monty's eyes widened.

"Look, I didn't just find my quill. I had to *catch* my quill." Parker turned her foot to show Monty the marks from the quills that had stuck her as they escaped last night. "That's not the half of it."

"Did you write magic?" Monty asked as a look of shock filled his face.

"No, of course not," Parker said. "I'm not a magic writer."

"That would have been cool, if you could write magic," he said. "Either way, if you figured out there's more magic writers than just Lazlo, the Plumes need to know. This is why we made this secret society in the first place. This *is* real."

"This is dangerous, Monty."

"Remember what *you* told me?" he asked her. "You told me that you can't write magic unless you can write. And if there's any chance that what you found inside the castle means a magic war is coming to Everly, you owe it to us, you owe it to me, to tell us. We can help."

"I never wanted the Plumes to have to write magic. That was never what I wanted."

"Then why did you teach them to write anything?" he asked. "This might be the only way for these kids to stay safe, Parker. Enchanted rooms, inscriptions, and flying books. It's not some accident."

"I came here to tell you this in person," Parker continued, knowing what she would say next would probably hurt him. "I want to disband the Plumes—"

"No. No way. *You* can't decide to disband after what you just told me," he barked.

"People could get hurt, Monty," she said. "The Illiterates aren't messing around; you know that. And magic writing—if that's what this is—it's way beyond writing a few letters in some sand."

"Yea, but it's *our* group. Plumes were as much my idea as it was yours. And you said it yourself, the quills and the library… they are telling us something, Pennymore. We all made our own decisions, and you can't just stop what we started."

"No," Parker said as she felt her heart beating in her fingertips.

"I'm not pushing for some army of writers," Monty said. "This is our home too. I'm just pushing for you to lead the Plumes. To tell them."

"You can't mean that."

"I can. And whatever you're worried about, we got your back."

Monty wouldn't say that if he knew I was running away from the fight. I'm not the leader he thinks I am.

She looked at the ground. "I'm just afraid that I'll let everyone down," she said, her hands shaking. "Okay?"

Monty put his hand on Parker's shoulder. "You're the bravest person I know, all of us know. The Plumes don't come for me. They come for you. You're the one who is willing to stand up to everyone, your parents, your teachers, your sisters, the Illiterates, everyone. We're all tired of being pushed around. They need to know what it's all for. You're the real deal, Pennymore."

She sighed. "I just came to tell you. You can tell them for me."

"No. *You* need to tell the Plumes too," he said. "You owe them that."

Parker bit her lip. *This isn't part of my plan.*

"Maybe—maybe you're right," she said, her hand touching her dress where she'd hidden the items.

"Maybe?"

"Yea, maybe they do need to know," she said.

"Yea, they do, Parker. They *deserve* that."

A quick stop doesn't have to change my plan, just a detour… for my friends. I share what we found last night. That's it.

"So, what are you thinking?" Monty asked.

"I'm thinking that in every story, there's that moment when you have a choice, a now or never moment, I guess," Parker said as she smiled slightly.

"Ah, the call to action, right?" Monty said. "You taught us about that one. Every hero needs to answer her call to action. So this looks like it's your call, Pennymore." Monty moved his eyebrows up and down at her.

"You know, I want to strangle you sometimes," Parker said, shaking her head.

"Is this gonna be the inciting incident?" Monty said, smiling.

Parker shook her head. "You're an inciting pain in my neck. But you're right. It's something important they need to hear and see for themselves," Parker said. "They deserve that."

She stared at Monty and then looked at the ground between them. With her foot, Parker traced a P into the dirt.

Monty raised his eyes to hers, nodded, and quickly scratched it out with his foot.

Parker was calling on all the members of the Plumes to assemble today. It was *the* symbol every member of the Plumes knew. Their members knew writing a P in the open to a fellow member required them to act.

They'd trained for this, and Monty knew she would not take this action lightly.

"Whew," said Monty. "That was way more intense than I thought it'd be."

Parker saw movement out of the corner of her eye, near the alleyway.

"What is it?" Monty asked.

"Did you see that?" Parker whispered, glancing to the alleyway.

Monty scanned the area. "There! Over there," he called out, pointing to an area near the entrance. She caught a glimpse of the shadow as it disappeared.

"Someone was watching," Parker said, shaking her head. "We can't stay here. It's way too dangerous. We have to go."

"We need to gather the others," Monty said. "If you're being watched, then someone may know something... about what's going on... or about us. Do you think your parents know about the room?"

"I'm pretty sure my parents are the reason it was sealed off in the first place. They know even more than they've told me. And if the Illiterates found the room—"

"They won't find the room, Parker," he said, putting his hand on her forearm.

"I'm worried they may already have," she said. "Okay, listen, if something happens to us, we need a way to communicate, to know who is with us. Something only Plumes know. Last night, the quills... it seemed like they were trying to tell me something, and it gave me an idea."

She drew back from him and placed her hand at her side. Then, taking her thumb and forefinger and connecting them into a circle, she fanned out her other fingers, like a peacock extending its feathers as she'd seen the quills do the night before. It looked like she had created a P, but he could see what she'd intended with her fingers splayed outward.

Monty's face lit up, and he mimicked her hand positioning.

"The *Plumes*," he said. "That's it. That's how we make sure who is with us. P and the feathers behind."

Parker nodded to him.

"I always knew we needed a hand sign," Monty said with a smile.

"Yeah, we need every Plume prepared for Drain Day… for whatever the Illiterates might be planning."

"We're coming out of the shadows, huh?" Monty asked.

"I hope not, but we started the Plumes to train and protect writers. If those idiots are planning something today, I have a pretty good feeling someone will need us."

"This is the Parker I know," Monty said, holding out his fist to her.

"And we need to figure out who or what is watching us," Parker said as she bumped his fist. "The Illiterates make my skin crawl, but if they are planning something, we'll be ready. That alley is on the way to Avenir. I've got to make a quick stop there first."

"Whew. I try to avoid Avenir at all costs, but you just want to march right in there? You know, you're either the bravest girl in the kingdom or the stupidest."

"I'm going to see Tatiana and the twins," she said. "We need to keep a sharp eye out for anyone who might be watching us. We can't be too careful."

Chapter Seven

Avenir

"Hey! Outta the way. You're blocking my way, kids."

Parker twisted around, her heart racing. Monty quickly pulled her aside as a man with wrinkled, weather-beaten skin and a large gray mustache wheeled a covered cart into the street in front of them.

"You know this place is bad juju, right?" Monty said as he scanned Avenir. The entrance to the neighborhood was identified by an old rope stretched across the buildings that lined the street with worn red flags hanging down limply.

Parker raised her shoulders and motioned to the street ahead. "You got a better idea?"

Avenir had a little bit of everything, and yet it was a place your parents would never take you. It was a whirl of people, animals, stores, homes, and carts, all moving in harmony as voices and noises echoed off the walls.

"Those flags are there because it's a *blood* street," Monty said. Parker shook her head since this was Monty's usual way of being overprotective, but as they walked past the entrance to Avenir, a man just beyond the flags pulled a long knife from his oversized jacket to hand to a potential buyer to inspect it.

"Two quick stops," she said. "Maybe three."

The pair pushed their way into the busy back-streets of the neighborhood, where many there seemed to be making last-minute purchases for the festival. Avenir buzzed with excitement.

"Why again did you think it was a good idea to meet them here?" Monty muttered. "Oh, yeah, let's meet on Blood Street… super smart, Parker."

"You did say I was either brave or stupid."

Tailors cut and measured next to blacksmiths who formed iron tools and utensils. Shopkeepers yelled out prices for everything from bread and potatoes to dresses and chairs. The echo from numbers, specials, descriptions, features, sales, and the rest made her head ache. More strange figures like the man selling weapons out of his jacket stood and watched, eagerly waiting for their next customer or whistling when a guard was nearby.

"All the yelling and screaming in this place makes it impossible to think," Parker said as they weaved their way through the streets. "Anyone ever suggest an exception to the no-writing rule for store signs and prices? With just that, I bet Avenir could save a lot of headaches from all this yelling."

"You get used to it," he replied. "Plus, the Illiterates aren't too keen on exceptions to the rules, as your dad found out."

Rumors were all seedy commerce in Everly played out on side streets and backrooms of this part of town. You could purchase nearly anything you wanted in this neighborhood for a price. Her parents definitely would disapprove of her being here, especially with Monty.

"One of the older news shouters said she heard stories where you used to be able to find scraps of paper, old books or quills, homemade ink, and writing contraband in here," Monty whispered. "The Illiterates put a stop to that and—" he motioned to a burned-out building on his left.

The pair moved through the crowd, eyes following them as they passed several shops selling baked pastries, varieties of fruits, and spices from throughout Fonde. Parker saw carpenters, bronze smiths, fletchers who sold arrows, bowyers who created and sold bows, potters, coopers, and barbers. Before long, they were standing in the center of Avenir among a large group of people, all waiting to watch three huge men perform the Changing of the Cobra ritual.

The Changing of the Cobra was a traditional ceremonial event brought to Everly from the Shadow Territories. Every hour outside of Three Eyes, the most trusted reserve in Avenir, the ceremony was performed as one part attraction and one part warning. Reserves like Three Eyes kept anything safe for its customers, from jewelry and coins to weapons and tools. These locations differed from the royal reserves with guards and protection from the kingdom; nonroyal reserves were on their own. Over time they'd become the center of commerce as these reserves would also allow you to trade, barter, store, borrow, swap, or transact anything and everything.

They'd designed the Three Eyes building to convey trust and power, with its three massive front columns supporting a triangular roof. Each hollowed-out column housed the tall, muscular individuals wearing brightly colored cloaks featuring the furs and feathers of unique creatures native to the Shadow Territories. Besides performing as the Cobra ceremony's entertainment, these individuals served as guards, enforcers, and intimidators, each having three interwoven snakes tattooed on their arms. Each hour they would rotate out from their post inside the columns while performing the ceremonial dance that included acrobatics, swordplay, and chanting from the region, often drawing crowds of visitors.

As this hour's Changing of the Cobra ritual concluded, Parker spotted her classmate, Tatiana Thrice.

"T!" Parker cried out, getting her friend's attention.

Tatiana had perfectly straight, jet-black hair that sharply framed her face. She rarely smiled, often appearing aloof and distant to strangers.

Tatiana saw Parker and Monty and glanced to a small hallway next to Three Eyes.

Three Eyes was the heart of Avenir, which made Tatiana's father the eyes, soul, and muscle of Three Eyes. Anyone trading, depositing, buying gems, coins, tools, weapons, and unique trinkets, or asking for a loan or a swap trusted the reserve to memorize the exact item and amount of their transaction or deposit. Conflicts and disagreements were common in most reserves without a way to write information down.

Three Eyes had been able to avoid much of that as Tatiana's father had brought a unique practice to his reserve from the Shadow Territories. The reserve's name—Three Eyes—referred to every transaction memorized and validated by three individuals, making it the most trusted location in all of Avenir. It still attracted its share of trouble, hence the burly guards out front.

Once in the small hallway, Parker and Monty followed Tatiana until they were all out of sight of the central street.

"It's good to see you two, but it's dangerous for you out there," Tatiana said with a smile. "Which means it's difficult for me, too, especially if my father sees us together."

"I wouldn't be here if it weren't important," Parker said. Parker nodded and drew the same P in the dirt between them. Tatiana quickly erased it with her foot.

"Today?" she said. "Drain Day's the busiest day at Three Eyes."

Monty had been the first to identify Tatiana as a fit for the Plumes: "She rolls her eyes whenever the Illiterates talk… so I think she'd be perfect." The pair had immediately bonded being strong-willed, quick-witted, and having a tricky relationship with their fathers—and both were excellent at eye rolls. Tatiana was one of the few Plumes who stood next to Parker when the Illiterates tried to harass her.

"The Illiterates are planning something," Monty said as he leaned toward Tatiana. "We think it may happen *at* Drain Day, but no one knows what exactly. That's why we're here. I have a feeling this may be what we've been training for."

Parker nodded. "Calm down, Monty, we don't know that yet."

"Tell her what you found," Monty said.

"Guess I can never tell you a secret, huh? I think Lady Julie was right. I found another inscription—a clue."

"No kidding," Tatiana said.

"Maybe I'm wrong, but this feels like a sign that magic writing may have returned here in Everly. More than just Lazlo. Way more."

She patted her dress, indicating the hidden items she had.

"Okay then... *now* you've got my attention," Tatiana said. "This sounds like a way better way to spend our day off than being here—I've watched the Cobra thing like a million times now. But you know my parents are not happy I'm spending time with you two—especially you." She pointed to Parker. "Said royals don't make friends with the rest of us. But I put a rest to that nonsense with my dad real quick... so don't worry, because now he is petrified I'll turn into some crazy teenager who freaks out on him all the time, which means he doesn't push me too hard on these sorts of things. You know... dads."

"That's good," said Parker, mustering a small smile. "You guys are all I've got."

"You think these are related?" Tatiana asked. "The Illiterates and the inscription you found?"

"I don't know," Parker said. "Maybe."

"Related?" Monty said. "You guys realize the Illiterates *hate* writers... and those inscriptions are *writing*. Of course it's related. I hate to say it, Parker, but your dad made these things related when Lazlo started scripting magic for Drain Day."

"I know. I know."

"Here's what I'm thinking," Monty said, looking at both of them. "Plumes meet, we make sure we're all ready for Drain Day, and Parker shows us what she found in the castle. You think the others will understand the importance then?"

"Yeah," Parker said with a slight chuckle. "You'll all get it. No question."

Monty looked at Parker. "Tatiana, we were being watched earlier. Parker and I. We didn't see who."

Parker shook her head. "So let's all be extra careful," Parker said to Tatiana with a smile.

"Are you saying I'm not careful? Fine. Fine. And so, what about today?" Tatiana asked. "You came to me because you need the bag you left here with the coins?"

"Yes. I had the twins making something special for me," she replied. "One of a kind originals."

"And I'll need your help to gather the other Plumes," Monty said.

"Okay then. My parents are asking a lot of questions too. Everything with Owen is making them skittish. I'll be right back," Tatiana said as she stood up and surveyed around them to make sure no one was watching. A few minutes later, she returned with a small pouch with the few coins she'd kept safe for her friend.

"Thank you," Parker said, stashing the coins in the hidden pockets she'd sewn in her dress next to her quill, inkwell, and journal. Then she and Monty showed Tatiana the same hand sign she'd revealed earlier, mouthing "bird watching" with a smile.

"Just be careful," Monty called as Parker stood and exited the hidden hallway. "Make sure you aren't being followed like before."

"Brave or stupid, right?" she called back to him.

"More brave and less stupid, P!" Tatiana called out. *"Please!"*

Parker quickly moved through the crowds again, aware of the watchful eyes and whispers.

A small part of her wished Quinn was here, as she always made Parker feel safe and protected.

"Pennymore!" a voice called out from a food stall. "You, Pennymore. We need to talk to you!"

From her peripheral vision, she could see the girl who had yelled her name with her white-blond hair with its cool, icy tones flanked by a bigger group of kids around her age on both sides of the street. The group was closing toward her. She quickened her step, hoping she could get past them before the group tightened around her like a noose.

"Pennymore! We just want to *talk*," the girl said.

It was Cassandra Waddle. Cassandra had been Parker's best friend, with the keyword being *had*.

Some of Parker's favorite memories were of the two of them sitting in the Hall of Resplendence, each offering the next idea for the story they'd imagine, with Cassandra always holding Boots, Parker's cat, in her lap. But once the king introduced Lazlo's magic writing powers to the kingdom, Cassandra's parents had been one of many who forbade their children from engaging with the Pennymores.

Cassandra's parents were now some of the most vocal of the Illiterates.

Parker spotted four small dots arranged in a square shape drawn on the back of Cassandra's hand. Unlike many adult Illiterates, kids mostly used coal to draw the Illiterates mark on their hands—less permanent, but no less terrifying when you spotted it. Cassandra had become her school's informal leader of the Illiterates, and other children who refused to add the dots would be harassed or worse by those who did. Six others who had dots on their hands closed around her, including Frederick Chickory, the boy who'd gotten her kicked out of school.

Now might be another perfect time for one of those blue lightning bolts to burst from my journal.

"Are you here alone, *Freeze Pop*?" Cassandra whispered, using the nickname she'd created for Parker. Cassandra put her arm around Parker, who raised her shoulders, attempting to move her hand from its place. "Not a good place to be *alone*. Lots of bad people hang out in Avenir. Glad we followed you in here and found you before one of them did."

"I—I am here with one of the castle guards," Parker lied, hoping to scare the group so she could escape.

"She's lying," hissed a boy with bright blue eyes. He was the one who'd chased Owen into the water that day it ripped him away. The boy stood beside Cassandra, scanning the crowd. "I saw her with the boy, the caller. I've been watching her the whole time. She's alone."

"Now, why was that so hard to say?" Cassandra said. "I had Muddle keep an eye on you, just to be sure nothing *bad* happened."

"I... I..." Parker froze.

"Again? Is this like when you stand in front of the class and get all choked up? Poor girl can't get a word out."

The other kids began laughing.

"But lying to Muddle and me, Parker, your friends. We're friends. Right?" Cassandra gestured to the blue-eyed boy and shook her head, her fingernails now pressing into Parker's shoulder. "You know what we do to liars. Right? It's a lot like what we do to writers—"

As she turned around, Muddle, the blue-eyed boy, was glaring at her. Parker took a deep breath and forced herself to smile.

"I wanted to ask, how's your nose, Frederick?" Parker said to the red-haired boy standing in the back of the group. She shook off Cassandra's grip, balled up her fists, and raised them in front of her chin. "You all remember how a *girl* beat up Frederick Chickory and made him cry?"

The other children snickered.

"Hey, that was a cheap shot," Frederick said, narrowing his eyes.

"Then don't make me take cheap shots at the rest of you!" Parker said, lunging slightly at the boy.

"Hey, hey, calm down, Freeze Pop. We don't want you to get expelled a third time," Cassandra said. "Mommy and Daddy can only rescue you so many times. We just wanted to make sure you'll be at the festival. Big day today, ya know? Got something special planned."

Was Cassandra part of the rumors Monty had heard about? Were these kids all part of the Illiterates' plan for Drain Day?

"And just a little warning for your little friends," Cassandra said. "I'd stay away from the torchbearer at the festival if you don't want to get that pretty little blue dress of yours burned. It turns out he's a *friend*."

Cassandra raised her fist, showing off the four dots, as the other children followed suit and began to laugh.

Phwwwwwhht.

Parker heard the low whistle and immediately spotted the Gazette twins across the street. The two tall, identical boys with thick, wavy dark hair raised their eyebrows and smiled at her.

You're kidding me. Those two are enjoying watching all this. Enough of it then.

Parker gave an exaggerated cough. "Ah, I thought it was supposed to be four dots, but why does Frederick only have three."

"What?" Frederick exclaimed before he began to fumble around, quickly turning his hands over to see what she was talking about. The others in the group looked offended and turned to examine him while Parker used the moment of confusion as her opportunity to escape.

"Welp, nice seeing you again, Cassandra," Parker continued. "Scratch that, *not* nice seeing you, any of you." She wriggled out of Cassandra's grip and quickly slid out from between the distracted kids now examining Frederick Chickory's wrists more closely.

Cassandra raised a hand to her group, a sign they took not to pursue her any further. Parker raced across the street and grabbed the hands of the two boys, pulling them away from Cassandra and her gang.

"Oh, don't worry! You'll hear more from us soon," Cassandra called after the trio.

Parker breathed a sigh of relief. *And I didn't even need the magical bolt.*

She and the Gazettes raced past the grocery shop and the unfortunate-smelling fishmonger before ducking into an unlit storefront and closing the door behind them.

Shoes, boots, sandals, and various leather scraps scattered on shelves and tables filled the room. Parker recognized she was inside the shoe cobbling store owned by the twins' parents. All the kids in Everly knew the Gazettes made the absolute best boots in the kingdom; however, the focus of most people was on Drain Day, so the ordinarily busy cobbler was quiet. If you knew their favorite colors, you could tell who was who by the accents on each twin's boots. This was pretty much the only way the Plumes could tell the twins apart.

"Took you guys long enough," Parker said, joking.

"We were watching the whole thing," Matteus Gazette said.

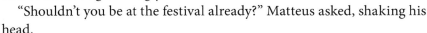

Marcus Gazette picked up where his brother had left off and said, "Whenever those kinda kids come past the red flags into Avenir, we keep an eye on them."

"A close eye," Matteus added.

"It's a red flag, eh?" Parker said. "So, what do you think that's all about?"

"Oh, come on, Parker. You know what it's about. We all do," Matteus said.

"And it's why you're a dolt for coming here alone," Marcus continued.

"Dolt? Them's some harsh words, boys," Parker said with a nod. "But thank you both for watching from afar while I took on six Illiterates myself. I know they aren't big fans of me... of us. You know that could have gotten ugly."

"Shouldn't you be at the festival already?" Matteus asked, shaking his head.

"I needed to talk to you both."

"What was so important to come here?" Marcus asked.

"I told you magic writers have returned," she said. "And now I have proof it's way more than just Lazlo and what we see on Drain Day."

"Hold on," Matteus said. "You didn't bring that proof here. Did you?"

"I did. But it's hidden. It's safe."

"Parker, you brought some magic things in here? Man, maybe it's safe for you," Marcus said, glancing around the store to ensure they were alone. "We aren't like you. We told you the writing and the secret bird watching writing club was fun and all for us. But—"

"We're street kids, Parker," Matteus said. "Me and Marcus, we've been pushed into walls, yelled at, and had our boots taken by those same kids Cassandra runs with. Don't underestimate what the Illiterates are capable of. Sure, people are afraid to mess with a princess, but they have no problem sending kids who live in Avenir away."

"Our mom said if we get caught doing anything, they'll just throw us into the drain with Owen," Marcus said.

"My father would never," Parker said, her eyes squinting at the suggestion.

"That's not what my brother meant. Calm down," Matteus said. "I mean, what do you think they'd do to the rest of us if they found out? We're not like you. They'd shut down this store and haul us away in a snap."

"This is why I am here," she responded, drawing the letter P in the dust on the floor.

Both boys quickly stepped forward to cover the letter, glancing around for anyone watching.

"For real?" Matteus asked. "Even after Cassandra and her goons tried to rough you up? You think this is still a good idea?"

"Before the festival, all of us Plumes are going to meet. I think you both need to see what I found," Parker said. "You have a right to see. No secrets, okay? That's all. Just see for yourself, and then you can make up your mind."

The brothers looked at each other.

"Or maybe since you're twins, you share one mind. Do twins share a mind?"

The twins smiled before turning back to her and nodding. "Fine. It's not like you leave us much choice anyway."

"And to be clear, Matteus borrows *my* mind now and again," his brother added.

Parker looked outside to see if any of the kids who had harassed her were still watching them. The twins appeared to have scared them away. "Do you have them?" she asked. "What I asked for?"

The twins looked at each other, nodded slightly, and then walked into an open door behind a table, dividing the store into a showroom and a workroom. They returned, each holding a boot.

"I made the left one," Marcus said, holding out one boot to her.

"And I made the right one," Matteus echoed, holding out its match.

"You each did one?" Parker said, taking the boots in her hands. "But how do you know they are the same?"

Both boys smiled.

"They aren't the same," Matteus said. "I make perfect right shoes."

"And I make perfect left shoes," continued Marcus.

"They are a perfect pair," they said in unison.

"Did you guys practice that?" Parker asked.

"Naw, we're bootheads, Parker," Marcus said, pointing to his boots that were identical to his brother's but with the colors and accents in the perfect inverse of his.

"We don't even have to practice."

She took her new boots and replaced the flimsy shoes she was wearing, knowing they wouldn't make the journey she had planned.

"They look like your foot is a wing," Marcus said, kneeling so his finger could trace the edges with their shapes and textures. "But subtle. Light and nimble so you can fly, but sturdy so you can pretty much stomp through anything. People won't even realize they are boots, especially for a kid from the castle district."

"Only pair like 'em in all of Everly," Matteus added.

"Wow, they are incredible," Parker said as she admired the design.

"They don't want us to write," Marcus said, "but they can't stop us from putting a story out this way, right?"

"Marcus thinks we should call them mayflys," Matteus continued.

"You *may fly*, right?" Marcus said, smiling at his brother. "Did you know the mayfly isn't just some bug? Where we are from, it's a symbol for the years of preparation you have for the brief moment when you can fulfill your destiny—your moment."

"Yep, the mayfly only lives a couple of days," Matteus said. "But if she does it right, she'll live her life to the fullest in her moment. That's why we joined the Plumes. Forget Cassandra. We have a feeling these are going to be special boots for your perfect moment too."

"I love that," she said, standing and walking around the room. "One-of-a-kind boots from two-of-a-kind friends. And they fit perfectly." She took out a few coins hidden in her skirt and handed them to the boys, who took them and high-fived each other. "My mayflys. They are perfect... perfect for *our* destiny."

"Now, you gotta go," Marcus said. "We'll come to see what you want to show us. And we will help gather some of the others. But you heard what Cassandra said. She's got something planned for today."

She nodded to them and, placing her hand at her side as she'd done with Monty, made her fingers into the shape of a P with the three other fingers fanned out with the peacock feathers.

"We're just bird watchers," she said with her wry smile.

The twins mirrored her hand and nodded.

"We're glad you're here," Marcus said. "We got you."

"Now, go out back," Matteus instructed, guiding her through the back workroom of the store. "It's safer for you this way, but be careful."

Parker peered out the door, looking for any signs of Cassandra before racing out the door to make her last stop.

She moved through the back streets behind Avenir until she exited the neighborhood, passing under the familiar red flags. She was glad she had on her new boots for this. *Why did her mother always insist on such impractical shoes?*

Ahead of her was the back entrance to the storarium—a place she'd spent nearly as much time in as her home.

The storarium was quiet other than the hushed voices of the storytellers relaying their stories to the patrons. It was an odd place, full of wonder and delight in the stories but missing the grandeur of the library with its books, shelves, and history, even without the flying books and flaming lanterns. The room had low ceilings to keep voices from echoing and distracting others. There were comfortable sitting areas, oversized plush chairs, and couches. The arrangement of the room had each of the storytellers seated at a round, cushioned circle in the center of the room. For storytellings, there were desks and tables for patrons and the storytellers they'd checked out.

Usually, Parker would get here before they even unlocked the doors, but today plenty of people were already inside the storarium. If you wanted to check out the mystery or adventure storytellers for the day—clearly the best stories—you must be here early. Otherwise, you'd get stuck with the history storyteller who looked like she was about a hundred years old, and everything she told was boring.

Maybe that's why teachers keep telling me that history repeats itself... and geez, if repeated history is that boring, I never want to be an adult.

"Miss Pennymore," a friendly young man greeted her, his voice fluttering as he spoke. "Back so soon. What story are you looking to hear, Miss Park—"

"Is *he* here?" she replied, scanning the room. "I need to check him out one more time—er, for a short time before..."

"Yes, he's expecting you," the curator said to her. "We had already checked him out to you as you'd requested. He's at the table to the left." He pointed to an elderly gentleman with a long, gray beard and a kind face who seemed to be muttering to himself.

Parker hurried over to him. She didn't know his name despite hundreds of hours together. Storytellers were supposed to remain anonymous, insisting it was the story, not the storyteller, who mattered. Parker thought otherwise and felt odd knowing nothing about him, especially since she'd come to view him as her only real mentor, given none of her tutors worked out.

Every hero has a mentor in their story. In moments of our greatest struggles, they help guide us. I could use some of that mentor guiding.

Parker took a seat across from him as the man absently stroked his beard. "Ah, I've been expecting you," he said.

"How do you know if you're doing what's right?" Parker asked, wasting no time.

He stared at her quizzically.

"I mean, how does *the hero* in these stories know what's right? How do they make the right choice?"

He paused and studied her face. "Well, Madam Pennymore, in the stories, the hero must often choose between what they know and what is unknown."

"I know they *must choose*, but how? Like, who tells them which path to take? To stay or to go? There has to be someone."

"There is. The hero herself," he said. "The hero alone must decide. That is why she is the hero, for if someone else instructed her to choose, it would no longer be the hero's story."

Parker let out a sharp breath. "I sometimes wish you'd just give me a straight answer."

He smiled and folded his hands. As he did, she noticed a glint or reflection from his pinky finger.

"I guess I came here for the story of the hidden library, the literati one," Parker said. "In the Northern Passage."

"But I have told you this one more than a dozen times," he said, tilting his head. "You practically know it by heart. Don't you want—"

"*Practically*," Parker interrupted. "*Practically* by heart." She wanted to hear the story one more time to make sure she didn't miss anything in the route, the path, the obstacles, the markers. She had to know everything for her plan to work. But a part of her wanted him to tell her whether even to go, even if she couldn't ask him the question.

"I need to know it *by* heart," she continued. "I need to hear it again. Every line. Every detail. All of it. So I won't forget anything."

The storyteller rarely argued.

"You are leaving. You are going to find the library."

"What?" Parker stammered. "No, no, it's—it's just a favorite story of mine."

He nodded. "Then you know the story is a tragedy. It's not an adventure. When the hero finds the ancient, magical library he seeks, it is in ruins, and he can't find the answers he sought. And those the hero left, they then suffered as well."

"I know. I know that, but you said it's a story," she said, eyes focused on the man. "Just a story. I plan to tell a new ending, not a tragedy."

The man's eyes widened. "And as I said, the hero alone, she must decide."

The man stood. As he did, Parker furrowed her brow. "Where—where are you going?"

"I do not need to tell the story to you," he said as he reached a hand into his pocket and withdrew his cupped hand, placing it on the table in front of her. "Instead of the story, I wish to offer you this. Take it. It may help you. You'll know when to open it."

Parker locked her eyes on the storyteller as she placed her hand over his, secretly taking a small, folded paper from him.

What has he given me?

"By heart," he said with a smile.

"What?" Parker asked.

"I should *not* have said 'practically.' It was wrong of me. Miss Pennymore, you do know the story by heart." He patted her hand, now holding the small folded paper. "But remember," he continued, "it's not the choice you make that will matter. It's what you do with the consequences of a choice. Good luck."

He returned to the center of the room to the circle, seeming to disappear entirely from view within the other storytellers. A young boy and his mother quickly raced by, rattling about flying horses.

She'd come here for answers but left with more questions.

She hid the folded paper in the pocket with her journal and raced away from the room.

Chapter Eight

The Rainbow Inkwell

Parker checked behind her to be sure she hadn't been followed before opening the door to her school. She reminded herself that no one would expect kids to sneak *into* school on a day off.

"You made it," Monty called out as Parker stepped inside the classroom filled with every member of the Plumes.

The only light came from a few candles burning in the corners. Schools in Everly had long ago banned windows because it distracted children from learning.

Chairs were lined up in perfect rows and bolted to the floor. The walls were blank. The air was stale. The only thing different from the castle's dungeon was the schoolroom didn't have chains. All classrooms were this way. Nothing more was needed when all they did was memorize and recite what the teacher had told them.

The perfect place to send kids for ten hours a day. I'm surprised more kids don't try to get themselves expelled. Maybe then those dungeon chains would be necessary here too.

As she joined the others, the hushed voices inside fell silent.

"We heard about Cassandra," Monty said.

The Gazette twins nodded.

Parker was both uncomfortable and energized seeing everyone. This was risky to all be in the school, and she wondered if this had been a bad idea.

"I'm okay. Really," she said, trying to reassure the dozens of kids who had come.

"I call this secret meeting of the Plumes to order," Monty said.

"We don't have a lot of time," she said, gently stopping Monty and remembering to breathe. "What I am going to show you is—well, I don't know how to say it…"

Uncomfortable with speaking to the group, Parker's fingertips began to throb with each beat of her heart.

"What Parker has been saying all along is *true*," Monty exclaimed.

She glared at him. He offered his "I'm trying to help" look back at her. Parker knelt in the middle of the room as the others silently gathered around her to get a closer look. She reached into the hidden pockets in her dress and pulled out the purple journal, her red-tipped quill, and the inkwell.

Gasps came from the group.

Most of them had never seen basic writing tools, and her heart quickened. Until today the Plumes only used bags of sand to spell words and maybe a twig to write with. These were minor risks, easily explainable as kids horsing around.

But these items were punishable by death, whether the king's daughter or not.

If this made them gasp, well, wait until what happens when they see what's next.

"If you want to leave, you should leave now," she said quietly, scanning the room. "I am putting all of you at risk. I know I am. But we are Plumes."

"*Plumes! Plumes! Plumes.*" The low chant rolled through her friends, led by Monty, Tatiana, and the twins. No one left. She raised a finger to her lips, urging them to keep quiet.

Parker took the journal and placed it in front of her, the black compass marks visible to the group. Then she put the inkwell on the journal.

The book glowed a yellowish hue, and then streaks of silver and gold shot from the inkwell like fireworks, spinning at the top of the ceiling and like a night sky of moving constellations of stars, comets, planets, and streaks. Bits of glowing dust hopped around the room, gently encircling each member of the Plumes.

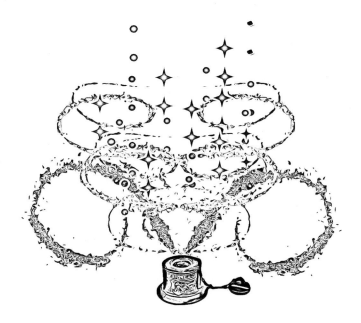

Whispers, gasps, and excited laughs surrounded her.

Monty said, "Whoa. What is that?"

"I—I don't know, but there's one more thing you need to see and you each need to do."

She looked at the room, letting the seriousness of her message sink in.

"Watch." She took the red-tipped quill in her hand, leaned forward, and gently held the quill over the inkwell. Then she slowly dipped the quill in it.

The room went dark as the candle flames extinguished, and only the inkwell glowed its yellowish hue before a rainbow of colors began circulating inside the inkwell. The colors spun with increasing speed until the room went dark. Then a red and orange glow from the inkwell exploded into red and orange glowing dust filling the room. The dust pulled together into a shape, flying above them around the room.

"Whoa, is it a cardinal?" one of the Plumes asked.

The beautiful bird with its distinctive crest flew around and around, weaving and floating, glowing brighter and brighter with each spin around the room.

Monty leaned over to Parker. "It matches your necklace."

She reached up and touched the stone she wore.

But the inkwell was purple this morning. Why did the color change?

"Parker Pennymore," a voice boomed from the inkwell. It was regal, warm, and inviting as it echoed off the walls of the room and shook the shadows from the candles. The red-orange dust swirled around her, illuminating her face and body.

It knows my name. She stared at it.

That voice hadn't happened this morning. Maybe she'd taken the quill out too quickly.

"Your story must be written," the voice continued. "You are the Order of Chronicle."

The voice fell silent, and the red-orange colors faded as she removed the quill from the inkwell.

They sat in stunned silence, illuminated only by the yellowish glow from the inkwell.

"Well, I just have to say, that was *epic*. Eh-pic. So, I'm nominating myself to go next," Tatiana said. "Order of Chronicle sounds pretty awesome, P."

Hushed whispers spread through the group.

"It's okay to be a little freaked out. Right? I'm a little freaked out. Okay?" Tatiana said with a shrug. "But come on, don't you want to see what the inkwell does when *you* dip the quill in?"

Another low cheer rose from the group as they struggled to hush their excitement.

"Now we are talking," Tatiana knelt next to Parker. "So, what do I do?"

Parker wasn't sure what to say but gave Tatiana a slight smile and a little shrug before handing her the quill and sliding over. "Wish me luck," Tatiana said with a smile as the Plumes began to chant quietly.

"Plume! Plume! Plume!"

Tatiana thrust the quill into the glowing inkwell. Again, the room went pitch black before the inkwell glowed, and the rainbow of colors blurred until it glowed teal, sparks bursting to the ceiling. The glowing teal dust formed a fox, darting and leaping through the room. Every detail illuminated from the fox's nose and whiskers to his fluffy tail and paws.

"Tatiana Thrice," the voice echoed again. "Your imagination must tell the story. You are the Order of Legend."

A quiet cheer came from the others. "Legend," Tatiana called out. "And sapphire is my color. I like this. Twins, get up here. You're next."

The tall boys stepped forward and knelt beside Parker as Tatiana stood and exchanged high fives with everyone. Parker smiled.

"Marcus Gazette," the voice bellowed as a silver horse galloped in the ceiling. "You are to discover the story. You are the Order of Scribe."

His brother followed. "Matteus Gazette," it echoed as greenish dust formed into an owl circled the room. "The meaning in your words will inspire. You are the Order of Poet."

Tatiana then pulled Monty forward, leading the group in a whispered chant: "Monty. Monty. Monty."

He smiled and sat next to Parker, taking the quill.

"I've never held a real quill before," Monty said. "Is this right?" He held it gently between his fingers and moved it over the glowing inkwell.

Then he dipped the tip into the inkwell. But unlike the others, the ink stayed a dark black.

Monty looked over at Parker, confused.

"Try again," she shrugged, unsure why it hadn't changed colors and spoke his name like when the others had dipped their quill.

He tried again, but the inkwell remained a dark color. "Must mean I'm Order of the Plumes," Monty yelled out.

And on cue, the entire room burst out chanting: "Plume. Plume. Plume."

Each member of the Plumes took their turn finding themselves segmented into the Order of the Chronicle like Parker, the Order of the Legend like Tatiana, the Order of the Scribe like Marcus, and the Order of the Poet like Matteus. The others who didn't see any change were welcomed boisterously by Monty into the Order of the Plumes. A few other children saw the inkwell turn a beautiful amethyst color like Parker had seen earlier, with the purple dust forming a raven that raced around the room before welcoming them into the Order of Enigma.

Hushed energy filled the room as each of these six new groups began to sit together, figure out what their order meant, and try to contain their excitement.

Parker looked at the others and felt relieved. She no longer felt alone. She was a Plume, a part of something that felt bigger now. That anxious energy she'd felt the last day since she decided to leave the island began to disappear.

Monty was right. This all feels good to be here.

"So what do our orders do?" Matteus asked Parker.

"I don't know what they mean, either," Parker said as she gathered her items and stowed them into her hidden pockets.

"We'll figure that out next meeting," Monty said. "Right, Parker?"

She nodded. "Sure. But for now, if we need to break up or separate, we can use our orders to help us. Things could get dangerous and—"

"And Plumes fly together," Monty added before she could continue. The room echoed his hushed chant.

The door to the classroom burst open behind them.

"Look what we have here, Muddle," said Cassandra.

Parker turned cold as the rest of the kids who'd surrounded Cassandra at Avenir, plus maybe a dozen others, joined Cassandra at the entrance to the classroom.

"What brings you losers here?" she asked, locking eyes with Parker. "Oh, you've all come to follow this frozen statue over there—you know she had to be rescued from us in Avenir, right?"

Her group chuckled.

"You're the one who'll need rescuing," Monty yelled back.

Cassandra laughed. "Oh, big words from the boy whose parents are so poor they make him be a news caller so they don't get kicked out of their house."

Monty's face turned red, and he shifted back and forth.

"Is *that* what you're wearing to Drain Day?" Cassandra asked. "Are you sure you aren't wearing something I threw away?"

"Leave him alone, Cassandra," Tatiana said.

Cassandra's eyes narrowed. "I don't waste energy on foreigners and border bouncers who shouldn't be living in Everly," Cassandra snapped back, drawing confident smiles and nods from the other children with her ready to fight. "Don't you know my parents and Parker's parents talk all the time about sending people like you back to wherever you came from? We don't want you here."

Cassandra turned and looked at Parker.

"Parker's parents aren't even *real* royals—surprised we let them stay in charge. Isn't that right, Parker?"

Parker shook her head. She could feel the others looking at her as her heart once again raced, each beat pounding in the tips of her fingers again. *Thump-thump, thump-thump.* She felt hot, her eyes began to get hazy with purple streaks, and she ground her teeth together as the words and sentences and letters jumbled and twisted in her brain.

"Cat got your tongue again, Parker?" Cassandra said. "Heard that cat of yours was smart enough to run away when Pennymores started getting kidnapped."

Parker lurched forward, but the other Plumes held her back. Parker noticed the candlelight flicker an eerie purple hue briefly before settling into its natural color.

"You're pitiful," Parker called out. "Pitiful."

"That's the best you idiots got? No wonder you guys come back to school on Drain Day. Well, don't worry. You're afraid to show your faces in public. We aren't."

Their group turned to leave, chucking at the Plumes.

"Oh, and Parker," Cassandra said. "You're going to want to keep a close eye on your friend Lazlo. A *real* close eye," Cassandra said, motioning to the others. "Let's go."

Frederick held up his fist showing off the four dots, while Muddle stared at Parker as if he wanted to say something but then smirked and followed the others.

The door slammed, and once again, it was silent, the dark shadows flickering across their faces from the candles.

Parker scanned the room. The Plumes, her friends, stared at her, their smiles from moments ago no longer visible. They were scared. She'd frozen in the moment.

"I'm so sorry," Parker said.

Tatiana put her hand on Parker's shoulder, and leaned in, whispering into her ear, "It's time. It's time to call them to action, P." Then she gently squeezed Parker's shoulder.

Parker inhaled.

Tatiana is right.

"No," Parker said. Everyone lifted their gaze to her. "No! She won't ruin this. She can't."

The others began to nod, and mutters of agreement began to fill the room.

"We know what we need to do," she continued. "You all saw what I saw. We all are part of something much bigger than people like Cassandra will ever realize. We won't be afraid anymore."

Monty and Tatiana nodded.

"You are legends, and chronicles, and scribes, and poets, and enigmas, and plumes. All of us are," Parker said as she saw the rest of the kids begin to nod with smiles returning to their faces. "I'm tired of getting pushed around by them. We all are."

"Yes, we are! She's right. Here's to Parker!" Monty said.

"No. No guys," she said, raising her palms in front of her. "No, we are *all* Plumes. All of us. I'm just like you guys—a writer, a troublemaker, a misfit, a Chronicle, and the girl who got kicked out of this school for punching Frederick Chickory."

The others laughed.

"You're the ones who'll stop Cassandra, the Illiterates, and whatever else is out there," Parker said. "Today. Today, they aren't just dealing with one of us. We taught you to write, so you're all ready for whatever comes our way. An important battle is coming today, and we've all got a part to play in stopping it," she continued. "We are all we've got right now. And we need to stick together."

"Right," Monty said, "Plumes fly together," leading the group on another whispered chant.

Plumes fly together. Plumes fly together. Plumes fly together.

"Now, let's fly!" Parker said. "Order of Chronicle!" she shouted.

"Fly," they responded.

"Order of Legend!" she called.

"Fly!"

"Order of Scribe!"

"Fly."

"Order of Poet!"

"Fly!"

"Order of Enigma!"

"Fly!"

"And last but *certainly* the best," Monty said smiling at Parker, "Order of Plumes!"

"We fly!"

Chapter Nine

Drain Day

"Straight and tall. Big smiles. One after another," the guard called out to the hundreds of children waiting to enter the amphitheater. "And stop touching each other with your boats!"

"It's almost noon," Parker said. "Where are they?"

Parker stood in line next to her friends in one of the waiting areas that opened to the amphitheater stage, nervously scanning for Cassandra and the other Illiterates.

"They've got to be here somewhere," Monty said. "The stage has two entrances, so they're probably on the other side of the stage."

"What if she's not?" Parker asked. "What if she's doing something, and we're missing it?"

"Chill, P," Tatiana said. "We got this." She formed the P shape with her fingers, her ring and pinky finger fanning out like feathers. Tatiana leaned forward to Monty, Parker, and the twins. "Can I talk to you guys for a second?"

"Now?" Monty asked

"It has to be now," Tatiana said as she inhaled deeply. Then she looked to be sure no one else was listening. "I wasn't going to say anything, but after what just happened with the inkwell and all, I realized I… I needed to."

"What is it?" Parker asked.

"Last night, I heard my mother and father talking. They talked about a boy… a boy playing in the forest and suddenly losing his speaking ability. They found a black etching or something, some charred inscription. Silent darkness, they called it, I think. They said that someone from the Shadow Territories had seen it in villages not far from Everly. The etching was burned there—a feather, with an eye."

"For real?" Marcus asked.

"Maybe it's nothing," Tatiana said, shrugging her shoulders.

"That's not nothing," Matteus said.

Parker shuttered. "That's the etching of the Ravagers, the evil magic writers I was telling you about. Lady Julie told us that's what they do. They silence your tongue or something. It's called the silent darkness. You lose the ability to speak, forever."

"Silence your tongue?" Monty asked.

"Yea, it's so weird," Parker continued. "Lazlo said that exact phrase this morning—silence your tongue. Now your parents talking about a kid going mute the very same day Lazlo would say that."

"And Cassandra was just talking about Lazlo," Tatiana said.

"He is creepy," Monty said. "Gives off that creepster vibe."

"I know and agree there's something off about Lazlo, but Quinn trusts him, and she's good at reading people. I don't know," Parker said.

"You think he's a Ravager?" Monty asked. "He's already a magic writer. And I mean, your parents accidentally let a Ravager into the castle before."

"Lady Julie isn't a Ravager," Parker snapped.

"Sorry—sorry," Monty said. "It's just, that's the rumor and all."

"I know," Parker said, lowering her voice. "And no, Lazlo is just… well, we've just never seen eye to eye, I guess. But whatever, I just thought we feel safer having a magic writer who can surround Everly by the water."

Tatiana shrugged.

"What else did you hear them say?" Parker asked.

"Not much. Just that things were getting dangerous, there's someone out there who isn't afraid to write in the open and attack a child, leaving these etchings even as the Illiterates are hunting writers. My dad isn't afraid of much, and even he looked spooked."

"See, I told you, Parker," Monty said.

"Wait, do you guys think all this is true?" Marcus asked. "You guys think the Ravagers, the evil magic writers, might be coming here to Everly?"

"My parents did something odd yesterday," Parker said, careful not to tell them her parents had decided to send her to live with her aunt. "It was weird, even for them. That was what led me to the inscription and to find the inkwell."

Tatiana raised her eyebrows. "Your parents being weird. My parents being weird. Cassandra, Lazlo, magic inscriptions and etchings—"

"This is what the Plumes was for," Monty said excitedly. "This. This is going to be great."

"Great?" Tatiana replied. "You and I have very different definitions of great."

"Lazlo came to our room this morning to warn us about the water's edge," Parker said. "He's never come, and then my parents assigned this guard chaperone guy to meet us at Drain Day. And the inscription. I think you're right. It feels like too big of a coincidence to be happening all at once."

"Plus, we know the Illiterates are planning something here," Monty said. "You heard Cassandra."

"Although it seems so weird that the people who hate writing would be doing something big when magic writers are reappearing," Marcus said.

"But maybe that's why," Parker said. "Remember, there was some Great War before that we learned about in school? Illiterates are trying to stop any writing, and now Serifs and Ravagers could bring back magic writing again... the Plumes could be at the center of something pretty scary."

"At the center? Whoa," Monty said. "Okay, that just got pretty deep, Pennymore. I always thought history class was super boring, but this makes some sense. I get why you were a little freaked out."

"Attention! Attention, children! You'll all be following the torchbearer to your spots on the stage!" the guard yelled. "You must always keep your eyes on him—only him. And smile. Big smiles. Everyone back in line!" The torchbearer raised a staff above his head as flames rose above it.

Parker squinted to see if she could see the four dots on his hand, but she couldn't make anything out.

"Okay," Parker said. "Just keep your eyes on Lazlo today. Can you two use your tallness to see if Cassandra is here?" She motioned to the twins.

The group nodded.

Parker stood on her tiptoes, trying to make eye contact with Aven again before their entrance. Parker winked and gave her a thumbs-up when she found her in the crowd of children waiting to enter the amphitheater.

Aven lifted her wolf-decorated lantern boat, mimicking it howling before she returned to her friends.

"There's no sign of her anywhere," Marcus said, returning after a few minutes now breathing heavily, having just sprinted through the waiting area.

"Being tall has its advantages," Matteus said. "We woulda seen her snow-white hair if she was here."

"We should have split up," Parker said. "We—"

"And enter!" called the guard as the torchbearer slammed his flaming staff on the white marble flooring.

Two doors swung open, and bright sunlight poured in, causing Parker to cover her eyes briefly.

"Big smiles. Straight lines, and keep an even distance. Your parents are watching," the guard said. "And do not get near the edge of the water. Stay in *front* of the torchbearers!"

The children meandered behind the guard, neither smiling, keeping straight lines, nor being at an even distance. It was a mass of short humans pouring onto the stage floor.

Parker tasted the salt in the air and smelled the cooked meats and sweets in the nearby festival tents. As she walked across what remained of the amphitheater stage, she scanned the other children entering from the opposite entrance.

"There!" Matteus said. "It's them."

Parker glared at Cassandra. Her smug smile plastered across her face just as it had been in Avenir. Parker watched as she whispered to those around her, as if she were giving them instructions. Many of them looked as if they hadn't even bothered to bring lantern boats.

"Watch out," a young boy said to Parker when she bumped into him, not realizing the line had stopped. The children formed into a roughly organized semicircle, looking up at the thousands of people waving and cheering their arrival in the stone seats. Columns, statues, and ornate marble carvings flanked the stage area. Just above the highest seats, the multicolored kites peeked over the edge of the amphitheater as if trying to get a glimpse of the festivities. She quickly scanned the crowd before turning her gaze back on Cassandra and the others.

"Pretty sure she sees us," Tatiana said, rolling her eyes.

Cassandra looked at Parker and the Plumes, and her hand raised into the air as if to wave, then closed it into a fist before rotating it so that the four black dots were visible on the back.

Muddle stood next to her, his awkward grin still plastered on his face. His grin turned into a laugh as the dozens of others around them all mimicked her raised fist with the four black dots. Tatiana let out an audible sigh.

The half dozen torchbearers stood behind them, preventing anyone from reaching the shore as Owen had done.

The amphitheater floor had once been a perfect circle with an alternating pattern of white and gray marble triangles that formed a radiating sun on the floor. Where the other half of the floor and stage had been was the craggy, broken shore.

"Boats behind you!" the torchbearers instructed the children. "On the ground behind you."

Parents called out to their children, who sometimes waved, mouthed instructions, or simply ignored their parents. A mass of decorated wooden boats began to form behind the children as guards roughly gathered them and moved them to the craggy shore.

"What was that about? The fists?" Monty asked. "There are a lot of kids, a lot more of them than I imagined."

Parker nodded. Forty or fifty children followed Cassandra's instructions.

"But how many of them are legendary?" Tatiana asked. "None. They are more likely unlegendary."

Whatever Cassandra will try today, I can't let it stop me. This is my only shot to escape and try to find Julie, my brother, and other writers. Otherwise, it's evil stepmother-ville for me.

Parker surveyed the amphitheater stage. The two double doors the children had entered were between the stone pedestal where Lazlo would script his Drain Day spell to vanquish the water. Directly behind the children were the torchbearers who were moving boats by the armful to rest on the shore before they would set them on fire.

There was a narrow gap between the seats and one of the columns to the left of the stage, just a few steps away from where she stood. Parker had discovered an overgrown path down to the water's edge there. The gap was obscured from everyone inside. Once Lazlo began scripting the drain spell, she'd slink away and run across the emptying seafloor to the other side. She'd calculated the distance, figured out the time she had while the Drain Day festivities were going on, and knew how to slip away undetected.

The story she'd heard dozens of times from the storarium storyteller told her of a route to an ancient literati library, giving her a rough idea of the monuments and landmarks to follow. It was just a story, but she knew there were truths in them. She'd stay off paths, avoid others, and hope to find a place to write again and hopefully discover some answers.

Now she worried Cassandra might ruin it all.

Monty's right. If she's going to try something today, she has her army now.

The ceremonial trumpets sounded.

The king and queen entered the royal amphitheater box, their purple robes with yellow piping flowing behind them. Her father looked tired with dark circles around his eyes. The king raised a hand to wave to the crowd as he walked to his seat. It was less of a wave as he seemed to high-fived the air in front of him.

Boos bellowed out.

Parker's father furrowed his brow and looked at her mother, surprised at the reaction.

"Aggressive," Tatiana said.

"That's never happened before," Monty nervously said.

More boos rang out as Lazlo followed her parents into the amphitheater. Parker squinted to see red lines or marks on his face. It looked like he had an injury.

Parker looked to Cassandra, watching as she encouraged the other children to boo and yell at her father. The children's boos were echoed by a growing number of people in the crowd, inspired by this act of defiance.

"They are booing. More people are joining in," Monty whispered from behind her. "What should we do, Parker?"

Her stage fright was on full display just as the eyes of the kingdom were on her.

I—I can't do this. This isn't what's supposed to happen.

A hand rested on her shoulder, fingernails glimmering in silvers and golds.

Quinn.

"Heard you could use a couple more bird watchers or whatever it is you guys do," Quinn said, her pink streak of hair covering her eye. "I brought a few more of us who like birds too, just in case."

Parker turned to see a dozen or more older children standing behind her.

"Nice to see you," Monty said as he awkwardly high-fived and then shook Quinn's hand. "We're glad you and your pink hair are here."

She raised her eyebrows.

"Oh, I came for her," she said, motioning at Parker. "We all did. I couldn't let my sister have all the fun without me."

As the boos increased in volume, Parker smiled at her sister, calming as her fingers no longer felt the beats of her heart. She looked at her friends, took a breath, then put her hands in front of her and pressed them down to try and calm the others.

"What's *her* problem?" Quinn asked, motioning to Cassandra.

The king stood, and his guards began to move toward the floor. Lazlo walked down to the altar to face the stone-carved, open book as more and more guards became visible, their hands near their weapons.

The king raised his hands to silence the crowd, though a few boos and yells continued. "Children, give your lantern boats as a tribute to the sea to welcome Drain Day!"

A smattering of applause came out from the crowd.

As the noise died out, someone shouted, "Like you *gave* Owen Wickerland to the sea?"

It was Cassandra. Their father glared at the girl, stunned by her public disobedience. More shouts soon came from the other children nearby.

"Will you give the rest of these children to the sea too? As a tribute? Sending your magic here?"

More boos from the crowd, louder now. People publicly agreed with her!

"We want Lazlo!" she called out. "Give us Lazlo!"

The children with Cassandra chanted his name.

Lazlo! Lazlo! Lazlo!

Cassandra cupped her hands around her mouth and shouted. "In chains!"

Behind her, dozens of the other children held up their arms, each holding a length of chain.

In chains! In chains! In chains!

Tatiana uttered, "They are going to take Lazlo."

Parker glanced at the horizon. Slivers of clouds began to form. Her father's guards were standing at the ready, their hands on their weapons.

Quinn leaned into Parker and whispered, "If they attack, the guards, if they attack them, this will be a disaster."

Thump-thump. Thump-thump.

Lazlo ignored the chants, reached into his cloak, and removed his brown quill, holding it above his head.

"Parker? Parker? Are we going to do something?" Monty asked as Cassandra's chants began to spread throughout the audience. "Parker?"

Thump-thump. Thump-thump.

Out of the corner of her eye, Parker saw a red flash. A majestic cardinal, identical to the one in the schoolroom, soared above, weaving and bobbing between the kites. It was magnificent.

Lazlo! Lazlo! In chains! In chains!

Calm washed over her. She knew what to do. She lifted her hand into the air, holding her thumb and forefinger in a circle, fanning the three fingers out like feathers—the Plume symbol.

"What are you doing?" Quinn whispered.

The other Plumes followed her lead. Chatters raced through the crowd as attention shifted from Cassandra to the group of children who stood with their arms outstretched, their hands in a Plume.

The cardinal flew, scripting a series of letters and words, sending her a message.

The bird was *communicating* with her.

Parker turned to Quinn and smiled.

Turning back to the crowd, she kept her hand in the air and yelled: "*We are the they! We are the they! We are the they!*"

The Plumes and the children with Quinn joined the chant, their words echoing off the walls. Those watching from the amphitheater seats also joined in.

"Form a circle around Lazlo!" Parker called to the others, her arm still raised. "Go now!" Tatiana, Monty, and the twins quickly raced toward Lazlo, forming their group in a half-circle around the stone pedestal to protect him.

"*We are the they! We are the they! We are the they!*"

The Plumes stood, hands in the Plume sign, chanting words few others truly understood. Parker stood in the center of the circle, looking directly at Cassandra.

Quinn's hand with her glittering fingernails once again rested on her shoulder, a gentle squeeze letting Parker know her sister smiled with her.

"Not bad," Quinn's voice called out. "Now, let me see if I can help. Watch this!"

Pop. Pop. Pop. Pop. Pop. Pop.

The rapid-fire sound rang out from where Cassandra and the Illiterates gathered. They ducked for cover, yelling, as high in the air, golden-brown circles flipped in near-perfect unison before being caught in the hands of the hungry, cheering crowd.

"Golden-brown, sweet doughnuts, served after four perfect rotations," Quinn said. "Exactly how I drew it up. The triple D!"

Lazlo lowered his quill to the stone book to script in the ancient letters, the dark clouds sending a wave of mighty wind through the crowds. The Plumes kept their hands high, a chorus of "We are the they" chants filling the air while the golden-brown pastries rained on the audience. Behind the children, the torchbearer lit the boats they'd placed on the shore's edge, then roughly kicked each flaming ship out to sea, where they bobbed and bumped into one another. Soon the boats would be sucked away.

Parker turned to watch Lazlo, but her mother made eye contact. Mother touched their father's arm and pointed down to them as Parker still had her arm in the air. Her father smiled at her.

Then Parker blew her father a kiss.

She hadn't done it in a long time, if ever. Her father was surprised and pantomimed, catching the kiss in his hand and placing her imaginary kiss on his wife's cheek.

She smiled at her friends.

Quinn nodded to her, saying, "You did good. *Really* good." More children rushed over to join the Plumes semi-circle protecting Lazlo.

"We should move a little closer to those dot clowns," Tatiana said, motioning to the others. "You coming?" she asked Parker.

"I'm good," she responded. "You're good, right?" Parker asked Tatiana, Monty, and the twins.

Tatiana and Monty smiled and gave her a thumbs up, then turned away to move toward Cassandra and the Illiterates. "Nice shoes," Marcus said.

"Mayflies for your moment," Matteus added before they followed the others toward Cassandra.

The Plumes continued their chant, Plume signs still in the air.

"Okay," Parker said to herself with an exhale. "They're good... they're all good, so *I'm* good."

It worked. I'll be halfway to the Northern Passage before anyone knows I'm gone.

She swallowed hard with the realization she'd done it. They'd done it. It all felt *good*.

This was her moment.

Her parents were still staring at the interruption, whispering to one another. She looked back once more at her friends and her sisters and took a deep breath.

I can go now.

Parker silently slid to the edge of the stage and out of sight through the small gap as everyone's attention remained fixed on the chants of the Plumes, the doughnuts flying through the air, and the white and blue sparks sprinkling from the stone as Lazlo scripted his magic letters. She spotted Major Cappa. He was scanning the crowd of children. He was probably looking for her.

This will just be better for everyone. Heroes find the truth and return better. Heroes don't get themselves locked away to rot until the end of time.

A blast of wind hit Parker, and the seawater along the shore began to swirl, pulling the flaming lantern boats away from the craggy coast. The swirling water began to recede from the beach.

Taking a deep breath, she climbed down onto the rocks below.

"You're going to miss the best part," a voice said over her shoulder.

"Aven! Why do you keep sneaking up on me?"

"Where are you going?" Aven asked.

Parker turned back to her sister. "Away. I just have to go."

"But you just stopped those other kids," Aven said. "That was you. Everyone is chanting your words. Why would you leave now?"

"You wouldn't understand," she said, pausing to find the right words. "They—they are going to send me away, our parents are sending me to live with some aunt I don't even know. Away from you. Away from everyone."

"But, why would they do that?"

"Because I'm an embarrassment, Aven. I freeze up. I yell, I get kicked out of school, my only friends are street kids, and I miss feeling normal. Okay? And because I just want to write again. I just have to." She shook her head.

A look of disappointment and pain spread across Aven's face.

"There's something out there, Aven," Parker said, gesturing to the shore below. "There's something more. Lady Julie told me it's my job to find the answers, the truth. I need to find out what happened to her and Riley. You saw it in the library. Some kids are being muted in the Shadow Territories. Something's going on that is way bigger than what anyone sees, and I've just got to go find it."

One explosion followed another.

"What's that?" Aven asked.

"I don't know. Lazlo must be scripting something new or the final letters. Maybe the rest of the water magic is going to start. Go and watch with them."

Aven shook her head.

"I've got to go now, Aven."

"Then I'm coming with you," Aven replied.

"You can't," Parker said.

"I can help. I can do it again. I can. I already got you the inkwell."

The cool breeze hit them, feeling stronger outside the arena. Drain Day was beginning, and soon the water would start to twist furiously into the hole formed in the center of the seafloor, sucking down everything, even the fog.

"Absolutely not," Parker replied. "I don't know if I can even make this trip. I can not take you."

"You promised you'd teach me to write," Aven said and reached out to make a cross over Parker's heart.

"But our parents—"

"If they are sending you away, then I'm going with you," Aven interrupted.

A roar bellowed from the crowd, followed by another explosion.

Why were explosions happening this close?

"You promised you'd teach me to write," Aven said.

"I know," Parker said. "I know I did—"

"You can't break a promise."

"But that was stupid. It was just a stupid promise I made," Parker said.

"A promise is a promise."

Parker let out a heavy sigh. "Fine. I can't believe I'm doing this," she said. "I made my choice already, and that means there's no turning back even if I have to take you, so come on. Now. We have to go now. And you have to do what I say. Promise."

Aven took her fingers and made a crossing motion over her own heart.

"Now!" Parker called out as another explosion boomed behind them.

Trying to keep pace with the rapidly retreating water, Parker raced down the squishy, sandy soil to the rocks on the shore. The sea retreated, leaving dry land, as it had been before the kingdom had become an island.

Energized and terrified, she looked out across the water toward their escape. The salty, cool air was a taste of freedom. She turned to check on Aven, knowing exactly where they'd go, the route, the stops, where they could hide.

It's just another detour. I'll make it work; the hero always overcomes the obstacle. This obstacle is more annoying than most, but it's just another detour.

As the vortex sucked the water away, the massive stone tower of the former armory emerged perfectly preserved, as if it hadn't spent a year under the harsh sea.

Grasses, clovers, and flowers sprung up on the seafloor, with butterflies and insects flying around them. Birds chirped, and squirrels and rabbits began to hop alongside as the sisters sprinted down the sloping grounds, the water receding in front of them.

Dark clouds rolled across the midday sun, creating an ominous, dusky color to this place. This was a valley again, a return to the world of a year ago. More features emerged from the receding water; the roof of a home peeked through, followed by windows, shutters, and a front door. More homes emerged, and entire streets of houses were becoming visible. A school, a grocery storefront, a tailor shop, gardens, parks, walking paths; everything you'd expect from a place people lived. Everything except the people.

The valley below Everly, preserved exactly as it had looked before the water had come, emerged in front of them

"Did people live here?" Aven asked. "What happened to them?"

"I guess. Just don't stop," Parker yelled.

Th buildings formed a barrier between her and the other side of the sea she hadn't anticipated.

Up ahead she spotted a path that led between the homes and shops, as if it were the main street of the village and appeared to be the only way through.

"This way," she called to Aven, urging her sister onward.

Everything was perfectly preserved with still-fresh bread in the store windows, clothing drying on laundry lines, outdoor tables and chairs with full place settings, and even children's balls and toys scattered about. It was a ghost town.

More like it vanished with a stroke of a quill.

"This doesn't feel right," Aven said, staring at the stone walls around them. "Creepy. It feels like we're being watched."

"These are just some old buildings," Parker said. "It's nothing. Let's just get across."

Another blast of wind rattled the homes. Ominous shadows crept through windows and open spaces.

Something moved in one of the windows, and a shadow caught Parker's eye. Something was inside; she was sure of it.

A shadowy figure moved again inside one of the windows of the homes to her left. The figure was a woman who seemed to be wearing a neat, braided bun of brown hair just like her mother always wore. *My mind is playing tricks.*

She turned back to the path.

Everyone is still in the amphitheater.

She grabbed Aven's hand, their pace slowing.

"Why is there a pond here in the middle of the street?" Aven asked. "All the other water is gone."

"It's probably nothing. Just leftover water."

"No," Aven said, pointing ahead. "That is not just leftover water, Parker."

Stretched across the cobblestone street lay a beautiful, clear blue, circular pool of water, with rocks outlining its edges. Lily pads with bright white flowers floated around the sides.

"This doesn't look right," Aven said.

Parker agreed. She loved adventure stories and remembered sea creatures, shipwrecks, and merpeople in the waters.

They're stories. Stories to keep children from swimming as Owen did. Just stories to keep us safe.

"It looks beautiful," Parker said. "Probably a place for people to just sit and relax, something we *don't* have time for."

She tried to pull Aven along, but her sister froze, listening to the melody coming out of the pond.

"You see that? Do you see that? The pond. It's—it's glowing," Aven said, tightly squeezing Parker's hand.

"We just need to go around it," Parker said, again trying to pull the young girl to the outer edge of the glowing pool.

The beautiful melody increased in volume. A shimmer clouded the surface of the pond, obscuring it before settling, leaving the water as clear as glass.

"I'm afraid, Parker," Aven said, attempting to turn back.

"I'm right here," Parker said. She paused, trying to place the music. She'd heard that melody before. "Do you hear this too?"

Aven nodded furiously. Parker stepped toward the edge of the pond dragging her sister as she did. Drawn to the music, she leaned over the water and saw *something* at the bottom of the pool.

"What the heck? Something is inside this pond," she said, her toes inching closer to the water's edge. "Are you seeing this?"

Was my mind playing tricks again? The melody grew louder, and the outlines at the bottom became clear.

"Aven, I think it's a room down there. A bedroom."

The water stilled, allowing her to see dressers, a mirror, and a bed with a crest on it with two crossed feathers. She leaned closer to the surface to get a better look, a light at the deepest part of the pond growing increasingly bright, the music echoing off the buildings.

"Pa-a-a-r-r-r-k-k-k-e-e-r-r-r!"

Light flashed as she was pulled into the pool, sinking into the darkness.

Chapter Ten

The Motsan

Don't let me drown. Don't me drown.
Please don't let Aven drown.

Parker's lungs burned. Water pounded into her nose and gripped her throat. She tried to cough but only managed to swallow another gulp of water.

Then, the air hit her. Parker coughed up the water she had swallowed as she struggled to catch her breath. She was lying on the floor, her sister strewn across her midsection, still gripping her hand. They both wheezed, coughed, and panted, feeling one another's racing heart.

"Certainly not my best landing, but I'm not used to doing two of you at once," said a muffled voice.

Parker and Aven tilted their heads to meet the eyes of the speaker. The flash before the fall had made Parker's vision hazy, unable to make out the figure. She squinted through splotches of fading purples and greens. The room she and Aven crash-landed in looked familiar. The floors were made of dark, well-polished woods, while the walls were cut from a white stone.

"Where are we?" Aven whispered.

"I don't know," Parker replied. "That pool… it pulled us in… and I think we are at the bottom of the pond," Parker whispered to Aven. "This was what I saw *in* the pool."

Across from them sat a large, elegant cedar chest with its doors spread apart, filled with pants, shirts, shoes, and other boy's clothing. The mirror had the family crest at its top center; two gold feather quills crossed in the middle. The bed had a gold frame, matching the mirror, with intricate grooves and waves that looked identical to the ones in their room.

Aven twisted her head toward Parker. "That's Riley's bed," she hissed. "His bed, his chest, his stuff. These are all *his* things."

"That can't be," Parker said, scanning the room. A piece of Aven's hair fell on Parker's face, and to her surprise, the strand was entirely dry. She was completely dry. She patted the top of her head, her face, and her stomach.

"Now, didn't I tell you both to stay away from the water?" the voice said, louder and more precise now.

Parker knew this voice anywhere. It was their *mother*. Though her voice was soft and gentle, the words were firm.

Parker bolted upright, brushing Aven off.

"Mom? But how—how did we get *here*?" Parker stammered.

"And where's *here*?" asked Aven. "Are we at the bottom of a pond?"

"You're safe," she said. "Come here, my little one."

Aven stood up and raced into her mother's arms. "Mom!" she cried. "I ran out of air. The water just kept coming, Mom."

Mother hugged Aven but gave Parker her *you two have some explaining to do look* and said, "Yes, Mom is good. Your sister calling me Pip this morning about sent me over the edge and you into some *big* trouble."

Parker's mind raced. *What just happened?*

"You're in a room under the amphitheater. You're safe, but we can't stay here. All right, up you go now, Parker," her mother instructed, waving her fingers at her.

"I was trying to leave," Parker said.

"You made a mistake, Parker," her mother said. "And it could have been a big mistake." She nodded to Aven. "I'm just glad you're safe now. Now, stand up."

Parker obeyed her mother and stood at the center of the room, realizing the woman she saw in the house on the seafloor *was her mother*. The glowing pool transported them back here. Mother had gotten here impossibly fast, unless…

"You're a… *witch*," Parker exclaimed.

Mom stroked Aven's hair and laughed. "Oh, stop it, Parker." She waved a hand, dismissing her. "Of course not."

Aven jumped up and down. "A witch? Wait, that's not Mom? She's a witch pretending to be our mom!"

Their mother laughed.

Aven stepped out of her mother's embrace, eyeing the woman.

"Wait, how do we know you aren't a witch who is pretending to be my mom?" Aven asked, cocking her head to the side.

"Ask her something only our mother would know?" Parker replied in a hushed tone.

"Okay. Okay. Uh, what did Quinn shoot like an arrow right at the wall at breakfast?" Aven asked.

Their mother paused, shaking her head, and smiled. "Why, poppyseed muffins, of course."

"O-o-o-o-o-o. Parker, it's not her," Aven said, turning to her sister.

"You two can't take a joke. If you must know, it was Quinndaline's doughnuts, and quite honestly, no one could get those stains and splotches off my walls. That sister of yours."

Aven's skeptical look faded, and she stepped back into the embrace.

"But how did you do all this? It's—it's magic? The house and the figure in the window and the pool transported us here, back to here. Are you a magic writer?" Parker asked.

"Ol' Pip wouldn't know the first thing about writing magic spells or potions," she said, referring to herself in the third person. "I'm a Motsan, if you must know—a completely nonmagical person, both your father and I are."

"But—if you're not magical, how were you in the village—the under-water homes—" Parker broke off, confused.

The door swung open. "That sure was stupid," Quinn said from the doorway. "Not the whole rebel salute you pulled off in the amphitheater, which by the way was awesome, but the... ya know, running away into the vanishing seafloor thing."

Her older sister was still wearing the goggles on top of her head, saying *I told you so* without having to say a single word. She pulled the pink strand of hair over her ear as she closed the door behind her.

"Did they fall into the transporting pool, or did it have to suck them in?" Quinn asked their mother as she walked to the center of the room. "You're so predictable, Parker. Something doesn't go your way, so you try to run away. Of course, we all knew."

Stunned, she replied, "No, I—I ran because they were going to send me away. I had to... I had to. Otherwise—"

Quinn cut her off. "No, you don't think, Parker. You just fly off the handle. No one was sending you away. You were going to a new place to study, but you just hear something you don't like and—"

"Enough," their mother commanded.

"That was a transporting pool? Can we do it again?" Aven said, beaming in a rush of amusement. "Can we? Can we? That. Was. Amazing!"

Their mother smiled, trying to balance the enthusiasm of her eight-year-old with the realities of an older daughter just caught running away.

"There's much we need to discuss," Mother said to Parker, touching her shoulder before stroking her hair. "And little time. Yes, the Illiterates have attacked the amphitheater to disrupt Drain Day."

"But how did you get here so quickly? How did you know? You knew I was going to leave?" Parker asked.

"I always knew," her mother said. "It's your destiny. We knew someday you would attempt to find answers. It's just who you are, Parker."

Quinn rolled her eyes.

"Now, Quinndaline, could you bring your sisters something to drink?"

Quinn sighed and moved toward the far wall of the room, balled her left hand into a fist, then pointed her fist at the table that held an empty pitcher, several glasses, and a small bowl of sugar cubes. Then she reached into her pocket and pulled out a turkey feather with flecks of gray and white and a blue circle at the top. Holding the quill in her right hand, she spread her fingers out on her left hand, her palm toward the table.

"Do you realize Quinn is holding a *quill*?" Parker whispered to her mother.

"Of course, dear. I asked her to get you something to drink," Mother whispered back.

Quinn paused for a moment, then lifted the quill to her fingernails—the same fingernails featuring the silver and gold etchings she'd seen earlier—and began to write on her nails.

The quill glowed; sparks of gold and silver burst from each fingernail. Quinn carefully penned a single letter on each nail before moving to the next finger. Her fingernails glowed; the beautiful patterns from this morning sparking.

Parker gasped. "*She's* a magic writer." Her mother placed her hand on Parker's and nodded.

As Quinn touched the quill to her thumb, silver and gold glitter spread from her palm, floating over to the table and enveloping the table, pitcher, glasses, and sugar bowl in a stardust glow. The items on the table levitated, rattling as the dust whirled around them before disappearing, sending the dishes back to the table with a thud.

"Whoa," Aven said.

"Why won't you just work!" Quinn yelled at the quill in her hand, the glowing silver, gold embers still spinning around her nails.

"How'd she do that?" an awed Aven asked.

"Magic writing normally requires an enchanted quill, ancient letters, and a writing surface," Mother answered. "If a magic writer wants to direct her spell, she simply turns her fingernails into the writing surface to direct her magic toward something."

"You—you can write magic on your *fingers*," Aven said. "That's. So. Cool."

"Yes. It's quite beautiful. Isn't it?" her mother replied.

"Uh huh. The beautifulest," Aven replied.

"Now listen," their mother said. "We haven't much time."

"But wait, wait. How is this possible?" Parker asked. "You said you're not a magic writer. If you and Dad are Motsans, you're not magical, then how can she write magic and be a Serif? In the stories, people are born with these powers."

"My dear, those are stories, and while much in the stories are true, there are certain things that you'll learn are much more complex and wondrous than the stories could ever tell."

"What's a Serif?" Aven asked.

"Magic writers. That's what we call them in the stories. Serifs," Parker whispered.

"Oh, and in real life too," Mother said. "Serifs are quite real, and there are quite a lot more of them than you'd ever realized. Quinndaline is already being *trained* to be a Serif. She's still not very good at levitation or cleaning spells to remove doughnut marks off walls yet, but it's still early—plenty of time for her. She'd rather invent and fix things than script any magic spells, it seems."

Quinn narrowed her eyes at her mother.

"You don't get it! I'm trying, okay," Quinn snapped, her lip quivering. She threw the quill on the ground.

Their mother walked to Quinn. "You don't have to be perfect, my dear. *You* are going to keep your sisters safe." She bent down, retrieved the quill, and placed it back in Quinn's hands. "You're doing great."

Quinn scowled and held out her palm again, fingers shaking as she began to script.

"You all have magic in your blood through me," Mother said.

The empty pitcher levitated as silver dust from Quinn's palm whirled around it. Filling with a red liquid and fruit, the pitcher began to wobble and shake, spilling the drink onto the table. Then, the glasses floated to the pitcher, tipping to pour liquid into each one. The cups were filled to different levels, from just a tiny dribble in the bottom to one overflowing the rim of the glass, before the pitcher floated back to the table.

Parker was furious. Quinn learned to script magic without her.

Why didn't she just tell me this was what she was doing?

"Many women in my family are born writers of magic," Mother continued. "Not every woman in our family is born as a Serif. You see, magic is tricky, selective. In fact, in our family, it sometimes skips a generation. Your grandmother had magic, but *not* me."

Their grandmother had always been full of surprises. Whenever she'd visited, she'd often struggle to explain how she'd arrived, seeming to pop up from nowhere and disappear just as suddenly. It was impossible to get away with any mischief; she always knew what trouble they were making. It made sense their grandmother was a Serif.

"Oh no, no, no," Quinn said.

Ice cubes of varying sizes dropped into the drinks, splashing liquid onto the floor, and Quinn, who knelt to wipe up the spills, looked around to see if anyone had noticed.

"Magic... well, it skipped me," Mother said. "We don't know to what degree or when your powers will come to light. But you'll each have it, no matter how strong or weak it may be."

Quinn walked to the table where the drinks were and touched her quill on the first cup. The cup floated to Parker, who grabbed it from the air. Then Quinn touched the second cup, and it floated to Aven, stopped, shot to the ceiling, and turned over, dumping the contents onto Aven's head. Then the cup threw itself against the wall and shattered.

"Oh my gosh," Quinn said.

Aven laughed, wiping the red juice from her hair. "Are you *sure* you weren't also using magic on your doughnut gun this morning?"

Quinn glared at her. "At least I can write," Quinn hissed.

"Some magic writers are more natural," their mother said. "Others, well, it takes practice."

"But I don't want to be a magic writer," Parker blurted out. "I didn't ask for this. I wanted to write normal things. Not this." She pointed at her sisters cleaning up the mess.

"I wish you had a choice, Parker," her mother said.

"But magic writing has just made everything worse," Parker said. "You saw what happened today. The Illiterates are attacking us—because of *magic* writing, not writing just normal stuff like stories or poems. That's why one of us have had a regular life since Lazlo brought the water here. We saw what happened to the library."

"You entered the library, our library?" Mother asked, her words sharp as she leaned toward her daughter. "What did you find? Did you remove anything?"

"My quill."

Her mother's expression softened. "Just your quill. Okay then. So you may understand that you girls descended from a line of magic writers who protect our world from evil," Mother continued. "You've been told the Ancients had outlawed magic writing, but this is not entirely true. Magic writing never stopped. It changed and evolved and went underground. No longer was magic writing used to heal, build, or entertain. Serifs use magic writing to protect us. You each are part of a group of Serifs tasked with protecting all of Fonde from those who seek to destroy it. Those magic writers remain hidden from the Motsans."

"I've been learning to script incantations and protection spells," Quinn said. "Lazlo has been teaching me how to keep us safe."

"Safe?" Parker asked. "Safe from what?"

Quinn and her mother exchanged glances.

"From. What?" Parker repeated.

"From *her*," Quinn shot back. "She kidnapped Riley and betrayed us all. And she could come back again."

Parker shook her head. It was Lady Julie. They were talking about her. But they were wrong; they'd always been.

"You can't possibly believe that," Parker replied, her voice shaking. "She's leaving us clues."

Mom squeezed Parker's hand and met her eyes.

"We... aren't safe," she continued. "I know it's hard to believe, but it's the truth. Unfortunately, you girls are all part of a battle existing in this world since the first Serifs learned to script magic. We all misjudged her, and then she kidnapped your brother, and now we fear she may be attempting to return with others like her."

Parker sank into her chair.

"We loved her," she said. "She raised you, and from the first moment I met her, I knew she was important in each of *your* stories."

Her mother stood and walked to the other side of the room. She stood near the cedar chest, its doors open, idly running her hand over its surface while looking into the mirror with their family crest of the two gold feather quills crossed in the middle that reflected her children.

She continued. "Before you girls were born, Lady Julie risked everything to reveal herself as a magic writer when our family was in dire need, and at that moment, she became part of our family. We trusted her. And this was why we asked her to teach each of you to write so when your powers revealed themselves, you'd be able to script spells and curses to protect yourself."

"But then, how come she never wrote magic with us?" Parker asked. "It was all just regular, normal writing."

"Magic writers cannot reveal their powers in the open, my dear."

"Except for Lazlo," Parker muttered.

Her mother ignored this. "We simply never expected what Lady Julie was capable of," she said, her fingers outlining the crest on the cedar chest. "Her actions changed everything the night she took Riley."

Something gnawed at Parker as she watched her mother. Something didn't make sense about the room, about that chest, and about her mother.

"I still don't understand. Why are we here, in this room?" Parker asked. "Why did you save these things from Riley and all his clothes?" She motioned to the chest.

Her mother folded her hands in front of her.

"These clothes aren't Riley's," she slowly said. "This room is Owen Wickerland's."

Chapter Eleven

The Enchanted Purse

Owen Wickerland is living in this room.

"He's alive?" Parker asked, shock filling her reddening face. "But how—how could you?"

"Owen is safe. He's here, and he's perfect," Mother said, turning back to her daughters.

The room fell silent.

"Perfect? His family thinks he drowned," Parker said, breaking the silence. "Why haven't you told his family or let him go home to them?"

"We couldn't. He was brought here through the transporting pool much like you were and we didn't know what to do. We had no idea Owen would enter the water or that he might possibly survive the drain, but—if today doesn't happen, we have no way to keep the Ravagers at bay."

"*You* kidnapped their son," Parker said, her anger pouring from her.

"If we returned him, clearly unharmed, we couldn't be certain the Illiterates would rise up and take the amphitheater."

"That's what you care about? The amphitheater?" Parker stammered.

"That was part of it, yes," she replied.

"But you know what it's like to lose a child," Parker said. "You know because of Riley."

"Yes, but this is different. Owen is safe, and when things are calm, we'll return him. He's well taken care of."

Boom. Boom.

Explosions shook the room, causing Aven to cover her ears.

"What was that?" Quinn asked.

There was a loud banging on the door, and then the door burst open.

"Queen, you and your children are not safe," Major Cappa stated as a dozen fellow soldiers crowded behind him in the entrance. "The Illiterates have brought more explosives and are about to take the amphitheater. We must leave before they find this room."

"A few minutes more," the queen demanded.

"We can only hold them so much longer, Your Highness," Major Cappa said and exited.

Why was the guard with the Illiterates mark here with them?

"Now, girls, we have very little time. The kingdom is under attack."

"Wait," Parker said. "Those explosions we heard, those weren't Lazlo?"

"The explosions are the Illiterates?" Quinn asked. "That whole thing from Cassandra was all a distraction for what the Illiterates were planning?"

"Today is a day when everything has changed in Everly," Mother said. "It's the Illiterates. They will be taking the amphitheater from us. That was always our plan, although your sister nearly ruined it."

"Me?" Parked asked. "I almost ruined it? I stopped your guards from attacking children and the Illiterates from taking Lazlo. Didn't you see what happened? I thought you'd be proud of what I did. I stood up to them and prevented something much worse."

Her mother shook her head, looking as she had when Parker had yelled at her tutor. "You could have been hurt," Mother said. "That alone is much worse."

Parker looked away, trying not to cry. Quinn put her hand on Parker's forearm.

"I know you think you were doing the right thing," Mother said. "We sent Lazlo to warn you. You didn't listen, and then your strong will nearly had disastrous consequences. We *knew* the Illiterates would attack. We needed them to. We chose to let this happen. We are choosing to let the Illiterates take the amphitheater from us."

"That makes no sense. Why would you let them take the amphitheater?" Quinn asked.

"We let the amphitheater fall, or the entire kingdom would."

"The Illiterates could take the entire kingdom?" Quinn asked.

"No. But Dagamar, Lady Julie, and the Ravagers could," their mother said.

"Dagamar?" Quinn asked. "Dagamar could come here?"

Mother looked at the floor and solemnly nodded. "We believe so. Lazlo saw a sign in the waning moon signaling Dagamar's return. Then attacks in the Shadow Territories began."

"The silent darkness," Parker uttered.

"Yes. We believe Dagamar and the Ravagers are planning to attack Everly soon. They have steadily moved toward Everly from the Grootten mountains. The beginning of this waning moon was the sign he seeks to attack our family and the entire kingdom."

"But can't you stop them?" Quinn asked. "Can't Lazlo?"

"The water was supposed to protect us," Parker said.

"The water is not a real barrier to magic writers," their mother said. "It's more of a display of magical power, but not nearly enough. Lazlo is but a single boy."

"How much time do we have?" Quinn asked.

"Days. A week, perhaps," their mother said. "The Illiterates may help us buy *more* time. With the Illiterates holding the amphitheater, watching the shores, and bringing all of Everly on edge, we'll have more time to stop the Ravagers. We fear they've already established a new home base in the Shadow Territories, and we may be next. We will need lots of help. The three of you must prepare for whatever comes."

"That's why you let it fall," Quinn said.

"And if it hadn't... I *could* have brought Dagamar here sooner," Parker whispered to herself. "You're right. I did—I did almost ruin it." She shook her head in disbelief and ran to the window as more explosions shook the room. And I got my friends involved in the fight. All of them," Parker stammered. "Are they going to be okay?"

"Yes," their mother replied. "The soldiers have been instructed to evacuate everyone else from the amphitheater. They are to fight the Illiterates but be prepared to let them take it. We hope no one will be hurt."

"But we saw Illiterates inside the castle. One of the guards had the four dots," Parker said. "And Cassandra said the torchbearers were Illiterates."

"Major Cappa," Mother said with a nod. "That was part of the plan. We had to let the Illiterates sense this opportunity."

"I still don't understand why Dagamar would attack us," Quinn said. "Why would Ravagers want to attack Everly?"

"This conflict began long ago. And as a result, we have enemies who want you children to pay the price for our family's mistakes."

"Mistakes?" Quinn asked.

Mother opened a drawer to the chest and pulled out a tiny leather bag. She brought it over to the table, motioning for everyone to sit down.

"There isn't time to explain, but my mother gave me these."

"Grandma?" Aven asked. "But I thought she couldn't come to visit us?"

"She can't. We believe your grandmother may have been taken or captured by the Ravagers."

"Wait, what?" Parker exclaimed.

"The Ravagers took her? And you didn't bother to tell us this?" Quinn asked.

Mother placed a hand on Quinn. "Your grandmother is a Scott, my last name before I married your father and became a Pennymore. Scott women are known for their wit and wisdom, and your grandmother has incredible magical writing abilities to keep her protected. Before your grandmother disappeared, she left these with me. I cannot create magic spells or potions on my own. I do understand how to use magic in items others have created. Powerful magic is enchanted into each of these items."

Mother held the leather purse in her hands and turned it over. Out fell three items, each too large to fit in the tiny coin purse. Each had a series of letters scripted, leaving a singed black mark magically imprinted.

Aven's eyes grew wide seeing the magic cave within the purse.

"Keep the bag, as you may need to hide items inside it."

Aven picked up the three items and began to examine them. After a few seconds, she coughed, drawing attention to herself. "Are we sure Grandma hadn't gone a little... you know, uhm," Aven twirled her finger in a circle on the side of her head. She held the first of the magical items and snickered. "I mean, she gave you a magical *oven mitt*?"

"Aven!" Quinn chided.

"And measuring cup and a tea ball?" Aven continued. "Are we going to cook our way out of trouble? *Here, evil people, drink some of this tasty tea, and you can't hurt us.* Why in the world would she give us an old oven mitt, this measuring cup, and a tea ball?"

"This is serious," Quinn said. "Haven't you heard anything we said?"

Her sister lowered her eyes.

"These items have capabilities far beyond their appearance," Mother answered. "Your grandmother enchanted common, simple, everyday things to hide them from others who want them."

Another loud bang on the door.

Quinn whipped toward the door, her palm pointing at it with her quill ready to touch her nails.

Was Quinn going to use her powers to fight? Could she even do magic writing like that?

Major Cappa's muffled voice came from behind the door, "Queen! We must go *now.*"

"It's okay, my child," Mother said, urging Quinn to put her quill away. "Please take them," she continued, storing the items back in the small purse and handing it to Quinn.

Boom. Boom. Boom.

"Are we safe?" Quinn asked.

"For now, yes. We hoped for the best, but anticipated the worst when your brother was kidnapped. Each day he is gone is another day closer to someone coming for you. We have strengthened one enemy in the hopes of holding off another. I hope you understand."

The girls nodded.

"You are all amazing," Mother said as tears formed in the corners of her eyes. "You must protect each other. You must trust no one but each other. Promise me."

Chapter Twelve

Owen Wickerland

The door burst open, and guards poured into the room.

More yelling could be heard outside, and another round of loud explosions shook the room.

"Take them somewhere safe," Major Cappa said, motioning to the girls. The group of guards surrounded their table and quickly ushered the siblings to the door.

"Get the boy," Parker heard their mother say to another guard before she disappeared. Then, in a blur of pushing, proding, and running, led them through dark corridors to emerge into the sunlight behind the amphitheater where smoke still billowed from inside.

Get the boy.

Her parents were *kidnappers.* They'd used Owen as a pawn to force the Illiterates to fight. A pang of guilt raced through her, knowing how he must be feeling, unable to see his family, trapped, alone in this room.

People *he* loved were taken away.

Parker knew *this* feeling… loneliness, loss, helplessness.

The guards herded her and her siblings on, shouts continuing all around them.

Boom. Boom. Boom.

The guards and her siblings flinched as the explosions echoed.

"This way!" the guards urged.

Parker thought of the heroes and monsters in her stories and how simple those stories were.

Good and evil.

Light and dark.

Writing had been something to fear until it wasn't.

Magic had been forbidden until it protected the kingdom.

Kidnapping had brought pain and chaos to her family until it was necessary to keep the peace.

War brought death and destruction until it was used to keep another enemy away.

She felt the hands of the guards pushing her forward. Step. Step. Step.

"We must hurry!" Major Cappa shouted.

Parker stopped, panic rushing over her. She felt trapped.

She'd been so close to leaving the island, to escaping from it all. Close to finding a new, safe place to write again. And now she was trapped, surrounded by guards, at the center of a conflict she wanted nothing to do with. The Illiterates won.

This can't be happening.

"No!" Parker said, and one of the guards following bumped into her back. "No more!"

"What are you doing?" Quinn said, turning to her.

"Where is he?" Parker asked. "Where is Owen?"

Quinn stepped toward her sister and leaned into her. "Now is not the time."

"I don't care," Parker said. "Did you know? Did you know they had him?"

"No," Quinn said. "I didn't know. I found out just like you."

Parker shook her head, unable to look her sister in the eye.

"Major," Parker said, wheeling around to address the man, "bring Owen Wickerland *here.*"

Major Cappa nervously looked from side to side. "But, Your Highness, your mother said—"

"I don't care what she said," Parker said. "He's safer with us. Where is he?"

"What are you doing? What is this?" Quinn whispered.

"I have to see him. I have to see his face to know he's alive."

"You see what's going on around us?" Quinn asked. "We aren't safe here."

"Major, where is he?" Parker asked.

The man pursed his lips. "He's been taken from the amphitheater. He's with the guards who took him. He's safe there."

"Send your men to find him," Parker commanded, "and bring him here."

Major Cappa turned to Quinn. "You heard what my sister said," Quinn said. "Bring Owen Wickerland here."

"As—as you wish," Major Cappa responded, nodding his head and then addressing two of his soldiers in hushed tones. They ran from the group back to the amphitheater.

Quinn never disobeyed our mother. Why would she agree to bring Owen here?

"Major," Quinn said. "Now, my sisters and I want to go back to the castle."

"I'm sorry," he said, shifting nervously again. "But that's not possible. The route is still unsafe. They haven't sealed the perimeter around the amphitheater for your return. We have identified a secure area ahead. The guards I sent back will meet us there, but we must hurry."

"Then take us there," Quinn said. "Are you okay with that?" she asked Parker.

"Yeah," she stammered, surprised to be asked. The group walked in silence until they were a mile away from the amphitheater. Parker knew they were now near the shoreline, where they'd often played as children.

As they walked, Parker replayed that moment from her dreams over and over, as Owen begged for help before the water dragged him under.

He was alive. I should feel happy. Why do I feel so afraid to see him?

Owen Wickerland is alive.

The guards spread out, forming a perimeter around the siblings. It was the first time the three sisters had been alone together in quite some time.

They sat on the dry seashore far from the castle and the amphitheater. They'd spent hours at this spot as children. The small stream usually emptied into the magic-made sea surrounding the kingdom. But with the sea gone for a few more hours, its water spilled into the clovers that had returned into the empty seabed.

"All these things, you didn't tell me. You didn't tell us," Parker said to Quinn. "I still don't understand why."

Quinn didn't answer.

"Mom and Dad are moat sand?" Aven asked.

"Motsans," Quinn corrected, trying not to smile. "It means normal people who can't write magic."

"Oh," Aven responded. "But *you* can write magic? So can you do the flying thing you were doing but with me?"

Quinn shook her head. "Maybe… well, not really."

"What about you?" Aven asked, motioning to Parker. "Can you do the flying thing with me? Oh wait, you already did that thing where you shot a lightning bolt from the book—"

"She did what?" Quinn asked.

"Uh, it was the coolest thing," Aven said, waving her arms in excitement. "We broke into the library, we stole this book and a quill, then a guard came, but it wasn't *that* guard, I think, and the candles all turned black, and then this crazy blue bolt shot from the book, and it destroyed the chandelier. Tell her how you did it, Parker, the whole thing."

"Whoa, whoa, whoa, you exploded the bronze chandelier outside the Hall of Resplendence?" Quinn said, sitting up on her knees. "*You* wrote magic, Parker? You cast a bolt spell that could explode something that massive?"

"I—I—no," Parker said, staring at the ground. "The quill just touched the book, and then, yeah, this bolt burst from the book, and I guess it destroyed the chandelier. But no one got hurt."

"On your own?" Quinn asked.

"Yeah, I guess. I was trying to get my quill. None of it makes any sense to me. I just saw it in my head, and then everything happened fast."

"This is crazy, Parker," Quinn said, her voice elevating. "That's next-level magic enchantment stuff, like bolts from a book to destroy things. You realize what this means, right?"

Parker shook her head.

"You are a Serif, and, like, a powerful one, I think," Quinn said and then exhaled a big sigh. "You thought they were sending you away. You thought it was because you'd been bad or because you did something wrong. But that wasn't it at all. You were being sent to a library, one of the ancient homes for magic writers. You were going to write again. That's what this was all about."

Parker looked up and turned toward her sister. "Why didn't they just say that?"

"Because they weren't sure where you were going," Quinn said. "You couldn't stay here in Everly and learn to write here because Lazlo is the Order of Legend. I'm a Legend too, so that's why he can teach me to write magic. That's how it works. Someone from your order teaches you."

"*You're* Order of Legend?" Parker asked.

"Yes," Quinn said, smiling.

"I'm a Chronicle, the cardinal," Parker said as she touched her hand to her chest.

Quinn looked surprised. "How? How did you find out? I didn't know you found out yet."

"That's what the inkwell told me," Parker said with a shrug.

"The inkwell told you? Wait, you found the rainbow inkwell?"

"No," Aven interrupted. "I did. I took it from the library."

"You *took* the rainbow inkwell?" Quinn said, her eyes growing wide. "How—where is it now?"

Parker's face grew pale, and she shrugged her shoulders. "It's been hiding in my dress all day…"

"You were going to *run away* with one of the most powerful magic items in all of Fonde?"

"I guess," Parker said. "We didn't know."

"Oh, I knew it was the best one," said Aven raising her hand. "I have good taste."

Quinn put her hands on her cheeks and shook her head. "Wow. The two of you have no idea what could have happened. That inkwell has for centuries told Serifs their order, to guide their training. Literati libraries for each order are hidden all over Fonde to help us learn how to write magic. You were going to one once they figured out what order you were in."

Parker bit her lips.

"What?" Quinn asked.

"So, I kinda let all my friends in the Plumes dip the quill in the inkwell and—"

"You did what?" Quinn asked.

"That wasn't a good thing to do?" Parker said.

"Oh my gosh, you just let all your friends find out which magical order they were in? You showed them the inkwell and let them do the Apportionment."

"What's Apportionment?" Aven asked. "Can I apportion—whatever you just said?"

"The Apportionment," Quinn repeated. "It's this ancient ceremony when Serifs discover their order. It's a huge, huge deal. Like the biggest event in any Serif's life probably. There's this entire thing, and visitors, and a ceremony around it. Then you receive your quill and meet your trainer, and there's some great food… Wait, you're being totally and completely serious right now?"

Parker winced and nodded.

"And all of them just got told their order," Quinn said, still shaking her head. "That makes them magic writers too, Parker."

"Wait, that's what it means when the inkwell talks to you?" Parker asked.

"Yeah. Now, you can't actually *write* magic until you learn how, but when the inkwell tells you your order, you are a Serif, a real magic writer," Quinn said, smiling as she nodded at her sister. "Your friends, just normal kids, are going to be able to *write magic*."

"Oh my gosh," Parker exclaimed. "I had no idea that's how you found out. The other Plumes all asked me what our orders meant, and I just told them it was a way to split into groups or organize ourselves."

"It's a bit more than that," Quinn said with a smile. "Now, when you tell them what that all meant, you'll blow their minds. Usually, Apportionment happens when you're almost a teenager. I did mine early because of this whole magical war thing going on, but you pretty much threw thousands of years of tradition out the window. You sure they can keep that all a secret?"

"They are Plumes," Parker said. "Remember, even *you* had no idea I built this secret group to teach dozens of kids to write?"

"Good point," Quinn said. "An underground writing society is the perfect place to reveal a secret this big."

"Hey, when do I get to do that apportiony thing with the inkwell?" Aven asked.

"Never," Quinn chided. "Not never, but not now. Thanks to Parker, we've got all these kids who just found out they are Serifs, who heard an inkwell speak, who saw dust. You guys all saw the dust and the animals. Right?"

"Yes," Parker said. "And then I saw the cardinal again at the amphitheater. It was flying, and it was weird... It spoke to me. It told me what to do."

"It told you what to do? Wow, that's a new one," Quinn said. "I've never heard of that before. This is so great that I can finally talk to you about all this." Quinn exhaled. "I feel like I've been keeping this secret from you forever. You guys all did the Apportionment and then scared away the Illiterates for a bit. So, the cardinal is what made you do whatever your rebel sign was all about. Huh? Wow."

Quinn held her hand up in the Plume sign.

"Guys, I think someone's coming," Aven said, pointing to a group of soldiers approaching.

"It looks like you're about to get your wish, Parker," Quinn said as they all stood up from the ground.

Major Cappa said something to Owen, and the boy nodded and walked toward the siblings. He was taller than Parker had remembered, but his round face, brown eyes, and chestnut hair were just as she'd seen in her dreams.

Owen really was alive.

"I'm Owen," he said, nodding to Quinn and Aven.

"You're the boy who survived the drain," Quinn replied. "You're pretty big news."

"I'm so sorry, Owen," Parker said. "I can't believe what happened to you. My parents—"

"They—they kept me safe. I'm okay," he said. "I'm glad you guys are okay. I heard all the yelling and the explosions. What happened?"

"The Illiterates took the amphitheater," Quinn said. "It was chaos. The guards took us here, but we don't know what happened to your parents or really to anyone. I wish we did…"

"Oh, okay," Owen said, a look of disappointment filling his face as his eyes looked off at the smoke still billowing from the amphitheater. "I—I… the guard told me you wanted to see me."

"I—we just had to see you," Parker said. "We all thought you drowned, everyone. And then to find out you're alive. I dunno, I just had to see you and make sure you were okay."

"I'm okay, yeah. Well, we are birthday buddies," Owen said with an awkward smile. "But yes, I'm okay. Thanks for checking on me. I'll go back now, and you guys can do whatever you're doing." He turned to leave.

"No," Parker said, grabbing his arm. "You're safer here, and this way, we'll make sure we get word about the amphitheater for you about anything that happens."

"Are you sure?" he asked, his face lighting up.

"We're trapped out here for now," Quinn said. "If you don't mind sitting around and throwing rocks into the creek, we've got plenty of rocks."

"Come on, I'll show you the best spot," Aven said, grabbing the older boy's hand and pulling him toward the creek.

The older sisters didn't speak as they watched Aven excitedly pointing out features of the creek to Owen. The pair looked like they were having fun, with Aven hunting trout in the stream much like she imagined a real wolf would do. She crouched down at the water's edge, spotted a tiny fish, and dove in face first. Owen laughed at their sister, who was clearly showing off, but thus far in her trout lunges, she had done little more than drenching herself and her clothing.

After a few minutes of silence, Parker said, "I'm not sure I feel better or worse now."

"We're safe, I guess," Quinn said. "And I want you to know that what you did at Drain Day was incredible."

"But—"

"No but about it, Parker," Quinn interrupted. "I was so proud to see you stand up to them. They were out for Lazlo, and who knows what could have happened. You were amazing. All those kids, they followed you."

"Yeah, but you heard what she said. I—I could have ruined everything," Parker said.

"She didn't mean that," Quinn said. "You may have saved us from something much, much worse. Without you, we might not be here now."

"I wish… I just wish it mattered," Parker said. "We're trapped on this island. The Illiterates won. And that means they won't be going away. Don't you feel helpless? Do you think they are just going to let us write ever again in the open? Fat chance. That ship sailed. We're involved, and so is our family. They took our brother and our grandmother. I don't even know what to think."

"Me neither. At least we're together, so there's that," Quinn said, smiling. "I'm just glad to have you back, sis."

Woof. Woof. Grrrrrrr.

Aven growled and circled Owen like a dog does when there's a stranger at the door. Owen looked at the two older siblings and shrugged.

"Uh, Parker. Parker. Pa-a-r-k-ER!" Quinn shouted.

"What?" Parker snapped back, tossing her hands in the air.

Quinn pointed. "Your necklace."

Parker reached for the stone. When she released her grip, the glow reflected on her fingers. The red-orange Carnelian stone felt hot and *alive*, the gem illuminating red to orange as it pulsated.

"Is it supposed to glow?" Quinn asked.

"I don't think so," Parker answered.

The sisters then heard a strange whisper in the wind.

Aven growled again, racing from Owen toward the stream where a series of spaced stones arranged as an informal bridge.

The whisper grew louder.

"Sisters! Sisters! It's me!" the whisper said.

Quinn stumbled back.

Parker's eyes widened, and she called, "Aven, did you say something? Owen, was that you?"

Aven stared across the stream, shaking her head, confused. Owen looked around as if he had heard it too.

"Sisters. Sisters. It's me." The whisper came closer.

Quinn looked at Parker. "Are the two of you trying to play a prank somehow? How'd you do that voice?"

Parker shook her head and said, "No. I promise. I thought it was you."

The two older sisters looked to the guards still in the perimeter around them.

"Look over there!" Parker whispered to her sister. She motioned to an area of tall grass. It bent and separated in rushed movements. They rushed over to Owen and Aven.

"Something's coming," Aven said.

"What do you think it is?" Quinn asked.

Parker raised a hand, shielding the sun while Quinn lowered her goggles. "I don't know. But I know I heard something and saw the grass moving. Be honest. You heard it too. Didn't you, Quinn? You heard the voice say 'sisters,'" Parker said.

Quinn bit her lip.

"Quinn," Parker pressed.

"I did," Quinn said. "What do you think it is, Owen?"

"Maybe someone's hiding over there," he said. Aven took off and raced toward the stream just across from the area where the grass had moved.

The others hurried to the bank to retrieve Aven. Both Quinn and Parker rested their hands on Aven's shoulder as though they were calming a riled and protective family dog.

One by one, they hopped along a few stones across the stream, toward the tall grass, careful not to fall in the water.

Aven followed close behind, pouncing on each stone and landing on all fours. They reached the far edge of the stream glancing back at their well-armored babysitters, and each took several giant steps to get to the grassy area above the bank from where they had heard the strange voice.

"We're fine," said Quinn as much for herself as for the group. "It seems odd because of all that's happened to us today. Right?" Then she stepped behind Parker and gave her a little push. "Well, go on. You're the brave sister wearing the glowing stone."

Parker nodded and pressed on, the grass tickling her shins and ankles. She waved her hands in front of her like she was wandering in the dark. She knelt to the ground, searching there too.

The grass was still.

Nothing was there.

The calm air fractured with Aven tumbling head over feet into the grass. She growled, waving her arms in a frenzy.

Parker and Quinn hurried to her.

Aven rolled over, facing the sky, then smirked and roared with laughter.

Pushing back the tall grass, Quinn and Parker saw Aven lying on her back with her arms raised in a circle as if she were holding something.

But nothing was there.

Chapter Thirteen

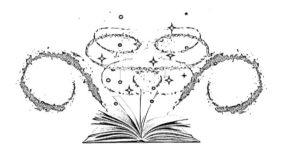

The Storyteller

"What is it, Aven?" Quinn asked, catching her breath.

"Parker, why is your gem glowing?" Owen asked, seeing the stone's pulsing light for the first time.

"I don't know," she said, reaching to cover the stone so the guards wouldn't see.

Aven laughed so hard tears flowed down the sides of her face. The sisters sat paralyzed, unsure of what to do.

Aven squeezed her arms tighter in the circle and tried to calm her laughter. "It's—it's—it's—him. It's Riley!" she said.

"What is she saying?" Owen asked. "Did she say Riley? There's no one there."

That laughter. I know that laugh. I know it. Where is it coming from?

"That's not funny, Aven," Quinn said. "It's not."

Parker felt the warm stone on her chest, the glow still pulsing.

Aven still lay in the grass, rocking back and forth, muttering words about Riley and laughing or crying or both.

Parker's heart raced as she knelt next to her sister.

Aven sat up and wiped her runny nose and wet eyes, her smile spreading across her face. She was shaking. "It's him," she said.

Parker felt a warm, gentle hand on her wrist. But when she looked down to that spot on her arm, nothing was there.

A chill crept over her body.

"It's me, Parker."

Parker, his voice echoed in her head, the R's in her name rolling slightly just as she remembered. She felt the pang of the space in their room, where the brother's bed had been. The tears her parents had cried. The anger they'd felt over the past year.

Everything stilled, except for the red-orange gem around her neck. It faded and brightened between the hues.

Aven, Quinn, and Owen stared at Parker.

"Riley? Is it really *you*?" Parker whispered, placing her left hand over the warm spot on her wrist.

The mere mention of his name made Quinn gasp, her cheeks beginning to flush. "Parker, stop. Aven's joke went far enough."

"But it *can't* be you. You're gone," Parker said.

Aven put her arms around Quinn and mumbled through tears, "It's him. It is Riley."

"Yes! Yes! Sisters, it's me. Riley. I'm here."

Parker felt another warm hand cup hers. The hands were smaller than hers, or Aven's, as Riley's, the youngest Pennymore, would be.

He was here. He was back.

Parker touched his shoulders, the back of his neck, his hair, and his face, remembering everything about him she'd missed, placing his features, even if she couldn't see him. She pulled him toward her, hugging him tightly, never wanting to let him go.

"I—I don't know what happened, but you can't see me," Riley said. "I—I know I'm—I'm invisible. But it's me."

"But how?" Parker whispered. "How did you find us? How did you get here?"

"I don't know," Riley said. "But I need your help. I'm in danger."

***

The guards led them back to the castle in stunned silence, no one wanting to say a word to the guards about the return of their brother, afraid of what could happen if they discovered him. The Illiterates had taken the amphitheater, but their father's guards now formed a secure perimeter around it, allowing them to return all of the Pennymore siblings, including the invisible Riley, to the safety of the castle and their room.

Now Parker, Aven, and Owen sat on the bedroom floor with a guard stationed outside for protection. Quinn paced, periodically placing her goggles over her eyes before taking them off again. She'd speak then stop herself, trying to find words.

"What's happening?" Quinn said, finally breaking the silence.

"You're the one who writes magic," Parker replied. "I—I thought maybe you'd know something."

"She writes magic?" Owen asked.

Parker nodded. Quinn shook her head and began pacing again, muttering as she did.

Riley seemed content to explore his old bedroom, as floating items and toys would levitate and move seemingly by themselves.

"So, this is new?" Owen asked, pointing to one of the levitating toys in the corner of the room. An awkward heaviness hung in the air as the older Pennymores tried to explain everything that had happened to Owen.

"Yeah," Parker replied. "It's new to us *all*."

"But are all of you are magic writers?" he asked.

"Yes," Parker answered.

"And your brother was kidnapped?" Owen asked. "By a witch?"

"A Serif," Parker said. "Yes."

"A witch," Quinn corrected.

"A Serif," Parker said. "Serif's can write magic. Some are evil—like the Ravagers. Evil writers would be a witch."

"Got it," Owen said. "And your parents let the Illiterates take the amphitheater to prevent Dagamar and the evil magic writers, the Ravagers, from attacking Everly?"

"Right," Parker said.

"Okay," Owen said, his lips pursed. "And you don't know why the Ravagers want to attack Everly?"

"Not really," Parker said. "Something about us being punished for mistakes in the past, I guess."

Owen clasped his hands in front of himself. "But isn't it just a little strange to you that Riley, who dark and evil writers took, just happens to show up the same day your mom—I mean the queen—told you Dagamar was trying to attack Everly?"

"He's our brother," Aven said.

"But it's weird, right?" Owen said.

A thought struck Parker. "Riley, how did you find us?"

"I just did, I guess," he said. "I'm not sure."

As Riley continued to answer their questions about his escape, his words at times were beyond a six-year-old. He'd been taken and was locked in a small room alone. Otherwise, he had almost no recollection of the past year. It was as if he'd skipped an entire year of his life.

"I remember always missing you guys," he said. "And being alone."

The girls each offered sympathetic smiles and returned the sentiment.

"Sometimes, I would hear voices outside the room. And they kept saying I was in danger. They kept using that word."

One of the voices he had heard outside his room was Lady Julie. However, he didn't see her face—not once while he'd been away. He heard her talking outside the room day after day.

He was treated well with food, clothing, and water for bathing. But he'd never left the small room and never saw another soul. "When she said I was in danger, I was afraid. I just wanted to come home so you could protect me. I tried to find how to get out, and then I did."

Someone pushed a food tray through the small window for him, but they forgot to lock the little window.

"I thought they'd come back to lock it like they always did. But they didn't. So, I went through it."

Riley told them how he had to squeeze to make it out of the small opening of his room. But with a long breath out and a painful wiggle, he was through the door. He crept out of the hallway and moved as quickly as he could, hoping to avoid anyone. He needed to find an exit to escape. He finally found a quiet stairwell and descended, hearing voices coming behind him and outside the stairs.

"I was trapped," Riley said, his voice shaking.

He stepped out of the stairwell and into the kitchen full of workers preparing the evening meal.

"They would send me back and lock me away again. I knew it," Riley said.

He surveyed the room and waited. They looked right at him.

"A cook yelled. I was scared. But then another walked right past me. I realized they weren't looking at me but *through* me. They couldn't see me," Riley said, as tiny drops—his tears—splashed onto the empty ground where he was sitting. "No one could."

Riley snuck past the workers, waiting for one of them to open the door leading outside, and was free.

For the first time in a year, he saw the sun and the sky, but more than anything, he wanted to see his family.

Wandering for some time, Riley came across a small stream and decided to follow a path marked beside it. He drank water from the stream and ate small handfuls of berries sprinkled on the ground. When their brother was tired, he would usually be able to find a small, warm space to sleep and could cover himself with blankets and furs he'd also found left for him. He shared that he was alone, but he wasn't scared.

"Someone watched over me," he offered.

Owen stood and began pacing. "None of this makes any sense. I get I'm new to this whole magical war world you're talking about, but—"

"You're an Illiterate," Quinn said. "How can we ever trust anything you say?"

"Whoa now," Owen said. "My parents are, sure, but do you believe all the things your parents do? I'm not my parents, and I'm not one of those kids who follow Cassandra and her stooges around drawing dots on myself."

"Yeah, but you tell your parents about this, and the Illiterates will try to tear down the castle," Quinn said.

"Listen, I got sucked into an ocean and wound up in a bedroom through some magical transportation thing. Okay? I'm not some writer-hater. I just want to know what's going on."

"He's right," Parker said. "He never was part of their nonsense. I know. Those were the kids I tried to punch."

"I'm just saying," Owen said, "that your little brother shows up here after traveling invisible and alone for days right as the ocean disappears, and it's *certainly* not a coincidence."

"You think it's a clue?" Parker asked.

"A clue for what?" Owen said.

"Lady Julie has been leaving clues for us since she left," Parker said. "We found another one in the library."

"Oh, here we go again, Parker," Quinn said. "You and your clues. There's no mystery. She took Riley. She kidnapped him. You heard it yourself from Riley. She said he was in danger. That danger was her!"

"But she told me I'm a storyteller—"

"I don't care what she told you, Parker," Quinn said. "She's evil. She's a Ravager. That's all there is to it. Get it through your thick skull."

Quinn stormed away, walking to her bed where she climbed under the covers. She pulled her inventing goggles over her eyes as if they were a sleep mask and covered herself with the blanket.

"It's how she *thinks*, I *think*," Aven whispered to Owen.

"What did Lady Julie mean, you're a storyteller?" Owen asked.

"Let me show you something," Parker said.

Parker led Owen and Aven to the nightstand beside her bed before pointing to the crack where she'd first hidden her journal, the quill, and inkwell. She reached in and retrieved another book, a small red one that she'd left there. She took the red book and set it in front of them.

"Where did you get that?" Aven asked.

"I got it from Lady Julie before she left," Parker said. "I was always supposed to return it to her, but when she left, I kept it over there."

"What are those?" Owen asked, pointing to the images on its cover.

"This is the *Book of the Seven Ancient Stories*, and inside it are the seven stories—each one," Parker answered, tracing each image as she spoke. "A compass, a fist, a book, a family, a defeated soldier, a wise elder, and a victor holding a sword."

"Oh, those are the stories they make us memorize in school," Aven answered. "They are *super* boring," she said, whispering to the invisible space where her brother was.

"They aren't boring," Parker chided. "They are simple, but simple is good. These were the seven stories, the seven destinies to guide us. There are only a few actual books like this one—this is one of the books the Ancients gifted to be sure we never forgot the seven stories."

"What do we do with it?" Aven asked.

Parker laughed. "You read it, of course. But I want to try something first."

She looked at Owen's face, his eyes wide looking at the forbidden item. Then she reached into her dress and felt around for the hidden pocket before pulling out her quill.

"Now, I know we're Serifs and can write magic," she continued, "but Lady Julie was very clear that you could never write in this book. I wonder if there was a reason why."

"Don't!" Aven called out, pulling Owen back from the book. "Those things shoot blue bolts!"

Parker smiled, held her red-tipped quill between her fingers, and gently moved it toward the book, Aven recoiling further. A flash of light filled the room, and the text opened itself, a red-orange color emanating from the pages.

"When Fonde was first created, it was chaos, violence, and conflict…"

The book spoke in a deep echoey voice like she'd heard earlier from the inkwell.

Parker looked at them and shrugged.

"The living creatures of Fonde were good but had nothing to guide them or protect them. And because of this, a great war occurred with good and evil tearing apart our world. We forbade the writing of magic, but we can't forget these stories to guide us. And in the trees, the wind, the sunlight, and the moonlight, they would discover seven ancient stories."

Each word or action brought about a glowing image or figure moving and performing along to the words. The book's pages began to flip as it announced each of the seven ancient stories, a scene illuminated similar to the icon on its cover.

The Story of the Traveler
The Story of the Will
The Story of the Storyteller
The Story of the Family
The Story of the Defeat
The Story of the Ancients
The Story of the Victor Who Defeats the Monster

The book stopped speaking and closed itself.

"And so, your story is the storyteller?" Owen asked.

"That's what she told me before she left," Parker said, keeping her voice low so Quinn wouldn't hear. "That day, Lady Julie seemed to want to tell me something that was weighing on her. I—I think she knew it would be the last time we would be together."

Parker opened to the page with the image of a book, indicating the storyteller.

"When I came to see her, she told me to take this book and go study it. Then she put her hands on my shoulders and told me, 'The storytellers carry an incredible burden. They must carry the burden of truth—a truth that may seem theirs alone and others will deny, will try to defeat, and may try to destroy.'"

Parker began to realize tears were building up in the corners of her eyes.

"And then she told me I was strong," Parker whispered, wiping her tears away. "I was strong, and I needed to go spend time with *you*. She said I should spend time with Riley."

Parker's head slumped into her chest. "But I didn't. I didn't spend enough time with you, and then you were gone, Riley. She told me. I—I'm so, so sorry."

Parker felt a small, invisible hand on hers. "It's okay," Riley said. "I'm here. I won't leave you again."

Parker took a deep breath. "Thank you. Ever since that day a year ago, I've been trying to right the wrong. I just didn't know how."

"You didn't know how?" Owen asked. "Do you know now?"

"I don't know," Parker answered. "But today, our mother told us about mistakes in the past that our enemies want us to pay for. Maybe that's what happened to Riley. Somehow those mistakes are why he's invisible."

"That's a lot to process," Owen said. "So, you think it's all connected— Riley, the kidnapping, the Ravagers returning, and some mistake your parents told you about?"

"I do. Storytellers must find the truth and right a wrong. Maybe those mistakes are what I need to right."

"Oh wow," Aven gasped, putting her hand on her sister's knee. "Look."

The book was still open to the *Story of the Storyteller*, and a familiar red-orange glow emanated from the book. In the glow, they all saw the face of Lady Julie, her kind eyes and warm smile framed by her white hair.

"Quinn, Quinn," Aven called out, realizing her sister hadn't been able to see or hear the book from across their bedroom.

"Shhhhhhh. I. Am. Trying. To. Think," came Quinn's muffled voice from under her covers.

"No, you've *seriously* got to see this," Parker tried again, wiping away the tears as their teacher's face appeared from the pages of the book.

"Hmmmmph!" Across the room, the voice yelled again, "Can you keep it down?"

Quinn's hand holding her quill emerged from a red comforter she had pulled over her entire body in the farthest bed from the window to think. She lifted her opposite hand up and turned the palm to the windows. Then the quill deftly scribbled on three of her fingernails.

A flash exploded over the bed, and then blue-teal sparks rained down from the window as the window shades unrolled themselves and partially darkened the late afternoon sun streaming into the bedroom.

"Grump-y," mouthed Aven, pointing across the room at her sister.

Guess we're doing magic in public now.

"Whoa," Owen gasped. "What was that?"

"Yeah," answered Parker, gesturing to the windows. "Now you see how we write magic."

"So that's why her nails have all those cool-looking etchings," Owen said. "Can you do that too?" he asked Parker.

Parker bit her lip and said, "No. I mean, at least not yet. Quinn's the only one who knows how to script magic."

One of the window shades was still struggling to unroll itself while the other two had made a partial covering for the window.

"Well, *sometimes* she can script magic, anyway," Aven teased.

Knock. Knock. Knock.

The children all looked to the door. "Children," called the muffled voice of Major Cappa. "You're summoned to the Hall for the celebratory family feast."

A big sigh emanated from Quinn's bed. She threw her covers back and stood up to face them, her goggles still covering her eyes.

"We need to go," she commanded. "We need to eat, and if we don't show up, they'll come in, and who knows what happens then. Then we'll try and figure out why Riley is invisible, how he got here, and what we do about it."

"But what do we do about Riley now?" asked Parker. "We can't just bring him to dinner."

"He stays here, of course," replied Quinn.

Parker shot her a concerned look.

"You just stay here. Got it, Riley?" Quinn pointed a finger at where her invisible brother had been sitting with the others.

"But I'm hungry," came a voice from behind Quinn's shoulder. She jumped and wheeled around to face the voice—nowhere near where she had been confidently pointing.

Parker and Owen smiled while Aven let out a grunt-laugh befitting a chuckling wolf.

"Can you *please* stay here?" asked Quinn, turning around to face her brother. "We'll bring you something. We can't risk you getting caught—the Illiterates could be here, inside the castle. It's just not safe."

Parker shook her head and followed the others.

This is never going to work.

Chapter Fourteen

The Dinner Guest

Parker knew something was wrong. Her parents were never late, especially for an important dinner with their children.

Food filled the table in the Hall of Resplendence: mashed potatoes, yams, buttery dinner rolls, green beans, fruits, roasted chicken, towering cakes, pies, and cookies. It was a dinner feast fit for a king, a queen, and at least three sisters.

The three sisters took their seats while Owen sat next to Parker and across from Quinn, and they all awkwardly eyed at the food, unsure if they could start eating.

The door to the Hall of Resplendence swung open. They turned expecting to see their parents.

It was Lazlo.

"Why is he here?" Aven whispered to Parker.

"You got me," she replied.

"What happened to his face?" Owen asked under his breath.

The three large scratches Parker had seen earlier ran down the side of his face, bigger and more ominous looking than when seen from afar. Fresh and deep, with puffy, pink skin around each of the red lines, they looked like they hurt.

"Children," Lazlo said standing at the head of the table. "The queen asked me to check on you and your *friend*."

"She's not coming?" Parker asked.

"She is indisposed at the moment," Lazlo said.

"Indis-what?" Aven asked.

"He's saying she has something better to do," Quinn whispered.

"Huh? What's something better than us?" Aven asked Lazlo.

"Why didn't you stop them?" Parker asked. "The Illiterates? You could have prevented this."

"Enough," Lazlo hissed, jarring the room. He regained himself. "I did as I was told, a lesson you may wish to learn from, Miss Pennymore." He narrowed his eyes at Parker. "Your father shall be joining soon, and I will pass along your well-being to your mother."

He turned and hurried from the room.

"Did they say we could start eating?" Aven called after him. "Yes, we should eat?"

"I just can't get past how much Lazlo hates me," Parker said. "I don't get it. I helped him today. Now the Illiterates are in control, but he probably could have stopped it with a strike of his quill. I still don't understand why they had to give up the amphitheater."

"I couldn't stop staring at those cuts on his face," Owen said. "It's like he got in a fight with a tiger."

"He's fine," Quinn said sharply. "Leave him alone. He's protecting this kingdom; otherwise, who knows what would happen to Everly. He can't just write a spell to attack anyone who is against us."

"Daughters!" Their father entered the Hall of Resplendence, emphasizing the "ters" of "daughters" with a robust upward intonation.

King Domn had been a boisterous man, full of energy, curiosity, and creativity. His inventive mind drew people and eventually turned him into a king after his inventions had saved the town.

As he used to tell his children, "I wasn't given the crown; I invented my own." But even Parker knew he heard the whispers about his non-royal bloodline from people like the Waddles. She knew these rumors weighed on him. This wedge between him and the people who'd once embraced their father as their own was only widening as the conflict with the Illiterates expanded.

With Riley's disappearance, this man who no longer had time for anything replaced the warm, imaginative man who had told them stories, run in the gardens, and built small castles with them. Parker missed those days.

He blew Parker a kiss as he walked toward the overflowing dinner table. Parker awkwardly shifted in her seat.

Lazlo had returned with their father and stood in the corner watching the meal with their father's other advisers.

"It's been quite the day," their father said. "You were brave today. I know it's been scary and a lot to take in, but we've got it all under control." He slid into his seat.

"Where's mom?" Parker asked.

"She's busy," he replied after a pause and then awkwardly looked away. "She is—she is negotiating with the Illiterates."

"About what?" Quinn asked.

"I'm afraid I cannot say more," King Domn answered. "Tensions are simply too high, and this is too much for the ears of children."

"But Father," Parker interrupted. "Owen's parents could be there—"

Quinn looked at her and shook her head, urging her not to press him on this.

Parker froze. Across from her father, a floating dinner roll was on the move.

Had her father seen it too?

Their father bolted upright.

"Aven!" her father yelled. "If it's not the howling, it's—"

Aven was hunched over her plate, scarfing down food and again, eating like a wolf—licking food straight off the plate.

Parker was grateful her wolf-eating sister was the center of attention.

A bite was missing from the top of the dinner roll as it continued to float around the room.

"Uh, fath-ER," Parker blurted out, emphasizing the "er" to draw his attention away from the runaway dinner roll. "Did you see Quinn's device today?"

Aven lifted up her head and grinned. Half of a piece of chicken poked out of the corner of her mouth, dangling just above the table. Her father waved his hands as if to try and instruct his wolf-child to sit up straight and use her utensils. But her distraction had been enough for the migrating roll to disappear under the table.

Whew.

Parker and Quinn exchanged relieved glances.

"Why yes, I did. A doughnut delivery device," he said to his daughter, filling his plate and nodding. "But it was reckless to try it in public. It worked, but what if it hadn't?"

Parker glanced at the wall, where streaks from doughnut stains remained.

Quinn slumped in her chair and nodded back at her father. Others often called her "her father's daughter," and the pair would work on her father's inventions together from the time she could barely stand. He'd get stumped by something, and his little helper would find the missing bolt or backward piece. During these times, Quinn had learned how to fix most anything—mending broken ropes, silencing squeaky doors, and loosening stuck wheels.

Now all he did was offer critiques, putting Quinn's insecurities on full display when he did.

"I—I tested it, and I guess you're right," Quinn said as she fiddled with her food.

"Father," Parker said. "When we spoke to Mother today, she told us about certain mistakes in the past. What did she mean? What mistakes?"

"She said that?" he asked. "When was this? What exactly did she say?" He stared at Parker, his face clenched.

"She said there were mistakes made, and she told us today our enemies wanted us to pay the price," Parker said. "Then she talked about our family and past mistakes. It was something like that."

"Enough," he said, stopping her. "We are not to speak of family matters outside of the family. You are not to speak of it again."

"It seemed important—"

"I said enough," their father said, looking at Lazlo.

Parker looked to Quinn, urging her to press this, but her sister's eyes were locked on a floating handful of pecans making their way toward a steaming bowl of green beans across from their father. Riley loved buttered pecans and beans. Quinn motioned to the doorway. *Could Lazlo see the floating pecans? Would their father?*

Their sister-wolf finished snarfing her food. They'd need another distraction, and quick.

Parker made a loud, noticeable cough, causing the pecans to pause in midair. "Ah-hem. Ah-HEM."

She coughed again, louder. The nuts fell from above the table and scattered as Riley got the hint.

Father shifted in his chair, glancing at the scattered pecans before turning to Aven and winking.

"Your device today, Quinn," their father continued, clearly distracted. "How did—"

The beans and the spoon right in front of him were on the move—slowly drifting away from their father toward the end of the table.

Quinn shifted to recapture her father's gaze.

"THE DEVICE, uh, doesn't have to only be for doughnuts," Quinn babbled, drawing her father's eyes away from his meal. "And I think with more time... uh..."

"... she could send food clear across the sea," continued Parker. "This way, we might not need to wait until once a month to transport fruit or salt or whatever to the kingdom."

Amused at his daughter's behavior, he paused then nodded in agreement: "It's certainly right. Keep us safer and more connected."

He reached down for his spoon and did a double-take. He looked all around his plate for the green beans he'd prepared, giving odd looks at each of his seated family members before looking back at Aven, who held up a spoon, licking it like a popsicle.

"Sire," Lazlo called from the doorway.

He smiled and reached for one of the legs of roasted chicken in front of him.

"Exciting day," their father continued with a sigh as he took a large bite of the chicken leg and stood. "We've got to keep an eye on the Illiterates and their hold on the amphitheater, as you can imagine. And your mother—" he trailed off, turning quickly with the chicken leg still in his hand, waving it almost like a baton. "Wish us well."

And just as quickly as he'd breezed into the Hall, he was gone again. Their father, Lazlo, and advisers rushed out as hastily as they'd entered.

"What was that all about?" Quinn asked.

"I was hungry," Riley's voice replied.

"No, I meant Parker. Why did you ask him about that—the mistakes in the past?"

"It was something Owen said," Parker said.

"Me?"

"You asked why Riley would show up and be invisible on the day that Mother told us evil forces were planning to attack Everly, and she said something about paying for their mistakes," Parker said. "I thought maybe he knew something. And from his response, I'm now pretty sure he does. Mistakes were made."

"I guess," Quinn said.

"She never misses a celebration dinner," Parker said. "Our parents are acting even more strange than usual."

"I'm sorry about your parents," Quinn said to Owen. "I'm sure that's not easy to hear."

"You're sorry?" he asked. "Your parents have my parents captive at the amphitheater, and for what? My mom and dad aren't anywhere near as bad as the other Illiterates."

"Do you want us to try and find them? Bring you to them?" Quinn offered.

"You can't. I'm better off here, with you guys for now. I mean, what do I say? 'Hi, Mom. Hi, Dad. Got sucked into a magic wormhole and spent the last month locked in a room by the king and queen until their kidnapped son showed up, who happens to be invisible. Hug?'"

"Well, at least you're taking this all well," Parker said.

"My parents and I weren't on great terms," Owen said. "It's kinda a long story. I just wish I knew they were okay. That's all."

Two pieces of fruit floated across the table.

"Riley! Do you realize we were almost caught?" Quinn hissed at her brother.

"I said we'd bring you something," Parker said, banging her spoon on the table and motioning to the fruit marching in front of her.

"And *I said* I was hungry," Riley said around another mouthful of food.

Chapter Fifteen

Boots

"Are you sure we have to go back in there?" Parker wondered, eyeing the tapestry hiding the ancient door to the library.

After dinner, the older sisters had sent Owen, Aven, and Riley back to their bedroom and, despite Quinn's reservations, had given them the purse containing three enchanted items to try to find the object's powers.

"You coming?" Quinn said, pulling the corner of the dingy tapestry back, allowing the two of them to enter the library together.

"I'm still a little concerned those blood-sucking quills haven't had enough time to forget I stole one last night."

"Listen, Riley is invisible," Quinn said. "We need to find something to tell us what to do, maybe figure out why that necklace you're wearing glowed when we found him."

"And we need to find out what our parents aren't telling us," Parker added.

"Mistakes were made," Quinn said, nodding.

"Right. I keep trying to figure out, why us? What is so important about our family that the Ravagers would hunt our grandmother and someone would kidnap Riley?"

"I agree," Quinn answered. "It doesn't add up. Someone isn't telling us the full story."

Parker let Quinn enter the library first, shrinking down behind her sister to avoid being seen by an angry book, quill, or scroll. After a few seconds, it became clear the enchanted library had forgotten her thievery of the night before. Books sporadically flew overhead, the quills zigzagged around, papers rolled and unrolled themselves on the floors. Parker watched as the inkwell orchestra struggled without its conductor, while stories were being told and retold with every fold of the writing papers. The library shelves—even those on the ceiling—shifted in a never-ending labyrinth.

A rumble-like rolling thunder came from the bookbindery at the far end of the library.

"Wasn't expecting to be back here so soon," Parker said. "Do you hear that?"

"Oh, the snoring sound?" Quinn responded. "You heard it last night too?"

Parker nodded her head.

"But you didn't investigate it when you were here last night. Huh?"

"No, we got distracted by the quills," Parker said.

"Come with me, but I want to warn you. It's going to be a surprise—and not the *good* kind."

Quinn led her sister past the writing desks, ducking to avoid leaping flames and the occasional low flying book. When they reached the back of the room, she moved to stand in front of Parker.

"Take a deep breath."

Turning the corner, the sisters came to stand in front of the arched entrance to bookbindery, the area where they'd learned to repair books and use threads to stitch book covers to bound parchment. The sound grew louder, but Parker couldn't tell where it was coming from.

"What is *that*?" Parker whispered.

"It's Boots," Quinn answered.

"Boots. My *cat*?"

"Let me show you," Quinn said. She extracted her quill and lifted it from nail to nail, her mouth moving as she did. Glittering snow fell from the library ceiling, illuminating the outline of a massive, breathing mound at least eight feet tall.

"But how do you know that's Boots?" Parker asked.

"Watch."

Quinn snapped her fingers, and the white, snow-like dust changed color, illuminating the hulking mound so the markings on the cat could be clearly seen. Other than being at least eight feet tall while still lying down, the creature was identical to the stray cat Parker had found hiding in the library that would curl up in her lap and purr while she did her writing lessons.

"I told you it'd be a lot to take in, but—"

"Boots is the size of an *elephant*!" Parker exclaimed as she stared at the enormous cat with dark, spotted fur and white paws.

"I know," Quinn said, trying to offer a calming voice. "And there's something else—"

"Boots. Boots!" Parker called out to the cat, who began to shift slightly upon hearing her name.

"Parker!" Quinn called, pulling her shoulders. "Step back *now!*"

The cat's eyes opened, murky yellow with a sliver of black down the middle, and the circular portraits hanging in the hallway.

"Boots," Parker said, reaching out her hand as she'd done when she'd first discovered the scared kitten.

Leaping to its feet, Boots arched her massive back and let out a hiss that became a roar ringing her ears. The cat's sharp, white teeth bared and snapped at them, her giant claws wildly lashing out.

Quinn grabbed her sister in an embrace. "Sometimes you're so stupid, Parker. You could have gotten killed. I told you, but you rush into things without a second thought. Use your head."

Parker pushed her older sister off and stared at the cat that no longer resembled the stray who had spent hours curled on her lap.

"Boots can't go any further than this," Quinn continued. "She can't touch us—can't hurt you if we stand here. You're fine."

"But what happened to her?" Parker asked.

"No one knows for sure. We just found her here, trapped at the entrance. It seems like she's guarding something in the bindery. Whenever we get anywhere near the entrance, she attacks as if she's a lion. This dust incantation is how we figured out who or what she was, and it'll wear off in a minute or so."

"What is she protecting?" Parker asked, trying to look over the cat's massive shoulders as it paced back and forth in front of them.

"You got me, but I sure don't plan to try and find out," Quinn replied. "Whatever it is, Boots is not interested in letting us near enough to get a closer look."

Parker sighed. "At least I know she didn't run away," she said, looking back at the cat as it spun around to find a comfortable spot to rest.

"We'll get her back and figure out what happened. But first, let's find what we came here for," Quinn said, pulling her sister back toward the maze of bookshelves.

Since Quinn had been studying magic writing, the sisters agreed she'd try to find any books she could to help them understand why Riley became invisible and what they should do about it. Parker would look for stories to teach them something about curses, kidnapped magic writers, or anything about their family's story.

"Lazlo says to watch out for the dictionaries," Quinn said. "They bite."

Parker tried to find any books with stories, journeys, or adventures related to the Pennymores. Looking for books in a library with a mind of its own was a challenge, but after a few wrong turns, she realized the library was guiding her.

"Uh, library," Parker asked. "You got any books with stories about curses?"

A shelf began to glow, arcing open to reveal a path toward another hidden nook within the shelf maze. Parker watched a blue book float down to it, nesting in the empty area. She picked up the text as frog flames jumped over to light the area for her. She saw the book was a collection of stories about numerous cursed heroes.

Well, you've clearly outdone yourself, library. Looks like there's no need for a librarian when you've got shelves like these.

"Thanks, library," she said, and on cue, the nearest shelf rocked forward, taking a bow.

After a few minutes, Parker had a stack of books and was seated at a table skimming through them. Her sister joined her, dropping a massive pile of books across from her.

After an hour of reading, the sisters decided to compare notes and see what they'd found.

"It's hard to find pictures of invisibility," began Quinn, "because what do you draw when something's invisible?"

If Riley had turned bright red or covered in purple feathers, they could easily search for drawings or pictures of people who were red or covered in purple feathers. But how in the world did you draw someone invisible? It was something Parker hadn't considered when they began their research.

"Then I realized something," Quinn continued. "Ghosts are invisible. Right? But they are covered in a sheet or something else to make them visible to us. If you remove the sheet, voilà, the ghost is invisible. Then I looked for floating sheets or floating bandages or other floating items."

Quinn continued to detail her search pulling out a heavy, black book with maroon binding.

"This book is called *A Definitive History of Dark Magic.*" She flipped through the book. "I'm pretty sure this is what we are up against."

She thumbed through page after page, showing floating sheets, floating candles, and some floating food reminding Parker of the evening meal they'd barely made it through.

"Oh, and there's one more thing," Quinn continued, opening the book to a page at the back of *A Definitive History of Dark Magic.*

Invisible curses on children are temporary until they are not. A child may be saved from the permanence of invisibility until the next moon wanes or may be made permanently visible or invisible with the ancient objects—all to avoid the clutches of death.

Quinn said, "When I read it, I realized there are a lot of words I'd never heard of—permanence, wanes, clutches."

"The moon," Parker said. "Mother said that was a sign, something Lazlo recognized. What does this all mean?"

"It's temporary until it's permanent," Quinn said. "This seemed to mean he's not invisible forever, at least not yet, anyway."

"And the waning moon can make him invisible forever unless we find the ancient objects?" asked Parker. "Do you think when Riley escaped, that was the sign that Lazlo recognized?"

"Could be," Quinn suggested. "Maybe others in magic realms did too."

"There are realms of magic?" Parker asked.

"I've heard there's an entire world of magical places out there," Quinn said. "I was hoping we'd get to see them sometime, but the only magical places I've seen since I got my quill is this library and Lazlo's study."

"Did Lazlo tell you anything about invisibility or dark magic?"

"I wish," Quinn responded. "I mean, I can barely even make the window shades all go down. So I don't even know what it all means."

Parker silently nodded in agreement.

"What did you find?" asked Quinn.

"The first thing I found was a book about our family," Parker said. "Our family is way more complicated than anyone ever told us. I couldn't follow the story because the book was damaged. Someone tore certain things and pages out of the text. It looked like entire sections had been removed."

"Why would someone destroy a book about our family?" Quinn asked. "And who would even know how to get in here to find it?"

"It's what I was trying to figure out too," Parker said. "We still have a few pages and pieces, though. I could follow a fire, and somehow our father was involved, but it didn't say how. It was clear that fire and the events surrounding it were bad, like, really bad. And Lady Julie and our grandmother were involved too. All I could figure out for sure was that some council had voted and eventually cleared our father of wrongdoing. But that was it."

"Our father was involved in a fire?" Quinn asked.

"I guess," Parker continued. "Something is important about that fire and everything after it that we need to find out about."

"Mistakes in the past," Quinn said.

"That's what I was thinking too. Oh, and there was something else peculiar."

"What was it?"

"Well, I couldn't take the book," Parker said, pointing to the stacks of the other books she'd gathered. "I saw it on the shelf, I picked it up and flipped through it, but whenever I tried to take the book or walk away from the shelf… well, it was like a rubber band and sling-shotted it out of my arms and put back on the shelf."

"The book did that?"

"I mean, I guess. But that book wouldn't let me remove it," Parker said. "Maybe that's why whoever was messing with it had to try and tear stuff out. They couldn't get the whole book out of the library."

"That's so weird," Quinn said. "An unremovable book about our family."

"Yeah, and a lot of it was written about the Scotts. I didn't know much about them. There was almost nothing in it about Pennymores. That seemed a little odd to me."

"Have you *ever* heard anything about Mother's family?" Quinn asked. "The Scott side of the family?"

"Other than Grandma, pretty much nothing," Parker said with a shrug. "I kinda thought we weren't allowed to talk about them, given how it always led to someone storming off in a huff when they did. Father slipped up yesterday and told me I have a cousin. Did you know we have a cousin?"

"I did," Quinn said. "Here, let me show you something." Quinn walked over to the massive mirror carved with Scott at the bottom and took out her quill. She examined the small square and circle shapes embedded in the frame, each containing a unique design, gem, tile, or carving. "Oh, here it is," she said as she touched a small circle that had a carving of two faces.

Her quill raced out of her hand and buzzed like a hummingbird in front of the mirror.

"This is Mom's family," Quinn said as her quill began to move in rapid patterns and motion, drawing an image on the mirror. "Meet the Scotts."

Parker looked at the drawing as dozens and dozens of people of all ages began to fill the mirror. It was so realistic Parker had to do a double-take to make sure it wasn't an actual reflection of people standing behind her. At the bottom, Parker saw drawings of the Pennymore siblings and their mother and father.

"Wow, Riley is there too," Parker said, pointing to the drawing of their younger brother.

"I know," Quinn said, her quill finishing the drawing and flying back to her hand. "This is every living Scott, the entire family. That's how we knew he was okay. We didn't know where he was, but I would check the mirror every day to make sure he was okay."

"Wow. I just thought it was a big mirror," Parker said. "Then what do all the other icons and carvings do?" She examined the frame more closely now.

"All kinds of things. Your quill draws whatever is happening at that exact moment, no matter where the person or place is. See, this drawing has my pink hairstreak, which I just added today. And it looks like some of our other relatives might have been napping or eating or even surprised at something the moment I touched the frame."

Parker could see now the faces were candid ones, nothing like the posed portraits in the hall. "Does every frame do this?"

"It depends," Quinn said. "Every mirror that has a frame like this can do something like this, but every mirror has different carvings in the frame, meaning it can do different things. Plus some paintings and portraits too, but you don't know. This mirror is the main one I've explored, and when I first learned about it, I spent hours and hours with it. I'm sure you're thinking the same, but we don't have time for that. I don't want to leave the littles alone with Owen for too long."

Parker nodded in agreement. She saw faces in that image that looked familiar, as if she'd met some of them before. She watched as the picture began to fade from view and return to the rainbow glimmering mirror.

"What else did you find besides the book about our family history?" Quinn asked "Did you learn anything about Riley?"

"I found a lot about invisibility and curses and stories of magic, but I'm not sure what any of it means either."

Parker summarized dozens of stories, fables, and poems, all touching on aspects of their situation. One had a family of sisters, another had wizards and sorcery, and still, another spoke about a cloak of invisibility. But none of them was *their* story.

"These stories are all related in a way, but I'm not sure they are helpful," admitted Parker.

"But you said there are rules, and magic helps enforce those rules," said Quinn to her sister. "Maybe something in these stories matches what I found about the invisibility magic?"

She nodded, encouraged by the idea, feeling a connection to her sister she hadn't in almost a year. She recounted the rules of magic in stories from Lady Julie:

Rule #1: Every story must have a hero or a heroine… and if you don't know who the hero is, it's probably you.

Rule #2: Every story must teach us something.

Rule #3: Every story must make us feel complete. It doesn't have to be a happy ending, but it must be complete.

"These are the rules of every story," continued Parker. "Once you know or decide which of the seven stories is yours, magic enforces these rules—or makes something happen. But I'm not exactly sure what our story is and how these rules fit."

"So, magic can only make the story?" asked Quinn.

"Well, mostly. The magic in the stories isn't like rolling a window shade or making water heat up. The magic is more significant—saving a life, protecting someone from harm, or things like killing. Magic can only be used in those ways to make the story complete."

Quinn nodded.

"And let's say if your story is the Ancients story—the story where you need a wise figure to come and show you the right way or path—you only use magic to help to find a right path, even if it harms or saves someone else."

"It's like an invisible force making sure the story ends, right?"

"Exactly," Parker answered. "Magic can only work in these big ways if used to get us to the end of our story."

"Lazlo said my story is the Victor story," Quinn said. "Magic will help me to defeat Lady Julie—"

Parker raised her hand. "You don't *know* you are the Victor story. Lady Julie thought yours could be the Traveler who brings back knowledge, and mine could be the Storyteller—"

"Lazlo said—"

"I don't care what he said," Parker snapped. "That's not how the stories work. No one can *tell* you what your story is."

Quinn's lip began to tremble. "*My* story is the Victor story. And I know *my* monster. That's what I've trained for. That's what Lazlo said. And he's right."

Parker stared at her sister.

"Maybe let's take a break and see what else we can find," Parker said.

"A break?" Quinn cut in. "We are kids, Parker. We don't need a break or more books or more clues. What we need is help. Okay?"

"I just meant—"

"I hate keeping secrets, from you, from everybody. Now here we are sneaking around trying to hide our invisible brother from the guards, our parents, the Illiterates, and from whoever may be trying to come back here to kidnap him again."

"But since you've been taught to write magic, you'd be able to use it to help or even teach the rest of us," Parker said.

"I don't know how to write magic, okay?" Quinn said, biting her lip. "You keep asking me things about magic like I'm supposed to know something. Don't you see? I don't know anything. All day, for ten straight hours, I get taught the same thing: protection spells. That's it. Yeah, I want to do magic that helps, but for the last year, I've practiced the same bolt spells until my fingers hurt. But I can't even fill a stupid cup or get the shades to roll down."

"I didn't mean—I just know you're always the fixer. You pretty much fix anything for us," Parker offered. "Maybe we go find Mother and talk to her again."

"I hate to be the one to say this, but can we even trust our parents right now? They kidnapped Owen Wickerland, they tried to blame you for standing up to the Illiterates, and they lied to us about whatever is happening today. It's like secret after secret after secret. You deserve to be angry. You find out they were sending you away without any explanation. You heard what she said—trust no one but each other—and I'm following her advice on *her*."

"Then who?" Parker said. "Who's left?"

"I want to see Lazlo," Quinn said then continued on before Parker could interrupt her. "I know. I know. You two have issues, and he still blames you for locking him away, but at least he knows more about magic writing than anyone else right now. Maybe he'll even thank you for what you did for him today. Right?"

Parker wanted to fight her and tell her all the reasons why going to Lazlo was a mistake, was rash, and felt to her like the last person in the world they should trust. She wanted to argue and fight and draw a line in the sand on this one. But something inside her said she needed to trust Quinn. At this moment, she might be the only person she could trust.

"You're right," Parker said.

"What did you say?" Quinn said, sounding surprised. "Did you just say I was *right*?"

"Yeah, I did," Parker said. "You knew I needed to see Owen, and even if you disagreed with it, you trusted me then. And it's my turn to do the same. So yes, Lazlo and I get along like oil and water, and I'm sure somehow he'll blame me for today, but I have to trust you. So you're right. We need to take Riley to Lazlo."

"I was ready to get in a fight over this," Quinn said, smiling at her sister. "That didn't go at all how I expected it to go."

"I'm working on introducing more surprising turns of events into my stories, Q. I keep everyone on their toes this way," Parker said.

Quinn pointed to herself and began nodding. "Surprised."

"And when exactly is this waning moon?" Parker asked.

"Four days from now."

"So, we've got to get ancient artifacts before then."

"Yeah, I know."

"And I'm guessing they aren't on this island?" Parker said.

"That would be way too easy—and you've heard every story out there. Easy doesn't make for a good story," Quinn said, smirking at her sister.

Parker nodded in agreement. "At least we've got a library to help us. But I still don't know what to think about the inscription in here." She pointed up to the glowing blue words: *Truth Inside.*

"Me neither, but we'll come back after we see Lazlo," Quinn said. "You can show me that book you found, the one you can't remove."

"And maybe we bring some catnip back for ol' Boots while we're at it."

Parker ducked when a yellow and green book flapped overhead. This waning moon wasn't giving her much time.

Chapter Sixteen

The Curse of the Invisible Quill

"We were only gone one hour," blurted Parker walking into their bedroom.

"Owen?" Quinn called out. "We left you in charge."

"They're monsters," Owen's muffled voice came from somewhere near the window. "You didn't warn me."

The leather pouch holding the three magical items from their grandmother was open on the floor. A twenty-foot-long pillow filled one of the room's walls. Aven was nowhere to be found.

"Please tell me you guys didn't try to hide in the purse?" Quinn yelled, holding up the purse to see inside.

"Already tried it," Aven's muffled voice called out. "It's like a gigantic cave once you squeeze inside, but it's boring."

Owen pulled himself out of a pile of blankets and sheets and stood up. "They put me in that purse and tied it so I couldn't get out. Then they threw it across the room, with me inside."

"It was hide and seek, Owen! We were hiding *you*."

"That's *not* how you play the game," Owen yelled back.

Where was Aven's voice coming from?

Besides the gigantic pillow, two tables had been pushed together with the three-bed frames perched on top. Precariously balanced on top of the bedposts were the three mattresses, the bedspreads, and sheets wrapped around them to form a makeshift fort.

Parker—who always prided herself on a tidy room—and Quinn—who would tidy things up to avoid getting scolded—both knew they didn't have enough time to start to put things back.

"At least they didn't leave the room," Parker said to Quinn.

"We need to get going," Quinn said to Aven, who was crawling under the tables. "Can you get ready and maybe clean up something?"

"Looks like you figured out how the magical items work. One of them makes something big, I see," Parker said, kicking the twenty-foot-long pillow.

"Oh yeah," Aven said, standing up. "The measuring cup is so cool. We didn't quite figure out the other ones, but you gotta see this."

Aven ran across the room and grabbed a chair precariously leaned against their fort. Then, placing the measuring cup upright on the floor, she picked up the leg of the chair and placed it inside the cup. The chair rattled and wiggled, growing until it reached the ceiling.

"Wow!" Riley yelled. "It's big enough for a giant!"

"But it's cooler than just this," Aven said as she picked up the cup from the floor and placed it upside down on top of her head. She shrank until she stood no more than three inches high, the cup completely covering her.

Parker leaned down and grabbed the measuring cup. A tiny Aven waved at her and motioned for Parker to put the cup back down, right side up. Aven ran and jumped, grabbing the edge of the measuring cup and pulling herself inside before growing back to her regular size.

"Do you want to try the cup now?" Aven said, eyeing an ant crawling across the floor. "I'd love to make you a guard ant."

"You guys didn't tell me you gave your sister enchanted magical items," Owen said, his hair a tousled mess. "A little heads-up next time."

"Let's bring the enchanted items with us," Quinn said to Parker, eyeing the giant pillow. "For protection."

Parker grabbed the leather pouch and placed all the items back inside. Then she stashed the bag in her hidden pockets with her journal, quill, inkwell, and the *Book of the Seven Ancient Stories*.

Next, Parker grabbed a spool of rope and a small knife, then ran to their window, tying the ends of the string to its frame.

"What are you doing?" Quinn asked.

"I'm getting a message out to Monty and the Plumes," she said, tying an extra piece of red fabric to the rope to look like the flags she'd seen at the entrance to Avenir. "I need them to keep their eyes open for something. *All* of their eyes. They'll know what it means."

"Okay, I guess," Quinn replied, shaking her head. "What about this disaster?" She pointed to the towering fortress filling half of their room.

"Owen," Parker called, stashing the rope and knife in her hidden pockets. "We've got to see Lazlo. *Now.* So I need you to stop playing around."

Owen rolled his eyes and shook his head.

"And Aven, where's Riley?" Parker asked.

Aven looked straight up.

At the peak of the wobbling tower of mattresses, they could see the shape of a head under one of the throw blankets. Parker looked at Quinn and said, "Like a sheet on a ghost."

"Why is Riley wearing the oven mitt?" Quinn asked.

Aven shrugged.

"Ugh, Riley," Quinn said. "Can you get down?" They saw the blanket rise and fall, rise and fall, and then the oven mitted hand waved to them.

"He's going to jump!" Parker yelled.

They saw the entire structure begin to shake and sway as Riley bounced his way down the left side of the monstrosity of mattresses, sheets, a dresser, nightstands, and pillows.

Wood shattered and splintered, and nails sheared off as the entire structure crumbled. It all came tumbling into a pile near the window.

Rushing over the mess, Parker and Quinn yelled, "Riley! Riley, are you all right?"

Knock. Knock. Knock.

"Pennymores! Pennymores!" the guard called through the door. "Is everything okay in there?"

"We're fine!" Quinn called out. "Building bunk beds."

"Building... Okay, very well then," the guard said.

Quinn grabbed Aven's exposed hand and foot, the rest of her still hidden beneath the remains of the collapsed fort.

"That. Was. Awesome!" Riley yelled from near the top of the pile, followed by a muffled, "H-ow-ow-owwwwwwwwwwwwl" from under the mattresses.

"How in the world were you not hurt, Riley?" Parker asked, surveying the wreckage.

But all she got was the oven mitt turning upward on his hand as if to say, *I don't know.*

"We—you guys—can get this later," said Parker, ushering them out the door before quickly closing it to make sure the guard couldn't see what had happened inside.

***

The stairwell was dim; the air cold. They reached large, heavy wooden doors at the end of a long hallway separating the basement and lower floors from the rest of the castle.

Guards regularly patrolled this corridor. Parker peered around each corner while her sisters stood flat against the wall like pieces of parchment paper.

"It's clear," whispered Parker, stepping from the wall to peek around the next corner and wave the others along.

When they reached the basement staircase, Aven whispered, "I feel like my *heart* is going to jump out of my chest."

"Don't worry," Parker said. "I'll catch it for you."

Aven smiled.

"Then we can use your heart as an offering," Parker whispered as she wiggled her fingers like she was casting a spell. "To the dark magician."

Aven's face went pale.

"Stop it," Quinn said. "We need his help. This is serious."

Owen laughed. "Creepy wizard jokes are the best."

They descended the stairs, walking into the dark, mysterious basement, where the only lights were faint, flicking candles—the dank air stank of old linens in an unused room. Parker tried to focus only on the dark, candle-lit path, not the darkness surrounding them.

"You come here every day?" asked Owen. "*Alone?*"

Aven squeezed Parker's hand a little tighter. Parker gulped. This place felt colder and less welcoming than when they'd come here for Lady Julie.

Quinn looked at the others and then knocked.

They heard rustling. A slot opened in the door, and a raspy voice bellowed out, "Who is it?"

"It's us," said Quinn. "We know we're not all supposed to be here, but we didn't know who else to talk to."

The slot quickly closed, and they heard the scraping metal as Lazlo twisted locks and undid chains. The door opened, revealing a brightly lit room.

"This is a surprise," Lazlo said, his sharp green eyes scanning the hallway. "I see you've brought someone with you."

Parker's stomach twinged. *Is he referring to Owen, or does he know Riley is with us?*

"Come in. Come in." He motioned to the children to step inside. He took another look down the long hallway, then closed the door behind them. "I was expecting you."

Handmade bandages covered parts of his scratches now as if he'd quickly slapped the coverings together without much care since they'd last seen him.

"What happened to your face?" Aven asked.

"I—I fell into the shelves," he said, his hand gingerly touching the bandages as he motioned with his other hand to the room behind him. "It's dark down here," he said with a faint smile.

Various hued lights, shelved potions, warm air, and vibrant rugs were a complete contrast to the grim corridor they'd wandered through.

"Sit down. I think I know why you've come."

"You do?" asked Quinn.

"Riley," Lazlo said, his voice warm. "Come here, Riley." Lazlo opened his hand and offered it to Riley. "I see you're also a boy who likes pecans."

He had seen what happened at dinner.

"Do you have any pecans?" came Riley's voice from near the door.

The other children smiled.

Lazlo snapped his fingers, and a feather flew over to him and hovered above his shoulder as they'd seen the quills do in the library. It circled him playfully, wiggling itself behind his ear before buzzing excitedly over his shoulder.

"Fetch some pecans for our friends, Crucis," he said. The quill raced to the small kitchen, sliding itself under a bowl of the nuts and carrying it to the table. Then, it wiggled its way out from under the bowl and floated back behind Lazlo's ear. An invisible hand picked up nuts, shoveling them into his mouth.

"Hungry boy, I see," Lazlo said. "Now, how did you escape the witch, Riley?"

"I just sorta did," he answered around a mouth full of pecans.

"You must tell me everything. The clock is nearly at eight, and I need to know what happened," he said, pointing to a large clock that read seven forty.

"What happens at eight?" Owen whispered to Parker.

"The Drain Day magic inscription wears off," she whispered. "The water is going to flood back again, and fast."

Riley detailed his escape, quickly retelling his harrowing tale, including the moment he'd realized he was invisible. Lazlo's hand closed around their brother's invisible hand, and his arm wrapped around Riley's shoulders as he spoke.

"The witch will soon discover you're gone, Riley," said Lazlo, his voice patient and calm. "And she will come for you."

"But we are safe here. You can protect him. Right?" asked Quinn.

Lazlo turned to her and shook his head. "Your father, the king, has shown my powers, but I am nowhere as strong as he wishes. Her powers are far beyond mine, far stronger than mine, and more capable with dark magic. The hidden library remains enchanted because of this. I wish it were otherwise."

"We found out about the curse," Parker said, motioning to Quinn. "We read about the waning moon and the ancient objects."

"Good. I've been studying it too," Lazlo said, his tone with Parker very different from earlier in the day. He took his quill and drew an X on a stone wall, which disappeared to reveal his hidden library filled with ancient-looking books. He studied the shelves before finding a black and maroon book he removed from one of his bookshelves. "But the most important line is at the end. 'All to avoid the clutches of death.'"

He pointed to the line in the book the eldest sisters Quinn and Parker had read in the library.

"This particular curse comes from an ancient, dark magic," he continued. "It's known in ancient texts as the curse of the invisible quill. This magic writing not only makes the child invisible from being seen but invisible from being detected by magical powers. Other than what you can hear and feel when you're with him, this curse makes it as if Riley doesn't exist."

"She made him disappear?" Quinn asked.

"She inflicted him with a curse, the curse of an invisible quill. This curse's power and permanence is simply terrifying to behold. We cannot undo his invisibility after the waning moon."

"That can't be," Quinn said. "Forever?"

"And this is why you are all in danger—far beyond my powers and the forces inside the kingdom. We have until the next moon wanes, just four days, to save your brother and the kingdom."

Parker's mind raced through the stories and books. "But what about the ancient objects? Can you save him with those?"

His bright eyes stared at the clock.

"No, but maybe *you* can."

***

Lazlo rushed to another bookshelf in the back of his room, searching for something.

"It's time to leave," he called to them. "We must go now before the witch discovers you've left the kingdom."

"What are you talking about?" Quinn asked. "Leave the kingdom?"

"Quickly now." Lazlo motioned for the siblings to come with him. The clock now read ten minutes to eight. "Before it's too late. You mustn't delay. Quickly children. Quickly now."

"Where are we going?" Parker asked, her heart thumping, unable to tell up from down and grasping for anything.

"You've brought your magical items?" he asked.

Parker nodded, placing her hand over the hidden pockets in her dress.

He smiled at her. "Good, you'll need them. Quickly now. Crucis, the bag."

The children raced to the hallway as Lazlo's quill shot out of view, returning with a maroon bag. Parker was the last to reach the doorway, but when she did, Lazlo stopped her.

"Wait for a second, children," he whispered, motioning with his hand for the others to wait for them in the hallway. He placed a hand on Parker's shoulder and knelt next to the door. "The stone," he said, pointing his finger at the red-orange gem on the silver chain around her neck. "Has it glowed?"

As he pointed at the stone, the sleeve of his cloak slid down, revealing another series of numerous deep scratches on his forearm.

"This stone?" Parker said as she tightly grasped the stone.

He nodded.

"Yes," she said meekly. "It glowed when we first found Riley. Or, when he found us."

"As I thought. The stone glows at times of greatest danger," he said. She heard kindness in his voice, seeing the face of the boy she'd spoken to that very first night.

"Danger?"

"Yes. And when it does, you must be aware trouble and strife will lie ahead of you. Trouble greater than you've ever known."

All to avoid the clutches of death.

"When the gem glows, trust no one," Lazlo warned. "I know you loved Julie, but she is not the heroine you seek," he continued.

She furrowed her face, and Parker saw he could sense her hesitation. His bright eyes studied her face.

"Uh, guys, I think we need to go. Now," Quinn called, looking at the clock.

Lazlo gently patted Parker's shoulder and leaned in to speak to her. "I am grateful for your... efforts at Drain Day," he said, his tone slightly ominous-sounding as he seemed to choose each word carefully. "I know... I know you were... well-intentioned. But know I do *not* need a child to protect me from other children. While I mean no disrespect by this admonishment, know I do not *need* your help, anyone's help for that matter," he said, standing up. "Do I make myself clear?"

Parker nodded uncomfortably.

"Come now," Lazlo continued, his previous tone returning. "We must hurry."

Parker's hand gently touched the gem around her neck. *Why are we going? Everything feels so rushed and sudden and...*

Thump-thump. Thump-thump.

Parker froze, unable to say anything, unable to stop them, her heart pounding again in her fingertips.

"We must hurry," he called, urging her to follow.

Parker's body moved independently of her will.

Lazlo raced ahead to the others, motioning for them to follow him into a narrow, dark passageway wide enough for the children to squeak through; he had to turn and squeeze to get through.

He came to a stop and wheeled on them.

"You must listen closely, children. You will have four quests leading you to the four ancient items. You'll only have until the new moon wanes—four days—or it may be too late. These are like the four directions, the four points, and the four elements. You must bring the ancient items back to me and only to me—all of them," he said, his words echoing off the walls. "All of them and *him*."

The Pennymores looked at one another, startled by Lazlo's harsh demeanor.

His voice softened. "I want you to be safe. Only I can save Riley and protect you. The four ancient items will—it will give *us*—the power to defeat the monster, to defeat Lady Julie, once and for all."

His green eyes narrowed and met each of theirs before he stood. "Hurry, the water is coming."

Their panted breaths echoed off the stone walls as they ran through the darkness.

Why isn't someone stopping us? Why doesn't Quinn say something?

Thump-thump. Thump-thump.

Soon the water would rush back in, trapping them here again.

"Run, children," he pointed across the open field in front of them to a space at the tree line. "Cross before it's too late."

"It's miles across, and there are the traps, the transporting pools," yelled Parker, snapping out of her daze. "How can we make it past?"

"Follow the pink stones. I placed the stone as a secret way in or out of Everly when the water is gone. You'll see," he called to them. "You *must* stand only on the pink stones, and they will transport you across the sea. It's much too far otherwise. *Only* the pink stones."

Parker, Owen, and Aven raced ahead, with Aven running on four legs.

"You'll see," he called. "The pink stones!"

"I'm coming," Riley called as Parker waited to grab his hand.

Parker ran ahead before finally peeking behind her only to see Quinn and Lazlo standing outside the door. She couldn't make out what they were saying. Her sister handed Lazlo a small, folded piece of paper, then Quinn and Lazlo raced to catch up.

The clouds were forming. There isn't much time left before the water floods back in.

Parker ran to the shoreline and turned back to see Quinn was only halfway to the tree line.

"Run, Quinn!"

Owen and the youngest Pennymores raced through the tree line and hurried down the rocks lining the shore.

"Step only on the pink stones," Parker instructed. "I think they are transporters, like from the pool, but in reverse." She whispered to herself, "At least, I hope they are."

Dark clouds obscured the ominous, yellowish dusk sky. The flood would come soon.

"There isn't time," whispered Owen. "She won't make it." Parker turned to see Quinn far behind them—not yet at the edge of the tree line.

Lazlo stopped, reached into his pocket, pulled something from his robes, and placed it on Crucis, who raced with the item to Quinn, dropping it at her feet. She stopped and picked up the maroon bag.

Whoosh.

The trees bent under a blast of warm air. Parker hopped ahead, each foot gliding from pink stone to pink stone. Each stone was a magical transporter connected to the next pink stone, enabling them to leap hundreds of feet with each step with a whooshing feeling like what she'd felt when sucked into the transporting pool.

There were explosions of pink, silver, orange, gold, and red as her sisters and Owen stepped on each of the stones as if fireworks launched them forward with each step. She wanted to watch but knew the water would soon cover the rocks and them if they didn't hurry.

They were only halfway across the seabed, even with the assistance of the transporting stones. The ground became soggy as streams of water erupted, swallowing the land.

"Go," Parker shouted to the others. "Go!"

Quinn was only a third of the way across, but Lazlo watched them from the rocky shoreline.

He won't let us drown. He can't.

Quinn's footsteps now splashed with each step on the pink transporting stones.

Parker turned to run. She could see the other side. A gush of water raced to catch her.

Quinn is going to have to swim. Where's Riley?

"Riley! Riley! Riley, answer me!"

Nothing.

Then—a scream.

"Help me!"

She whipped around, scanning for him. His voice was coming from *behind* her.

"Help me!" Riley called out again.

Parker looked at Owen, her mind seeing him in her dreams again, being dragged under the waters by that invisible creature.

Finally, she saw it. Water splashing at least two hundred feet behind her.

"Just go," Quinn screamed out. "I've got him."

Quinn dashed toward the splashes. Parker knew she needed to turn and run, feeling the rising water pour over her boots. But she couldn't take her eyes away from where Riley was. With the grace of a water bird, her elder sister bent down in stride, picked up her brother, and ran for their lives. Each pink stone was leapfrogging them over vast swaths of the rapidly rising water.

The pink stones were now engulfed by dark water.

Run. Just run.

Aven and Owen ran ahead of the rapidly rising water line. Aven reached the shore first and scrambled up the rocks and to the other side, Owen right behind her. She couldn't look back again for fear of missing a stone or falling.

Step. Splash.

Step. Splash.

Step. Splash.

The water deepened, making Parker's run more like jumping over hurdles. But she could still see the rocks. Twenty more feet. Ten.

The elevation of the seabed changed. She'd made it too, scrambling up and reaching out for Aven's arm.

"Parker, your gem. It's glowing again!" Aven cried.

The gem was warm against her chest.

They were still in danger.

Parker scanned the water for her older sister.

Where is she? What's she doing?

Then she saw the splash—Quinn's face between waves. She gasped for air, Riley holding on around Quinn's neck, making her head bob below the surface. The water was up to her chin.

"Hurry!" Parker yelled.

The water was at Quinn's chin, her nose, over her face, her head.

"Where are they? I don't see them. Where *are* they!" Parked cried.

Chapter Seventeen

The Magic Compass

The seawater stilled. Parker scanned for any movement, any sound, any sign of Quinn and Riley. Finally, a hand broke through the water at the edge of the rocky shore, followed by another and the familiar face of her older sister.

"Quinn!" Aven yelled out, running down to help. "Riley!"

Their eldest sister rolled over onto her back and coughed out some water before she sucked in a big breath and finished pulling herself up the shore, her hand gripping Riley's.

Parker raced over to help. "I—I thought you were gone. That—that was so *not* good."

Quinn laughed, shaking the water from her hair and smiling at her sisters.

"Well, at least we made it," Quinn said, letting out a sharp breath. "Plenty. Of. Time."

Parker shook her head. "I think we have a different definition of *plenty*."

"How did you do that?" Owen asked.

"Yeah, I didn't think you were going to make it," Parker said to her older sister. "You swam?"

"I think so," Quinn stammered. "It felt like the water was behind us, pushing us forward. I'm not sure, but the water, it propelled us ahead... It was weird."

"Water propelled you? Yeah, that's definitely not called swimming," Owen said. "It's more like the opposite of what happened to me on Drain Day."

Parker reached down to her necklace, and it was no longer glowing. Danger had passed, and they were safe. But they were trapped and there was no way back home.

"And *this* was why it took me a little longer to get here," Quinn replied, tossing her sister the maroon bag she'd received from Lazlo.

Parker unwound the string around the bag. She reached inside and pulled out the small black octagon shape with cream-colored trim and a small gold latch. When she opened it, the interior lid had a night sky blue circle, and below were the points of direction traced in deep golden lines and a spinning hand like a clock. The others leaned over to examine it.

"Our compass," Quinn said, still short of breath. "Lazlo said it is our guide. I guess we use it to find the four objects."

"Hang on," Parker said. "These markings inside aren't directions."

"That's because it's a magical compass."

Of course it's a magical compass.

The five of them looked at the compass. Like a normal compass, there were four different directions, but instead of N for north, it had an enscripted Z.

"Z? What is Z?" Owen asked.

"Zuma?" Parker suggested. She'd already planned to try and find the hidden city of Zuma herself on the way to the Northern Passage. Perhaps she *was* on the right path.

"The lost animal kingdom?" asked Quinn.

"If we have to recover an ancient item," Parker responded, "wouldn't you expect it to be in a lost kingdom?"

"Plus, Zuma has talking animals!" Aven beamed.

"Wait, wait," Owen said. "You're kidding. Right? Talking animals—we're trying to find a lost place that has talking animals?"

"You've never heard the storytellers talk of Zuma?" Parker asked.

"Sure, but it's a kid's story. We all heard it. Imaginary, right?"

"Have to tell you, Zuma's real, bud," Quinn said, raising her eyebrows. "At my Apportionment ceremony, two hyenas, a flamingo, and a talking sea lion showed up."

"Apportion—what?" Owen asked. "Talking sea lions? A magic compass? This day can't get any weirder."

They had a magical compass, oven mitt, measuring cup, and tea ball. They'd barely made it across a magical sea, and they were trying to save their invisible brother from a dark and evil witch. What else could this day throw at them?

"Zuma is near to the location of the ancient library for the Order of the Legend, my order," Quinn said. "It's a magical animal kingdom where animals are anthropomorphic."

"That means they wear pants and walk on two legs," Aven said to Owen. "I know a lot of big words."

"The stories and fables you heard as a kid are all true in some way or another," Quinn said, "but they are just told in stories, so we don't forget them. A lot about the magical world is right in front of us. You just never knew to look."

"Okay, but how will we get there?" Parker asked. "We have four days, and we can't make it to some faraway kingdom."

"So, this is where it gets a little weird," Quinn admitted. "Lazlo told me to find a chain to take us there."

"A chain?" Parker asked. "How is a chain going to help us find it?"

Parker had heard every adventure story in the kingdom, but none of them ever talked about chains other than tying up prisoners or attaching to anchors on boats. One of her favorite stories was an entire underground city where dwarfs and elves would use a chain to pull their elders through the tunnels in wagon trains hundreds of wagons long.

"I don't have any idea," Quinn said. "We didn't have time to talk about it, but he said, 'When you find the chain, you'll know what to do.'"

More clues. The last thing we need is more clues.

"We should go," Quinn said. "We don't have much time, and Lazlo says a dark witch is hunting us."

"I have to ask," Owen said, "isn't it a little weird he just sent a bunch of kids across the magical sea that's supposed to be protecting Everly?"

Parker looked back across the dark, stormy water separating them from their home and family. They were alone. Only Lazlo knew they had left.

"We have to save Riley," Quinn replied. "You heard what he said about the four items, four quests, and four days."

"Okay. But why not tell the soldiers or your parents or go himself? Does he think it's a good idea to send us?"

"I've been training," Quinn said. "I can write magic to protect us."

"Owen's got a point," Parker said. "This all happened pretty fast. Maybe we could go back and get help or something? Maybe there are more clues Lady Julie left? I mean, can we trust Lazlo?"

Quinn let out a sharp sigh. "Parker, *you* were running away this morning." Her tone became more aggressive. "Alone. I mean, you, of all people, should be excited about this. You got your wish—we're all running away. Just what you wanted, okay? At least he's trying to help us save Riley rather than lock him in some prison cell."

"I just wanted to find answers," Parker said. "That's it. I don't know why you are mad at me right now."

"Because you're being ridiculous," Quinn replied. "Listen, you can go or you can stay. It's your choice. We weren't safe on that island anyway, so I'd rather do something to try and help someone. Okay?"

"This isn't helping," Aven said.

"Okay, okay. Look around us," Owen said, his hands gesturing to the water. "We can't even get back across the water. This is all we got right now. Your mother told you guys to trust no one, and here we are, trusting some weird wizard. Either some dark witch is hunting us or maybe the Ravagers. Who even knows what the heck is out there. I'm a kid whose parents told him all his life that writing got you locked up, so what do I even know? We are where we are, and it's late, and we gotta get moving."

"And I'm hungry," Riley said. "When do we eat?"

"Owen's right. We follow the compass. That's the best we can do," Quinn said, looking closely at the octagon-shaped device in her hand. "You okay with that, Parker?"

"Fine," Parker said.

"Then it's settled," Quinn said.

"I feel like this is a moment you two should hug or something," Owen said with an awkward smile.

They glared at him.

"We get going," Quinn said with a sharp exhale, "and hopefully, we find somewhere to rest for a bit. I'm not sure how the compass works, though." She shook it a few times.

"Let me hold it?" said Riley, quickly grabbing the compass from his sister.

The compass floated, its face glowing. The night blue sky on the interior lid began to move, mirroring the sky above them. The stars and constellations were colorful, illuminated, specks of light shooting across the compass's blue face. The floating arrow spun faster and faster and faster.

"Looks like we just let the invisible kid hold it to make it work," Owen said with a shrug.

As quickly as the arrow had begun glowing and spinning, it settled on a direction, the Z turning from gold to white.

"Looks like it's this way," said Riley, handing the compass back to Quinn. "And is anyone else hungry?"

Quinn motioned to the others to follow. Aven let out a howl and scampered off in the direction the compass had pointed.

"You and your sister got something going on," Owen said to Parker once Quinn was out of earshot. "I'm new to all this magic stuff, but as far as I can tell, you're on team Lady Julie, and she's on team Lazlo. And I'm on team 'just don't get us killed.' Okay?"

"She just doesn't get it."

"Your sister is no dummy," Owen said. "But the two of you need to put whatever is going on between you aside. Your brother's life depends on it."

He began to follow the others.

Maybe Owen is right. Quinn has been learning to write magic. She'd met the other Serifs, she knew about things like the Apportionment, and she'd been the one who found the inscription about how to save Riley. All I have is some random clues. What else does Quinn know?

Parker inhaled deeply, then said, "Guys! Wait up."

∗∗∗

"It's getting late, and I'm tired," Aven said.

"We've only been out here for an hour," Quinn said. "Can we keep walking for another half an hour?"

Some sort of a grunt or snort came from Aven—definitely not the enthusiastic howl she'd let loose when they started. Parker took her grunting snort as an agreement.

She was tired too. It felt like weeks since she'd entered the enchanted writing room, but they needed to keep moving. Lazlo had been clear: follow the compass, return by Sunday at dusk, bring him the four ancient items or Riley would stay invisible forever... or worse.

My gem will glow when we're in danger, like when someone is about to drown or who knows what. No pressure.

As dusk turned into night, their group continued onward, the compass leading them along the shore of a choppy river.

They'd been unprepared for the journey, but Aven and Riley had stashed a few pieces of fruit, bread, and an entire loaf of cinnamon pulls into the tiny magical leather purse while building their bedroom fort. Enough for them to eat for now, but it wouldn't last long.

"I had been listening to all the stories about Fonde, the adventure ones," Parker said to Quinn as they walked together. "There are quite a few stories about the route to the Northern Passage. And if the stories are true, the hidden kingdom of Zuma is on that path northern travelers take. I thought it was probably a day's walk from the Everly, at least. And from what I can tell, the compass seems to be taking us along this river. The storytellers talked about a couple of bridge crossings to get us over the canyon between here and there. I was planning to find one and cross there since the river's current looks pretty strong."

Quinn nodded and gave Parker a concerned look. "Why did you try and run away? I could have helped or done something."

"Helped?" Parker replied. "Ever since Riley disappeared, you were gone. How could I have known you even wanted to help? When they took away the library, it's like they took you away from me too."

"I know. I wanted to tell you everything," Quinn said. "I did, but I couldn't. They wouldn't let me. Mom and Dad just kept telling me they'd tell you, too, soon. You'd learn magic writing. You'd hear everything. That's what they said, so I just didn't know what to say to you about any of it. And then I saw you with your friends like Monty and your writer kids, and it was like you didn't need me anymore."

They walked in silence for a few minutes.

"Why do you think she took him? Why did Lady Julie kidnap Riley?" Parker asked.

Quinn rubbed her hands in front of her as they walked. "I am not supposed to tell you this. I swore I wouldn't. I swore it." She turned to Parker. Her brown eyes filled with sadness. "It wasn't just Riley."

"What? What do you mean?"

"It was supposed to be all of us. She was planning to take us all, Parker," Quinn said. "Julie *meant* to kidnap us all."

"That's impossible."

"I know it seems that way. No one told you because… well, because they wanted you and Aven not to be terrified and worried all the time. When the black etchings from the Ravagers started to appear, they wanted to protect you and get you to one of the literati libraries, where our aunt and other teachers could keep you safe. All of this was to keep us safe."

"But how do you know that?" Parker asked.

"Lazlo. When Lazlo found the hidden room, a lot more was there. He found Lady Julie's plans to kidnap each of us, all the Pennymores. It was all arranged, and then something happened. Riley was the first, but they were coming for us all."

"But that doesn't make any sense. Lazlo told me and Aven our father came to him in prison the morning of that first Drain Day and gave him a choice," Parker replied. "He told Lazlo if he could bring the water to protect the kingdom, he would free him. There was no hidden room."

"No, you must be confused," Quinn said. "He said—"

"Then what about the clues she left—"

"It was part of her plan too. She wanted us to find them, to think there was a chance of hope. She used us, Parker, all of us."

"And you—you're sure?" Parker asked.

"I wish I weren't. That would be so much easier."

"But why?" Parker said in a hushed voice. "Why would she?"

"I don't know," Quinn said. "After a year of asking myself why, I just had to stop looking for answers. Bad people do bad things. Who knows why she did it, but now that we have him back, I can't let him go, not now."

Parker's face grew hot, and she felt her heartbeat in her fingertips. Something still didn't make sense, but maybe she'd make a mistake. Tears filled her eyes. How had she missed the signs?

"My friends. We just left them, and if she brings Dagamar and the Ravagers to Everly…"

"Lazlo stayed," Quinn said. "He told me what you did for him, how you told Father about him and urged him to let Lazlo stay."

"He said that? I don't get that. But if he knew I didn't try to get him locked up, then why would he be so hard on me, threaten me, call me stubborn, and refuse to help me?"

"You just don't know him," Quinn said. "I got to from the training and lessons. But I know he stayed there to protect Everly if she comes back.

And you heard what our parents said about the Illiterates... As long as they hold the amphitheater and keep the place on edge, the Ravagers won't... they shouldn't try. They'll be okay."

"I just feel so stupid about all of it."

"I told you, your magic abilities are even stronger than mine. You've already done things that are insane," Quinn said, putting her arm around her sister as they walked. "You're going to learn. And I can try and teach you what I know, so you can help keep us safe."

Parker wiped her sleeve across her eyes, drying her tears.

"Okay," she said. "I'm sorry for everything."

"No, you don't need to apologize for anything. Our parents should have told you. I should have. It's unfair they let you think she was something she wasn't. Now we need to keep the others safe and save Riley."

Parker took a deep breath. "Looks like we are stuck with each other. Right?"

Quinn nodded.

"We've got a long way ahead of us to find the items, a long way for those two," Quinn said, motioning to their younger siblings who were struggling to keep up.

"I've been thinking about that," Parker said. "Maybe I've got an idea. Aven, Riley, you guys want a shoulder ride?"

Quinn hissed at her sister, "No, no, no. We can't carry them to Zuma!"

A smile crept across Parker's face, and she raised an eyebrow. She waved the enchanted measuring cup she had pulled from the leather pouch.

"Think you could carry a miniature girl who howls once in a while?"

***

Dawn filled the early morning sky. They continued, following the river until the compass guided them to a bridge. Parker and Quinn had found it easier to keep walking through the night while their now-three-inch-tall siblings rested comfortably on their shoulders. Quinn had the idea to cut small slits in their clothing to act like seat belts to let them rest and not fall off while Owen and the older Pennymore siblings walked, guided by the twilight sky compass.

But as the sun was rising, Parker's aching feet let her know how much time had passed.

"Are we there yet?" asked Aven, in her squeaky, mouse-like voice.

The girl rides on our shoulders all night sleeping and now is complaining about the trip.

"You guys, I think food tastes *better* when you are small," Aven said as she bit into a crumb of cinnamon pull the size of her head. "Here, try it." She held out a crumb.

"Look. Up ahead is a bridge," Parker said. "I knew there would be one soon. We'll need to cross to get to the plains leading to Zuma. We're probably not far."

Quinn craned her neck, quickening her pace as the bridge came into view. "It'll be best if the two of you *miniatures* are back to your normal sizes in case something happens as we cross," she said. "A stiff breeze and you guys will float away like a kite."

After returning Aven and Riley to their natural heights, the five of them made their way to the rope-and-wood footbridge stretched across the canyon's fifty-foot gap. It was much farther down to the floor of the canyon than they'd anticipated.

"Well, definitely don't look down," Aven said.

"Are you sure this is the best bridge to take?" Owen asked. "Maybe there's a better one further down."

"The compass says this is it," Quinn answered, leading the group over the first steps of the bridge.

Riley called out, "No. Wait. Do you hear something?"

A loud rumble came from the cavern.

"Is that thunder?" Aven asked, looking for the source of the noise.

"There's not a cloud in the sky," answered Parker. "I'm not sure what it is."

"It's probably nothing," Quinn said, placing her other foot on the bridge, a noisy creak giving them all pause.

"We should wait," Riley repeated. "Something's not right."

"I'm with the kid," Owen said.

"I don't see any other way across," Quinn said, bending down to survey the ropes holding the bridge together. "But better to be safe. Give me a couple of minutes. I think I have an idea. Parker, do you still have the spool of rope?"

Parker handed the rope to her sister, who took it and pulled her goggles down over her eyes. Quinn pulled a small knife from her pocket and carefully cut the wooden spool into four parts. Her hands flew over the spool, threading the rope through the pieces, creating loops in the string where she attached the spool pieces. She unwound the entire length, marking three spots along the way to make four equal sizes.

The claps of thunder were more frequent and felt like they were getting closer.

Could that be Riley's stomach? That kid asks about snacks every fifteen minutes. I wonder if being invisible makes you eat like crazy?

"This is a climbing rope," Quinn said, standing back and admiring the knotted rope.

"Will this work better than your doughnut thingy?" Aven asked, tilting her head.

Quinn narrowed her eyes at her. "Owen, you, and Riley are in the middle. I'm going to tie these pieces of rope to you, and this way, we are all connected. Parker and I will be on the ends, and we'll go slowly, so we don't put too much weight on the bridge. Riley's right. It looks... old."

Once everyone was attached, Quinn carefully stepped onto the wooden bridge.

She checked the compass and confirmed it still pointed directly over the bridge.

"See, nothing to worry about," Quinn said.

Aven, energized after eating the massive crumb, gave a hearty, "Let's do it!" followed by her usual howl.

"Woo hoo!" Parker cheered.

"Uh, Parker," said Aven. "Your necklace. It's glowing again."

Of course there's danger. Even the gem can see this rope bridge is a million years old.

"You guys, Lazlo told me it glows when there's danger nearby. And pretty much every time it's glowed so far, something pretty ugly has happened."

"Except when we found Riley," Aven chimed in. "That wasn't dangerous. It was great. Right, Riley?"

Parker clenched the gem in her hand and said, "Okay, just be on guard, everyone. Quinn, keep your eyes on the other side of the canyon. It seems like something… or someone might be over there."

Quinn pulled down her inventing goggles, gave the group a thumbs-up, and continued over the first few feet of the bridge.

Boom.

Thunder echoed, shaking the entire bridge.

"Did anyone bring an umbrella?" Owen said. "It sounds like rain is coming."

Boom.

"Guys!" Aven said. "That's not thunder! Look down." She motioned to look beneath them.

The children screamed as a large rock hurtled toward the rope bridge. They all fell to the wooden planks, covering their heads.

Parker saw another rock hurtling toward them, peering through space between the boards. "Not! Thunder! That's a troll! A canyon troll is trying to knock us off the bridge, Quinn."

"You've got to be kidding me!" Owen yelled. "Trolls are real?"

"You had to have heard the stories about bridges?" Aven called.

"Those trolls are always asking for money, not tossing boulders!"

"Hang on, everyone!" Quinn called out.

At the bottom of the canyon, a fifteen-foot-tall, green creature wearing leather battle armor and holding a wooden club on its shoulder was bending down to grab another boulder the size of one of their beds. Its broken and jagged teeth jutted out of his mouth in all directions, visible even this high.

The thunder was boulders bouncing off the walls and canyon floor.

"Run, Quinn!" Parker screamed, watching the troll grimace as he hurtled a rock at the swaying rope bridge. Quinn scrambled to her feet and urged her siblings forward.

The rock grazed the side of the rope bridge.

Snnnaaaaapp.

Quinn ran, reaching the far edge of the bridge first.

"Hurry," she called, pulling the rope connecting them toward her to help the rest of the party across.

Creak… snnnaaaaapp.

The entire left side of the bridge frayed and split, sending Owen, Parker, Aven, and Riley careening down, grasping for pieces of the bridge.

Aven screamed.

The troll grabbed another rock and hoisted it up to finish the job. Then the troll blew into a makeshift horn, alerting others of his catch. As the rock flew and exploded on the wall, they could hear a deep bellowing laugh.

"Riley? Riley? Do you have him?" Quinn yelled, holding on to the rope connecting them

"I've got him," Owen said, "I *think*…"

"Hold on," Quinn called out. "We're all still connected. Move slowly, but do not let go." She held their climbing rope in one hand and reached for Aven's outstretched arm with the other, trying to bridge the gap between the edge of the canyon and where Aven dangled from the rope.

Her siblings hung in the air, the bridge rope continuing to fray beneath them.

"Now might be a good time to script something with your quill!" Parker called Quinn.

Her gem's red-orange glow illuminated the rope and pieces of board she clung to. The handrail rope snapped under their weight, leaving a single cord connecting the two sides.

"Hold on. *Hold on*," Quinn instructed. She swung her feet to the wooden beam at the edge of the rope bridge. "The rope is going to snap, but do not let go!"

Parker's eyes widened as Quinn held the rope, her feet firmly pushing into the posts connecting the bridge to the land.

Pop. Pop. Pop.

Just beyond where Parker clung to the bridge, the worn rope frayed, dropping them against the side of the canyon wall with a thud.

Another rock flung by the troll exploded below them, the horn sounding again. His aim was getting better, and if they fell, they'd be hurt… if they were lucky.

"Do. Not. Let. Go," Quinn commanded. "Everyone, I'm pulling now!"

Quinn's muscles shook, and the rope slipped in her hands. The gem around Parker's neck pulsed the brightest it had seen yet.

"Don't. Let. Us. Go," Parker called to Quinn.

Another boulder exploded a few feet from them at the top of the canyon wall. The troll aimed for the bindings at the top, hoping to knock them off.

Parker looked into Aven's terrified, teary, red face.

Quinn took another breath and grunted, heaving her three siblings and Owen over the edge, tumbling them into the dirt beside her. The mass of children piled onto one another, sobbing through their labored breathing.

Aven scrambled over to Quinn, wrapping her in her arms. "Oh, thank you. I love you."

"How? How did you do that?" Owen stammered. "You just lifted, like, four people and, like, two hundred and fifty pounds. *By yourself.*"

"I—I—I, don't know how it happened," Quinn stammered. "I just—I'm glad we're all okay. We've got to be careful. I don't want to lose you."

Parker looked down at her boots from the Gazettes.

Good work on these boots, boys. Mayflys sure did fly.

They were alive but had no way back across the canyon now, and even if they could, their home was no longer safe unless they could find the items. There was no turning back.

Owen stood and began wiping the dirt off his pants then knelt to examine one of the bridge's wooden posts.

"Guys, what's this on the beam?" he asked. "This charred mark?"

Parker knelt next to Owen. "That's the mark of the Ravagers, a black etching. Someone scripted that."

"But why would they leave that here?" he asked.

"Because whoever left that mark also left something else," Quinn said, motioning to the cavern. "They left the troll here too. They scripted magic to put that canyon troll here to guard the bridge."

"Why didn't you warn us, Quinn?" Parker said angrily.

"You think I knew there'd be an angry troll trying to knock us off a bridge over some random canyon? I didn't even notice the mark until Owen found it."

"Do you think they left that—that thing—for us?" Owen asked. "I mean, could someone know we were coming on this path or going to take this bridge?"

"It's one of the only bridges to get to the Northern Passage, but who would know we'd be here?" Parker asked. "Lazlo? But he wouldn't want to make this quest harder for us to retrieve these items. No one else even knows we left. Otherwise, I—I dunno who."

"Dagamar has something against our family—the Scotts and the Pennymores, remember?" Quinn said. "They already kidnapped our grandmother, so we're probably on their list too."

"Oh great," Owen said. "You're saying evil magic writers can just drop fifteen-foot trolls around wherever."

"We should be on the lookout for more black etchings," Quinn said.

"You could have used your magic or been ready for him," Parker responded, trying to calm the situation.

"I can't use my magic," Quinn snapped. "It's not just like you snap your fingers and do it. I can't lift ice cubes, so you think I want to trust my quill to save you?"

"You're supposed to know how to protect us."

"I don't. Okay? I don't know how. I can't fill up a stupid cup, let alone stop some huge boulder. And you keep telling me to use it, try, and write. You don't get it."

"I'm—I'm sorry," Parker said.

"Go. Just go," Quinn said with her head down. "That horn may mean more of them are coming."

Why didn't she at least try to script magic? She has powers none of the rest of us have.

The gem warned them of the troll. They'd just missed the warning, and now the entire bridge was gone.

Quinn looked shaken, and Parker smiled at her sister.

Why isn't she prouder? She saved us.

"We've been hiking all night," Quinn said as she brushed herself off and stood. "We need to find a place to rest."

Chapter Eighteen

The Chain Station

"Aren't we supposed to see something resembling a kingdom?" Quinn asked Parker.

"*Hidden* kingdom," Parker said. "Two days ago, I had no idea if all of the stories we'd heard were just stories, but I'm pretty confident every story is describing real places and real things."

"You all saw that troll," Owen said. "Real rocks. Very real rocks."

"It's real. I know. But Parker's right. It just won't be out in the open," Quinn said. "I remember that flamingo told me Zuma was hard to miss." Quinn looked down at the compass and shook it. "Stupid thing just keeps telling us to keep walking."

"Maybe we need another break," Parker said, sensing her sister's frustration. "I need to think through the stories again and see if I can remember any detail or landmark we can use to figure out where we need to go."

"What did Lazlo mean by take the chain?" Quinn asked. "I know what he can do with his stupid chain."

As she lowered herself onto a mound of dirt, Quinn closed her eyes to try to rest.

"Uh, guys," said Aven. "*Guys!* You need to see this!"

From the corner of her eye, Parker saw Quinn jump to her feet, holding her open palm in front of her with her quill inches from her fingers. She quickly lowered them when Aven darted after something only she could see.

Aven ran on four legs, keeping her face a few inches from the ground. Then she stood up from the long grass and pointed down at the ground.

The other children came over and looked at where Aven pointed. "Look," she said.

A single file line of mice walked past the toe of Aven's shoe. Each mouse held the mouse's tail in front of it in its tiny paw.

"Are you thinking what I'm thinking?" Parker asked, smiling at Aven.

"A chain," Aven said, smiling like she'd found a treasure trove of cinnamon pulls.

"Of mice," Parker finished. The two sisters did their elaborate fist-bumping routine.

"Lazlo said to *take* the chain," Quinn relayed. "So, I guess we should follow them?"

"Can we ride the chain?" asked Aven.

"I don't—" Before Quinn could finish, Aven raced off on her hands and feet, following the tiny chain of mice marching tail to paw through the tall grass of the field.

Aven reached the end of the line at a small hole in the base of a solitary tree. She watched mouse after mouse reach the tree and disappear into the small gap at the bottom of the tree where the scraggly roots and the trunk met.

"They're going into this tree," she said when the others joined her. She dropped to her knees, inching closer to the small gap the mice were wedging into. Her sisters and Owen followed, each studying the hole for any clue how this might lead them to Zuma.

"What are you looking at?" asked a soft, gentlemanly voice from behind them.

Startled, they jumped, scrambling to their feet.

"Did you not hear me? I asked what you're looking at."

"You have horns," Aven said. "Are you a goat?"

"Why, of course I am. What did you expect?" the goat replied with indignation. "Well, I'm no lion or hippo or hedgehog, but a goat is a perfectly respectable creature to meet at the chain station."

"What's a chain station?" Aven asked.

"Why, it's a chain of mice who guide you where you're going, of course," the goat replied, a hint of disdain in his voice.

While a talking goat was most certainly befuddling, this goat was dressed in a tan tweed jacket and vest, bright red tie, and a hat with a colorful feather perfectly sewn to leave a spot for his two horns to poke out.

Parker eyed the goat closely, recognizing something about him. "You look strangely familiar. Have we... have we met?"

"Met? Us? Why, of course not," the goat said. "Unless you've visited Zuma before, which seems highly unlikely."

The goat smiled then winked. *He was the escaped goat from the yard outside the castle in Everly. It had to be him.*

Parker smiled back at the goat, nodding as she did.

"And mom said wolves couldn't wear clothes," Aven announced to her siblings. "If a goat can do it, why not a—"

"Wait, you can talk?" Owen asked, interrupting Aven.

"I suppose if you call this dreadful conversation we're having 'talking,' then yes, I'd say I talk," continued the goat. "My name is Beauregard, Beauregard Dondula, but my friends call me Beau."

"Nice to meet you, Beau," Aven said, stretching out her hand to shake his hoof.

"Oh, dear girl," he said, jerking his hoof back from her. "We are *not* friends. You shall call me Beauregard."

"He's silly," Aven said. "Beau the billy goat. I like it."

The goat snorted. "I'm certainly curious as to what three girls and a funny-looking boy are doing chasing the chain of mice entering Zuma."

"Did you say entering Zuma?" asked Parker, unsure what to make of a talking goat dressed in a perfectly fitted suit.

"Did he call me funny-looking?" Owen asked.

"Of course I did," Beau continued in a slightly offended tone. "Zuma. It's the three o'clock chain, and they are right on time, as usual. Never late, never ever late. And you must admit you're a bit funny looking."

In stories, Zuma had been a regal, majestic animal kingdom. Parker leaned in to speak to Beau. "We thought Zuma would be bigger," she whispered. "We didn't expect a tree. We were looking for a kingdom."

The goat laughed.

"You are not from around here," he said, taking off his hat and hitting it to knock off the dust. "We were forced to go into hiding many, many years ago," Beau replied. "As those dreadful Illiterates—scoundrels, they were—began to hunt for writers of all shapes, sizes, and demeanors, they seemed to think any magical creatures like the zumans must be magic *writers*, which as you all clearly must know is not the truth. As if. We feared for the safety of our kingdom and decided to use a little magic to keep those dreadfully impolite Illiterates away from us."

"The Illiterates have been here?" Quinn asked, looking around.

"Of course. They are always lurking around here," Beau continued. "Recently, we've had more attacks on our creatures who do come out of hiding than ever before. Ravagers, Serifs loyal to Master Dagamar, have kidnapped zumans, lit fire to our homes, and destroyed our crops. We have heard rumors of *The Story of the Defeat* being upon us. It's why I was dreadfully concerned to see three girls and a funny-looking boy standing alone waiting by the chain of mice."

Quinn cringed at what the goat said.

Was someone else after the ancient items too?

"Do you think I'm funny-looking?" Owen whispered to Aven.

Reaching into her pocket, Quinn pulled out the compass.

"This," she said, pointing to the compass Lazlo had given them, "led us here. But we are looking for an ancient object we must find to save our brother."

The goat ducked at the sight of the compass, looking around for anyone who might see them. Then he gave a bleat-like stutter.

"B-b-b-brother? Why, you look nothing like one another," Beau said, leaning in to get a closer look at Owen.

"Nope. No, we're not related," Owen said, pointing to the Pennymores.

"Well, that's a relief," the goat replied. "Then who is this brother? I don't see any brother, just three girls—some of whom have dreadful manners, I might add." He tilted his head in Aven's direction. "Who among you requires saving, and from what are you being saved?"

"Me," a voice came from near the compass, forcing the goat to scurry back.

The compass from Quinn's hand began to glow and spin.

"What in the dickens is this magic?" asked Beau, taking another step away from the floating compass.

"Me. I'm the brother in danger," Riley said to the confused billy goat.

Quinn followed Riley toward Beau. "The invisible quill has cursed our brother. We are under threat of magic writers, and the Illiterates have attacked our kingdom."

"And before the waning moon, we must find four ancient objects," Parker said.

"Or I'll be stuck this way forever," Riley added.

"This is certainly troubling. I see," said the goat. "Magic writers have been hidden from men for centuries. Never understood this silly fear of writing, you men have."

"I'm not a 'men,'" Aven said with a grin.

"Look, can you help us?" Quinn asked the nervous goat.

"You must first know you are not the first to search for these ancient items. We've heard stories of others seeking Zuma for what we have. We've had attacks, and many zumans are afraid."

"But you know what the ancient item is? What do you have?" asked Parker excitedly. "We don't know what we're looking for, and we don't know where to go."

"It's not what you seek, but *who*," the goat answered. His face had grown severe and sad. "Come with me, but quickly now. Those who seek what you've come for are not good. We've remained hidden to protect ourselves. Hurry now."

He reached out his hooves, gathering them in front of him while facing the tree where the mice had entered Zuma.

"Come, invisible prince, come here," he said to Riley.

"He's not a prince," said Quinn, correcting the goat. "None of us are princesses, either. Our father told us he invented his crown. We aren't real royal blood."

He shook his head. "Whether you call yourselves a prince or princess or not, the curse that has fallen upon your brother is a curse of magical royal blood, and he is most certainly the invisible prince of legend. Now come quickly—all of you."

"Where are you taking us?" asked Quinn.

The goat gestured to the chain of mice steadily running into the tiny hole in the base of the tree. He motioned with a hoof for the children to follow him.

"There's no way we'll fit in this mouse hole," Parker said.

Beau rested his hooves on the shoulders of Quinn and Parker and continued to nudge them onward. "All right, all of you stand here. Trust me."

Parker froze, but the billy goat was solid and determined, pushing the eldest two directly in front of the tree. Before she knew it, Parker was standing on an invisible platform that slowly inched forward.

"The mice are pulling us like a sleigh ride!" Aven exclaimed, as inch by inch they disappeared into the tree's bark. The tiniest gap in the tree opened to a ridge looking over a vast, beautiful cityscape. Parker instantly felt the warm sunshine on her face. The mice continued to march tail to paw, pulling the invisible sleigh down the ridge and into the city below.

"Welcome to Zuma," Beau said.

The land stretched on, well beyond any kingdom they'd ever heard of or imagined. It was a world that blended the human and the animal perfectly, with buildings resembling tall, snow-capped mountains, paths and roads woven into the landscape, and expansive parks filled with sand like a desert, tree canopies, and savanna grasses. Parker could see tiny castle-like buildings that must have housed all types of rodents, mice, and squirrels. Bridges connecting the treetop jungle canopy sections opened into homes built into the trees. Scattered throughout these unique areas, they saw cobbled streets with street signs and stores with vendors. The kingdom stretched for what seemed like miles and had everything you could want if you were a goat wearing pants and a top hat, a rhino going for a jog, or a busy bird looking to buy worms at the grocery store for her chicks.

"Zuma!" Aven shouted with a smile as she stepped off the sleigh and broke into a run. The others followed her and ran ahead until they saw buildings and homes with animals moving in and out of them.

"How did you do that?" Parker asked. "How did we suddenly get here?"

"Ah, these connections exist all over—doorways between the magical and nonmagical world," Beau replied. "We call them Ellipses, these hidden doorways, and they are how the magical world can remain hidden right in front of your eyes. What you've seen is not what you've seen, Madam Pennymore. Now go ahead and look around. I'll catch up."

The landscape shifted into a bustling city with paved streets, shops, gardens, houses, and the noises of a city—quite different from the quiet they'd experienced outside the tree.

What struck Packer was the writing. Buildings and streets had written signs on them while stores and stands were selling books and newspapers.

"Look," Aven whispered, pointing to an open-air building where a mix of young-looking animals sat at desks of varying heights, each creature with an open book and their quills in front of them. The room was bright, filled with natural light and colors; books lined every shelf in the room. Words, signs, and letters covered the walls. A teacher stood in the front holding white chalk and writing letters on the dark gray chalkboard.

"It's a school?" Parker asked Beau who'd joined her in admiring the activity.

"Oh no. That's an elementary library. I attended this very one many moons ago," Beau said, watching the Pennymore children's fascination. "We study and learn in libraries such as these all of our lives. Center of Zuma, they are. These places are the keepers of knowledge here and everywhere, you see. Notice all the picture books—those are the books that speak to you, the voice books. Children come here every day to learn to write."

The teacher in the elementary library said something aloud, and five or six books leaped from various shelves in the room and flapped like birds toward the teacher, just as Parker'd seen in her library. The teacher grabbed one of the books and waved her hand to the others, who fluttered back to perch on the shelves. Then she opened the book and began reciting from it. While the teacher spoke, an otter hunched over a desk, frantically scribbling into a book with a quill when a bright glow burst from the book, filling the entire classroom with a rainbow of colors. It looked like what the *Book of the Seven Ancient Stories* had done when Parker had touched it with her quill.

The teacher hurried to help the young otter, embarrassed at the other students giggling and pointing.

It's just like the enchanted library I found in the castle. Maybe that wasn't so unusual.

"Come along, children," Beau called as he led them through the entrance to the city, engulfing them by the sights, smells, and sounds of Zuma.

They passed a lion wearing a suit and reading from a small blue book.

A family of at least two dozen rabbits wearing dresses and fancy hats hopped in front of them, each carrying their little picture books while their father had a folded newspaper under his furry arm.

Citizens could read in the open without ridicule, punishment, or fear.

"Mama, what's this word?" one of the littlest rabbits asked.

The rabbit in the front, far taller than the rest, said, "Sound it out. This is how we learn."

The littlest rabbit stopped looking at her book and turned to examine the Pennymore children, her nose twitching wildly and an excited smile filling her face. "Mama. Mama? Is that a people?" she said, pointing a paw at the sisters.

Aven smiled and waved back to her.

The mother rabbit stopped, hopped over to the young bunny, and studied their faces curiously. "Why, I think they are. Yes, I do think those are a people. Honey, honey, look."

The father rabbit carrying his paper joined them as the entire family of dozens of bunnies began to line up immediately across from the Pennymores to examine the strange visitors. "My dear, those aren't *just* a people. Those, my children, are Pennymore people. The Pennymores, yes? Your grandmother is a Scott, right?"

"How do you know our grandmother?" Parker answered, trying to hide the surprise in her face. "Parker, Quinn, and Aven Pennymore," she said, gesturing to her sisters as several of the younger rabbits began running in and out of their legs as if they were playing a game.

"Of course we *all* know her," the mother rabbit answered. "Why, of course. Honey, honey, let's draw a picture with them."

"Wonderful idea, my dear," the father rabbit said, whistling loudly. "Lepus, here, Lepus."

A fluffy, white feather burst out of the father rabbit's tail and hovered excitedly in front of him.

"You children don't mind if we draw a picture of us all, do you? It'd only take Lepus a moment or two."

"Sure," Quinn said, looking to Beau. "Is that okay?"

"It would be rude to say no, so as long as it's quick, it's no bother," said the goat with a slight nod to the father rabbit.

"Hooray," shouted the littlest rabbit, who hopped over and leaped onto Aven's shoulder. "I've never seen real people before." The rabbit sniffed Aven's ear and hair. "She smells different, Mama."

The rabbit family hopped in front of the three Pennymores as Owen and Beau watched from the side. The father rabbit held out his newspaper. "Lepus, just find a blank page and use that. Just be quick about it. They're in a hurry."

The quill raced and slid itself inside the folded newspaper before exploding out with a single blank page that Lepus held upright with its glowing tip, moving in fast, frantic movements as if it were trying to keep the piece of paper afloat.

"Say carrots," the mother rabbit said.

"Carrots," the group said in unison as the quill whizzed from corner to corner of the piece of paper before coming to an abrupt stop.

"Now, let's just see how it turned out," the father rabbit said as he hopped over to his quill and held the paper up in front of himself, pushing his spectacles up from his nose. "Wow, this is just terrific. I think this might go over our fireplace in the burrow. Mama, what do you think?"

He turned it around, and they all leaned in to get a look at the near-perfect full-color illustration. "The quill drew that?" Quinn asked, leaning in to get a closer look.

"I know," the mother rabbit said. "I wish you didn't try to rush him next time, Harrold. It's—well, there's a streak and—but otherwise, kids, we got our picture drawn with the Pennymores. What a day."

Parker leaned down to a small rabbit standing directly in front of her. The rabbit had been staring for quite a while now. "Hi, what's your name?" she asked, reaching out her hand to shake the small bunny's paw.

"Oh, sorry," said the mother rabbit, racing over to the bunny and pulling him away from Parker. "He's—well, he just can't say much of anything." She leaned toward Beau and whispered, "Boy's got the silent tongue."

Parker looked at the goat, who politely nodded to the rabbits before offering an understanding look to Parker.

"Come along," the father rabbit said. "You too." He motioned to the youngest rabbit now standing on top of Aven's head. "They've got lots of important work to be done. Come, come. And we are all pulling for your grandmother."

The rabbit family hopped away, with many of the youngest ones turning back to them, offering waves and glances as they did.

"That was... interesting," Owen said. "So, they know you. But how do they know who you are?"

"I have no idea," Quinn said. "I've never even heard anyone talk about Grandma other than our family."

"Well, turns out you guys are a big deal in the rabbit world," Owen said with a smile.

"Hurry along," Beau said. "There are less friendly creatures than the bunnies in Zuma. I'd prefer we avoid them."

Beau motioned them to follow, leading them deeper into the city. Outside a fruit market stood two towering giraffes talking, each wearing what had to be the tallest pair of pants the sisters had ever seen.

"Wow," Aven said. "I bet those giraffes' pants are as tall as the castle!"

An elephant wearing swim trunks crossed the street opposite the girls.

"This is even more amazing than in the stories," Parker said.

"And it's all in a tree?" Owen added.

"Well, not *in* a tree," Beau said. "I'm not sure you realized, but it's simply an enchantment to keep us hidden from outsiders. We aren't in a *real* tree."

Owen looked at Parker and rolled his eyes.

"I'm hungry," Riley said. "Can we go into the market?"

"Shhhhh, child," responded Beau in a hushed tone. "While they cannot see you, you must not let them hear you or know you are here. This is not a welcome visit, mind you. None of you should be here."

They noticed more than the species and attire of the townsfolk, but their expressions too.

The giraffes, elephants, and lions seem stunned and interested in us as we are in the animals wearing clothes. Had they never seen kids before?

"Quickly, this way," said Beau, corralling the children and pushing them down a series of small and winding streets. "You need to speak to Droma. She's the only hope we have of saving your brother."

Chapter Nineteen

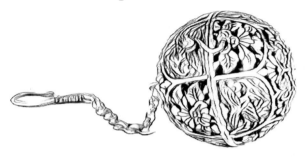

The Ancient Zuman

"Let's get off the main streets to avoid someone seeing us," whispered Beau.

The children quickly adapted to being hurried along by a well-dressed goat, but hearing a stranger refer to "saving your brother" had made Parker's heart race.

After twisting and turning through the streets, the goat led them into a small alleyway tucked in the shade, which gave the mysterious red door at the end of it an unsettling appearance.

"There," Beau pointed to the door at the end of the alley. "This is as far as I can go."

"What do you mean? You're leaving us?" Quinn asked.

"This is not safe for any of us, me included," he replied. "I've gotten you in. I've gotten you here, and now I must go before harm comes to us. I must leave you."

"Harm? To us?" Owen asked.

"No, of course not," he said in a wheezy voice. "I'm simply saying in harm lies valor, and I'm not very valiant and… I must be going. Droma will help you. She was once a curator."

"A curator?" Owen asked. "Curator of what?"

But the goat was gone, racing away, leaving Owen and the Pennymore siblings to stare at the small design etched on the surface of the door.

"Curators with a capital C. The curators organize all the ancient books, I think," Quinn said. "They are, like, some of the highest-level magic writers—I never got to meet one, but they're like a big deal, I guess. The ones who to make sure books and knowledge aren't lost. I might have skipped over some of that when I was supposed to be learning."

"So, a curator lives here?" Parker asked.

Quinn shrugged. They had already seen houses and buildings of various shapes and sizes—some featured massive doors and high windows for creatures like elephants, giraffes, and buffaloes. In contrast, others were built to be subterranean accommodations for animals like snakes, weasels, and badgers. They'd seen buildings with pools, waterfalls for the hippos and flamingos, and homes with wide doors for animals like horses, cows, and warthogs.

This building looked to be a home for something sized from a gorilla to a tiger—maybe that's why the goat had been so skittish.

Parker chewed her bottom lip and looked at Quinn.

"Maybe we knock?" Quinn said.

"That goat said something about harm coming to us," Owen said. "Let's not just go around banging on doors inviting some rabid polar bear to open the door and have us for a tasty snack."

"Oh, come on, Owen. I mean, you do look the tastiest of all of us, though," Quinn said with a smirk and raised a hand to knock. However, before she could, the red door swung open.

A tan creature scurried out, almost knocking Aven to the ground. Owen let out a shriek. Everyone turned, expecting to see the beast behind them, snarling and lunging for them.

"I've been expecting visitors," a kind voice said. "The mice... well, they aren't good at keeping secrets, and when young humans show up, it's obvious where they'd be heading. I'm Droma, and you'd better get inside before anyone else sees you. It's not—"

"Safe," continued Parker. "We keep hearing that. We're sorry, but we don't know why we are here, either. A wizard gave us this compass and told us to let it guide us, and here we are."

"Come in then," Droma said, "although I'm worried you may be too late."

The children followed her inside, moving cautiously, avoiding the sewing equipment, weaving looms, spools of thread, fabric, and pieces of unfinished dresses, suits, and shirts that filled the space.

Parker thought she might be a llama or perhaps a camel but couldn't be certain since Droma was dressed in a beret, a raspberry-colored hat that was slightly askew, and a yellow shirt that seemed to be alive, patterns moving in the fabric as the light reflected on it. She couldn't recognize many of the items hanging from walls, ceiling beams, and furniture, as they were sized for all varieties of zumans. Part of the fun of looking around her home was figuring out which garment was to be worn by which species of animals.

Droma motioned for the children to sit, although the piles of clothing and fabric made deciding exactly where to sit a challenge.

"You must be starving," Droma said, locking the door behind her. "I'll prepare food for us. It's getting late, and you should stay here."

Parker exhaled in relief as she sat down in a massive pile of clothing that enveloped her in a soft hug. They'd spent the past day outside running across a filling seafloor, hiking through a forest, and running from an angry troll and a falling bridge. Now she was at a place with food, warmth, and a creature who seemed willing to help if she could.

Droma cut thick pieces of bread, laid out fresh cheeses, and sliced fresh tomatoes, cucumbers, watermelon, and other fruits for her guests.

Quinn waved off the food. Parker saw her hesitancy and directed Quinn's eyes to her gem that *wasn't* glowing, indicating it was probably okay for now.

"Are you a camel?" Aven asked between bites of watermelon. "I just can't see your hump—or your two humps under your clothes. Do you have two humps?"

"No, my dear. I'm a llama, actually, a cousin to the camel—but yes, all of us are part of the camelid family, and, well, those humps are where my camel cousins just let themselves go a bit... one too many sweet potatoes for them, if you understand."

"Droma the llama. That's easy to remember. It rhymes," Aven said as she gave Droma a thumbs-up sign.

"Would any of you like some tea?" the llama asked.

"No, thank you," Quinn replied.

Aven raised her hand. "I'd like to try tea, I think," she replied.

Quinn stared at her quizzically.

"I've never had tea," she said with a shrug. "But we have a tea ball from our grandmother, so…" Then Aven leaned down and made a poor attempt to whisper, "And it's enchanted, you know."

"Shhhh," Parker hissed at her sister.

"Hey, guys, since Grandma is magical, can I call her my fairy god-mother?" Aven asked aloud. "Get it? She's like a grandma but a magic one, so fairy godmother."

"Aven! Fine, fine. Take the tea ball, but less sharing with strangers. Just be careful with this." Parker reached into her hidden pockets, pulling out the leather purse and extracting the tea ball.

Aven grabbed it and began fiddling with the small metallic ball. It had small holes drilled into the metal and was cut into two perfect halves neatly fitting together and creating a hollow cavity to fill, with a chain at the top to hold to dip the ball into hot water. Droma handed Aven a tray containing a pot of hot water, a bowl of sugar cubes, and some loose tea, while the others quickly ate without saying much.

"I know your grandmother well," Droma said as she served the children. "A magnificent woman, powerful of spirit. She's one of the most amazing people I've ever known."

"What's this?" asked Riley in a squeaky voice as a bowl of dark brown pellets floated in the air.

"Ah, and you must be the invisible prince I've heard so much about. You, my boy, are in for an absolute treat, a true and absolute delicacy in Zuma," Droma answered, her voice filled with delight. "Why, it's dog food."

"Gross!" Aven called out. "Don't eat it, Riley. *Ewww*. Why would you serve us dog food?"

The llama began to laugh. "You humans think quite differently about your dogs. Zumans know dogs and other canines have the absolute sweetest teeth in the world. It's far superior to even the sweetest of sweet potatoes."

A handful of the kibble floated from the bowl and into Riley's mouth upon hearing the word sweet. The room paused, waiting for his reaction.

"Mmmmmmmm. Dog food!" came his reply as the boy began shoveling handful after handful into his mouth.

"Seems like the boy likes it," Droma replied as she winked at Aven. "We've got several more bags of dog food and dog treats, which are divine if you'd like to try them."

Aven shook her head. Riley paid them no mind, pouring dog food from the large bowl straight into his mouth. The crunching and chewing sounds made his sisters and Owen chuckle.

"They've come here already. I tried to tell them I couldn't help them, but they didn't believe me and smashed everything. They came chanting of the coming Incendio as if it were a celebration." She pointed to the back of the large room where a spinning wheel made of dark wood and held with silver metallic pieces sat mangled.

Droma stood and removed a large piece of fabric hanging over some painting. As she did, Parker could see it was a large mirror that reminded her of the one hanging in their library. Droma studied the frame until she found a small square with a green gem inside. She removed a quill from her pocket and touched its tip to the rock.

"I refused to help them—told them I wouldn't—and they made sure I could help no one, including you."

"Ravagers?" Quinn asked.

Droma nodded her head.

As she spoke, her quill hovered in front of the mirror and drew a series of illustrations, each as a panel detailing key moments. In each one, the quill drew hooded individuals, each with a quill bearing the dark eye of the Ravagers. They scripted bolts that destroyed garments and fabrics. Eventually, in the final panel, the quill depicted a scene revealing the destruction of the spinning wheel that now lay in pieces in the next room.

"Were we supposed to collect the spinning wheel?" asked Parker. "Is that one of the four ancient objects we need to save our brother from the invisibility curse?"

Droma raised her head and looked Parker in the eye. "I am the ancient object you seek. My family line is unbroken from the days before Zuma, long before there was an animal kingdom, and long before our kingdom was enchanted, allowing us to live this way. Ours is *The Story of the Traveler*—a story where the animals were suffering through drought and famine, and my ancestors set off on a journey. They returned to save the zumans and received the power of speech as a reward. From then on, we have lived in peaceful harmony with your people. Until recently."

"Aven," Parker whispered to her sister, who had taken the tea ball and filled the two halves with sugar cubes and was spinning the ball around her head. "Pay attention."

"How are you supposed to get the sugar out?" Aven asked.

"She's talking about one of those stories from the book. Right?" Owen asked Parker.

"Yes, my favorite stories are of the traveler."

Parker saw *The Story of the Traveler* yesterday when she'd touched her quill on the *Book of the Seven Ancient Stories*. Lady Julie had said Quinn was likely to be the traveler. The traveler set off to a strange place or land to help her people. The traveler must overcome the threats during the journey and prove their bravery. While they were tempted to remain once they've succeeded in the trip, the return created transformation.

"That's how all the Zuman creatures in your kingdom learned to speak?" Parker asked.

The llama nodded. "My ancestors returned to save us, and now we are blessed with the power to speak to you."

Parker had assumed magical rewards were simply stories, but seeing the kingdom and speaking to a distant relative of the traveler made all those hours she'd spent listening in the storarium feel even more worthwhile.

"There is a reason you are here," Droma continued. "Our family was the first—the ancient family—and has been an unbroken line since the beginning of the kingdom. I am this line. This is why you're here."

"But who came here, and why did they destroy your spinning wheel?" asked Parker. "Is the wheel ancient too?"

"I don't know who came here, but they knew. They knew the spinning wheel was how to create the ancient item. You need the ancient fabric to save your brother. This is what you seek. My family are the keepers of the ancient wool, but there's nothing to be done to create the cloth without the spinning wheel from your people to spin it. I'm sorry."

Why would the Ravagers want to destroy it? Didn't they require these items too?

"They sure look like whoever came here wanted to make sure no one else could get the item," Owen said as he surveyed the broken pieces strewn everywhere. What remained was either bent, mangled, or in shards.

"Surely, there's another spinning wheel. We have one at our home we could bring here," offered Quinn. "We could try and fix it."

"The wheel was a gift to our animals from our human neighbors—your people—when we first established our kingdom," she replied, unable to make eye contact. "The inscription reads, 'From ancient wool, the ancient circle will only spin.' I've tried everything, but they knew what they were doing when they came here. Nothing is even left to repair. I'm sorry."

Parker glanced over at Aven, who shoveled sugar cubes into her mouth from the bowl in front of her.

"I m-m-l-o-o-v-v-e m-u-g-a-r-r-r," murmured Aven through her entire mouth and chipmunk cheeks.

The bowl of sugar refilled and began to overflow right before Parker's eyes. Every few seconds, sugar cubes would duplicate, spilling out of the bowl onto the tray Droma had brought. Within moments, sugar cubes covered the entire tray.

"Aven, what did you do?" Quinn asked.

So many sugar cubes filled her mouth she couldn't speak. Instead, she mimed what had happened, holding the tea ball she'd filled with sugar cubes up out of the hot water pitcher. The sugar cubes stopped multiplying when she pulled the tea ball out of the water. Then she dunked the ball into the water. The sugar cubes returned to replicating.

The tea ball makes exact copies of anything inside.

"Woah," Parker gasped, reaching over to gather a handful of sugar cubes as more appeared in front of Aven.

Quinn took the chain from Aven's hand and removed the tea ball from the water, and the cubes stopped.

"The enchanted tea ball is a replicator," Quinn said.

Aven held up the overflowing tray of sugar, asking if the llama wanted any, but Droma politely refused.

"Is there anything left to try?" Parker asked Droma.

"No. Of course, you can stay as long as you'd like." Droma said. "I'm so sorry, but I can't help you any further without the spinning wheel."

Droma stood and gathered up the plates and trays from their dinner before disappearing into the next room.

"Sleep well, children."

Chapter Twenty

The Spinning Wheel

N-n-n-n-n-s-s-s-s-t-t-t! went the metallic buzzing sound.

N-n-n-n-n-s-s-s-s-t-t-t!

"Could somebody please turn that *down!*" Parker said groggily from the heap of fabric piled near the door.

"How about I turn it *up!*" Quinn snapped her fingers, and the volume rose as if a giant were drumming his fingers on the roof.

The children all sat up.

In the corner of the room where the mangled mess of dark wood and silver chunks of metal had sat now stood a spinning wheel whirling round and round.

"It's fixed?" Parker asked, hoping it wasn't a dream.

"Remember my doughnut device? This gave me an idea," said Quinn.

Droma raced out from her bedroom. "How in the world? You've done it."

"Aven figured out the tea ball," Quinn said with a smile. "I wondered if our tea ball, a little hot water, and a couple of the unbroken pieces could be enough to rebuild it, and sure enough, I was right."

"This was from tea?" Droma asked, confused.

"I didn't know exactly how to make a spinning wheel, but I improvised. I began to sort through the broken pieces and bits, looking for anything I could use, hunting for a wooden dowel and a metal spindle in a pile of broken junk."

The spinning wheel was beautiful.

"I kept duplicating anything I could find," she continued. "If you put just a shard of one broken piece, it will make a new unbroken copy, just as it was before it had been broken. It's wild. I had no idea how many things to make, but then I remembered a whirlpool, and once I understood how it worked, I kept trying various pegs and metal pieces until voilà."

She waved her hands in front of the new spinning wheel.

"And then it was a snap," she said again, pulling out her quill and touching it to her thumb, snapping her fingers to slow the wheel back down.

Her sisters and Owen raced over to her. "You did it!"

"Well, what are we waiting for then?" Droma said. "We've got some ancient fabric to make for your brother."

There was a knock at the door. Everyone froze.

"Children," Droma whispered. "Hide."

The children hid themselves under the piles of fabric while Droma pulled a curtain across the room, hiding the new spinning wheel.

The door creaked open. Parker only heard murmurs and muffled sounds from under piles of fabric and clothing.

"Well, you should tell them yourself," Droma shouted loud enough they could all hear her voice.

As they emerged from their fabric piles, they all saw a familiar face.

"Beau!" Aven called out. "You came back." She jumped up and let out a howl.

"No, no, it's utterly unnecessary, especially in light of my horrid behavior," Beau said. "I—I—I owe you an apology. I most certainly should not have left you here and cowered away as I did. I was afraid, and I simply did not behave like a goat of honor. I owe you my deepest sympathies."

The goat removed his hat and dropped to a single knee, showing the open hat as a peace offering to them.

"The laws of Zuma do offer an answer," Droma replied to the kneeling goat.

"Oh no, I was merely here to express my sympathies and be gone."

"This is not what the rules say, Beau," Droma said, grinning. "You are to accompany them until your debt is forgiven."

"But, Curator, they aren't from Zuma," the goat protested. "Surely this can't apply to four human children?"

"Five," Aven chimed in. "And since we are friends now, I'm calling you Beau. Or maybe B or perhaps BB. Do you like BB?"

"Children," Droma said, turning back to the Pennymores. "Seems like it might be nice to have a little help on this journey. Am I right?"

Aven began spinning around and let out another loud howl.

"Thank you for coming," Riley said as Beau wobbled slightly from the boy squeezing his legs with a hug. "I'd like you to stay."

The goat stammered, "Well, I am a goat of the law, and I am in your service until you forgive this disgraceful debt."

"Oh great," Owen whispered to Parker.

"Having him around is going to come in handy," Parker replied. "He knows things none of us do."

The Pennymores and Owen shared what they'd done since he'd left them with Droma while the llama quickly worked the spinning wheel, carefully threading a tiny bit of hair and fur from her wool coat and turning it into a fine thread winding around onto a wooden dowel. From there, the llama worked the loom in the adjacent room, weaving the beautiful wool thread back and forth until she'd created a perfect square of fabric, almost a yard on each side.

"Now for the best part," Droma said as she waved the tan square of fabric in front of the group. "Riley, please come here."

The boy made his way to the llama.

"I'm going to place this on your shoulders. Are you ready?"

"Yes," he said.

Ready for what?

In a blinding flash of light, sparks exploded off the fabric in purples, reds, oranges, pinks, whites, and blues. The girls, Owen, and the goat covered their eyes as the flashes popped and whirled all around. Droma enjoyed the moment until the sound stopped and the fabric remained draped over the shoulders of the invisible boy.

"Whoa," Aven said. "We need you to come to do this for the next Drain Day."

"Look at the fabric," commanded Quinn. The tan wool fabric square had become a beautiful collection of colors, weaving patterns that reflected the room's lights with stitched edges of gorgeous stars, moons, and animal patterns. Parker ran over to Droma and threw her arms around the llama, who grinned.

"Thank you," Aven whispered. "For everything."

They encircled Riley, his outline now visible under the ancient cloth. A rattling sound began to emanate from one of the piles of fabric. It grew louder. Wearing the material, Riley made his way to the pile, reached down, and pulled out the maroon bag.

The compass.

"It's telling you to go," Droma said. "Now that you've obtained the first item, it knows you must continue. And you must leave now, as magic with this strength may draw the eye of those you do not wish to follow you. But you must hurry."

Scratch. Scratch. Growl.

"Did anyone else hear that?" Quinn asked, staring at the door. "The scratching sound…"

A roar echoed from the street. Owen nervously nodded his head.

"You definitely all heard that," Quinn said, turning to pick up all their items while frantically looking at Droma.

"Tigers. Hunting. The tigers have now certainly found us!" Beau said.

"I thought you said all the animals here were the kind who wore pants and drank tea?" Aven asked as roars and scratches rattled the door.

"Yes, Madam Pennymore," Beau answered. "Animals here do wear pants and drink beverages. This does not mean they won't use their animal teeth and claws to do terrible things at times. Especially the tigers. We must hurry, children!"

"Take them out back, Beauregard," Droma said to the goat. "I'll hold them off as long as I can."

"Wait, I've got an idea," Quinn said. "Aven, bring me the tea ball and the sugar cubes. Droma, do you have any matches?"

"You must not burn down this house, Quinn Pennymore," Beau snapped. "Your parents would be ashamed of such a terrible houseguest."

As Droma handed her several long wooden sticks with a white coating on the ends, Quinn shook her head. "Don't worry," she said. "It's a little trick I think might scare them off."

Quinn took a sugar cube from the bowl and handed the rest to Parker, motioning her over to the covered window near the door.

"Parker, hold this, and when I tell you to, I want you to throw the entire bowl outside. But try to make sure the cubes get around the tigers. Make a circle around them."

"Do tigers like to eat sugar?" Parker asked.

"No, but they are afraid of fire," Quinn responded as she lit one of the matches and held it under the sugar cube, which burned with a low, blue flame. Then she dropped the burning sugar cube into the tea ball and closed it shut.

On cue, Quinn dunked the tea ball with the burning sugar cube inside into a nearby teacup, and the bowl of sugar cubes in Parker's hands burst into flame.

"Now, Parker," Quinn commanded. "Throw them around the tigers."

Parker pulled back the window and threw the entire burning bowl toward the pair of pacing, lumbering striped cats. They fell in a near-perfect circle around the cats.

"It's not working," Parker called, looking at the cats as they bent their heads to sniff the tiny burning cubes.

"Wait for it," Quinn said, spinning the tea ball faster and faster in the cup. Parker watched as the cubes began to multiply while Quinn spun the tea ball, the burning sugar cubes popping and jumping as the flames rapidly grew higher and higher until blue flames surrounded the tigers.

The tigers winced and recoiled from the flaming walls surrounding them.

"Quinn Pennymore, today you are my most favorite of the Pennymores," Beau exclaimed before looking at the others. "Just for today, mind you. Now, we must flee before others follow. Madam Curator, we are in your debt."

"Sorry about the mess, Droma," Quinn said quickly, following the goat. "But the pleasure has certainly been all ours!"

Parker removed the cloth from her brother's shoulders, placing it with the other magic items in the leather purse. They didn't need to draw further attention to their group with a beautiful, floating cloth in their party.

Beau pushed the Pennymore children out the door, past the growling tigers. "This way, children," he called as they raced through the streets. "Do have a warm and toasty day, tigers!"

As Parker hurried past the trapped tigers, she saw a spot where the fur looked discolored and different. Someone had made a dark etching on the tiger.

The Ravagers had found them.

Chapter Twenty-One

The Literati Library

"It's a shame, but I haven't the slightest clue where this compass wants us to travel, Lady Pennymores, Prince Pennymore, and you," Beau said as they walked in the midmorning sun.

"'You'? What is that goat's problem with me?" Owen whispered to Parker. "Just you? I have a name, ya know."

"Maybe he's jealous of the way you dress."

"Hey, what's wrong with the way I dress?" Owen said, surveying his own clothes before looking at the well-dressed goat.

"I saw something as we were leaving," Parker whispered. "I think I know why the tigers tried to attack us."

"Like what?"

"They had black etchings with the eye in the feather," she said, "the etchings of the Ravagers… like it had been burned into their fur. Someone must have sent them or led them to us. It's like what you found at the canyon bridge."

"But who?"

"I still don't know. But we need to find out, and fast."

The group hurried ahead, following the route of the compass. A good night's sleep, the first of the ancient items, and a new traveling companion had helped the children immensely. Beau treated this job as their guide and steward with absolute professionalism. As they'd left

Zuma, he'd purchased a cluster of carrots, a few pullover sweaters for the cool evenings, several loaves of bread, freshly baked cookies, and materials for making a fire from a lion wearing a suit. He'd also gathered several bags of dog food and dog treats, much to Aven's chagrin and Riley's delight.

It wasn't hard to be in a better mood when cookies were involved.

He was very particular that they must stay away from the open areas and insisted on referring to them as Lady, Madam, and Prince Pennymore.

"*Lady Pennymore*?" Aven said, mocking his tone. "Does he think we drink tea with our pinky fingers sticking up?" She held her pinky up, mocking a formal tea drinker.

"Your interest in tea did lead us to the first item," Quinn said.

Beau knew more about the area's history than any of the children. "Madam Parker, perhaps a dozen places beginning with B lie between the Grootten Mountains and the water's edge," he said, referring to the *B* that had replaced the *Z* on the compass.

"But are any of them ancient?" Parker asked. "Places with ancient items from around the time when the *Book of the Seven Ancient Stories* was originally written?"

"If it's ancient, magical, and mystical you're after," he said, lowering his voice and eyeing the others, "you may not like the places I know that begin with a B. There's the Bone Keep. I know of Burnside. And certainly, the demon people have called their home Blade Hollow. Maybe we get lucky, and it's Baskerville. The dwarfs are certainly a rowdy bunch, but I'd much rather take my chances with them than Bones or Blades or any place called Burnside.

"I must warn you, Pennymores," Beau said as they neared a clearing in their forest path. "What you'll see ahead is disturbing, but there's no other way forward. I recommend you keep your eyes facing forward, as I cannot say for certain what you'll see otherwise."

Parker walked near the goat as they entered the hollow, trying to keep her eyes forward but unable to resist the temptation to look.

To the left of the path was the charred footprint of a large building. The stone foundation was still visible, but stones were scattered and knocked over, and dark ashes blanketed the entire space. She looked closer, seeing scraps of white sprinkled throughout the ash.

"Is it paper?" she asked the goat in a whisper.

"Madam Parker," he replied. "I urge you to avert your eyes."

Laying askew on the ground was a dark-colored flat piece of rock. On it was letters and numbers written in white chalk, identical to what she'd seen in Zuma.

That was a chalkboard. The burned building was another library.

"Beau," Parker said with a hush. "I know what this is—a library like what I saw in Zuma. I saw the chalkboard. Did someone burn it down?"

"I didn't want to worry you," Beau said, his voice low. "It's not simply any library. It was a literati library, a hidden magic writing home for Serifs and one of the last few in Fonde. Someone must have discovered its Ellipse, as it was hidden for a long time, but someone who knew told the Illiterates. We know this for certain. And…" He trailed off, unwilling to say more.

"And what?" Parker urged. *What had happened to the children? Did they escape? Were they too terrified and hiding? I understand how they must have felt.*

The goat looked at her before deciding to speak. "I know fire plays an important role in your family's past."

That's what the book I found in the library—the one with the missing pages—had said too.

"You… you were in Everly," Parker said. "I saw you. I saw you… being a goat. Why were you there?"

The goat paused as if thinking what to say next. "Creatures like me must stay hidden, and so yes, we do change to fit our surroundings," he said, running his hand over his clothing. "We were sent there by others who want to keep *you* safe. There are more creatures, magical ones, who are watching and protecting you, even now. Yours is a family of great importance in Fonde, Madam Parker. We knew this day would come."

"You knew?"

"We suspected but did not know when. And so, we've been watching… to keep you and your siblings safe. You are simply a most clever one. Most humans would never realize a boring old goat eating clovers could be more… sophisticated."

Parker smiled. "The mother rabbit said the small bunny had the silent tongue. Was that from the Ravagers?" Parker asked, changing the subject.

The billy goat inhaled. "I'd suspect yes. We don't know for sure, but that is certainly what it appears."

"You said Zuma went into hiding. Is that because of the Ravagers?"

"It's because of many things, child. The Ravagers seek our support to bring magic creatures out from the shadows again, while the Illiterates seek to harm those magical creatures that are not hidden. We are not all magic writers, Zumans, but we began to see our kind attacked, taken, murdered. It was more than we'd seen in thousands of years. We fear this darkness will return to the chaos before the seven ancient stories. I have heard whispers this is the beginning of *The Story of the Defeat*."

"How can that be?"

"Your brother was kidnapped, and the rise of these attacks—they are most certainly related. More and more creatures are on the side of Master Dagamar. Invisibility is dark magic, and its return is something we must not let happen. There are rumors of the return of death's clutches, the Silent Darkness brought by the Ravagers."

A chill raced over her body. She and Quinn had seen the magical incantation and inscription that spoke of death's clutches leading them to seek out Lazlo and flee the kingdom to save Riley. "Is that why you ran away earlier?" she asked the goat.

He stopped walking and looked at her. "It is why I came back."

They continued in silence.

"I'm getting tired. Do you think we could rest for a little while?" Riley asked as the sun beat down on the group.

"We shouldn't," Quinn said, checking the horizon, partially covering her eyes with her hand. "The compass is pointing ahead, and we should follow it until it's dark. We have matches to build a fire if we need to camp for the night. We can rest then."

"You're right," Riley said. "I'm just not used to walking so much. I spent my time sitting in a tower."

Quinn frowned. "Here," she said to Riley. Quinn put one leg back and knelt into a lunge. "Hop on my back. I'll carry you along. We don't need the measuring cup for now."

The older children took turns carrying Riley. Beau was kind enough to carry Aven despite her multiple attempts to scare him with well-timed growls and barks, something the goat was never quite prepared for.

By early afternoon they'd been on an upward climb for nearly an hour until reaching a ridge. Quinn continued to check the compass. At the bottom of the hill, about a mile down, was a clearing that opened to a massive river.

Beau pointed to the horizon. "We'll need to go to the river and find our way across."

"How do we cross?" Parker asked.

"I'm a great swimmer," Aven replied. She looked at Beau. "All wolves are."

Beau shook his head and made a *tsk, tsk* sound as he thought. "No. No. It would be much too dangerous. I know this river, the Pediment River, and it's known for its strength and its unforgiving current never slowing until it reaches the sea."

"But we can all swim," Aven offered. "Well, maybe not Riley."

"If we swim, we'll surely drown," Beau answered. "The Pediment is deep, and the water is much too forceful today. We'll have to find another way across. Perhaps there is another point upstream to cross." He seemed confident in the selection, and their earlier experiences with water made them hesitant to try and make it across on their own.

Quinn eyed the compass. "Come, we need to be quick," she yelled.

The terrain began to change, and soon they spotted a wider river area with flat landings on each side. And a boat.

As they got closer, Parker saw a boy, who must have been about her age, asleep inside the boat.

"Excuse me," Quinn said as they inched closer to the boy sleeping in the boat.

He jerked and scrambled to his feet when Quinn spoke, his hat hanging low enough his expression wasn't visible.

"Oh. Oh. I'm sorry," he stammered. "My father was supposed to be back and—"

"We are looking for safe passage," Beau said in a calm voice.

The boy stared at him and then looked back at Quinn. "Did a goat just talk?"

"Yes, it's—well, it's a very long story," she replied. "We are hoping you could ferry us across the water."

"We could pay," Owen added.

The boy pondered the offer. "Pay? I like the sound of that. The name's Alan. Alan Nerudit." He held out his hand, his red, curly hair pouring out from under his hat. "And I'll ferry you across, but you'll each need to paddle as it's too strong for only me. Hop on board and grab an oar."

Parker sized up Alan, aware they were putting their lives in his hands, and tried to motion to Owen to do the same.

Everyone loaded into the boat and was handed an oar to paddle.

"What in Grootten is going on?" Alan yelled.

The children turned to see an oar floating in midair. Riley had picked up an oar, and Alan stood horrified.

"My dearest boy," Beau said. "It's neither trick nor magic. But an invisible boy we have set out to save."

"I'm Riley," his voice called out. "I can row too."

Alan muttered, holding the oar up to defend himself. "An invisible boy and a talking goat?"

"He's an invisible *prince*," Beau corrected. "You, my maritime guide, are in the presence of royalty."

Parker glared at Beau. "No, we're not real princesses or royal," she responded. "Just looking to cross."

"We just need your help," Quinn said. "Could you just take us across, please? We'll be gone before you know it."

The boy rubbed his hand over his face and stepped past Parker to the back of the boat.

"Fine. Let's go," he gruffly said. "Each of you start rowing quickly upstream, as the current gets much faster if we float too far down the river."

Alan's red curls blew behind him as he pushed the boat off the riverbed and hopped in. The wind and rocking waves beat and swayed the ship.

"Stroke! Stroke!" Alan instructed.

They obeyed their captain as he hollered above the blustery wind to get everyone rowing on the same beat.

They made some headway, tearing their oars into the aggressive water reaching the middle of the river. There, the current was more potent, shoving the boat downstream.

"I need you all to paddle. Push the water," Alan yelled. The boat wrestled the current.

Parker panted as she paddled, the familiar red-orange glow emanating from her necklace.

"Parker, your necklace is glowing again," Owen called to her.

She reached down to touch it, calling out, "Everyone! We're in danger—the river—we've got to row faster."

She turned to look to Alan for reassurance or instruction.

"What are you doing?" she screamed.

Alan had his arm bent across his chest, and a knife in his other hand pointed just above his elbow. On the back of his hand, she saw four dots.

Alan was an Illiterate.

"No one stop rowing," Alan called. "Anyone misses a stroke, and he dies. Then you all die."

"Don't hurt Riley," Parker said. "You don't want to do this."

Alan grinned. The gem pulsed faster on Parker's chain.

"Why? Why are you doing this?" she asked.

"A prince fetches a high price—especially one who is invisible thanks to some magic writer," he said with a chuckle. "And a talking goat. Your kind isn't meant for these parts. My father is an Illiterate, and when he's back, he'll help me take all of you to the highest bidder. This crossing is going to be valuable for our family." He squeezed his arm to his chest, shaking and trying to choke their brother. "Now keep rowing," he called.

"What do we do?" Owen whispered to Beau in the front of the boat.

"I'm sorry, but I don't have the faintest idea."

"Now, hang on, everybody," Alan said. "Time to shift our angle. Watch the water!"

Parker saw a wave heading straight for them.

"We're going to aim for that wave," Alan said.

"Are you crazy?" Quinn shouted. "It will swallow us up."

"It might swallow *you* up in the front of the boat, but it's the cost of getting across."

Parker had read about maintaining a course and used her oar to create a zigzag in the water. "This is how we'll move," she shouted. "It will lessen the impact and give us enough control to keep our direction."

The wave was inches away. "Okay, everyone, to the right, hard left," Parker called out. "Again!"

The gem continued to pulse.

The others followed her orders. The boat shook, lifting Aven from her seat and dropping her back on the wooden bench.

"Ouch!" Aven said, rubbing her head.

"You're a better crew than I'd expected," called Alan. "Too bad we couldn't take another ride."

They continued to zigzag, approaching the wave at a sharp angle and riding over. Beau placed a hoof on Aven's leg to keep her seated as they topped the wave.

"Only a few more strokes," Alan called. "Then we'll wait. Now grab the rope."

Parker looked back to see Alan loosen his grip on Riley's neck and push what looked like Riley's shoulder down to the seat. Alan still clutched the knife. He lifted a foot and slammed it on the bench, presumably to pin Riley's leg down while reaching for the rutter stick behind him.

"Stay," he hissed.

Then something caught Parker's eye upriver, and she turned to see it.

"Wave!" she shouted. "Hold on!"

A ten-foot wall of water raced to their boat, and everyone grabbed whatever they could find to hang on.

Water poured over them, drenching the boat.

Alan and his knife were flung over the side of the boat, bobbing downstream.

"Wait, no—" he called out, as the water spun him further downstream until he was only a speck.

The water around the boat was calm, the current slowly guiding the ship to the shore, its bow settling into the soft, silty soil.

"Are you all right?" Parker raced to where Riley was pinned down by Alan's foot.

"I'm here," Riley said. "I'm okay. That was scary."

Parker reached for her gem, seeing it no longer glowed.

"Lady Pennymores," Beau said, raising his voice. "Are you all right?"

They all nodded.

"But what was that?" asked Quinn. "How did the water—why did the water do that?"

"It wasn't you?" Parker asked, still holding her brother.

"No, I couldn't do that."

"We don't have time to figure out the seasons of the river," Beau announced. "We need to leave this boat before his father returns. If he's anything like that nasty child, I don't think we want to be around to meet him."

They departed the boat, pulled it further onto shore, and tied the rope to a tree.

Alan's hat was still in the boat, but Parker had no idea what had become of the boy.

Chapter Twenty-Two

Houses of Bask

The children and their billy goat guide were wet, cold, and shaken. It was early evening now. They'd traveled almost all day, and still, the compass pointed them to **B**.

The terrain was rougher on this side of the river. It was a dry, dusty space with large boulders pocking the landscape where much less vegetation grew.

They knew the threat from the Illiterates followed them, and Alan and his father could find them and bring others. Parker watched Beau talking to himself, realizing he was talking to Riley. She wondered what they were saying.

Beau walked closer to her. "I think your little brother needs his big sister right now."

Parker made her way over to Riley. "Can I hold your hand while we walk?"

The boy took his sister's hand. "If I die, will I go to heaven?"

Parker gripped his hand tighter and then put her arm around her brother and pulled him into her body, feeling Riley shiver.

"Sometimes I worry it's something grown-ups make up so we don't feel so scared. Riley, listen to me," Parker said in a soft voice. "We are going to make this all go away. And we'll do it together. And then, we'll go home, and it'll be like it was before—better than before."

Riley squeezed Parker's hand three times. It was something the Penny-mores had done throughout their childhoods. "I. Love. You." One squeeze for each word.

"And all the cinnamon pulls you can eat."

Parker saw Beau look back at her and mouthed "thank you" to the goat.

Beau nodded and spoke loudly, "Given all that has transpired today and the late hour upon us, perhaps we find shelter. I have materials for fire and—"

"I can go find some wood," Owen offered.

"We have one," Quinn answered him sharply. "We have one of the ancient items. One. How can we stop now? There isn't time. We have until the waning moon, the waning moon, and that's it. We have to keep going."

"But I'm tired," called Aven.

"I'm cold," Riley said.

"Maybe a rest will—" Parker stopped. She'd been holding the compass since they'd crossed the river, but the arrow was no longer pointing straight ahead. She turned, following where it led.

"Oh wow," Parker called out, holding the compass in front of her. "Look!"

"Why is it spinning?" Aven asked, her head trying to track its jerky motions.

"This is most certainly a wonderful sign," Beau said. "Or a terrible one." He looked over at Parker, who he'd discussed the various B named places they could find themselves seeking. "I think we are here."

"But where is here?" Parker asked. "Nothing is here."

They looked around their surroundings and saw only mounds of rocks and boulders littering the area, creating small caves and blocking the view of the horizon.

"Could this be another hidden place, Beau?" Owen asked. "Like Zuma was?"

"I'm afraid I simply don't know," Beau replied. "This looks like absolutely nothing if I'm being my most honest self, but as you'll see, an Ellipse can be truly anything, which is quite actually the point, you see."

"How does an Ellipse work?" Owen asked.

"Think of it as a book," Beau said. "If you turn a closed book on its side and look at the stack of pages in it, the book appears solid with no way inside it. But you, of course, know the book is not a solid mass, but with a delicate thumbing, you can enter into it. That's an Ellipse. To most, it's a solid mass, but to the trained eye, it's entering a magical world."

"I still can't believe people are afraid of a book," Owen said. "Maybe they just don't know what they are missing—like my parents."

"There's gotta be something more than we're seeing. There has to be," Quinn said. "Everything is evident after the fact. The chain of mice looked like just a bunch of mice. The tree looked like a tree, and Alan looked like a nice boy."

"He looked like a brat, actually," Aven said. "What should we look for? What should I sniff for?"

Parker took a seat to think. She held the compass in her hand and watched as the needle jerked around and around.

Where is it trying to lead us?

She looked all around her and found herself idly spinning the compass in between her fingers. She was holding the edges of the circular compass upright between her thumb and middle finger, spinning it around and around, watching as the light of the compass face cast an eerie illuminated glow around and around, flashing in her eyes with each turn.

She squeezed her thumb and middle finger, stopping the rotation. She slowly rotated the compass face to her and smiled. "Guys! Come see this!" Parker shouted. They rushed over to her, and Parker slowly turned the compass until the B was right above her thumb toward the ground.

There it was.

"Down!" shouted Quinn. "The compass is pointing down!"

"Oh, dear me," uttered Beau as a realization rushed over him. "This. Oh, yes, this is most certainly it then. The compass has brought us to Baskerville or Bone Hollow, but I'm almost certain it's Baskerville. Nearly. Oh, dear me, yes."

"Baskerville?" asked Quinn.

Beau looked at Parker. "Dwarfs? Yes, we are here to find a dwarf. I am certain."

He pointed to a small rock about two feet high. A detailed carving was on it—an arrow pointing down. "Well, hello there," Beau said to the rock. "This must be our welcome."

"You know a dwarf?" Parker asked.

"Well, don't we all?" Beau replied with a shrug. "I didn't say I knew the dwarf *well*, but I'd say we are friendly. As friendly as dwarfs can be. You see, dwarfs are quite dreadfully rude, simply awful. Worse than a walrus, but slightly better than a rhino, which as you'll see are despicable and smell nearly as bad."

"Rhinos smell worse than sea lions?" Quinn asked.

"Oh, much worse."

"Are dwarfs like in the stories?" Parker asked. "Dwarfs and elves, are they the same?"

"The same? Oh dear," the goat said with utter shock. "My dear, saying a dwarf and an elf are the same is like saying a goat and sheep are the same. It's like saying a horse and a zebra are the same. If you ever said such a thing to a dwarf or an elf, well, they'd most certainly be offended and never speak to you ever again, which is a long time since dwarfs and elves live hundreds of years."

"But we're going underground?" Quinn asked. "Dwarfs and elves both live underground in caves or caverns. Right? We always heard they were miners and builders, but dwarfs are only this tall," she said as she held her hand two feet from the ground."

"Finally, a girl with some sense. Thank you, Madam Quinn," he continued. "Why yes, the dwarfs are simply spectacular builders and inventors. I'm quite sure you'll feel right at home in Baskerville. The dwarfs and animals have long been friendly with one another, and the dwarfs have given us some of their greatest inventions to make our lives in Zuma a bit more exciting."

"Does your dwarf have a name?" Quinn asked.

"Oh yes. Bralwynn Bronkuhk," he replied. "She's quite remarkable. Her skills with vegetable husbandry are simply unbelievable."

"Husbandry?" Aven asked.

"Oh, why yes," Beau continued. "Husbandry, her ability to raise and care and grow plants of all types, are simply unbelievable. She says she can hear them and they can hear her, which seems hard to believe, but it's quite remarkable. Her work has helped feed an entire civilization of dwarfs for centuries with only those tufts of weeds and grasses visible to the naked eye." He pointed to the few clusters of plants, each with a dozen or fewer grasslike stalks.

"Underground?" Quinn asked.

"Oh, wait until you see it," Beau said affectionately. "It's unexplainable what dwarfs can accomplish. You, humans, have simply missed out on all of their splendor because you've been too busy trying to stop any creature from holding a quill in her hands.

"Now, I must warn you," the goat continued. "Bralwynn is an exception, as she is a ray of sunshine, but the rest of the dwarfs are no-o-o-o-thing like what you probably heard in your stories. I'm sorry to say. Pure propaganda is what that is, letting kids believe those angry dwarfs are whistling while they work. Well, dwarfs are simply unpleasant, rude, and obstinate. They do not listen. At. All."

"We know a bit about that," Quinn replied, motioning to Aven, who was chasing around the stick her invisible brother was waving.

"Are you certain you don't have some dwarf blood in you?" Beau asked Owen.

"Me? No, of course not. Just two normal human parents. Do I look like a dwarf to you? I'm, like, way bigger than two feet tall." Owen leaned over to Parker. "Is he saying I'm rude like a dwarf or something?"

"You and Beau need to put your differences aside," she said as she raised her eyebrows. "I'm on 'team staying out of it.'"

"Just one thing, children. It's going to be impossible for us to visit," Beau said. "Dwarfs are much smaller than us. You could scarcely get your foot in Baskerville. Perhaps we could wedge your brother in, but I suspect he'd get stuck as soon as we got his waist inside."

"I've got an idea," Parker said. "Would it be unusual for them to see a two-foot-tall goat?"

Parker hadn't quite mastered using the enchanted measuring cup to make something a particular size. Aven and Riley had created a giant pillow, and Parker and Quinn had shrunk Aven and Riley to a couple of inches high, but it had taken about a dozen minor corrections to get their siblings back to their original height. Shrinking seemed a bit more of an art to Parker. Too small, and they could fall into an anthill. Too big, and they wouldn't fit into Baskerville.

"Tell me when," Parker instructed Beau, relying on his experience with the proper dwarf-like height as she held the cup over his head.

"This sounds like a b-a-a-a-d ide-a-a-a-a-a." The goat began to shrink. "Now!" Beau squeaked frantically, waving his hooves to get Parker to remove the measuring cup over his head.

"Okay," Parker said. "This is a dwarf goat. I think I can work with this."

She shrank each of her sisters and Owen down to similar sizes. She saved Riley for last because he would need Quinn to keep her hand on Riley's head until he was the right size. And once everyone had been dwarfed, Parker held the cup over her own head and felt a warm, pulling sensation, as if someone had clipped a clothespin on her hips and gently pulled her outward as her body shrunk downward.

"That was not what I was expecting," she remarked, shifting and stretching her new body. "Okay, now how do we get in?"

"You simply ring the bell," Beau answered without a hint of irony.

"The bell?" Parker replied.

"Yes, we find bell six—which is the address, of course—and we'll ring the bell. It's simply not the least bit complicated. This is a one on the scale of difficult Ellipses."

"How high does the scale go?" Aven asked.

"Well, I've never thought about that question," Beau answered. "Let's just say quite high."

The Pennymores looked at one another and let their goat friend walk over to the rock with the arrow. He leaned in closer, looking for something in or around the arrow carved into the rock. "Ah, here it is." Beau pointed to a barely visible carving into the stone.

BELL 6

Once he found what he was looking for, he took his hoof and drew a circle, and a melodic note grew louder and louder.

"Quick, over here," he called to them. "This is another Ellipse and quite a delightful one, I must add."

Whoosh.

In an instant, they were tumbling on top of one another through a series of pipes, taking each member of their traveling party and separating them into an appropriate tube. Then they'd looped around and around for at least a minute before being spat out from their five individual tubes to land on a colorful array of pillows.

"This should be part of version two of the cask-carriage," Parker said to Quinn.

"Definitely. I'm taking a mental picture."

Parker's eyes adjusted to the dim light underground.

"This is Baskerville?" Quinn asked.

"I think so," Parker said, motioning to a huge sign glowing on the rock wall to their left:

"Seems friendly," Owen said. "I'm surprised they don't have more visitors."

"Are you guys seeing this?" Quinn said, her voice cracking. "This place is incredible. Parker, it's like we got to do everything we wanted in the tunnels under the castle. Except, like, a million times better."

"It's like a real life hamster maze," Parker said. "Did you guys know we once built a series of tubes to let a family of hamsters run freely throughout the outdoor barn? That way, they couldn't run away or get chased by our barn cat."

"You trap this family of hamsters in a maze for your entertainment?" Beau exclaimed. "Unacceptable, Madam Parker. Simply unacceptable."

Realizing how offensive this might sound to a well-dressed goat, she clarified, "It's a luxury maze with exercise equipment and some wonderful spaces."

"Still on 'team staying out of it,' huh?" Owen whispered to her.

But the analogy was entirely appropriate. When Parker had thought of underground caves filled with dwarfs, she assumed simple caves and tunnels built into hills. These walls were smooth, and perfectly spaced braces lined the insides to prevent collapses or falling debris. There wasn't a single spec of dirt anywhere or any wasted space.

"All this hidden under some rocky field," Quinn said to no one in particular, pulling her goggles down over her eyes. "Someone here knows what they are doing."

"I think you'll get along quite well here," Beau said.

Parker stared in wonder at the complex systems, machinery, and technology operating entirely underground. Quinn was right. This was a million times better than the tunnels under the castle. Motorized sidewalks and varieties of multi-wheeled contraptions dwarfs rode in. Clear pipes filled with fireflies ran throughout the tunnel to keep it well-lit. Water was gathered in drains and piped to holding tanks for drinking. The tunnels had extensive underground planting and farming sections where root vegetables were cultivated and sucked from the surface into the tunnels when they were ripe.

"Those planting and farming tunnels up there," Beau said, pointing to the watering systems and lighting woven into the tunnels, "are all the work of Bralwynn."

Parker studied the detailed written instructions, signs, rules, and messages placed in every wall, intersection, window, and corner. The signs instructed how many steps per minute you could take, permitted jumping but banned skipping, and arrows pointed in all directions guiding them toward the critical aspects of Baskerville from the libraries, the reserve, the stores, and even a fire department and hospital.

"Why is everyone unhappy?" Aven asked.

"And mean?" Owen added.

Almost every dwarf walked past glared at them with a deep-set frown, and in the few minutes since they'd arrived, dwarfs had engaged in heated yelling matches over seemingly trivial things.

"This hat is blue!"

"No, it's turquoise!"

"You fool, it's blue-green!"

These fights would often escalate to someone throwing their oddly-colored hats or commencing a full-out kicking and screaming temper tantrum. The Pennymores had undoubtedly heard of a grumpy dwarf or two in their stories, but it seemed like every dwarf was grumpy.

Beau lowered his voice. "Dwarfs are never the most positive of creatures, but this place is perhaps the worst of the worst. You see, two brothers have ruled Baskerville for two hundred years. And for the last one hundred and eighty years years, the brothers have not spoken."

"How is that possible?" Quinn asked. "This place is incredible. How could they create such a place with two rulers who don't speak?"

"It's quite the conundrum," Beau agreed. "And what's more befuddling is neither brother remembers what the argument was about. They simply refuse to talk, operating in a perpetual state of brotherly silent treatments."

Inside Baskerville, the compass behaved much less erratically. Parker guided the group using it in three dimensions, navigating tunnels up, down, left, right, forward, and back. Baskerville would have been impossible to navigate without the compass despite each tunnel, corner, staircase, and ramp labeled with extensive signage, arrows, and distances.

"Beauregard?" a woman's voice called out from one of the alley-tunnels. The group paused, trying to find where the voice had come from.

"Why yes, I do declare," Beau responded.

Hurrying out of the alley was the first dwarf they'd seen who wasn't frowning. She wasn't smiling, but her neutral expression was a welcome change. She was round, her orange dress reaching to the floor, with plants and flowers bursting from the dozens of small pockets littered throughout it. On her head was a wide-brimmed hat with at least two feet of the most exquisite flowers perched on top.

"Are her flowers moving?" Owen asked, unable to take his eyes off the hat. The flowers constantly rearranged themselves on her head, moving in unison, braiding into ornate patterns, organizing into colors and shapes. "Tell me it's not just me seeing this. I think they are smiling. Can flowers smile?"

"I think this flower waved at me," Aven said. "Guys, did the little flower in her hat wave at me?"

"Bralwynn, this is a delightful surprise," said Beau.

"You," she said, squinting at the goat, "got short, I think?"

The goat laughed and introduced his friend to the children.

"My absolute pleasure," the dwarf said. "And these are my children." She raised her hands to point to the flowers in the hat on her head. As she did, her flowers each gracefully bowed to the children.

"Nice to meet you too," Aven replied.

"Well, children, that was quite a formal greeting of you," Bralwynn said. "They usually don't meet many celebrities down here in the tunnels," she whispered to Beau.

"Don't touch," Parker chided as Aven stepped closer to the dwarf and attempted to pick one of the smiling flowers off her hat. "You too," she added to Owen, who leaned in to smell one.

"We are grateful to have found you," Beau continued. "We are seeking an ancient item and have been told it resides here in Baskerville. Might you know where the compass is leading us?"

Bralwynn's face contorted to mirror all the other dwarfs. "You're not going to like where you're heading. If you are to find an ancient item residing here, it will be in the hands of the brothers of Bask."

"Oh, dear my, this is terrible," said Beau, turning to the elder Pennymores.

"The brothers of Bask?" Quinn repeated. "Why is it so bad?"

"These are the rulers of Baskerville I had mentioned to you. They are not ones to collaborate, and if you seek an ancient item, you'll need them to speak to one another, and that's something they have refused to do for two centuries, it seems."

"I can get you in to see them," offered Bralwynn with a shrug. "Both the brothers love my squash, and my radishes, my muskmelon too, come to think of it. They have never complained about a single fruit or vegetable I've provided them. But once you get inside, it's entirely up to you."

"I'm getting hungry," came the voice of their always ready-to-eat brother. "Flower lady, do you have anything I can eat?"

"You must be the invisible boy your siblings seek to save, and you're most certainly in luck. I've been making something you may find an absolute pleasure," the dwarf replied. "I'm not sure there's enough for all of you, but I have a freshly made pea, lima bean, and turnip shake."

"Those are all vegetables, not good ones, either. That's disgusting," Aven blurted out, the mere mention of a shake made from her three least favorite vegetables causing her to contort her face as if she were in pain. "No, thank you. We'll pass."

Bralwynn ignored her and quickly scurried inside, returning with a mug of a thick greenish liquid with more colorful chunks floating on the top. Parker had to admit that it didn't look like something she'd ever want to drink. But their brother took the mug from her and hungrily gulped down the entire concoction.

"It's better than the dog food," he exclaimed, a greenish smear from the frosty lima bean shake floating in the air.

"Why, the boy has great taste," Bralwynn said to Beau. "But we should hurry."

The party followed Bralwynn, since they no longer needed the compass to guide them. She led them to a section of Baskerville featuring ornately carved signs advertising the services inside each: from the bars and restaurants where dwarfs were busily eating and drinking to stores selling shoes, clothing, quills, and books to open areas where it seemed debates and arguments were settled by a judge in some type of courtroom. Further on, they came to a series of learning or library rooms filled with young-looking dwarfs who hung from the ceiling using quills to write upside down. The teacher held a long stick and would gently hit their hands when their words began to get the tiniest bit diagonal.

"Why are they hanging like that?" Parker asked Brawlynn as she watched some of their quills glowing and sparking as the magic writers scripted on a chalkboard. "Are they writing upside down?"

"Ah, you never know when you'll need to write," the dwarf replied. "Scripting can be needed at any time, Parker. Anytime indeed. Imagine you're in a cave or in the sky or underwater, which I have to tell you is truly memorable. You can never be too certain where you'll need to write perfect characters, you see, and our libraries are simply known for perfect quillmanship."

Parker watched a group of dwarf children playing a game in the small gymnasium in the next room. In the middle of the room, dozens of quills hovered like she'd seen in their hidden library while children lined up with their backs against the walls directly across from one another, each child holding a small piece of wood carved into a Y shape.

"What are they doing in there?" Parker asked, pointing to the small, open gymnasium.

"Haberdash," Beau replied, his face contorted in surprise.

"Haber—what?" Owen asked.

The goat shook his head. "My boy, have you never played Haberdash? Every child must have played Haberdash in the library yard. No wonder you seem a bit sad. It's the way children bond and build skills for life." He looked down the row of children who each shook their heads. "And you, Pennymores? Have none of you ever played Haberdash, either? What an absolute shame, a disaster of the highest order. What kind of punishment are they inflicting upon you humans?"

"Dash!" yelled the teacher, organizing the game. On his signal, the dwarf children sprinted toward hovering quills from each side of the gym. They each attempted to grab one of the quills as the quills tried to avoid capture, reminding Parker of her own experiences the first night in the magical library. These quills seemed even more naughty, dipping, diving, and moving sporadically to make grabbing one a challenge. After a few moments, children began to capture quills in their hands.

"These teams are wearing blue and green Haberdash uniforms," Beau said. "Which means it's a game of legends and poets on the pad today."

The pad was a rectangular-shaped court with a line in the middle separating each side. Parker could tell that neither team was allowed to set foot on the other side of the pad, even if a quill had floated there. As children gathered a quill, its tip turned the color of their uniform, blue or green, and they'd sprint back to their side. Many children touched their quills to their fingernails and flew up and around after the dancing quills.

"Wonderful scrawl, boy," Beau called out. "Wonderful!"

One of the poets, a boy about Aven's age wearing floor-length green robes a size too large for him, placed his glowing green quill into a sling-shot, the small piece of wood carved into the shape of a Y she'd seen earlier. Then the boy pulled a strap toward himself and launched the glowing quill from one corner of the court to the opposite end, striking a girl who had momentarily turned her back to him. A green spot exploded on her back, covering her clothing with thick ink.

The boy jumped and yelled, "Haberdash." He pointed to the teacher, who raised his hand, signaling the direct hit. The quill he'd fired toward the girl then fell to the ground, and another girl on the legends' team standing nearby picked it up. As she placed it in her slingshot, the tip turned blue. The girl with the green ink spot on her back turned and left the pad, shaking her head and sitting next to her teacher.

Haberdash looks like a game the Plumes would love. Is this where my parents were sending me? Although I don't remember any of our aunts being dwarfs. But with all the weird things in our family, who knows who we're related to.

"Wonderful game," Beau continued. "You should see when the zumans are playing. It's a sight to see a collection of primates, birds, bovines, lizards, and cats all scrawling together. Builds quite the comradery. Ah, I miss my days on the pad. I still keep my Haberdash bobbin with me, as a memory." Beau reached into his jacket pocket and pulled out a small Y-shaped, carved stick that had a small Z written at the bottom of the handle.

"Can I hold it?" Aven asked. Beau nodded and offered it to the youngest sister to inspect.

"We should hurry on," Bralwynn called out to the group, with Beau nodding and trying to get a last look at the game as the intensity increased with more quills flying across the gymnasium and striking the players.

Bralwynn guided them to an area with guards stationed outside. She and Beau left to speak to her contact at the court, and when they returned, Bralwynn led them through a maze of small chambers and antechambers until they reached a room with two identical double doors about ten feet apart.

"Pennymores, this will all seem quite unusual," Bralwynn admitted. "And it is to outsiders. But you must not let anyone you meet from here on out realize you find any of this to be the least bit unusual."

"Unusual how?" Quinn asked.

"You'll be speaking to the brothers of Bask," Bralwynn said. "Both of you will."

"Me?" Parker asked. "I have to?"

"Yes, each of you will be asked to speak to the brothers. And your words must be identical. You must each recite the identical words and phrases without error or mistake. No exceptions."

"I—I can't," Parker said, looking at Quinn. "No, there has to be another way."

"There is none," Bralwynn said. "No errors. No mistakes. Perfect recitation. It should be as normal as smelling a fresh-cut rose on a snowy day or growing a squash inside a thousand-year-old cave filled with bat dung."

Thump-thump. Thump-thump.

The guards motioned to the travelers and opened the doors allowing them inside.

"Quinn," Parker whispered, "I can't do this."

In the Hall of Bask, everything was a perfect mirror images divided straight down the middle of the room: two doors, two carpets, two thrones, two identical sets of guards, and two green, miniature parrots in cages.

Beau leaned over to the elder sisters, "I told them you are princesses," he said in a whisper. "This way, the brothers will be less vile to you. You should prepare yourselves, though. They'll still be absolutely rude, but it'll be better than it could be."

The sisters exchanged exasperated looks, but if they had to use their royal standing to try and gain their favor, they would. Beau told them the fastest way to be removed from the mirror throne room was to make any indication to one brother that the other brother was also in the room.

"Oh, and one more thing," the goat continued. "No eye contact with your sister, none, absolutely none, zero. Even a peek at her will get us all thrown out and perhaps tossed into a jail cell."

Thump-thump. Thump-thump.

"You mean—" Quinn asked but was cut off before she could continue.

"And one more crucial thing—very—simply do *not* mention your invisible brother," Beau continued in a whisper. "This is the absolute last thing to mention. Good luck!"

"You got this," Owen whispered, flashing Parker a double thumbs-up.

Thump-thump. Thump-thump.

Beau guided Bralwynn, Owen, Aven, and the invisible Riley to the doorway to avoid further attention. Parker heard Riley's voice ask, "Why are there all these silly rules?"

This was Parker's worst nightmare, someone asking her to memorize and recite something. Her heart pounded, the pulsing in her fingertips quickening and the pain spreading to her temples.

"I've got an idea," Quinn said, pulling Parker closer and grabbing her hand. "This will help keep us in sync… I think."

Quinn took her quill and scripted a letter onto Parker's pinky finger, a jet of blue dust whirling around each of their pinky fingers, twisting into a bow as if shoelaces tied them together. Parker admired the silver and gold etchings on her nail. Then, she took a step away from her sister, feeling like she had puppet strings now controlling her movements.

"Don't fight it," Quinn whispered as Parker found her lips forming the identical movements as her sister's. "Just follow my lead."

If I didn't appreciate Quinn bossing me around before…

Trumpets blared, making all of the children jump. Two identically dressed dwarfs sporting long, braided beards entered and announced the sisters. "On this glorious day," both of the dwarfs said in unison, their voices melodic, "we welcome the princesses of the kingdom of Everly."

Each dwarf removed his navy, puffed hat with a yellow feather plume and bowed to the respective princess standing in the identical doors at the ends of the identical carpets, which mirrored one another. Then together, the dwarves said:

"Princess Parker Pennymore."

"Princess Quinn Pennymore."

Owen whispered to Beau, "Don't they realize we are all in the same room? They're saying the same things."

"It's been this way for one hundred and eighty years," he replied.

The sisters tried to embrace their princess responsibilities. They walked forward toward the brothers of Bask, keeping an identical pace and avoiding any eye contact with their mirroring sister as instructed.

"Welcome to Baskerville," the two royals said in unison. They each wore multicolored robes, bejeweled crowns, and held a staff in opposite hands.

"You come to me in need?" they echoed.

Each sister nodded, Parker feeling as if an otherworldly force pulled her head up and down.

"I have come with important news from Everly," the sisters announced in unison.

Parker began to say "kingdom" at the end but caught herself when Quinn didn't. Her fingertips buzzed. The words she'd memorized had started to jumble and twist. *Breathe. Breathe.*

"Our party has been led here by an ancient compass to retrieve an ancient item to save my family from danger. Do you know what I seek?"

The brothers each slammed their staff down on the floor three times.

Each of the bearded dwarfs announcing the princesses ran to the center of the room and picked up two corners of a green rug, neatly folding it and placing it near the door. They returned to the carpet and lifted a large stone to create a pedestal. Then, two female dwarfs, each with a dozen braids flowing out from under beautiful plumed hats, each carried a maroon fabric pile to the center.

The ornately hatted dwarfs placed the maroon cloth on the pedestal and unfolded it, allowing a bright, shimmery glow to project to the cathedral-high ceiling.

"You seek," the brothers said, slamming their staffs again three times in unison, "the halo."

The single glow split into flashes on the ceiling.

Parker lowered her gaze from the ceiling to the pedestal, seeing the women holding large silver rings.

The women each held up a ring and moved in a series of identical, scripted movements.

"Thousands of years ago, our forefathers discovered the halo," each woman sang in unison. "In that tunnel of Bask, we found you, and we followed where the halo guided. We built the house of Bask. And today, we continue our commitment to follow wherever the halo directs. The house of Bask is the halo, and the halo is our house."

The brothers each slammed their staffs down three times. Then they spoke in perfect unison.

"My brother keeps a halo as his claim as the rightful King of Bask. He shall pay."

"Yes, I seek the halo," the two elder Pennymores said. "I seek the ancient item."

At these statements, the brothers slammed their staffs again, and the women placed the halo bracelets back on the pedestal and covered them.

"And I request a private audience as I wish to deliver a message only for your ears. May I whisper my message?"

The brothers each pondered the request, awkwardly pausing as if waiting for a sign of what to say.

I wonder if this is why Brawlynn said nothing gets done. They don't want to answer differently than the other brother seated less than five feet away.

"Approach, princess of Everly," they responded.

The sisters stepped forward in unison and bent down to speak in the ear of their respective brother.

Each sister used what they knew would appeal to the brothers, aware they'd need to get both to agree to something without the other one knowing.

"Your kingdom is the most advanced we have seen," Quinn whispered, expressing her honest and pure thoughts. "Your farming, transportation, water, health, and safety here are the finest I have seen in the known world. My father and I are inventors. I wish to propose our kingdoms work together to bring these marvels to others and request the halo as a show of good faith."

At the exact moment, Parker whispered into the other brother's ear, "Your kingdom has a story to be told. Your rule for two hundred years is unparalleled and unrivaled. Our kingdom contains the finest writers and a bookbindery. I wish to propose we understand your story—to harness *The Story of the Storyteller* to discover the truths and share the stories to others throughout the known and unknown worlds, and I request the halo as a show of good faith."

The sisters stepped away from the ear of their king and waited for a reply.

In unison, the brothers spoke. "I have listened to your request. I am sympathetic to your plight. However," continued the kings, "my heartless brother would never allow such a request to a Pennymore."

"*Hmmph*," Riley exclaimed from the back of the room. The others shifted awkwardly to try to cover the noise.

Parker saw Quinn open her mouth. She tried to mimic her as she spoke slowly, each syllable carefully said. "May I ask you to re-con-si-der? Dagamar and the Ravagers—"

"Silence! You must not speak of this again," the brothers spoke, each slamming their staff down three times. "Begone."

The brothers stood, and each exited the room in a rush. The elder Pennymores stood, unsure what to do next.

What had gone wrong?

The sisters paused at the front of the room. Then they turned and walked back down the carpets to the entrances, the inscription forcing them to continue to mirror one another.

"They don't seem good at sharing," Riley said. Bralwynn offered an uncomfortable smile and nodded.

"What just happened?" Owen asked.

Bralwynn looked at the sisters. "The Scott family of your mother's side is ancient one in the realms of magic. With such history comes differing views on your family and their actions of the past. For that, I am sorry."

"What does that mean?" Owen whispered to Parker.

"Dwarfs are jerks," Parker quietly replied, the feeling of being out of control of her body still there. "I want to stop this, Quinn." She felt her head jerking back and forth as Quinn shook her head. "Now."

Quinn nodded and took Parker's hand. Aven watched as her sisters continued to move in odd synchronicity as they'd done with the kings. But Parker resisted, creating an awkward movement in her actions like she was trying to move through mud.

"What happened to her?" Aven asked Beau as Quinn took Parker's hand and examined her sister's pinky fingernail, now etched with an ancient letter.

"Your sisters were magically connected—they synced. That was how they were able to fool the brothers," Beau said. "Magic was written, and now the magic remains, embedded in Parker's body—in her nail. This is where things about magic writing get somewhat scary."

"Scary?"

"What your sister Quinn must do to remove the magical incantation," Beau continued. "That removal, well, this is an act of unwriting."

"Unwriting? What does that mean? Like erased or something?"

They watched Quinn hold her quill over Parker's fingernail and delicately trace the shape she'd written in reverse, as a black, smoky glow came from the quill's tip.

"You see, you cannot just erase magic," Beau said. "It can only be unwritten. Once it is unwritten, it can never be written again. Ever. Magic has a memory, almost like a scar left even after it is unwritten."

"So, Parker has a scar?" Aven asked as Quinn lifted her quill from Parker's nail, and Parker shook herself, free of the synchronicity with her sister.

"There will always be a mark, however faint, for that spell," Beau continued. "Once it's been unwritten, you cannot change again to the way it was before."

"So, they can't do that sync—whatever you called it—again?"

"No," Beau said. "It's been unwritten. And unwriting is permanent. The scar is all that remains."

"Let's just go," Quinn said, frustrated. Parker examined her nail and looked at the faint traces of the remaining etching.

Their group left the house of Bask, navigating through the royal court. After several minutes, they were back where they'd first met Bralwynn.

"What do we do now?" Parker asked. "We did everything right."

"Can you talk to them?" Quinn asked the dwarf. "Could we ask Droma to speak to the kings since she's of an ancient line?" she pleaded with Beau.

The pair shook their heads.

"Maybe I can help," came Riley's tiny voice.

"We appreciate it, Riley, but I think we need their help to figure out what to try next," replied Quinn, motioning to their guides.

"Maybe we try for an audience tomorrow," offered Beau.

"You could each try to approach the other brother, perhaps," suggested Bralwynn. "The halo bands are an ancient source of conflict. And—"

Ch-ring.

A metallic ringing echoed.

The group turned to see where the noise came from.

Floating in front of the group were two silver bands, a familiar iridescent glow coming from them.

"What are those?" Quinn said.

"Those are the halos," Bralwynn whispered, lowering her voice.

"Didn't we just—" Owen asked.

"Yes, we just," Bralwynn said, the flowers on her hat all moving in tandem, holding their leaf arms up to their flowered faces in terror.

Parker echoed. "But how—"

"Those rings they had," said Riley as he twisted his wrists to shake them. "They weren't sharing, and when I don't share, our parents take the things from us we aren't sharing. So, I took them from those two."

"You *what*?" Beau asked incredulously.

"I walked over and took them."

Aven smiled and held up her hand, waiting for a high five.

"Oh, this is not good," Quinn said. "Do we take them back? Or maybe this is okay; we just need to borrow them for a few days. Right?"

"Well, on the bright side, the halos were covered up by a cloth, and maybe they won't notice they are gone," Owen said.

A whistle blew.

"Thieves! Come back! Stop them," voices yelled from the direction of the throne room.

"Or *not*," said Quinn. "Run!"

"I supposed this means we aren't returning for an audience with the kings tomorrow," Beau said, scurrying ahead.

"Follow me," Bralwynn called. "I know a way out."

"Are you sure?" Beau asked.

"The young prince had a point about not sharing," she replied. "Someone should have taken away their toys one hundred and eighty years ago. Maybe it is about time. Now, this way, *quickly*."

The group raced through the tunnels as the chasing voices grew louder. Bralwynn bent down to open a small metal grate at the base of a farming pod where tangled roots were visible.

"In here," she called to the group.

One by one, they crawled into the tunnel on their hands and knees for about twenty feet until they reached an open area where they could stand.

"It's humid here," said Parker.

"And it smells terrible," Aven said, holding her nose.

"This is a beet farming pod," Bralwynn said. "The first crop of beets has been harvested, which is why we can stand in this spot. And the smell is, well, it is because we use natural fertilizer, Aven."

Aven looked at the flowers on the dwarf's hat, who each pointed a leaf at their backsides.

"Ewwww," Aven groaned.

"We will need to climb up here," Bralwynn said, pointing to the spaces above them.

Parker looked up and saw it was much too high to reach. There were no ladders or boxes to climb on.

"I was thinking we can get four of us on shoulders and—" Bralwynn said before being cut off.

"Wait," said Parker as she pulled the leather bag off her shoulder. "I think there's a faster way."

She reached into the bag and proudly displayed an item.

"A measuring cup?" asked Bralwynn as Parker smiled, waving it to the others in their group.

Bralwynn was first. The yellow glow enveloped her as she morphed into a six-foot-tall version of herself, just tall enough to reach the beetroots and climb out.

"You look like us now," Aven exclaimed, seeing the stretched version of the dwarf. "You could come to visit us in Everly now!"

"I'm quite happy as I am, my dear, as most of us dwarfs are," she whispered. "Now, quiet my child. They could hear us."

"I suppose the brothers won't be pleased with our little activity," Beau said.

"Oh, they will be *furious*," said Bralwynn, looking up at the others once they'd returned her to her standard dwarf height as she'd requested. "It's quite something to see an angry dwarf. Those two will say words that will make your parents blush."

"Naughty, naughty dwarfs," Aven said, shaking her head as she rubbed her forefingers against one another.

"And when they find out a fellow dwarf helped you," Bralwynn continued, "I can't imagine what they'll do to me."

"Can you come with us?" Aven said. "Pretty please?"

"We could use your help," Quinn said. "And we all need to get away from here as fast as possible."

Bralwynn looked down at the massive hole they'd created in the former beet farm. "They'll find out how we escaped in no time."

The girls all looked at Bralwynn with wide, begging eyes.

The dwarf sighed. "I suppose my plants will be fine for a few days. You say you have two more ancient items to find." The flowers on her hat gave high fives to their neighboring flowers in celebration. "Where to next?"

Parker pulled the compass out of her leather pouch and held it out. "Riley, how about I trade you the compass for the halo bracelets. For safekeeping."

The bracelets floated to Parker, who placed them into the leather bag with her books.

As soon as the compass touched Riley's hands, it glowed, illuminating another letter on the dial.

"What's S?" Bralwynn asked.

"We don't know yet," Parker responded. "All we know is we need to go this way." She pointed in the direction of the arrow.

"Let's get out of here," Quinn said. "It's late, but we spent another full day gathering the second item. We only have two days left before the waning moon."

Beau added, "Plus, I am almost certain the dwarfs will be after us in…" He checked his watch. "Ten minutes, give or take."

"Then what are we waiting on?" Owen called.

The compass floated ahead, the party following it into the evening.

Aven ran on all fours and let out a small howl.

A distant howl echoed hers.

Parker saw Owen, Beau, and Quinn huddled together just ahead of her. Their entire group turned to look at her, each quickly turning away once they realized she'd caught them.

Are they talking about me? And if they are, what were they talking about?

Chapter Twenty-Three

The Flowers of Aeonik

"I don't wish to worry my traveling companions," Beau said, "but I'm quite certain this compass is trying to lead us into a valley none should venture to."

"How can it be any worse than where it's already led us?" Owen asked. "Tigers and trolls and Illiterates, oh my…"

"I'm guessing that was a joke, Mr. Wickerland," Beau said. "And if it was, I must say it was not a very good one then. Not very good at all."

Owen shook his head. "Why do I even bother?" he said.

"Still 'team staying out of it,'" Parker whispered to Owen with a wry smile.

"We need to hurry," Quinn said, urging the others.

Bralwynn dragged her small feet through the dirt with glimmers of sweat covering her hairline and upper lip. Her flowers were wilting.

Though their new companions were helpful, offering support and carrying the younger Pennymores for brief periods, darkness made this part of their trip difficult. Their feet throbbed, sweat made clothing stick and itch, and the lack of sleep made their eyelids heavy. Parker noticed Beau's head hanging low, nodding as sleep tried to lull him in.

"I'm so tired," Aven said.

"Me too," Riley groaned.

"We have to keep going," Quinn instructed. "The dwarfs could be on us, and we don't have much time until the waning moon in two days." She pointed up into the sky where the moon hung low, yellow, and nearly complete.

Once it reached its peak and began to fade away, Riley could be invisible forever.

The howls in the distance were closer, which meant wolves by the sound of it.

"I worry the compass may be leading us to a troubling place," Beau said. "This area we are coming upon is Aeonik, the valley of flowers."

"A valley of flowers sounds lovely right about now," Parker replied.

"It's, in fact, the exact opposite," Beau continued. "While the flowers are most certainly beautiful, the night is most definitely not the time to see them."

Bralwynn continued, "Wolves guard this valley."

"Really?" Aven asked, perking up.

"These are not the wolves of your stories, my dear Madam Aven," Beau said. "These wolves are protectors of the flowers. They've roamed this valley for hundreds of years, hunting thieves and magicians who seek their powers. It's not a safe place for children and goats."

"Or dwarfs," Bralwynn added.

"We could travel around the valley," Beau said, "but it may take much more time, and time is something not on our side."

"The compass points this way, and it's the fastest route," Quinn said. "We have only two items and need to return to our castle before the moon wanes. We aren't after their flowers, and maybe we can lose the dwarfs chasing us through the valley."

"Oh, the dwarfs will avoid anything to do with this valley," Bralwynn added.

"And so would a very smart and very uncourageous goat in normal circumstances, but since I am in your debt, we will proceed as you wish," Beau replied. "But they are not simply protecting the flowers. They dislike anyone stealing the scents of these flowers too."

"Scents?" Quinn asked. "Meaning we can't smell the flowers?"

"This is what the legends say," Beau replied. "The power of these flowers extends beyond the flowers themselves to the majestic pollen they produce. The wolves protect even a single grain of pollen from being taken from the valley."

"Do we hold our noses?" asked Aven.

"It would certainly be a good way to start," Beau continued, reaching up with his hoof to hold his nose.

"We're going through the valley," Quinn said. "It's settled."

"What do you mean, it's settled?" Parker asked. "It was settled when *you* led us across the bridge. It was settled when you made us take the Illiterate kid's boat across the water."

"Fine," Quinn said. "You made your point."

"No, I haven't. It was also settled when—"

"Enough," Quinn interrupted. "Then what's your great idea, Parker?"

"I don't have one. I just know this is a terrible plan. So how about we go around the valley filled with wolves, maybe? How about that?" Parker said, shaking her head and glaring at Quinn.

Parker was tired and out of patience after holding herself together through the recitation in front of the dwarfs. No one ever seemed to question her older sister. She only wanted to avoid danger and for the group to follow her.

"I said we're following the compass," Quinn hissed.

"No, I'm done listening to you."

"Of course you are," Quinn quipped. "You always do your own thing, but now you're part of the group. This is why tutors and teachers keep leaving. This is why our parents were trying to send you away. No one can reason with you when you get like this."

Parker angered, sensing the others' stares.

"No, I—I don't do my own thing," Parker said gruffly. The moonlight flickered in the corners of her eyes. Paurple-colored moonbeams began to dance in front of her.

"Yes. You tried to run away from us, your sisters, Parker," Quinn yelled. "Us!"

"Whoa," Owen said. "Let's take a breath."

Parker shook her head, trying to hold back tears, the eerie lights pulsing around her. "You were supposed to know magic to protect us, and you can't even fill a glass with ice."

"And you ran away from your friends and all the Plumes. You ran away from our parents. You're trying to run from Riley now. You are constantly trying to run away. Listen, it is not about you. It's about Riley and saving him, so stop with this selfishness. This is not about *you*, Parker!"

Tears poured down Parker's cheeks. Her head felt like it would explode. She turned and raced away from the group.

Parker ran until she found a place to sit and cry. She buried her face in her hands, sobbing. She'd only tried to run away to protect them, to find answers, and to find someplace she belonged. Now, she couldn't trust anyone. It had built and built, and they'd all abandoned her. Maybe it was better if she let them go on their own.

She felt better when she could stop and think. Alone. It was quiet here. Maybe too quiet, as even the familiar forest sounds were missing. Something felt wrong about this place. She looked for the night sky through the forest canopy, but the thick trees and leaves sealed her from the outside world.

A high-pitched sound forced her to her knees, the pain burning in her head. She covered her ears, barely muffling the painful noise, as she looked for the source.

A stone's throw in front of her were two bright red circles.

Eyes.

"You've wandered off alone," said a hissing voice inside her head.

Another high-pitched sound brought her to the ground. "Stop," she begged. "Please."

"Come closer, child," the voice commanded.

Parker stood and slowly stepped toward the eyes. As she did, the creature formed in her mind as a giant bat, its red eyes following each step.

"Your name, child," the bat commanded. "Who are you lurking in Namor's forest?"

"Parker," she meekly answered. "I am Parker Pennymore."

"A Pennymore? A Pennymore child," the bat responded, a chuckle in its throat. "This is a surprise—a wonderful surprise." Another high-pitched screech wailed.

Parker heard sets of wings all around her as thousands of bats rushed into the area, their leathery wings brushing against her. Her heart raced, and she felt the pulsing in her fingertips.

"These are Namor's children," the bat hissed at her.

She'd run from her sisters and her friends, who had no idea where she was. She was trapped.

"You are afraid. We can sense it," Namor continued. "You need not fear. Instead, you must kneel. Master will be happy with Namor." The screeching and the beating of their wings echoed all around her. Noise from thousands of bats forced her to the ground, writhing in pain.

More bats flew over her, their wings and claws scraping her back and moving her hair. She clenched her eyes tight, balling up her fists to her ears.

Another wail rattled every part of her.

The noise no longer sounded powerful but scared and frightened. The bats fled, scurrying above her.

Namor called out, "No, trespasser! No, these are Namor's children!"

Silence.

Parker lay on the ground, not wanting to move in case Namor and the bats were still there.

Eventually, she lifted her head. The red eyes were gone. Flaming columns surrounded her, illuminating the canopy. The bats had been scared off by fire.

She glanced over to one of the flaming columns.

Flaming arrows? Where did the flaming arrows come from? Who or what saved me? Was it my sister or someone else?

Parker rose to her knees and looked around, ears still ringing as her eyes adjusted to the light. "Hello?" she called out. "Hello. Who's there?"

"I am no one," the voice responded.

Parker stood and looked at the outline of the figure. The voice was masculine and stood as tall as an adult male but had long dark hair. He had no beard or facial hair, but she was sure he had pointed ears sticking out from the long hair.

"Are you a dwarf?" Parker asked.

"Are you a snake?" the figure snapped back.

"I'm—I'm sorry," Parker replied. "No. Thank you for saving me. It's just, I've never seen a creature quite like you."

"My name is Juventan," the figure replied, placing his bow over his shoulder like a sling. "And I'm an elf, from the elven kingdoms. And you should not be wandering here, as this is not safe for a human."

"I know. I wasn't alone," she admitted. "But now I am."

"You are a Pennymore—a Serif," Juventan continued. "Namor could sense your powers. He would have certainly turned you over to the Ravagers and to Dagamar. I could not stand by to see you taken by Namor."

"Thank you, truly," she said. "My family—we are here, on this journey to try to stop him, to stop Dagamar and the Ravagers. To save my brother."

"Why?"

"Why?" she repeated. "Because Dagamar has attacked Serifs and is planning it again. He's coming to Everly."

"And yet many Serifs agree with his cause," Juventan said. "His methods, not always. But his cause is a noble one to many of us."

"Us? Are you on *his* side? Dagamar?" she said in disbelief, her hand reaching up to touch the gemstone. "But you're not evil. You rescued me. You can't be evil."

Why isn't the gem glowing?

The elf laughed. "Ah, to be so young and naive," he said. "The villain of your story may not be the villain of mine. Dagamar has built a coalition of the disenfranchised, the misunderstood, the hunted, the hidden, and the condemned."

"Misunderstood? Of what?"

"You're a writer, a magic writer, yes? And yet, as a human, you live in the open, in the free, in the living. You are seen to be one of them. You may hide your gift, but you do not require to hide. Your people see me, an elf, and know I am different. I am to be feared. I am to be condemned. I am magic. Animals, dwarfs, giants, fairies, trolls, trees. They see us as creatures to be feared. So they hunt us, our people, our children. For centuries they push us to the shadows."

"Not everyone thinks that way."

"The Ancients did us no favor, child. Do your Illiterates embrace us? Do they want us to return, to live amongst you?"

Parker shook her head and looked at the elf, sensing his anger.

"Dagamar was first a poet, and his words spoke to the many of us hidden and hunted by the Motsans," Juventan continued. "The creatures were told we were lesser and we were only to be in the shadows. And many joined him, including the elves. We simply wanted to be equal, to be in the light again after centuries of hiding and running in fear. Others in the realm of magic disagreed, willing to stay in the shadows or able to hide amongst you, and this conflict escalated until it erupted. Lines were drawn, alliances forged, and conflicts raged. Until this uprising was tamped down, smothered."

"In the Grooten mountains," Parker said.

"Yes. But the embers of that conflict, that desire to be seen, a hope to no longer be feared, were not snuffed out. Now again, that flame rises. And because peace did not work before, the promise unfulfilled, now there are more who believe his message, his goal to unite the magical creatures under the Master Curator and silence those who disagree, the silent darkness. To build a master race of Serifs to rule."

"All the Ravagers want that?"

"No, not all of us, but more now than before, child. Many do. But there are those such as us, the elves, those who follow him, who align with his cause, who simply want to be equal, to live in harmony with Motsans once again, to be in the light. To stop being hunted. They do not want Dagamar's way, his ambition and thirst for power. They have not lost hope."

"What do they want instead?" Parker asked. "If they don't want to wipe out Motsans?"

"Those are the Ravagers who seek *you*."

"Me?" she replied. "What would they want with me?"

"If Dagamar captures you, it will fulfill his destiny," Juventan said, waving his hand to the sky. "There are those of us who seek to stop this. *You* are what Dagamar needs to rule."

"Ravagers are working to keep us away from Dagamar? To keep him from becoming the Master Curator and wiping out the Motsans?"

"Yes," he answered. "They seek to stop you from this quest you are on. They hunt you and your siblings, hunt you to keep you from him. They won't stop until they've kept him from realizing his true power, no matter the costs or the bloodshed. Yes, to them, you are the prey."

A chill ran through Parker's body. This was why they'd seen the black etchings, why the Ravagers had followed them and tried to harm them. The canyon troll, the tigers. It all made sense now. To those Ravagers, they were the hunted.

"And that's why you rescued me? Because Namor would have given me to him?"

"Precisely. And that simply cannot be. My people, the elves, are aligned with the Ravagers," he said. "And that is because we have long been in conflict with the dwarfs, and so we align with the Ravagers in our conflict with them. But we do not seek destruction. We seek equality, to come out of the shadows. We seek to live in harmony with the Motsans. Yes, we elves are a peaceful people."

"And so you see another way?"

"Maybe I am foolish, but we lived in peace before—Motsans and Serifs— for many centuries," Juventan said. "And so I must believe there must be another way, child, for all of us. You see, I do not simply seek a new master. I seek no master. So I must believe there is hope, we all must, to bring Motsans and Serifs into harmony once again. It is that hope I see in you."

"Me?"

The elf sighed. "Dagamar will not stop, and so preventing you from falling into his hands by whatever means only stalls the inevitable. He will not stop until he has wiped away every Motsan and established a new magical Fonde. He no longer sees a peaceful path. You and I share a hope for one, a peaceful path. And so I saved you, child, because the conflicts of the past have not yet colored you. I fear your unique connection to him is our only hope."

"But how?"

"Magic is leaving the shadows," he said. "That is your truth to discover, storyteller."

Storyteller. The message from Lady Julie. My burden; to discover the truth.

"And you must know the Ravagers have infiltrated the Illiterates," he continued, "and now they work to overthrow your father and your kingdom. Nothing is as it seems. Alliances are being drawn."

"But why would people who hate writing work with evil magic writers?" she asked.

"Discover the truth, child. And remember, the villain of your story may not be the villain of mine. Now let me lead you to your group, and then we shall hope never to meet again as the next may not end as this has." The elf held out his arm and pointed ahead. "Follow me."

Parker's thoughts shifted to the others; of Droma, Beau, Bralwynn, and even Juventan now—how they'd been forced into hiding and hunted by the Illiterates. Parker suddenly realized the danger she'd been in, they'd all been in, and how a stranger had saved her. Now she needed to find the others.

The elf moved with absolute grace as silently as the forest creatures themselves as Parker tried to keep up.

The elf paused after several minutes and motioned to Parker to join him. Juventan grasped Parker's fist. "Your party is ahead. I have saved you, and this debt may be called at some point. Until then, you must never speak of this, even to your party, your family, and your friends. Do you understand?"

Parker nodded.

"I see hope in you," he said as he stared into her eyes before turning and quickly vanishing into the thick forest brush.

She was sad that she could remain free as a Serif and magic writer, while Juventan, Beau, Bralwynn, and the other magic writers could not. These magic creatures had been forced into the shadows by zealots afraid of magic and its power. They made creatures who were kind but different become monsters. An unfathomable alliance between the Illiterates and Ravagers was building—all thanks to their shared hatred of the Penny-mores and the Kingdom of Everly. It was clear why Lady Julie had warned that war was coming.

It was already here.

Parker heard her sisters calling out for her and raced to them.

"Parker!" Aven squealed. "Where were you?"

"I needed a walk to clear my head. I was over there," she pointed off in the distance. "Never far."

Quinn put her hands on Parker's shoulders, leaning her forehead against hers. "I'm sorry for what I said," Quinn said. "I just—"

"You were right," Parker replied. "I need to trust you—trust them." She pointed to the others gathered nearby. "We'll be okay."

"We will?"

"Of course, we will," Parker smiled, trying to forget how close she'd been to danger in the forest and what she'd learned about the Ravagers and elves. "We're Pennymores," Parker whispered to her sister. "Now, where's the compass saying to go?"

They continued to follow the compass until the valley below filled with white daisies.

Beau turned to the girls and Owen and said, "This is it, the Aeonik, the valley of flowers. A valley guarded by the great wolves."

The girls were nervous and pulled each other close. "How do we make sure the wolves know we're not here to harm them?" Parker asked.

"Remember, they're not simply protecting the flowers," Beau repeated. "It's also the scents of these flowers."

"How do you protect a scent?" Owen asked.

"He means you can't smell the flowers," Quinn reminded. "None of us can."

"Our best bet is to rouse no attention," Beau said, his voice squeaking as he spoke through his now-pinched nostrils.

"Touch nothing," Quinn instructed. She looked at Aven and where she anticipated Riley to be. "You two in particular. Take nothing, touch nothing, say nothing."

"Smell nothing," Aven added, chuckling at the sound of her voice as she held her nostrils shut.

The scene enthralled Bralwynn and her flowers. These weren't simply daisies; they had streaks of golden light pulsing through the stems, leaves, and flower petals. Each time they brushed even just the tip of a petal, a musical tone sounded as the group made their way through the flowers.

"Whoa, this is incredible," whispered Aven through her pinched nose.

The howls continued in the distance.

"You all are certainly doing wonderful," Beau said once they were half-way across the field. "Please accept my sincere apologies for doubting your ability to refrain from sniffing—"

A child's squeal came from their right, the flowers moving in a circular pattern.

Riley.

He spun around with his hands stretched as far out as they could go. "This is amazing!" he squealed.

"Riley! Riley!" Quinn called out to her brother, racing through the flowers. "Cover your nose. Don't breathe in!"

"My gem!" Parker called out, seeing the red-orange glow pulsing.

The howls doubled, tripled, and in seconds wolves circled the group.

They barked and growled, their jaws snapping. They tightened the circle around them.

Parker could imagine all too well how ferocious these beasts could be. "Run!" she called out, racing to pick up Riley and carry him.

Beau hurried to Bralwynn, kicking in the dirt and lowering his horns. "You and Aven, get on!" Together, they scrambled through the flowers toward the edge of the valley.

Parker saw the flowers moving ahead and shouted, "This way. Go left!"

The growls intensified into furious, ferocious snarls.

The wolves had found them.

The flowers parted as the wolves gathered around the travelers.

"The boy," an angry, deep voice said. "He dared trespass and steal from us?"

A lone, brutish-looking wolf broke from the pack as the numbers in the pack behind him continued to grow.

Parker guessed there were hundreds.

"I am Dante," the wolf snarled as he stepped forward, his shoulder muscles rippling with prominent veins. "We watched you from the hills and let your party pass through our land. And now you've taken our generosity and tried to humiliate us by stealing from us. Who are you?"

Despite the terror in his eyes, Beau stepped forward and said, "Your sirness. We've passed through your valley following the guidance of an ancient and magical compa—"

Dante lowered his head and snapped his jaws inches in front of Beau's bearded face. "Silence, you lying billy goat."

The goat cowered back.

"But it's true," Bralwynn began. "I'm Bralwynn of Baskerville. We know the wolves are good creatures, rightfully protective of their land. We mean you no harm."

Dante released a vicious bark. Bralwynn jumped back, grabbing the girls' hands.

"You dwarfs have stolen our flowers, sneaking in, using your petite bodies to weave in and out of the fields, weakening our pack."

Bralwynn shook her head to protest, but it was all she could do to respond. Fear had stolen her voice.

"It was me," Riley moved to come face to face with the wolf, its wet breath fogging the outline of his invisible figure.

"What is this magic?" he bellowed, as growls emanated from the other wolves surrounding them.

"He did not come to take your flowers," Quinn said. "He's just a boy, and we warned him, but before I could stop him—"

"I smelled them," Riley said. "They're the most beautiful thing I've ever smelled."

"Enough," Dante commanded. "This child has taken from us. He must face punishment."

A much higher-toned howl broke through the pack. *Awwwwwwhhhoooo!*

Dante turned to the source. It sounded like a wolf cub.

Aven.

On all fours, her teeth bared and her eyes narrowed and sharp, she stepped nose to nose with the great wolf.

She howled again. This time, in perfect pitch and as loud as the howls they'd heard echoing from the valley walls.

The great wolf stood unflinching as puffs of warm breath came from his nose and open mouth, blowing back Aven's hair.

The wolf reared back on its massive hind legs, threw back his head, and began to let out an ear-piercing howl, so loud everyone in their party covered their ears.

Everyone except Aven.

The hundreds of other wolves followed suit and echoed Dante's call.

Aven stood her ground, her arms crossed and head tilted, admiring the first wolf she'd ever encountered, who now stood directly in front of her and seemed to be admiring her as well. She reached out and stroked the snout of the great wolf.

Dante's body went rigid, but Aven continued with her gentle caress until the wolf bowed his head.

Aven's love of wolves looked to be much more than simply a cranky, young child causing mischief. It was pure, just like Quinn had for fixing things and Parker had for writing.

Aven smiled, lifting the wolf's massive face to meet her eyes.

"Yours was louder, but mine was better," she said to the great wolf king.

The wolf let out a snort of hot air, again blowing back the curls framing Aven's face.

"Yes, child," Dante responded with a gritty laugh. "Perhaps it was."

The wolf stepped back and addressed his pack. "The child is one of us," he bellowed.

The pack let out a barrage of howls, with Aven joining in.

"Children, why are you crossing this valley when you know of its danger?" Dante motioned to what the goat and dwarf had said.

"Our brother is cursed," Aven said, stepping close to the wolf. "And only we can save him."

A series of short barks and growls came from the other wolves. Dwarfs' shouts bellowed in the distance.

"Someone followed you," Dante said. "Torches in the distance. We can protect you in the Aeonik but not beyond. We can help you escape, but where will you go?"

Parker stepped forward, holding the compass in her hands, passing it to their brother. As Riley took it in his hands, the face of the compass again glowed, and the arrow pointed to the *S*.

"We don't know, but we know we only have until the waning moon to save him," said Aven.

Owen leaned over to Beau, who was still cowering beneath the flowers after the near bite from the wolf. "How is this happening?"

"Each of the Pennymores was born with magical abilities. They are Serifs," Beau replied.

"But I thought they only *wrote* magic, like write with a quill?" Owen asked.

"Serifs have magic that is beyond what they write. Some can see visions of the future. Others can levitate. Still, others can communicate through their minds. It appears that Madam Aven has the power of the wolf howl," he said with a shrug.

"Like, just wolves, or can she talk to you?"

"You are talking to me, Mister Wickerland," Beau said with a concerned look.

"But I mean, like, not-you animals—like a normal goat."

"Well, I shall not take offense to you calling me abnormal and instead be the bigger goat who takes that as a compliment. But to your question, we don't know yet. She has expressed her power to communicate with the wolf, it's their ancient language beyond what our ears can hear, and her connection is unmistakable. Their histories must connect them. This is all I can imagine."

The alpha wolf scanned the hillside, examining the dozens of torches moving toward them. "Quickly now. There isn't much time," Dante responded, eyeing the moon above. "We will guide you where you seek."

"How?" Aven asked.

The wolf let out several low growls and barks. Then six wolves joined Dante. They each sat with their noses pointed in the direction of the compass.

Aven turned to the others. "He's telling the other wolves we will ride."

"Wait, wait," Parker exclaimed. "You got that from their growls and barking?"

Aven raised her shoulders as if to say, "I guess."

Parker raced up to her younger sister and hugged her. The gem on her necklace no longer glowed.

"Why did you ever think howling at him like that was a good idea?" she said, not wanting to let her sister out of her arms.

Aven leaned back from the embrace. "You pushed me," she said with a confused look. "I was standing there, felt your hands on my shoulders, and then you pushed me, so I simply ran to the wolf."

I didn't push her. But if I didn't push Aven forward, who did?

Aven climbed atop Dante. The alpha wolf's muscles rippled down his back as he raced through the pack.

"Hold on tightly," he bellowed. "Grasp the fur on my neck and don't let go. You won't hurt me."

"Is she serious?" Owen asked Parker. "You want me to get on that?" He pointed to the row of wolves standing in front of them.

"I mean, it's either this, or you can take your chances with an army of angry dwarfs."

"Just when I thought this couldn't get any stranger," Owen said with a shrug.

The others followed Aven's lead and pulled themselves on the back of their wolves. Owen struggled to climb up the wolf's back, forcing him to grab the boy by the back of his shirt as if he were a cub and heave him onto his back.

"You're doing great," Parker said to him with a smile as she reached down to grab the fur around the neck of her wolf.

How different could it be from the back of a horse?

Parker looked as Aven steadied herself in a low, crouched position on the back of the alpha wolf and then stood up, arms stretched like a bird ready to take off for flight.

"We are the they!" she yelled out.

Dante growled at the circle of hundreds of wolves again.

"They'll keep your pursuers at bay," he called out. "Now, are you children ready?"

Aven leaned her head back and let out a howl, which drew echoes from the wolves in the circle.

"Aven, sit down!" Quinn yelled in a panic. But the alpha and Aven raced away, howling with glee.

Though it frightened her, Parker had to admit, her little sister looked more beautiful than ever. Their group moved in unison, their movements fluid and fast.

This is even better than riding a horse.

"We will carry you as far as the compass instructs," Dante yelled out to the wolves and their riders. "We may split and separate, but wolves are connected even if you can't see one another."

"I'll keep my eyes on the compass," called Beau, still noticeably uncomfortable on the back of a reddish-brown wolf.

Parker looked over at Owen, his knuckles white from gripping the fur with all his might. She smiled at him and flashed him a thumbs-up sign.

I guess we are the they, huh?

The children each lay down on the back of their riding companion and buried their faces into the warm fur. They'd not felt this warm and safe in the past days, and soon, the rhythmic motion and body heat helped each quickly fall asleep as they moved deeper and deeper into the forest ahead.

Chapter Twenty-Four

Serpentine

The compass behaved differently, shifting and moving them in opposite directions as if multiple forces were competing to guide them.

The goat awakened the children as dawn broke.

"Lady Pennymores and Prince Pennymore," he said in his too formal way. "I request you wake. The compass, it seems, believes we have arrived. Therefore, so do I."

Quinn raised her head from the soft fur she'd slept on and looked around. "Where are we?"

A massive rock jutted from the landscape, and the ground gently sloped from the rock down to a small creek.

Serpentine Rock.

Beau wobbled his head back and forth. "It is a strange thing, Madam Quinn. The compass turned and twisted and shifted throughout the journey. It's a wonder our wolf guide didn't throw me off as I instructed us to turn left, right, go back, and circle around."

"That was surprisingly relaxing," Owen said, sliding down his wolf's back and stretching his arms. The wolf turned its head and licked Owen's ear, face, and side of his head, then trotted off to join the others in the pack.

"I see you two are getting along," Parker said with a smile.

"Ummm, Mister Wickerland," Beau said. "I must advise you that wolf saliva is known to cause one's hair to fall out, all of it, which wouldn't be a good thing for a boy of your age."

Owen sighed and began frantically rubbing his shirt on the side of his head where the wolf had licked.

"I thank you, kind wolves," Beau said, bowing slightly. "The compass was certainly not our friend last night, but it seems here is where we are to be, although *here* is probably not where I would choose to be."

"It was no trouble, goat," came the voice of Dante. He sweetly shook his back to wake the still-slumbering Aven. "You have been delivered here, child. Now we must go and keep your pursuers away."

Aven slid down the back of the wolf with a yawn before she circled to put her face inches from Dante.

"But you can't go," she said with tears welling up in her eyes. "I just found you."

"You'll never lose us," the wolf replied. "And if you do, we know your call. We are but moments away. Always."

Aven rubbed her cheek against the muzzle of the wolf.

Dante bowed his head. "The dwarves are still seeking you children, but we've received word from the other wolves that elves have been seen. The elves have been fighting with the dwarves, those who followed you. Strange it seems, but their distractions were a help to us in avoiding a confrontation with the dwarves."

Juventan. It had to be. He must have decided to help us.

"Thank you for everything," Parker said.

"Be safe, Pennymores," the great wolf replied. "We won't soon forget you and hope you save your brother. Fonde depends on it."

Aven threw her hands around Dante's neck in a big hug. He nestled his nose over her shoulder and looked to the others, giving them a nod of goodwill.

She laughed as she turned to her sisters and said, "I've been doing it all wrong. My tricks come much more naturally with wolves than horses. Or maybe I needed the right wolf."

With that, Dante licked Aven's face, eliciting a concerned look from Owen. Then the alpha wolf called over to the billy goat while the children and Bralwynn surveyed the area.

Beau and the great gray wolf spoke for only a few moments, passing a few glances at the children.

"How did they carve a snake's head into that mountain?" Owen said, squinting at the carved snake embedded in the top of the massive rock.

"Magic writing," Quinn answered. "Most of the great buildings and monuments of Fonde were done by magic writing before it was outlawed. There were thousands of years where magic writing was part of all of our lives. But then it stopped, and soon all writing with it. It's a shame, really."

Beau returned to the group and nodded to the wolves. Then, the wolves each bowed their heads in turn, howled, and charged back down the path they had come. Aven chased behind, howling in her booming wolf voice.

"They'll keep others away," Beau shared. "They don't believe we were followed, and the other wolves have tried to throw the dwarfs off our scent."

"Did they tell you anything about this place?" Parker asked.

"It is called Serpentine, the serpent's tongue, and the Ancients called this Serpēns. There are rumors that the Order of the Enigma was first established here."

"But I thought the Enigma was a raven?" Parker asked.

"In ancient times, the raven held a snake in its talons," Quinn said. "You sorta have to pass a test to do the Apportionment, which you conveniently got to skip. But the orders are fascinating. The Enigma are one of the oldest, and... well, let's just say there's a lot of stories about them."

"That is a kind way to say it, Madam Quinndaline," Beau said. "The snake and the raven are fighting one another in many ancient pictures of the order. And that feeling certainly is given off here." The group watched massive birds circling the top of the Serpentine Rock. "Our wolf friends have expressed a preference we practice extreme caution here. The compass, it seems, fears this place almost as much as the wolves do."

"I've never heard about this place in any of the stories," Owen said. "Is there a story about a snake castle built into a mountain I somehow missed?"

"There's a reason it's not in the stories, Owen," Quinn said.

"I know this place," Riley quietly said.

"What?" Parker said, turning to where his voice had come from.

"This place," Riley continued. "I was here. I here before. We, we have to leave!"

Parker recalled each step of her brother's harrowing tale of return. And as he had said, they found themselves surrounded by each haunting detail: a split tree, a small creek, a path, and a fortress built into a hill with a door on the side.

Why would the compass take us here—bring Riley back to a place with the sorceress who had taken him away and who had wanted to take all of us away?

"How do you know?" Quinn asked. "Riley, how do you know this is the place where you were? You said you never left the room."

"No, but this is *exactly* what he described before," Parker shared.

"I remember it," Riley said. "I can't forget it."

"Then we go in," Quinn said firmly. "We follow the compass."

"Uh, that witch who was going to kidnap all of you… She's here," Owen said, motioning to the sharp rock faces. "You can't just give yourself up to her. We can't risk that."

"I must agree," Beau said, raising his hooves. "We scarcely are ready for our party to take on a dark witch. Perhaps we wait for the wolves or something else. But this is simply unwise."

Quinn screamed.

Everyone stared at her.

"This can't be happening," she said, pointing her fist at the sharp rocks. "We can't let her take him away again. We can't let her."

"Maybe we get Lazlo," Owen said. "We get him, and he can help us. There's still time."

"They're right," Quinn said, her eyes staring at her shoes. "You heard what Lazlo said, even he's nothing compared to her. There's no use. We can't just charge in and take her on." She sat on the ground and buried her face in her hands.

"No," Parker said, raising her voice, clearly trembling. "No."

Quinn looked at Parker.

"No. Quinn's right," Parker said, nodding. "She's right. We can't just let her take him away *again*. She took him once, we have him back, and I am not waiting to see what happens. It's on us. We are enough. The compass led us here. The waning moon is in two days. Riley knows it's here. We go."

Owen stepped forward. "I go where Parker goes."

"Me too," Aven agreed, with Beau and Bralwynn nodding in agreement.

Quinn lowered her head again, and her voice shook as she said, "I don't think I can."

"What do you mean?" Parker asked. "You don't think you can?"

"Protect you. I can't protect you."

"But—"

"I have to protect you. That's what I'm supposed to do," Quinn said, her lip quivering. "I'm supposed to know what to do, to know how to write magic, to keep my family safe. But I can't."

Aven sat next to Quinn, putting her arms around her, with Parker and Riley following.

"You're our big sister," Parker said. "And we protect each other. All of us." She motioned with her arms to the others. "You all too."

Owen, Beau, and Bralwynn joined in the group hug.

Parker turned to the others. "We don't confront her. We just need to get the ancient item. We listen to Riley. We trust the compass. We work together and stay out of sight. We are here together now, and we trust no one but one another."

Quinn wiped her eyes.

"And maybe you can do that lightning bolt thing with the book again, Parker," Aven said smiling.

"Maybe," Parker said, squeezing her shoulder. "Riley is invisible. He can sneak in and make sure the route is safe. We leave if we see a soul or if anything feels off. Okay?" Parker looked at Quinn, who smiled at her, tears in her eyes. "And you," Parker continued. "You just keep that fancy quill of yours ready in case we need it. Deal?"

"Deal."

"Won't she be expecting us?" Owen asked.

"Maybe not. Riley escaped, and I'm sure that's gotten the Ravagers up in arms looking for him. Our mother said the Ravagers were threatening Everly, and the Illiterates would hold their plan at bay. The witch might not even be here," Parker offered.

"Wouldn't that be nice?" Owen muttered.

Beau smiled. "Our new friend, Dante, gave me some advice and guidance. Wolves had found tunnels in this area, ancient tunnels from when Serpentine was first built. Even if she knows we're here, she won't expect us to have such knowledge."

The goat pointed to an area near the stream. There they could attempt to gain access to the hidden castle built into the face of the cliff. The ancient builders had done such a magnificent job, even knowing it was there it was still difficult to see any trace of it. This was the perfect place to hide from prying eyes and lock away the most wanted kidnapped child in the known world.

The hidden castle of the Serpentine Rock was monstrous. Its battle walls had been carved from the natural stone of the mountainside, and at the top sprouted vines with sharp thorns like teeth in the vast, hungry mouth of the roof. The very top of the castle, presumably a tower of sorts, came to a sharp angle that looked as if a snake was ready to strike, its fangs exposed with a V-shaped split in the rock face, reminding Parker of a serpent's tongue.

Dante must've had some type of run-ins with the witch to know of the secret entrance. They'd escaped from Baskerville's tunnels, and here they were going back underground.

"We can do tunnels," Parker said to Quinn. "You and I have spent more time than any normal kids exploring tunnels."

Quinn inhaled. "Plus, we have a dwarf. And you have a gem that glows if we're in trouble."

Parker nodded as if she were trying to convince herself this plan was a good idea.

It was still morning, the sun still making its way up the horizon while clouds swarmed the grim castle, making the place appear particularly dreadful for its visitors.

Taking a heavy gulp, Aven said, "You sure I can't call the wolves to come back?"

Joining hands, the group made their way from the rock face and crossed the last few rows of flowers, which became more wilted the closer they were to the castle. The dark stone of the castle expanded around to a large lake full of murk and moss.

Beau pointed to the water. "The far side of the creek and the still pond are connected and will lead us to the tunnels, I hope."

Parker saw movement in the water beneath the mud and stringy weeds.

All of them were afraid, and rightfully so. They had never faced anything like the witch or been somewhere so formidable as her castle.

At the edge of the lake were expansive cave openings into infinite darkness.

Bralwynn grabbed some dry branches and packed wet leaves around the top. She had some matches and lit torches.

"There, this should help light the way," Bralwynn said, the flowers in her hat giving a celebratory cheer.

They followed Bralwynn into the tunnel. A few feet in, the smell of rotten eggs paired with the musty scent of damp clothes, like when Aven forgot to hang her riding pants to dry after taking her horse through the stream, all but bowled them over.

The walls narrowed, closing in on them. The ceilings became lower, forcing everyone, even Bralwynn, to their hands and knees.

The wet tunnel floor squished between their fingers. Aven grabbed the front of her shirt and pulled it over her nose as the putrid smell worsened.

Several moments later, with cuts on their hands from the pebbles in the tunnel, they saw an opening.

"There!" Aven called.

"Shhh!" Beau scolded. "This is an opening to the inside of the castle. We must continue undetected to find the item and exit before the witch finds us."

Aven nodded and whispered, "Sorry."

They followed the light, and the stone above them expanded, allowing them to stand. However, with each step forward, the dank water rose until it reached their waists and to Bralwynn's nose. She tilted her head back, coughing at the stink and grime.

"Here," Quinn said to Bralwynn. "Hop on my back."

Bralwynn smiled and obliged. "Thank you."

Above them, they heard the echoes of slamming cabinets and the collision of iron cookware. Beau raised a hoof, signaling everyone to wait. They froze and listened for the kitchen staff to hurry along.

"How does a witch get a castle?" Owen whispered to Beau.

"Rumors are she's mighty, and for her, this would be child's play."

"Great to hear," Owen muttered. "This massive castle is just child's play... just great."

When the servants passed overhead, Beau whispered, "This is where we'll go in."

"Riley, you okay with this?" Quinn asked.

"Yeah, I think so."

Quinn and Owen shimmied the grate open, and its groan traveled through the tunnel, bouncing off the stone walls. When no one rushed to see what the noise was, the children stood on their tiptoes to lift Riley to the kitchen floor and let him climb inside.

After a few seconds, he said, "It's clear," into the grate. Quinn and Owen lifted Bralwynn next, and once she was inside, her small hands returned to the opening, ready to help the others.

As Beau, Owen, Quinn, Aven, and Parker climbed inside, the smell of garlic and turkey replaced the sour, disgusting smell of the tunnel. The castle's occupants must've just finished their breakfast and been preparing for lunch.

This feels off. I was expecting a place much more terrifying: bubbling cauldrons, newt eyes, and dripping moss. But the kitchen is homey.

Fresh bread sat on a counter, and the group tiptoed behind the oven for cover. Quickly, they broke the bread into small bites and stuffed it in their mouths. Bralwynn snatched two more loaves, split them in two, and buried them away in her pockets for the journey home.

Parker held the compass in front of her, letting it guide them across three dimensions. "It says we go up," she whispered to the group.

A member of the kitchen staff walked by the entrance.

"Get down!" Beau said.

The sisters and dwarf ducked.

"She's insisting the room be cleaned each day and remain exactly as it was left," a male staff member said to another trailing behind him. "The boy's room is not to be touched otherwise."

The man departed the room.

"Do you recognize them or anything?" Parker whispered to Riley.

"I don't know," he admitted.

"Come on!" Beau said, hurrying through the kitchen. "Then we'll follow the servants."

Only the man was too fast. He was down the hall and took one of the turns.

"Hmmm…" Beau said. "Where do you think the witch would go? We should go the opposite, I suggest."

Quinn said, "Did you guys see the tower when we reached the castle?"

Owen shook his head, "It looked like a nasty snake's tongue."

"Exactly," Parker said. The compass's arrow pointed straight up. "I think it's taking us to the tongue of the witch's tower."

The compass continued guiding them upward as they traversed floor after floor, with Riley serving as the lookout around each corner. Besides the servants in the kitchen, they'd seen no one.

Why haven't we run into anyone? Why are there no guards? It was strange that the kitchen was empty at this hour; their kitchen bustled with people from sunrise to sunset. Why are the hallways and stairwells so quiet?

The compass spun like an angry funnel cloud. Parker turned the compass on its access, and the spinning stopped with the arrow pointed straight above them.

Quinn looked at her sisters, "I think the compass knows what we're seeking is right above us."

"Then let's get whatever we're looking for and get out of here," Parker said.

Quinn took charge. They pressed their backs to the corridor walls. Like the tunnel, the halls were wet, and water swished under the sticky wallpaper.

"Why let a place look like this if you could use magic to fix it?" Aven asked, pinching her nose to block the moldy stench.

"Sometimes magic, especially dark magic, can only make interpretations of a person's wishes," Beau offered.

"What does that mean?" Aven said.

"Well," Bralwynn said, continuing for Beau, "if an evil or wicked witch used the spell of a good witch when she built this castle, it's possible the good magic gave her the castle but refused to omit the hideous characteristics of the caster."

"They are saying this witch is probably really, really bad news," Owen offered.

Dark, decaying ivy webbed the ceiling, and cracks snaked through the wooden floors. Serpentine was as rotten as the tunnels beneath it.

As they reached the top landing of the stairs, they saw signs of life. A few guards meandered in and out of the rooms, each too busy to suspect any intruders.

Parker said a soft "thank you" to Dante.

"There," came a small voice from Riley. "This is it."

At the top of the castle, hiding in the serpent's tongue, was a hallway with a closed door with a small window with a golden latch.

The window Riley had escaped from.

"It's where the compass is telling us to go," Parker whispered, still holding the glowing compass.

Why would the ancient item be in the same room Riley had been locked in and escaped from?

The party crept down the hall to the door. Quinn reached for the handle and turned it. Locked.

"This door must have some type of special lock on both sides, maybe to keep people in or out," Quinn offered. "Riley, think you could crawl back into the room?"

After a minute of grunts and groans, a click was followed by a long *creeeaaaakkk*. The door opened.

Footsteps.

"Hurry, someone's coming," Beau whispered, ushering the group inside. "We've got to hurry. Parker, where is the item? Use the compass."

Standing in the center of the room, she held the compass and slowly turned until it pointed to an empty wall where a key hung from a rusty nail in the stone.

"A key?" Parker said. "Was it there in the room the entire time?"

"No," Riley answered. "It's new."

"Well, the compass thinks it's what we want," Parker responded, "so let's get it and get out of here before someone finds we've taken it."

She walked forward to the key and carefully removed it from the wall. *Click.*

"What was that?" Beau asked.

Quinn ran to the door. "We've been locked in." She banged on the door.

"Why didn't someone stay outside and watch?" Parker asked.

"Why didn't you?" Quinn asked with a sigh. "I can't figure out everything and—"

Parker hung her head.

Of course, everything had felt too easy inside the castle. Because it was too easy. She must have brought us here with the key. The witch knew we'd come. How did I miss it?

Riley sighed, "This was all a trap."

Now she had them, all of them.

"Riley?" Parker asked. "I—I can see you."

Riley was visible again.

"I'm sorry," Quinn kept saying over and over. "I missed it. How did I miss it?"

"We all missed the signs," Parker said. "Not listening to the wolf, not asking why it was too easy, failing to listen to Riley. All of us. We all missed it."

"Uh, guys?" Owen said, awkwardly raising his hand. "You guys can all, like, see him too, right? Like, we all realize Riley's visible again—isn't that what we came here to do?"

"Yes, but it's just an enchantment," Quinn said.

"What do you mean? Isn't all of this some enchantment?" Owen asked.

"Yes, but this room must have some kind of spell on it, and as long as he's locked inside, everyone can see him, but as soon as he steps outside, he'll be invisible again. So, it's not what we came here for."

"And once he escaped the room, he only had until the waning moon to reverse it," Parker added. "Plus, *we* are all trapped too."

"We've got to find a way out," Quinn said, pacing back and forth as she fiddled with the goggles on her head.

Parker walked to the window in the corner of the room and sat, running through ideas in her head. Then she removed each enchanted item from the leather pouch, hoping one of them might help them escape.

She put the measuring cup on her head, but nothing happened. It seemed as if all enchantments, not just the one that made Riley invisible, were blocked inside the room.

After some time, food slid through the door slot on trays. They were all hungry, and despite their anger, filled their bellies, eating in relative silence.

Parker might be able to think on a full stomach.

Quinn stared out the window, looking at the sun as it moved lower in the sky, a sign that they'd been there too long. They were running out of time and ideas. They'd pushed every brick, stood on shoulders to look for a loose ceiling beam, anything they could think of to get out. There were no bars on the window, but they didn't need bars to keep them from escaping at this height.

They were trapped.

Click.

Quinn and Parker looked at one another.

Parker felt the hot pulse of the gem. "We're in danger," she said.

Quinn bolted to her feet and raced to the door. Holding the handle in her hand, she turned it.

"It's unlocked," she said, turning to the others. "Everyone, come here."

They all raced toward the door, each of them standing on one side or the other.

"Parker," Quinn said. "Your quill, get it."

"I don't know how to use it."

Quinn reached into her pocket and pulled hers out. "Let's just hope you don't have to."

"Owen, take the others away from the door," Parker instructed, and he moved the others toward the window, standing in front of them.

"I'm going to open it," Quinn said, her palm outstretched and her quill in her fingers.

She pulled the handle and opened it, expecting to see guards, but the hallway was empty.

"I never meant to hurt you, any of you," a voice echoed down the hallway.

It was Lady Julie. The witch.

"Keep them all back," Quinn instructed Owen.

Quinn stepped into the door frame to face Lady Julie, her palm fully extended, tightly gripping her quill. Parker stood behind her as the beats of her heart pounded in her fingertips.

"Stay back," Quinn yelled. "Do not step one foot closer."

"The gem," Parker whispered to Quinn. "It's getting brighter. We're in danger, Quinn. Don't do anything stupid."

"My child—" Lady Julie said.

"I am *not* your child," Quinn yelled, taking a step into the hallway. "None of us are. We never were."

"You don't understand, I—" Lady Julie said.

Quinn muttered, the blue tip of her quill glowing.

"I am not armed," Lady Julie said, raising her hands and exposing her palms.

"Parker, watch for her quill. Watch her hands," Quinn shouted.

"You all may go, and I will not harm you or stop you, but I want to tell you—"

"Bolt!" Quinn commanded, raising her palm to Lady Julie and scripting a curse on each of her fingernails as her quill flashed teal and blue, and an explosion rocked across the hallway, striking Lady Julie squarely in her chest. She stumbled back but did not fall.

"I want you to know—"

"Bolt!" Quinn commanded again, the quill jumping from finger to finger as another flash raced and struck Lady Julie again, this time sending her down to one knee.

The smell of sulfur and burning fabric filled Parker's nostrils, causing her stomach to tighten. The hot, pulsing stone now burned her chest, its red-orange glow illuminating the entire hallway.

"Please," Lady Julie begged, her breath labored. "The gem. It does not glow when you are in *danger*."

"Liar!" Quinn yelled.

"The gem only glows when I am near."

Parker touched the stone. Its warmth was the same as before.

"Monster, you lie," Quinn screamed, her face red and flushed. "It was you! You kidnapped our brother. You tore apart our family. Bolt!" Her quill angrily danced across her fingers.

The woman stumbled and fell to both knees, her hand up and outstretched, clearly in pain.

Lady Julie brought a single hand down to her chest where the blasts struck her. "Please, listen to me, child."

"No. More. Lies."

"Lazlo," Julie said, swallowing hard. "He told you yours was *The Story of the Victor*. He told you I was your monster. He trained you for this moment. He pushed you to feel your rage."

Quinn stepped forward toward the woman kneeling before her, her palm now trembling.

"No! You were never there for us when we needed you," Quinn said. "You left us afraid. You kidnapped our brother. You did this! You left us alone."

Lady Julie raised her eyes to meet Quinn's.

"My child, you were *never* alone. Never," she said meekly. "Think of the stone's glow. It glows *only* when I am near. In those moments of great danger."

Quinn shook her head. Her palm fixed on Lady Julie, her quill now quivering.

"The gem. When you first found Riley, I was there, leading him back to you and keeping him safe on the journey. I returned him to you. He was never alone."

"No, you couldn't!"

"And I was there when the water rose, pulling you and your brother under. I gave you my hand to pull you to shore. I was that water's push."

"No," she mumbled. "You left us. You left me."

Lady Julie shifted and raised herself to a knee. "I was there when your sisters hung from your arms over the crevasse as the bridge crumbled and you held their lives in your strong hands. I was the wind lifting you from danger."

Julie pulled herself back to her feet.

"I was there when a knife was at your brother's throat when he could have been taken away again in an instant. I was that wave."

Parker reached for the pulsing stone around her neck, feeling its warmth increasing as Lady Julie walked toward her.

Quinn began to sob as her palm fell, holding the quill loosely to her side. She looked at Parker, who still held her gem, her fingers white as she gripped it tighter, remembering each moment.

Parker nodded to Quinn as tears welled in their eyes.

Julie stepped closer. "And I was there beside you urging and pushing Aven forward to speak to the wolf, to share her gift, and to save you all." Lady Julie's arms were outstretched. She stood face to face with Quinn. "You were never alone. I was always with you. All of you."

Quinn brought her hands to her face, her body shaking.

"I had to flee, to leave to protect you. But you were *never* alone. I was *always* with you."

Quinn sobbed, her quill falling from her hand to the floor as Lady Julie took her in her arms.

"Always."

Chapter Twenty-Five

An Unchoosable Choice

"I'm proud of you. It wasn't easy to gather these ancient items," Lady Julie said, admiring the items they'd placed on the floor, "even if you had a little help," motioning to Bralwynn and Beau.

The group circled close around her, buoyed with a renewed sense of optimism. Quinn stayed particularly close to her former caretaker and kept checking with her to see how she was feeling after their magical "run-in" a few minutes earlier.

"These ancient items are critical for what we have to do next," Julie continued.

"We just find the fourth and then you'll save Riley from the invisibility curse," Quinn said, her voice hopeful, as she placed the items back in the enchanted purse. "We use the compass and get it before the waning moon."

"My child," Lady Julie said, locking eyes with the eldest Pennymore. "I wish I could give you better news, but the quest you've given was never a quest meant to save your brother."

"What—what do you mean?" Quinn asked. "We can't save him?"

"I didn't say that. I simply said *this* quest was never about your brother," Julie replied. "You see, he is not a foe to defeat easily. He's been planning this for many moons, and if he suspects you have found me now, he will show us no mercy."

"He?" Parker asked. "You mean Lazlo?"

"No," she replied. "Far worse than Lazlo, I'm afraid. There's much you don't understand about that boy. He's but a pawn in something much more powerful, much more sinister. Lazlo is under the spell of Master Dagamar."

"I don't understand," Parker said. "Dagamar is behind ... our quest?"

"You see, it's Dagamar who has been pursuing your brother," Julie said. "And the purpose of this quest was always intended to help *him*, to aid *Dagamar* in his pursuits. And now that you've gotten this far, Dagamar seeks all of *you*."

"But how—how could we have missed it?" Quinn muttered. "Lazlo—he lied to us."

Silence hung in the air.

"You did the only thing you could to try to help your brother. No one can fault you for this."

Quinn buried her face in her hands.

"That day—the day I fled with Riley was the day I knew Dagamar had returned to power. We suspected Dagamar was healing and rebuilding his army to return someday. That day I discovered the truth of his rise."

"But how?" Parker asked.

"Your parents and I argued then," Julie answered, staring in the distance. "You remember—the story I told you of Dagamar's return and how your parents fought in the hallway as I did. And how they quickly dismissed me from your room. I told them I suspected the Ravagers had taken your grandmother. That was the sign—if they could overwhelm her, there was simply no way to stop him from what was to come.

"Dagamar had regained enough power to capture your grandmother, certainly no small feat," Julie continued as she withdrew her quill and held it between her fingers. "That day, she was supposed to visit Everly. I knew it was unlike her to simply not show. She never would do that, so we went to find her—going to the only place she could be. And we found this." She drew a series of lines and shapes in the air, the symbol of the black etching.

"We know we are Serifs," Parker said. "We know."

"I have known since your births. It has been your destiny, your legacy," Julie continued, a proud smile stretching across her face as she studied them. "I suspect your grandmother was protecting you. That was why she let herself be taken then, perhaps. You see, you children have always been at the center of Dagamar's aims for destruction and a new magical war in Fonde."

"But why does he even want a war?" Owen asked.

"Power, anger, revenge," she replied. "These are the reasons why once good men do terrible things. Yes, some seek a world where the magic writers, all of the Serifs, can return to the world and are no longer forced to hide only in the realms of magic. They seek an understanding between us where magic doesn't need to be feared and hidden. They seek a return to the before times, a time when Serifs and Motsans lived in peace together. That is a promise I had even hoped for."

"But you said Dagamar wants a war," Owen said.

"He does," she replied. "There are others within the magical realm who believe peace with Motsans is no longer possible, a farce and a false hope. They believe magic creatures and magic writers will always be hunted by men who fear those unlike them, those with mystical powers, those who are different. Many have joined with Dagamar, convinced by his rhetoric that magic writers are meant to rule Fonde. They are to come out of the shadows and build a new world as they are tired of being trampled down and hidden. They follow Dagamar to destroy anyone who *forces* magic writers into the shadows. They want war."

"The Illiterates," Parker muttered, "they've created this with their hatred and anger."

"No, it's not only the Illiterates," Julie answered. "Yes, they have certainly stoked the anger, but many Motsans fear those unlike themselves. You see, it requires bravery to stand up for the trampled and hidden. It's not only those who attack magic writers… it's also those who don't have the bravery to bring the magic back into the light."

"This is why Dagamar and the Ravagers already have an army," Owen said. "And now they want to use them to wipe out everyone and create a new world for the magical to rule."

"Yes, to destroy every nonmagical creature or any magical ones who dare stand up to him," she said. "They want to make Dagamar the ruler of Fonde, the master curator of her powers."

A chill raced over Parker, realizing the weight of what she'd heard from Juventan the elf. She finally understood why he'd said magic *was* leaving the shadows.

"We can stop him, can't we? We've seen Zuma and Baskerville, the wolves, Serifs, and others would stand with us, right?" Quinn continued. "We can build an army to fight him, right?"

"You have an army already," Lady Julie said with a smile. "You, the four of you, are an army greater than Dagamar can ever truly build. Quinn, your powers are growing, and you'll harness your potential with training. Parker, your writing has always been your gift. You've already realized it even without any training in the ways of magic. One can rarely write magic without *writing*, but you have, and you share this distinction with few other writers of magic."

That must be why Quinn was so surprised when Aven told her of the bolt that destroyed the chandelier without writing anything. But Lazlo and I both have this ability.

"And you've summoned the power of the Apportionment for a group of gifted children, a remarkable feat that some Serifs will shun while others will celebrate. With time, we can build those to stand up to him."

Lady Julie took her hand and raised it above her shoulder, forming her thumb and forefinger into a circle, fanning out the others into the feather-like shape.

"We are the they," she said with a tender smile.

She knows about the Plumes!

"And you've brought another with you who will serve you well in this fight," Lady Julie said, motioning to Owen.

He looked at the others with a smile, sitting up straighter.

"You've each done far beyond what I could have hoped," Lady Julie said as Quinn reached over to rub Parker's shoulders.

"What you did not realize, Parker," Lady Julie continued, "is your efforts have helped dozens of children realize their magical powers."

Parker looked at her skeptically. "Wait, so all of them *are* magical. They are Serifs too?"

Lady Julie nodded and gently wrote a script on her forearm, illuminating a glowing map in the air. "Yes, Fonde is gracious with her powers, and each child who was told in the Apportionment ceremony by the inkwell of their order has the potential to be a magic writer, a powerful and good one. They'll need training, and there are libraries where you'll learn, five ancient locations to help you harness the power of your order, with curators, storytellers, and custodians that train each writer to realize their potential."

"They will be able to go to the literati libraries?" Parker asked.

"Of course, all of you will someday attend the ancient libraries for magic writing if you wish. A library of chronicles, a library of legends, a library of scribes, a library of poets, and a library of enigmas. Your magic writing powers are varied, but each writer will have unique skills tied to their order, remarkable things that enable wondrous powers if cultivated. Powers to bend heart, mind, object, and energy. Other libraries of lesser significance are throughout Fonde, but each order has its own home to train its members."

As she wrote, brightly colored quills rose from several locations, with dozens of tiny colored dots illuminating other sites on the map.

"Where are these ancient libraries? Is one of them in our castle?" Parker wondered as she examined the map for clues of the locations of the colored quills.

"Oh, no," Lady Julie said, smiling. "These ancient libraries are some of the greatest wonders in the world, far more splendid than in Garamond castle." The map transformed, revealing an image of the hidden library she'd found inside Everly. "Writers are, of course, trained wherever we can. You all were to be trained in Everly, and in fact, Quinn began hers there. And despite his dark loyalties, Lazlo is a strong, young wizard in the Order of the Legend. He's trained you well in many areas, child."

Quinn mouthed, "I'm sorry," as Julie touched her chest where Quinn had attacked her with bolt spells.

"To realize your full potential, you'll need access and training from the most powerful curators of magic writing," Julie continued.

The map transformed to reveal a circle of five individuals. Soon their outlines transformed into a grand and majestic cityscape filled with library-like structures, arches, walkways, stairwells, and floating books.

"These are the keepers of knowledge, keepers that Dagamar seeks," she continued. "Your powers are but one part of what Dagamar and the Ravagers want. Each of the libraries is hidden in the stone originating its magic. The places with these ancient items you've obtained are home to some of these great academies of magic writing. Parker, you are Order of Chronicle. You'll find the library where the stone you're wearing—the carnelian stone—is buried. This stone powers and fuels us as well as the library. Quinn is Order of Legend, and the sapphire fuels the library."

"What about Aven?" Quinn asked. "What orders are she and Riley?"

The woman smiled. "They are still too young to know for certain, but soon they'll discover their calling. Aven has already found a piece of her powers. She has a special connection to animals, something that will serve her well."

Parker thought about Monty and how the inkwell had not changed color. "What about when the inkwell doesn't give someone an order?"

"Not all children are born with magic," Lady Julie replied. "Most are not. They are the Motsans, nonmagicals, like your father. But as you will learn, being born without magic does not mean one can never become a magic writer. You are here because of this very fact." The glowing scene on the map became filled with flames before it disappeared from view.

"So then, how do we save Riley from the curse?" Quinn asked. "That's why you brought us here."

"By bringing the ancient items back to Lazlo exactly as he instructed," Lady Julie said, holding her palm out and scripting on her nails to create four glowing orbs that floated in front of her.

"Wait, what?" Parker asked. "We bring *him* the items? Why would we do that? He'll just give them to Dagamar."

Inside the orbs, the children could make out a cloak resembling the one Droma had made in Zuma and the two rings of Bask. In the other two spheres, they saw a blue flower and what looked like a small knife.

"Yes, we *must* return the items to him," she replied, the seriousness in her voice creating a chill in the room. "Our only hope is for Dagamar to *believe* you retrieved these items *and* that he has captured you."

"We fought off trolls, Illiterates, water, wolves, dwarfs, and now we just hand ourselves over to the bad guys?" Owen asked. "That's just a crazy plan."

"Yeah, if Dagamar is controlling Lazlo, he'll just deliver us to them," Quinn said. "Isn't that exactly what he wants?"

"I know. But there's simply no other way for us to stop him without putting the four of you in harm's way. Dagamar must *believe* he has won. He must believe you have brought them the items."

Quinn shook her head.

"We must be in two places at once," she said, holding up her palms. "Here *and* here." Images of Serpentine and the Garamond castle illuminated above her hands.

"But how do we do that?" Quinn replied.

"Lazlo instructed you to collect four ancient items," she continued. "And while he told you these items could save your brother, that was not true. These items have a much different purpose."

"They can't save Riley?" Quinn asked.

"Not alone. These are four ancient items Dagamar has sought for many, many years. The cloak of Zuma, the rings of Bask, the flower of Didot, and the Ancient Awl used to create the *Book of the Seven Ancient Stories*. Once Dagamar gathers all four items, he could use them to unlock a powerful force inside himself to take control of all the dark magic and dark magicians, witches, and wizards. This would unlock the silent darkness… for *all* that remains of Fonde."

"And we have three of the ancient items," Quinn said, patting the purse that contained the items. "But where is the key we took from here, from the room?" Quinn scanned the four orbs with the cloak, rings, flower, and the small knife.

"You only have *two*," Lady Julie corrected. She waved her hand, and the orb with the small knife disappeared before all the spheres faded from view.

Quinn took her finger to count the items they'd collected.

"Yes, *two*. And that difference is our only hope of defeating Dagamar."

Aven raised her hand. "Wait, Lazlo is helping Dagamar. So he's bad? I mean, he was kind to us and gave us the compass to find you. And those pecans too."

Lady Julie awkwardly paused at the question.

"Lazlo's story is complicated, my child," she answered. "He is young. He has not had what you did growing up. Dagamar's powers seduced him," Julie responded. "His story remains to be written."

Aven raised her hand again. "But then Dagamar is super bad, like evil?"

"Yes, but not in his beginnings," Julie answered, smiling. She whistled, and her quill darted from her hand and hovered in front of her face. "The book, Veritas."

The quill raced across the room, wedging itself between a series of books before a green book popped out and her quill delivered it to her. She smiled at her quill and set the book in front of them, opening it where a flash of yellow light glowed from between its pages.

"Dagamar was a young boy, and much like your sister Parker, he grew up loving the power of words," she continued as the book illuminated a scene showing a happy, young man. "You see, Dagamar was a Motsan."

"Really? So that's why you said not every magic writer is *born*," Parker said.

"Correct. Dagamar was the most gifted storyteller I've ever seen—his writings, stories, and poems filled the shelves. But his gift was not magical. While he was a Motsan, his mastery of writing was so exceptional he was trained to become a writer and would eventually become the curator and trainer in one of the small literati libraries."

The book showed scenes of the young man teaching rooms of children as they'd seen in various places throughout Zuma and Baskerville.

"Dagamar was not teaching magic writing but simply the power of writing, much as Parker and Quinn were first taught. He was brilliant, and many of the most gifted Serifs studied under him to learn how to harness words beyond enchantments and inscriptions. His stories are those of legend and remain told by many storytellers today throughout Fonde."

The book showed the young man writing and filling book after book on the shelves behind him, as behind him people picked up these books with smiles, tears, and laughter filling their faces as they read.

"But one day, Dagamar left one of the books he was reading in the land of Motsans, where books and words were never to be revealed. His actions that day accidentally revealed the Ellipse secretly connecting the real world to a magical realm. Sadly, a Motsan discovered it and was afraid. They waited and watched, eventually uncovering the passage into the library and all that was inside. The Illiterates soon brought more men, hunting the library entrance until they found it."

She paused and gathered herself as the illusions grew darker, colored by a purple hue.

"That day, the Illiterates set fire to his literati library. There were children still inside who Dagamar was supposed to take from their hiding places, but he refused. He hoped to save his work, the years he'd spent writing the books and his stories. The fire quickly raged, burning the books, the writings, everything. It was a day of great tragedy in the magical realm. Many were lost. Serifs still remember this day as Incendio; a day to remember all of those lost."

A fire in a hidden library. A mistake. Wrongdoing. A Motsan. Was this the fire mentioned in the book in our library? Was that referring to the Incendio?

"Droma told us the Ravagers were celebrating it," Parker said. "Celebrating the *return* of the Incendio."

"That's right. The Ravagers celebrate it now, believing it's a day that will mark the full return of Dagamar and the destruction of all those who don't follow him."

Aven gripped the billy goat's hoof as Dagamar's illuminated face grew darker.

"After Dagamar's actions led to the tragedy at the library," Julie continued, "his rage and anger transformed his writing from love, joy, and triumph to wickedness, hatred, and retribution. His rage began to turn his writing into something more, and his quill began to write magic. He unlocked powers as a Serif, unusual and destructive powers. He'd not been trained, and his inscriptions were wild and uncontrolled, unlike anything we'd ever seen. He hunted the men who'd set fire to the library that day. His rage began to manifest as a unique ability to silence the voices of others, a power we now call the silent darkness."

The book showed Dagamar's inscriptions turn person after person into these mute, almost zombie-like beings.

That's the silent darkness. Parker turned away, unable to watch.

"For the first time in Fonde, a Motsan learned to harness magic writing without training using only deep anger, hatred, fear, and resentment. Soon he was able to show others the same abilities, to teach them. And yet, as he learned to harness his power, he also began to see their limitations—powers harnessed only through his anger. We always knew his dark magic could not defeat the light magic... unless..."

Lady Julie inhaled deeply.

"Dagamar discovered an ancient scroll containing a powerful prophecy that would allow him to *take* the magic of a born-writer and harness it for his own. If he did, he'd be unstoppable."

Lady Julie motioned to Riley as a wave wiped the glowing images away from the book in front of them.

"The prophecy requires the four ancient items and a *born* Serif. This is why Dagamar sought your brother."

"So that's why you took him," Parker muttered under her breath. "You were keeping Riley from Dagamar."

"I had to take Riley, and it's also why I've brought you all here—to try and stop Dagamar from taking the rest of you."

"But I still don't get it," Quinn said. "If Lazlo told us about the ancient items and gave us this compass to find them, why doesn't Dagamar just send his own people to get the items himself?"

"Because he can't," she answered.

"He can't?" Quinn asked. "But he knows exactly where they are."

"He can *find* them, but he cannot *touch* them," she answered.

The four orbs appeared above the book, and the children watched as Ravagers attempted to grab each one, only to be stopped as the invisible enchantments around each one burned their hands.

"You see, we discovered what Dagamar was after and his desire to use them to steal the power of a born-magic writer through this ancient prophecy. When we did, the most powerful Serifs in Fonde—the curators from the five ancient libraries—joined together and scripted a nearly unbreakable enchantment."

The book illuminated a ring of Serifs scripting a powerful spell protecting the ancient items.

"This enchantment made it impossible for Dagamar or those trained by him like Lazlo ever to touch the ancient items. That means even if he or the Ravagers found them, he couldn't *use* them in the way he intended."

"Of course," Quinn said. "Since he can't hold or touch the ancient items, Lazlo needed us. He needs us to gather the items and bring them to him."

"But if those enchantments protect the items, then we're safe, right?" Parker asked. "Even if we bring them to him, he can't use them."

She shook her head. "Dagamar discovered how to break the enchantments."

"How?" Parker asked.

"The unwriting," she said. "He discovered that if he used the power of the unwriting, he could destroy the enchantments." The book revealed a series of powerful flashes exploding around each of the enchantments around the items, destroying the enchantments visible around the objects.

A chill ran over Parker.

"I did not take your brother to keep him from *Dagamar*," she continued. "I took Riley to keep your brother from being *unwritten*."

The book in front of Lady Julie began to glow again as she touched its corner with her quill. A glowing image of Serpentine appeared, and the children watched as Ravagers started to close in on the castle, their quills leaving dark etchings in trees, homes, and rocks.

"I kept your brother safe and hidden here for a year," Lady Julie said as the book illustrated her words. "But I knew it was only a matter of time. The Ravagers were getting closer to finding him and finding me. They were growing stronger, I could sense it, and if they had found us, there would have been no hope or way to prevent this."

"Is that why you let Riley escape?" Quinn asked.

She nodded, and the image in the book revealed the outline of a small figure fleeing the hidden castle, following the small stream outside Serpentine's walls.

"This very moment set everything in motion. The moment Riley stepped foot from Serpentine, the match was struck."

"How?" Quinn asked.

"Riley's escape unlocked the waning moon, a magical moon instantly visible to everyone throughout the magic realm. That waning moon signaled the beginning of the unwriting. And at that moment, Dagamar would see his opportunity to harness the unwriting and return to power."

"Then why would you just let Riley escape?" Quinn asked.

"I realized letting Riley escape was our only hope to stop him."

"I mean, what exactly happens if Riley is unwritten?" Parker said. "Doesn't that just mean he can't do some spell again like what Quinn did to me with the synchronicity inscription in Baskerville?"

"This type of unwriting is far, far worse," she replied.

Parker eyed the faint etchings still in her fingernail.

"Mistakes have been made in your family's past," Lady Julie continued, her tone growing darker. "Your parents upset those forces when they attempted to change the story of another. I sadly played a small part in these mistakes, actions I regret to this day."

"Our family is cursed or something?" Aven asked.

"Yes, but curses are not what they may seem in the stories you've heard," she said. "Curses are magic's way of returning our stories to the natural order."

"You mean this unwriting is some cursed thing to change Riley's story?" Quinn asked. "Making his stories different or something?"

"No," Lady Julie replied. "It's changing his story *back*. Back to the way it was before the mistake. Returning the stories *back* to the natural order."

"But what does that mean for Riley?" Quinn said. "What happens if he is unwritten back to the way his story was *before*?"

Lady Julie stood and walked over to a mirror that filled much of the far wall, and like the mirror hanging in their library, this one had hundreds of tiny icons, carvings, and images embedded into the frame. Julie studied a corner of the frame until she saw what she was looking for and touched her quill into the square dot with an hourglass inside.

"This shows the unwriting," she said as her quill drew a portrait of the four Pennymore siblings.

"Riley's legs are missing," Aven said, pointing at the drawing.

"It's because your brother's unwriting has already begun," she said.

"He's already being unwritten?" Aven asked.

"Yes, the process began as time ticks down until the waning moon," she said. "And we can see what happens as we speed up the time to go forward into the future." She put her finger into the spot in the frame she'd touched with her quill, and the quill began to remove lines and dots from each of them, starting with what remained of the illustration of Riley, and then Aven, Parker, and eventually Quinn until nothing was left.

"It will unwrite us all?" Parker asked.

"Yes," she said. "For you children, there is no *before*," she said.

"No before?" Parker asked.

"But why? Why us?" Quinn asked as she rubbed her temples.

"You see, Quinndaline, we all have free will over our own stories," Julie said. "None of our stories are set in stone. And your story will continue as you change and evolve."

The book showed the outline of an individual standing before a single, straight line. Above him were the seven icons Parker had seen on the cover of the *Book of the Seven Ancient Stories*. Lady Julie took her quill and touched one of the icons, which began to branch out the line from that point. As she tapped another icon, new points and branches grew on the expanding tree-like structure. Then Julie waved her hand over the book. Dozens of unique images of the exact figure, all slightly different from the original, were now visible at the end of every dot.

"Your story is always being written," she continued. "Your choices determine the story and the millions of potential destinies you *can* fulfill. When your parents met, their story was one of love and happiness, but with challenges and obstacles as most love stories have."

The book glowed, showing images of their parents when they were much younger, smiling and holding one another's hand, a branching line now standing before them. She touched one of the icons above them that Parker recognized as *The Story of the Defeat*.

"Before any of you were born, your parents made a difficult choice to change the story of another. It was by no means an easy choice—it was an impossible choice, but a choice nonetheless. Magic can only help us with our story but never *change* another's story. We simply cannot use magic to alter another's free will. That is a choice they cannot take back."

A powerful light exploded around their parents as they held hands, and part of their branching line in front of them evaporated. Then, their mother's body fell to the ground after the flash. The children watched as the image of their father picked up her body and ran with her until they both disappeared from the page, leaving only a broken, partially branched line now on the page.

"What happened?" Quinn asked.

Lady Julie continued, "A horrific price is paid when magic changes the story of another. History cannot be forgotten; it can only be unwritten. You children, each of the Pennymore siblings, are to be unwritten as punishment for those acts."

"But we didn't have anything to do with it, those choices," Quinn protested.

"Your family—the Scotts and now the Pennymores—have a complicated history. And while you were not privy to the choice, this history cannot be forgotten, and it cannot be removed."

Parker remembered the unremovable book she'd found in the library. The one about her family. Perhaps this was why she couldn't remove it from the shelf.

"And so, this story is to be *unwritten* in reverse, beginning with your youngest brother and eventually reaching their eldest," she said. The branches of the line now began to slowly disappear until only the first single line they'd seen in front of their parents remained.

"I warned your parents of this day, but they hoped to find another way. But finally, I knew the only way to delay the unwriting was if I took Riley to protect him. I hoped it would buy time to save his life and yours. He was afflicted with an invisible curse, shielding him from it. All to save him from the unwriting."

"You can't have brought us here just to tell us this. We have to try to save him, our brother, and our family," Parker said. "There has to be another way."

"In two days, your brother is to be unwritten at the waning moon," Lady Julie said. "The unwriting will produce an extraordinary amount of energy, a power rarely seen in the world. It's with that energy that Dagamar will attempt to destroy the enchantments and complete the prophecy, taking the powers of a born Serif."

"And in that single moment, we'd lose everything," Quinn said. "Dagamar breaks the enchantments and harnesses the magic of our brother... forever."

"You kept him safe for a year," Parker said. "He was invisible, and that protected him. Why can't you do that longer? Protect him that way."

"As you've discovered, invisibility is temporary until it is permanent," Lady Julie said. "The unwriting, however, cannot be stopped."

"You're saying if we leave him invisible, then he's stuck that way forever," Quinn asked, "and the magical forces would just move onto Aven, and Parker, and me?"

She nodded.

"But if we make Riley visible, he gets unwritten, and if he's unwritten, he's wiped away forever, and Dagamar gets his powers."

"Yes."

Parker looked at her younger brother, oblivious to the decisions and discussions about his future and the role he might play in the end of all Motsans. She sighed.

"But you said you found another way," Owen said. "You said it. I heard you say there was some other way, right?"

She paused. "I have scoured all of Fonde for some way to stop this, to give us a path to prevent this unchoosable choice," Lady Julie said. "And I may have found it hidden in the ashes of a fire."

"Found what?" Parker asked.

"The way to save you all."

Chapter Twenty-Six

Didot Forest

"Do we *all* have to be here?" Aven asked, clearly tired from her days of being away from comfort. "I didn't even get to finish my dinner."

"Don't worry, I ate it for you," Riley replied.

The walk hadn't taken more than a half-hour from the enchanted Serpentine castle thanks to an hidden Ellipse. The compass had stayed true in its path, unlike the winding, confusing route that first brought them to the hidden key in the castle. They all followed behind Lady Julie as she kept a sharp eye out for others along the path.

"What order is Dagamar?" Parker asked her as she and Owen walked beside Lady Julie. "Is there an evil order or something?"

The woman paused. "We choose our paths, Parker. As you saw, nothing about our path is set, and nothing is certain. The Ravagers can be chronicles, scribes, legends, poets, and enigmas. It's what they choose to do with their power that makes them good or evil, much like all of you children."

"Then what order did the inkwell assign to him?" Parker asked.

"He's never been apportioned. But we believe Dagamar is the Order of Enigma, the raven is his creature, as his quill glows a deep purple color when his rage is fullest."

Parker thought back to the first day she'd put the quill in the inkwell and saw the purple color and the streaks when she froze. *Could her own anger do the same?*

"Remember, we are not but one thing. You will write your story and be your own magic writer," Lady Julie continued. "Things are not always as they seem."

"Are we there yet?" Aven called to the group. "And where is there?"

"We're going to retrieve the last item," Quinn replied.

"But not Dagamar's last item," Lady Julie corrected.

"What do you mean?" Quinn said, confusion filling her face. "Not Dagamar's last item? You said we had to bring him the four ancient items he was seeking."

"I said we needed to bring him four ancient items," she said with a wry smile. "Not all of them are the items *he* is seeking."

"So, a slight of hand?" Owen said, seeing the smile on Julie's face.

"Clever boy," she said, patting him on the shoulder. "The first two items—the ancient cloak spun from Zuman wool and the silver rings of Bask—are the same items Dagamar had you seek. As is the flower of Didot, which we are to obtain next."

"Uh, I got us the rings," Riley said.

"You did, my child." Lady Julie ran her quill across her palm, and the four orbs again emerged: the cloak, the rings, a flower, and the small knife.

"Where's the key?" Quinn asked. "The key we collected from Riley's room in Serpentine?"

"The key will replace one of the items," she said. She moved the orb with the small knife to the side, and in its place, a new orb appeared containing the key.

"And you need us to convince Lazlo we have the items in one place ready to help Dagamar," Owen said, "while you're with Riley in another place at the exact same time of the waning moon to harness the unwriting to try to save *him*."

"Precisely."

"That's why Lazlo can't know that we know," Owen added.

"There are rumors that unwriting can be stopped only through a magical act of true regret," she said. "This key is the original key to the Ellipse that led to the Incendio."

"You can unlock an Ellipse?" Owen asked.

"The magic threads between this world and that are as unique as grains of sand on the beach," she replied. "This key once unlocked the magical door to the library that was the site of the Incendio, and it was that door that the Illiterates accessed to destroy Dagamar's library, sending him on this vengeful path. This key was central to the Incendio. When I discovered it in the ashes and studied its power, I realized it may help us stop this."

"An item of regret... this item is filled with regret over the losses at the Incendio," Quinn said. "But does Dagamar even have regrets?"

"He doesn't need to," she answered, her fixed gaze distant.

"What about the real item, the knife?" Owen asked. "How do we know he can't find it or that Lazlo or Dagamar won't find out and replace it?"

"The key has already fooled the compass," Lady Julie smiled and nodded to Beau. "These items share certain histories, and that was why the compass behaved so strangely on your journey with the wolves to Serpentine. But it led you to me, and I've kept the true ancient object hidden from you and from him to protect us."

"This way, no matter what happens, Dagamar can't get the fourth item he needs?" Quinn asked.

"Correct," Lady Julie said as the orb that held the small knife turned to dust that spread to the four corners of the room. "I've hidden the fourth item he needs in a safe place, protected by both a powerful magic enchantment and by the power of love. You see, even if Dagamar were to find the ancient item, his magic would be useless. He no longer knows how to love. And unless he convinces one of you to join the Ravagers, he'll never, ever be able to get his hands on it."

Aven looked at the others and shook her head as if to confirm she would never join the Ravagers.

"But this item," continued Lady Julie, "the key—is the item I searched for. If we can use it with the others, I'm hoping we can undo the unwriting and save all of you."

"Hoping?" Parker asked.

"These are ancient powers, my child," she replied. "And I'm not sure what will happen when we harness this power, but I'm hopeful we can fix the mistake you children are to be punished for."

Owen made eye contact with Parker and held up two crossed fingers. He mouthed "fingers crossed" and shook his head.

"I saw that, Mister Wickerland," Beau whispered to the boy. "Sadly, you cannot cross a hoof."

Parker's heart thumped, the nervous energy flooding her and beating into her fingertips. "This is our best bet?" Parker asked. "You want us to go back to Lazlo, convince him we have the items, and you'll stay back at Serpentine and perform this other incantation?"

"It is not without risks," Lady Julie said. "But we need Dagamar to believe you're still on your four quests and will bring the items back to Lazlo before the waning moon. And this will require a sacrifice. That is certain, I'm sorry to say."

"A sacrifice?" Quinn asked.

"Yes. Now, ahead is Didot, the kingdom of the living forest," Lady Julie announced. "Someone we seek is holding the final item"

"Where?" asked Quinn, squinting across the tree line. "I just see trees everywhere."

"The eye often misses what it isn't searching for," Lady Julie said with a smile. She whistled, and her quill shot into the air above them. "Veritas. Illuminate!" Glowing dust flew from the quill and danced in the trees in front of them, revealing hundreds of hidden ropes, ladders, platforms, boards, and devices.

"Whoa," Aven called. "I want to climb around that!"

Quinn pointed to naturally occurring tree houses, buildings, streets, shops, and much more. Signs, springs of water, slides, canopies—an entire city hidden from Motsan eyes. "There are steps and bridges above, but nothing down here."

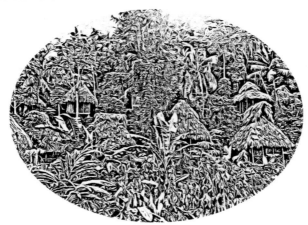

The flowers on Bralwynn's hat reconfigured, mirroring the features of the tree-city above.

Aven began climbing the nearest tree. She couldn't get much traction, and every few inches she advanced, she dropped back to the ground.

"Come now, Aven. I know how to get up there," said Bralwynn. "It's a little-known secret, but there's only one way up to Didot. We dwarfs know things. Here, let me show you."

Bralwynn shuffled past the tree Aven tried to climb and pointed to the frailest, tiniest tree they'd ever seen.

"We can't climb *this*," Aven said. "It's like one of those scrawny house-plants we have in the grand hall!"

Bralwynn grimaced, and her hat top flowers looked at Aven with disapproval. "You don't climb it," the dwarf instructed. "You sit in it."

She pushed down on the little tree until it folded itself into a sort of makeshift seat, and Bralwynn motioned for the ever-so-adventurous Aven to take a seat.

"Is this going to be like Quinn's cask-carriage?" Aven asked as she sat on the tree seat. Before she could say a word, Bralwynn pulled a rope.

The little wolf-girl flung into the air, legs kicking in panic.

"Oh no, this is certainly not a good idea! What have you done!" Beau shouted.

Aven tumbled through the air and trees before landing high in the canopy tree with a thud, a pile of leaves exploding into the air.

"Aven! *Aven*, are you all right?" Quinn called.

Aven peered out from behind the tree.

"Yes! Can I please, please do that again?" She smiled and waved down to everyone below. "That was awesome!"

"Is it the only way up?" Parker asked, hesitant.

"Yep, there's only one way up, but don't worry," said Bralwynn. "It's quick and fun!"

"And *awesome*," Aven called to Parker.

"I've heard that before," Owen said, shaking his head.

"I'll go next," Riley shouted. Riley once again became invisible outside the room where he'd been held. The visibility enchantment only worked inside Serpentine, shielded from the outside world.

Before long, Owen, Beau, Lady Julie, and the Pennymore sisters got on the ride into the soft netting above. Then, Bralwynn seated herself, gave a big tug, and laughed the whole way to the net.

As they exited the netting, Parker saw it was an entire hidden town woven into the fabric of the tree canopy, so well organized it took magic to reveal its contours. There were stores, workshops, buildings, complex homes, water fell from falls and into streams weaved throughout the city, and pulley systems to move effortlessly throughout.

"Now, we need to find the fourth item?" Beau asked, gazing around.

"Finding the fourth item won't be the problem," Lady Julie replied. "Getting the item will be the problem."

"Someone's over there," Aven said, pointing to a little girl sitting on a bench alone.

The group crossed the sturdiest bridge they had come across thus far to reach her.

Aven spoke first, "Hi, there. We are on a quest…"

A hand shot up, interrupting Aven, and pointed to a bridge leading across from her. Then the little girl stood up and quickly walked away, disappearing into the canopy.

The compass pointed to the exact location across the bridge where a small door hid in the bark of a large oak tree.

"I told you, finding the item won't be our problem," Lady Julie said, urging the party across the bridge.

Knock! Knock! Knock! Quinn rapped on the door.

A rustling came from inside the room. A plump woman with gray hair opened the door and stood in the doorway. She smiled at them, the wrinkles around her eyes and mouth deepening. Her smile grew wider when her sweet brown eyes met the Pennymore sisters.

"I was hoping you would come to visit me," she said, motioning for them to join her inside. "I'm Mary. Come in. Come in."

Then, almost as quickly as her smile had appeared, her eyes narrowed, and the smile faded. "Except her," she said, motioning her chin at Lady Julie. "She can wait outside."

"Go on," Julie said, motioning for them to go inside. "I know where to find you."

The Pennymores, Owen, and their two guides entered the small room.

"Sit. Sit," Mary instructed as she hustled into the next room. Off the dark sitting room was the kitchen where Mary fumbled with dishes. She hollered into the sitting room, "We'll have tea and cookies while we go over everything!"

What was that about with Julie?

The children snugly sat around the fireplace in soft, cushioned seats. Mary came in with a piping hot pot of tea and a basket full of fresh cookies full of jams and nuts, chocolate chips, and peanut butter. A piece of tree bark from the basket floated in the air.

"Don't eat it, Riley," Aven said. "Looks like some old tree bark fell into the basket."

"My child, it's the best treat in the basket," Mary corrected. "Rotting oak bark is a delicacy of our people. It's wood from an ancient tree left to rot for hundreds of years until it is the perfect savory, sweet, nutty delight. Oh, I get chills thinking of how much you children will love the Rotted Oak."

Aven's face filled with horror at the thought of eating rotted anything, but Quinn shook her head at her youngest sister, discouraging her from saying it.

Riley thought otherwise, taking a huge bite.

"She's right," he exclaimed, delighted. "It's like a good rot, like really rotten." He quickly devoured the rest of the bark.

Facing the travelers, Mary said, "Please, keep munching and sipping. I know you have questions, but let me begin with a story I think will help clear things up a bit."

Aven carefully continued to sort through the basket of treats, sniffing each.

"The woman you have brought here is my sister," Mary began. "I am a Windhorn."

"Lady Julie has a sister?" Aven exclaimed. "But shouldn't you be happy to see each other?"

"I am here in Didot because of my sister. For her punishment, I will never forgive her. More cookies?"

The teapot rested in the center of the table with steam pouring out of the spout. Mary bent down and inhaled the steam into her lungs. She sat up, blowing the moisture out of her mouth. It formed into a small two-story home, where two gleeful young girls chased one another through the tall grass. A woman appeared in the home window calling to the two girls.

The house looks eerily familiar. Where have I seen this house?

"Ours was a happy family, the Windhorns. Two sisters and one brother. Our parents worked hard to care for us. But our father fell ill and died, leaving three young children under the care of our mother."

The happy scene turned dark as the figures aged, and struggle wove into their faces.

"Our mother was forced to do what she could to earn money, which is when we learned our grandmother had magic inside her, passed down to our mother's daughters."

The scene again transformed.

"My mother was desperate and fought with my grandmother about us. Our grandmother wanted to keep us from magic, especially until we were of age to make our own choices. But our mother won out, and she pushed both of us—Julie and me—to show her our magical abilities. I was the elder sister and was unable to script any magic. Yes, I was a Serif, but I could not learn to harness my powers. My mother cursed me, saying I was weak of mind. Perhaps she was right."

The steam revealed this conversation, and the pain of a young girl's mother scolding her was hard for Parker to witness.

Lady Julie said very few Serifs could script magic without training, but her mother must not have known.

"But Julie, my sister, was strong of mind, and my mother used her magical powers to earn money for our family. She would bring her to towns and cities, showing the powers of a magical girl to entertain. My mother treated her like an animal in a cage. She took her from village to village to be shown off for a few coins. My sister was on display until one day; then, she couldn't take it anymore. Julie ran away without a trace."

The steam vanished. Mary bent down to suck in another breath of hot steam and blew a new circle.

"Without Julie and the money she could bring her, our mother became desperate, broken, and erratic. When I was about Quinn's age, I returned home to find my mother killed by some of the Illiterates. My mother couldn't write, but they killed her because they knew her daughter could."

Mary looked away before continuing.

"My mother left me alone to care for my younger brother. Julie, my sister, never returned, never even paid her respects to our mother after her death. My brother and I would scavenge for scraps, steal coins, and beg."

Their brother appeared in the steam, a handsome young boy but dirty and malnourished.

"We found our way. Cleaning houses, fixing broken walls and tables, growing and selling vegetables. We built a good life for ourselves, and then she returned."

The siblings in the steam grew into adults. Lady Julie became a younger version of the woman who had brought them here.

"She had returned from the kingdom of Everly where, eventually, she would care for you. She promised to help us, get us work, and visit more. But her promises were all lies."

The steam moved in sharp angles and grew darker in color.

"Then she fled, kidnapping Riley. Your father's soldiers came looking for our help. We told them what we knew, but they were not satisfied. They took my brother, and I never saw him again. He vanished like my sister."

Parker looked at Owen, watching him process what they'd just heard. She placed her hand on his, eliciting a faint smile from him.

"And then," Mary continued, "they decided to take everything, including the home where we'd lived all our lives. They warned us of the flood— said it would protect us from the Ravagers. They gave us one hour to leave, to gather my entire life up. They promised they'd help, but it wasn't enough time."

The steam formed a massive wall of water that rained down into the valley, enveloping what she now recognized as Mary and Julie's childhood home. It was the home from the seafloor, the house she'd seen when she'd first tried to run away. The wave of water washed over Mary's home, vanishing it beneath the dark and stormy water.

"I fled," Mary continued. "I took everything I could, but that water buried my memories. I came here. My sadness unleashed something hidden inside me, and these people, these plants and trees protected me, saved me. These creatures are alive and have kept me alive."

The steam showed the trees walking and reforming the treetop canopy. This was a living kingdom of trees.

"You seek my help, our help," Mary said as the steam faded away. "But who was there to help me? I cannot forgive your parents for what they have taken, and I cannot forgive my sister. She left us. She took my home. She took our brother. This is my family now."

Parker placed her hand on Mary's, holding Mary's and Owen's hands in her own.

"But why should I give you my help?" she asked. "By helping you, Didot and our people put all that we've built at risk. For what?"

"For family," Parker said. "We give you our word. We will do everything to make this right and to keep Didot from falling into darkness."

"Without your help, all of us will be unwritten," Quinn continued. "And maybe all of Fonde."

Mary closed her eyes and nodded her head as she did.

"I will help you," she said with a sigh. "I cannot bear the thought of you being alone, losing one another. I cannot fix the past by continuing to live in it."

"Thank you," Quinn said. "Truly."

"I will bring you the item you seek to save yourselves and your kingdom."

She rubbed her fingers together, and a blue flower appeared.

"This is the blue lotus," Mary said. "It's an ancient flower that only grows here. I'll bring it to you by tomorrow's dusk so your family will not suffer the same tragic fate ours has. Now you must go."

The flower image faded, and Mary stood to collect the dishes.

The sisters and their companions silently stood and walked to the door.

Parker turned to Mary. "Thank you for everything. When you are a sister, you are never alone. We are grateful for you helping us save our brother."

"I just hope it is enough."

Chapter Twenty-Seven

Flames of the Tongue

"How could they take her brother? Wipe away an entire village?" Parker asked. "Our parents use magic to protect us, but for what?"

"You'll never understand how much your parents love you until you have a child," Beau offered. "It's the circle of life and love. You only understand the love you've received when you've been able to give the same."

"But they destroyed *her* family to do it," Parker said. "They took her brother and her home."

"They were trying to protect Everly," Owen said.

"But they took *you* from your family, too, all to protect us," she said. "Us."

Parker stormed away, slamming the door to Mary's home, and stomped into the night.

Angry and confused, she raised her glistening eyes to the haze-covered moon and said, "How could they?"

Quinn placed her arm around her. "When they lost Riley, they couldn't bear the thought of it happening again. You know how we felt. Imagine the hurt and pain. They did what they thought they had to do to protect us."

Parker's heart ached, and her hands shook. "But they drove a wedge in her family for ours? It's not right."

The fire at the library, the council, her father, Dagamar's rage, Lady Julie and Lady Mary's brother, the waters of Drain Day and their home, Owen. Her parents no longer felt like protectors. She winced. They destroyed others to try and fix their mistakes.

Her mother's words echoed in her head: *And sadly, we do not understand who our friends are and who are our enemies.*

These moments repeatedly played in Parker's mind as they walked silently from Didot back to the hidden castle at Serpentine.

Parker tasted sulfur in the air.

A man ran toward them.

Quinn drew her quill and extended her palm. "Get behind me, everyone," she called, the group huddling around her as she scripted on her nails. "Celare!"

Blue dust whirled from her palm, forming a transparent, glowing field around them. "Very impressive, my child," Lady Julie whispered to her, placing her hand on Quinn's shoulder.

The man approached, breathing hard, his face covered with dirt and soot. His clothes were ripped, and a speck of blood pooled at the corner of this lip.

"Clovis!" Lady Julie called out. She placed her hand on Quinn's wrists, pulling them down, the glowing field evaporating as she did.

Parker recognized the man from the Serpetine's kitchen.

"They found us!" he shouted. His breathing was shallow and frantic. "We tried to keep them away, but they ambushed us. They ransacked everything, tore the castle apart, tortured the guards for any information about you, and then…"

He sobbed. Through quivers, he said, "They are gone. My friends and the others from the castle… gone."

Julie placed her hands on his face and peered into his eyes. "Who?" she asked. "Who did this?"

The man's pained eyes shifted to the Pennymore sisters standing beside Julie.

"We need to know," Quinn said.

"He asked where *they* were," he said, his trembling finger pointing at the children. "And when we told him we didn't know, his soldiers—" He put his face in his hands and wailed.

Our father's soldiers? They found the castle. But our father isn't some violent tyrant who would attack innocent people.

"Did you see him?" Quinn asked. "Our father. Is he here?"

The man shook his head. "No, the soldiers, they set fire to the castle and left."

Lady Julie nodded her head. "I'm so sorry. I cannot ever repay you. This sacrifice is more than I could ever repay," Lady Julie whispered to him. "Now go. You must protect yourself and find any others who escaped. Please hide."

He turned and ran. Parker watched him flee, the scents and sounds of fire filling her senses.

Lady Julie took the hands of the Pennymores in hers. "Children, come with me and stay in the shadows. We aren't safe here. We must find a place to stay and see what we can save."

"Why would your father destroy Serpentine?" Owen asked Quinn. "You could have been inside."

"He wouldn't," she answered. "He's never been like that—destruction and war. That's not him. It can't be."

They followed Lady Julie through the dark woods. Quinn and Julie held their quills in their fingertips until they came to the top of a hill, still hidden but in sight of the Serpentine castle.

Flames rampaged out from the open areas, creating a heavy black ash cloud. Everything crumbled to ashes. The serpent's tongue was ablaze, the castle destroyed.

Lady Julie looked at her home, the glow of the orange and yellow flames reflecting on her stoic face. Then buried her face in her hands.

"Lazlo," Julie said. "Lazlo knew you were here. He knew."

"No," Quinn said, her voice filling with rage between her tears. "This can't be."

"I—I could never have imagined," Julie muttered.

"Was *this* the sacrifice you were talking about?" Her hands motioned to the flames that poured out. "Back there? This was the sacrifice? This."

Lady Julie looked to the ground and nodded.

"It was the only way. I knew that," she said. "There had to be a sacrifice, so they didn't discover our plan, get suspicious. I wanted them to know you were here. To know you completed the quest, so they'd bring you home. I just didn't believe they'd destroy, destroy everything."

"You didn't have to—not this," Quinn said.

"Dagamar had to believe we would return with the items to Everly," Parker said. "And so, this leaves us no choice but to return. Maybe they figured it out with the compass or… who knows."

"It was me," Quinn said. "Lazlo knew about this place because I told him. I'm so sorry. I led them all here. I wrote all of it down for them. I wrote down what Riley said, the details of how he'd found us. Every landscape, every marking. I didn't know he was a Ravager. I thought he could bring the soldiers to find you and punish you. I gave him a map to find you. And he destroyed everything." She broke down crying.

Parker placed a hand on Quinn's shoulder. "This isn't your fault. You were trying to protect us."

Watching the embers and ashes float overhead, Parker remembered Beau's words about the fire's role in their past and present. "But we still have the items," Owen offered, pointing to the bag slung over Parker's shoulder.

"Yeah, I have them all," Parker said. "And tomorrow, we'll have the blue lotus. We still have everything to fix this, right? Listen, all is not lost… it's not."

"Not everything," Lady Julie said dejectedly. She turned from the flaming castle to the others. "I told you it would require sacrifice, but I never expected them to destroy Serpentine. I hid everything inside the castle. Now I no longer have the ancient texts to script the incantation. The books, the herbs for the ancient ink, the preparation—it's all gone. I can't do the inscription without it."

Aven placed her arms around Lady Julie.

"They—they won," Quinn said quietly. "All of it…"

Parker clenched her fists and gritted her teeth. "They can't. It can't be," she said. "I don't believe it. There has to be another way."

"My child, I can't perform the incantation without the preparations. Those are gone," Julie said as she pointed to the remains of Serpentine.

"What if there's another way?" Parker asked. "You said we need to be in two places at once. But maybe we don't have to. You said we needed to return the items, right? Maybe we still return, but we rewrite the story when we get there."

"Huh?" Quinn said.

"We confuse them. We change the story on them; surprise them with something they never expected."

"You heard what Lady Julie said," Quinn answered. "We don't even have what we need anymore."

"But maybe we don't *need* them," Parker said with a smile. "Lady Julie, you taught me every great story has a plot twist, some misdirection, and a climax. Remember, it's not the obstacle; it's what the hero does after the obstacle comes that matters, right? Maybe we just need to write a different ending. Our climax."

"But I'm not sure what we could do, my child," Lady Julie said.

"They expect us to return," Parker continued. "They are counting on it, but they aren't counting on what we do *when* we return. I mean, I thought I had to do this myself. That's why I tried to run away, but then the Plumes, and you guys… we have something they don't have."

"What's that?" Quinn asked.

"Something we care about," Parker said. "We already have an army… the four of us Pennymores and Owen, but there's even more of us now with everyone we've met here in Fonde and the Plumes. It'll take us all to play a part, but it might work."

"I'm not sure it's worth the risk for all of us to return," Beau meekly offered.

"Yes, there are many in these magical realms who may be lost if we fail," Bralwynn said.

"You guys always said Parker was the best storyteller," Owen said. "Heck, I don't even know what a plot twist is, but we got to do something. Does anyone have a better idea?"

Quinn shook her head.

"Okay, then to pull this off, we'll need all of us. And these," Parker said, holding the enchanted measuring cup, tea ball, and oven mitt in her hands. "Oh, and Aven, I need a piece of your hair."

"My hair? But I love my hair," she said as she let out a dramatic sigh. "But I suppose I can contribute one hair… all in the name of a good story."

"Deal," Parker said. "And then we'll just need a lot of luck."

✳✳✳

The early morning of the waning moon, the early glow of dawn beginning to show on the horizon. The two eldest sisters had stayed up with Lady Julie much of the night, sitting around her quill as it floated in front of them, emitting warmth like a fire to cut the night's chill.

"We don't have to take such a risk.," Lady Julie whispered to Parker and Quinn. "There is another way."

The others slept nearby. The smell of the smoke from Serpentine hung in the air, obscuring the dawn.

Quinn nodded her head. "Yeah, Riley remains invisible," she said. "He could live—not be unwritten, right? That was why you kidnapped him, to keep him hidden and safe. Could you take him and find another place, further hidden in Fonde, and so long as the Ancients didn't see him and never found him, his story could not be unwritten?"

"We could try," Lady Julie agreed.

"And until they decided to unwrite the other Pennymore siblings," Quinn continued, "the rest of our family could continue to live in peace."

"Eventually, you'd all need to become invisible to stay alive," Lady Julie said. "To avoid the unwriting."

"And then what? What if they found Riley or us," Parker asked, "even when we are invisible?"

"You could still be unwritten," she said.

"You said he won't stop until he finds us—until Dagamar can harness the unwriting," Parker said. "What happens when he finds us?"

"That will be the end of Fonde as we know it."

"You told us he was stopped before, in the mountains," Quinn said. "You said a *brave* Serif stopped him before. Can we find that person to do it again?"

"No. That Serif sacrificed their powers that day. Forever."

"Maybe we are the new brave Serifs," Quinn said, her eyes revealing a glint of hope again.

"That's right. If all of us joined together," Parker said as she looked at the others, "you, Mary, me, and Quinn. We heard about the curators like Droma. Others may join, right? Could we all stop him?"

"We have to try," Quinn said. "We have to."

Lady Julie looked away. "Dagamar was among the most powerful wizards on the planet. He seeks to become the master curator. His power came from anger and vengeance, which led to his defeat before. We must count on that, though I'm not sure we alone are enough."

Aven sat up and stretched. "You have the four of us, the Pennymores," she said through a yawn.

"And me," Owen said, joining them.

"And you said we've got an army of Plumes," Parker added. "None of us know how to write magic yet, but let me tell you there ain't a braver group in Fonde. We can write and aren't afraid of a little rebellion."

"While I admire your optimism, I still don't think that all of us could defeat Dagamar. He's much too powerful, and his followers are strong," Lady Julie said. "Our best hope is to keep Lazlo from fulfilling his goals. Then we can buy time to gain the support of other Serifs and bring more to Everly's shore."

"Maybe Lazlo would listen to us," Parker said. "I don't think he wants to hurt us."

"Defeating Lazlo and preventing Dagamar from coming to Everly is our best hope, children," Lady Julie said. "Even so, I must warn you, once unwriting begins, once that concentration of magic begins, it'll be too late to stop Dagamar from returning."

"We have to try," Parker said.

"You also have the billy goat and me if it counts for much," Bralwynn laughed, joining the group huddled around the warmth of the quill.

"We are grateful for all of you," Quinn said. "But first, we need you both to return to your homes. You must warn the dwarfs, the animals, and other magical creatures. We'll need your help to save them if we fail."

"Oh, Pennymores," Beau responded. "I do not believe you are capable of failure. Your stories have not written it." He winked at Parker. "And we shall be in your service here forward."

The girls hugged their new friends, grateful for their friendship and loyalty.

"We will do as you've asked," Beau said. "We know the way through the magical realms, through the hidden Ellipses."

Bralwynn and Beau said their goodbyes and quickly departed, knowing the plan would require the support of their kingdoms and a bit of explaining after their hasty departures from Zuma and Baskerville.

Parker watched Owen whisper something to Lady Julie, and the two of them stood and walked away from the rest of the group. After a few minutes, Owen returned and sat next to Parker as Lady Julie stared at her smoldering home.

"What were you talking about?" Parker asked.

"About my place. About my role, what I could do to help."

"What did she say?"

"She said to be patient and said my story will be revealed when it is my time, but that now was not it. She said mine is *The Story of Will*, a story that has now brought me something powerful and dangerous. And I will have a choice."

"A choice?"

"That's what she said."

"Well, I'm glad you're here," Parker said. "You could have left us, but you didn't."

He looked up and turned to her, a seriousness in his eyes. "Parker, what I didn't tell you before was I wasn't even brave enough to run away how you did. I had seen some written words and wanted to learn about them. My parents and I had fought about writing. I told them the Illiterates were going so far beyond what the Ancients ever wanted. I couldn't take it anymore. I ran into the water that day, so someone would notice, someone might see me finally. Someone might help me. I never realized I'd be sucked away. That moment changed everything for me."

"But your parents think you drowned."

"And maybe it's better that way. Part of me is glad this happened. I know you're angry with your parents for what they did, for what they did to me, Mary, and her brother, but at least they tried. I mean yeah, sure they kidnapped me, but they were always kind, and they did it for *you*. I was never going to be the son they wanted. I always just wanted to know someone cared for me, and I wasn't some bother or someone they wanted to use for their cause."

"But don't you miss them?"

"I want them to know I'm okay, but I don't think they'll change their minds."

"About writing?"

"About listening," he said. "I'm never going to be who they want me to be."

"We write our own stories," Parker said, nodding. "Family, huh?"

"I'm grateful for this new family," he said as he waved to the group. "It's weird, but at least it's *my* weird."

The pair sat together as Julie returned, a sad look on her face. "It's time," she said. A friendly voice bellowed, "Isn't this a sight for sore eyes?"

Dante, the magnificent wolf, strode toward them.

"Dante," Aven said, racing to him and burying her face in the warm fur of his neck. "Thank you for coming."

"I will always come when you speak," he said, bowing his head to acknowledge the others.

"You don't have to do this," Quinn said to him. "You've already done more than we could ever repay."

"A code binds us," he bellowed. "When one in the pack is in need, all in the pack are of service. She is one of us." He motioned to Aven, who had moved to speak to Lady Julie.

"We must go, child, as the sun is rising," Dante said.

Aven and Riley climbed on the great wolf's back as he circled the others.

"You'll know it's me," Aven called back with a smile. "My howl is the loudest of all."

She tipped her head back and howled. Dante raced away in a blink of an eye, carrying the two younger siblings.

"You ready?" Parker said to Owen.

"I already felt like an honorary Pennymore, and this just seals the deal." He flashed two thumbs-up to the elder Pennymore sisters before walking away to give them time together.

Alone with Lady Julie, Parker and Quinn leaned in close in a circle, their foreheads pressed together as they hugged one another.

"We finally found you again," Parker said, "and now we have to lose you again. It's not fair."

"My child," she answered. "You're never alone. Remember, I'm always near you." Her hand touched her heart, and the gem began to glow.

"Never alone," Quinn said.

"This will work," Parker said assuredly. "It has to. And then it's going to make a good story."

"No, a *great* story," Quinn corrected.

"It's our time now, children," Lady Julie said, holding them tightly. "You must do it and never hold back despite your feelings for me. They must believe you."

Owen rejoined them, and they all made their way down the hill, Lady Julie leading followed by the sisters and the honorary Pennymore.

The last moments together were somber without discussion, smiles, or happiness.

***

"Who goes there?" a voice bellowed at them.

"We are the sisters of Everly," Quinn replied authoritatively, her face illuminated by the guard's torchlight.

"We've captured the witch."

Chapter Twenty-Eight

The Broken Quill

"Here. Take it," Quinn said, holding two pieces of a broken, gray quill in her outstretched hand. "It's hers."

Their father ran to them, throwing his arms around them.

"We thought we'd lost you," he said, ignoring the broken quill as he embraced them. He had met them on the shore where his boats had landed. His guards, who had walked with them from the ruins of Serpentine, left the Pennymore sisters alone with their father.

Behind him, Lazlo kept within earshot.

"Dozens of soldiers and my daughters captured her," he said, beaming with pride. "She kept our kingdom on edge for a year, and you return with her in chains. I'm so proud of you. You must be exhausted. We will get you home to recuperate."

"Yes," Quinn answered. "Just tired. It's been hard."

"You are *so* brave," he said, kissing each of his girls on the cheek. As he leaned down to kiss his youngest daughter, he recoiled. "What's this? Owen Wickerland?"

"Uh, hi, Your Highness," Owen said awkwardly, the hood still covering his head, pieces of curly, blond hair sticking out.

"How did you—" Their father examined the boy's face.

"Yeah, so I'm probably a little shorter and smaller now than you remember, like eight-year-old me, but it's still me. And the hair, well, yeah, this is actually Aven's hair too. It's just kinda stuck on in here. It's cool, right? I think I look pretty good with blond hair. All Parker's ideas. You like our dramatic irony?" Their father stared at him until Owen leaned over to Parker and whispered, "This *is* the dramatic irony part, right?"

Parker smiled at him and nodded. "Yeah, you nailed it, Owen. Aven is safe, Father," Parker said. "This was our decision, a way to protect her and us." She pointed to Owen.

"Where is she?" their father asked. "How do you know she's safe?"

"We found help and split up," Quinn answered. "But she's safe. We need you to keep this all a secret, to keep us all safe. Aven will join us at the castle. You need to send a boat one hour before dusk to the shores across from the amphitheater. She'll be there with her protector."

"How do you know?" he pressed. "How can you be sure she's safe?"

"She's with someone we trust, Father," Parker said. "We couldn't lose anyone else and knew what we were trying was extremely dangerous. "

"And you both?" their father asked. Parker studied him, his eyes those of the kind man who'd told them stories and protected them. "You—you're both not hurt. You're okay, really?"

Lady Julie, her hands and feet bound by thick chains, was led past them onto the boat that would return them to the island of Everly.

Parker wanted to scream at her father. *His soldiers hunted her, hurt innocent people, and now Lady Julie is bound and being treated like a prisoner.*

Instead, Parker forced a smile on her father. She felt exhausted, the days of little sleep and the weight of their actions heavy on her.

Their father took each of his daughters by the hand and led them onto the gangway of his ship. Owen followed.

"We lost Riley," Quinn lied, ensuring Lazlo, who also followed, heard what she'd said. "We had him, but he slipped away. Riley is alive. We just lost him…"

Their father bent on a knee, taking Quinn's face in his hands. "You did everything you could, everything. We will find him."

"You can't stop searching," Quinn said.

"Say no more," their father said. "We'll have plenty of time to discuss."

He took the broken quill pieces from her hands and put his arm around Lazlo.

"Amazing, aren't they?" he said proudly. "Captured the witch without soldiers or any fancy magic even. Can you handle this now?" He placed the broken quill pieces into Lazlo's hand, walking past him up the gangway onto the boat.

Lazlo examined the quill in his hand.

"It's hers," he said. "The quill, it's hers. I know it's markings. They've broken it, and she'll be unable to script magic now."

"I know. *They* did it. Is there more?" their father said. "Do you need something?"

"No, sire," he meekly answered.

"The soldiers have already taken her below deck. You are dismissed. My children have returned," the king said, a smile on his face.

Lazlo nodded to their father and looked down again at the broken quill in his hand with sadness. He quickly turned and walked up the gangway, leaving them alone with their father.

"We must get you children home," the king said. "Your mother hasn't been able to sleep since you left. She'll be happy to have you safe."

"Father," Parker said, drawing back to look him directly in the eye. "We'd rather not be alone tonight. We'd like to be with you, our family, your advisers, and the important people of Everly. We'd like a small celebration to thank those who aided our journey."

"So soon?" their father asked.

"Yes," Quinn continued, "it's been a trying few days, and with our family back together and this chapter behind us, we want to remember this day. It's important to us."

"Then it shall be arranged," their father said, and he walked the three of them into the main cabin of the ship.

***

Mother raced to their boat as it docked at Everly. "My girls! My girls! Where have you been? Are you hurt?" She threw her arms around them as Owen stayed back, his head covered by the hood to ensure he wasn't seen. "I—we were so worried. What is Aven doing?" she said, eyeing Owen.

The girls told Mother about Owen and assured her they were all safe.

Quinn said, "We went looking for Riley. He spoke to us. He's alive."

"I've instructed our soldiers to continue their search," their father offered. "We know where he was kept. We found her hiding place."

The queen pulled them in tighter.

Over their mother's shoulder, Parker saw the guards drag Lady Julie off the boat. She ached at how Lady Julie was treated, desperately wanting to call out to her.

Their mother turned to see the commotion.

"Guards, take her away from our sight!" she ordered, her hands quivering.

The guards roughly grabbed the metal cuffs on Julie's wrists and led her away. Their father smiled at his family, then set off after them.

Lazlo followed their father and the guards, glancing at the sisters as he passed.

Word had already spread of their return, and crowds of people were waiting for them.

"Our children are safe!"

"Heroes!"

"Burn the witch!"

"Into the drain with her!"

Their return to Everly was a triumph; these girls captured an evil villain who had thrown the kingdom into chaos. Smoke still billowed from the amphitheater, as the conflict with the Illiterates had escalated since they'd left. News shouters shared snippets and highlights of their return.

"The castle has been fortified," their mother said. "We've doubled the protections, and your father's forces have surrounded the amphitheater. It's only a matter of time before we end this conflict with the Illiterates."

"And our friends," Parker said, "are they safe?"

"Of course," Mother answered. "This was their demonstration to distract us, and we let them take the amphitheater without bloodshed. I told you, this was always the plan."

"What happened when you negotiated with them?" Parker asked.

Her mother looked at her quizzically. "Me? Negotiate with the Illiterates? I haven't spoken with them," she said. "I have stayed far away. I've never left the castle."

The sisters glanced at one other. *Our father told us she was speaking with them during their dinner. He sent her. Why would he tell us that?*

"But you're safe now," Mother said. "This can all be over soon now that Lady Julie has been captured. When their leaders hear of what the two of you have done and know their children are safe once more, it'll be all over."

"Over?" Quinn replied. "You told us there was an attack coming... Dagamar," she whispered. "Dagamar and the Ravagers were coming to Everly. That's why you let the Illiterates take the amphitheater. To delay that attack."

"But you already defeated her," Mother said. "You snapped her quill. You stopped it. All that's over now. We've won. Once Aven returns and Riley is found, everything will be back to normal."

Parker bit her lip.

"We've won because of *you*," she said to them as she put her arms around their shoulders. "It's finally *over*."

Quinn locked eyes with Parker, both fully aware they were on their own for the coming fight.

***

All morning following their return, well-wishers came by the castle to congratulate the sisters, offering them words of encouragement, small gifts, and tokens of appreciation. Some asked the sisters to show their children the Plumes sign, now the most famous symbol for school children in Everly. The castle was still on alert, but the well-wishers seemed to see their return as a source of hope.

It is exhausting.

"This is so much fun," Quinn said. "We are famous, and it's all thanks to your hand sign. Why doesn't anyone seem to remember they had delicious doughnuts delivered to them, too, from yours truly?"

"I feel like we are missing something big," Parker said.

"Why are you so worried? Usually, I'm the worried one," Quinn said. "We've got a plan. Owen is back and regular-sized. Lady Julie is here even though she's locked in the dungeon. Mary and the others are coming here tonight. We have the objects, and the true fourth item is hidden away and protected. Riley and Aven are safe. Your plan is going to work, Parker. It's a good plan."

"I hope so," she said.

They had little time for additional consideration. Once the special visitors and dignitaries had finished greeting the sisters, Monty, Tatiana, and the Gazettes arrived at the Hall of Resplendence.

"Hey, bird-heads," Quinn called out. "You came."

"We're looking for the girl who silenced the Illiterates!" Monty boomed as he walked in.

"Hey, don't forget the girl who delivered the doughnuts," Quinn said to him.

Monty blushed while the other children waved back at her.

"Monty!" Parker called out. She ran to the door to see them all.

"You said you wanted to get away from the Plumes for a bit," Monty said as he embraced her. "We didn't expect you'd wind up running away from the kingdom. You guys are all anyone is shouting about. You gotta give me an exclusive."

"Was this all part of your plan?" Tatiana asked.

"This plan involved a bit of a detour," Parker said, smiling at Quinn. "A pretty *big* detour."

"You're the one who always says every good story needs a big obstacle, P," Monty added. "But we got your message—the red flag from your window. Marcus and Matteus knew *exactly* what you meant the moment we saw it. Clever, real clever."

"Yeah, and so we started tailing all the kids who cornered you in Avenir after that," Matteus said. "And those kids haven't taken a drink without us knowing what was in their cup. Four days straight, no gaps. None."

"We rotate shifts," Marcus continued. "It's like a well-oiled machine, chronicles, legends, poets, scribes, enigmas, and plume orders."

"Did you find anything?" Quinn asked.

"Frederick Chickory is a real crybaby. He's got some serious issues," Matteus said, his brother furiously nodding. "But the big thing was we saw ol' four dots herself, Cassandra Waddle, meeting with *your* Lazlo. It was quick, just a few minutes, yesterday. I couldn't even tell if it was planned or just a random meeting, but they were talking. None of us could get close enough to hear what they said, but it felt…" He paused.

"Inappropriate," Marcus continued. "You don't want the castle wizard in some awkward meeting with that crackpot school ringleader from the Illiterates. I almost started booing at her just to show her what I thought but didn't want to blow our cover. That was mostly it, though."

"That's great, *really* helpful," Parker said, nodding to Quinn. "There's a lot to update you about, but first, we're going to need your help." She motioned to Quinn.

"We found out Dagamar is amassing an army," Quinn said. "*The* Dagamar."

"I knew it," Tatiana said.

"Yes, the muted child. The black etchings in the Shadow Territories," Quinn continued. "We think those were a signal to the rest of the Ravagers."

"But there's more. We are also pretty sure Lazlo is working with him," Parker said.

"No way," Monty said, slapping the arm of the Gazettes. "You guys *were* right. Inappropriate isn't the half of it."

"I know," Quinn said. "People seem to believe us capturing Lady Julie means this is over—"

"But it's *far* from over," Parker continued.

"Julie *didn't* kidnap Riley," Quinn said. "She was protecting him."

"But you just put her in the dungeon," Monty said. "Shouldn't you tell people she's not, like, evil or something?"

"We can't," Parker said, "at least not yet anyway. No one would believe us."

"Yeah, my parents freaked out when I asked them about the Ravagers after Drain Day," Tatiana said. "I'm not even allowed to mention that name in our house again. Whoever they are, they seem like super bad news."

"Dagamar wants to be the master curator," Quinn said. "Wipe out any nonmagic creatures and rule all of Fonde. He's every terrible story villain you've heard about all rolled into one."

"And you think *your* Lazlo is working with *that* guy?" Matteus asked. "I thought he was protecting us with the magical seawater and all."

"Trust me, this story is turning out to be full of surprises," Parker said, looking over at Quinn. "And get this: We think the Illiterates may be working with the Ravagers somehow. That's why the meeting with Cassandra and Lazlo is a big deal. That's proof the elf was right about it."

"Wait, did you just say elf?" Monty asked. "Like, a legit, real elf?"

"Yeah, when did you meet an elf?" Quinn said, her face shocked at the admission. "I was with you the entire time…"

"It doesn't matter," Parker said, trying to brush off this revelation. "It's just that what the Plumes saw means we've got to keep our eyes open for anything strange. Unusual alliances are being drawn."

"But you've got to be kidding, right?" Monty interrupted. "The Illiterates and Ravagers are on the total opposite sides of this writing rule thing. Uh, no writing and *magic* writing…"

"Yeah, that doesn't make any sense," Marcus replied. "Why would people who hunt writers help some evil magic writers?"

"We've been trying to figure that out too," admitted Parker.

The Pennymore sisters relayed the rest of what they'd learned, leaving out parts about their roles as magic writers in the conflict.

"We think Dagamar is still trying to come to Everly," Parker said. "And we think he may try something tonight. "

"Tonight?" Monty said, scanning the room for any signs.

"Tonight is the waning moon, and the waning moon is a powerful moment when Dagamar… well, let's just say it's a moment when things can get ugly for all of us. We want to keep him from getting here," Quinn said.

"We understand the Illiterates are angry for the return of magic writing, but what would Dagamar want with you guys and Everly?" Tatiana asked.

Quinn looked at Parker, then answered, "We don't know for sure, but we think our parents have a history with Dagamar. Something happened that led him to discover his power, and we think our parents were there when it happened. Now we're in the middle of it too. We can't tell you everything…"

"Because part of the plan is going to require some secrecy and major luck," Parker continued.

An awkward silence hung in the air.

"Maybe this is an inappropriate question, but I sorta have to ask it," Monty said. "Are you magic writers? Like, are you *real* Serifs?"

Quinn and Parker looked at one another, smiles creeping across their faces.

"Of course it's inappropriate, Monty," Parker said. "And yes. We are magic writers."

"I knew it!" Monty exclaimed. "I totally-totally knew."

"For real?" Tatiana asked.

"It's real," Parker said.

"But that's not all," Quinn said, looking at her sister. "We aren't the only magic writers in this room. So are *you*." Quinn looked at them and then paused to let this sink in. "Parker had you dip a quill in the rainbow inkwell," she continued. "And then that whole magical dust thing happened. Well, none of you knew it at the time, but you were taking part in an ancient Serif ceremony called Apportionment. That inkwell has helped magic writers find their orders for thousands of years. That ceremony is how you learn you're a magic writer. I'm Order of Legend. And this means soon I'll get to attend one of the ancient libraries to study how to write magic. Parker too."

"Quinn actually knows how to write *some* magic already, but I can't write magic yet," Parker added. "I'll learn, and Quinn promised to teach me… and you guys too. I've made her an honorary Plume since I'm pretty sure she can keep our secret safe."

Monty, Tatiana, and the Gazette twins flashed Quinn the Plume sign, who curled her fingers into the same shape.

"We are magic writers? *Real* magic writers—I can't believe it," Marcus said, shaking his head. "Just normal kids can be Serifs?"

"Looks like we *aren't* such normal kids, Marcus," Tatiana said.

"And now we just need to make it through tonight to get our quills and learn how to make things fly," Monty said.

Quinn glanced at Parker. They both knew inkwell didn't apportion him, and he had to give the other Motsans the titles of Order of Plume himself. Monty couldn't learn to make things fly; he wasn't a magic writer. *But Lady Julie said not all magic writers are born. I'm going to help Monty find his magic too. I owe him that.*

"Tonight is important," Parker said, nodding to Monty. "We think something is happening here in the castle. We don't know what, but there's a chance it's dangerous, really dangerous. And listen, we can't tell you to come tonight. I wouldn't ask you to put yourself in danger—"

"Did those mayfly boots I made work well on the trip?" Marcus asked. Tatiana glared at him. "What? I—I just wanted to see how the boots did," he continued.

"My brother's awkward change of subject is important to talk about," Matteus added. "You just said it's dangerous, and we already did our part. We followed those Illiterate kids, but you know our mother would kill us both for something like this. Plus, none of us know anything about magic writing yet, so what do we do if that evil guy shows up?"

"Are you two bootheads trying to get out of this?" Tatiana said, rolling her eyes at the twins. "No chance. You boys are in," she said. "I'm Order of Legend like Quinn, so I'm prepared to be legendary tonight." She winked at the nervous twins. "You'll both be great. Your moments of greatness await. You are *not* normal kids anymore, Gazettes."

"And we don't need any of you to write magic or to fight some evil writer," Quinn continued. "We just need everyone to play their part in the story. But we know this is our fight."

"Everly is our home too," Monty replied.

"And Pennymores *are* Plumes," Tatiana added. "Plumes fly together. Remember?"

All of them curled their fingers into the Plume signs, with both the Gazette twins even joining in.

"You promise you'll teach us how to write some magic after this is all over, Quinn?" Matteus asked.

"I'll teach you everything I know," Quinn said, "which isn't much *yet*."

"I'm ready," added Monty. "You heard what Tatiana said. We are all coming. So will all the rest of the Plumes when they hear what's happening."

Parker put her arms around them, and the others followed suit.

"You all are going to be great tonight," Parker said. "Trust me—even better than great."

"Where are they?" Parker asked, staring into the choppy water surrounding the island. "They should be here already. It's dusk."

"I've got Plumes lined up all along the shore," Monty said. "When they spot a boat coming this way, they'll give a bird whistle. We have our own bird whistle, Quinn. Did Parker tell you?"

"Nope, but yeah, it sounds great. Whistling makes sense for birdwatching, I guess," Quinn said, scanning the water. "Don't worry, Parker. They know the plan. They'll be here."

"I can't wait here any longer," Parker said, exhaling loudly. "I have something I need to do."

"Where do you need to go? This is happening as soon as they arrive. Waning moon?" said Quinn, gesturing to the darkening sky.

"I'm going to see Owen."

"Owen?" Monty asked, his eyes wide. "Like Owen Wickerland, Owen? The kid who drowned, Owen?"

Parker looked at Monty. "Owen didn't drown. He's alive and in the castle. I have to talk to him before tonight; something about this all still doesn't feel right."

"What?" Quinn said, recoiling at the idea. "Owen's safe. We snuck him back here. He did his part, and now he just needs to hide out while the real Aven returns. Do you realize we have one opportunity to stop the unwriting of Riley—to save him? And you need to see Owen?"

"I know you don't get it, Quinn, but I just have to see Owen. Now," Parker said. "I can't really explain it. Monty is here, and he's got reinforcements. You don't need me."

Quinn shook her head. "I like Owen. But you realize his family thinks he *drowned*. And what if his family finds out you're with him? Or what happened to him was from a magic writer? What do you think happens to us?"

"You don't understand," Parker said, her voice shaking.

"You're right. I don't," Quinn snapped. "We risked our lives. And now there's more risk. It seems like every time we all have a plan, you need to go and do your plan. I—just go. Go, okay!"

"I'm sorry," Parker said. "I am."

"Just go," Quinn said, shaking her head. "I'll catch Monty up. Go."

Maybe Quinn is right. Parker headed back to the castle, stopping to glance over her shoulder at the shore. Monty smiled. Then he mouthed the words, "You got this. Now fly!" back to her, flapping his arms as he did.

I sure hope it isn't a colossal mistake to involve my friends in what's about to happen.

∗∗∗

Parker found her mother in their parent's bedroom.

"Where's Owen?" Parker asked. "I need to talk to him."

"Why? He's safe," she said. "I can show you where he is staying, but no one knows he's here."

"I just need to talk to him."

Mother walked over to a dark wooden chest with brass edging in the corner of the room. She removed the red scarf lying on top and pulled a small key from her robe, unlocking the chest and opening it.

The chest was full of her mother's formal clothing and dresses.

"Why are you showing me this?" Parker asked her.

"Once the chest opens like this," she said, placing the key back into the lock and turning the lock a full rotation to the right, "it becomes an entrance."

The clothing inside folded onto itself in smaller and smaller halves until it disappeared. A long, winding brass spiral staircase extended fifty feet below, lit by a series of torches at the bottom.

It's an Ellipse, a perfectly enchanted place to hide an Illiterate boy. She sure uses a lot of magic for a Motsan.

Her mother placed her hand on Parker's shoulder.

"I know you don't understand. But I've replayed the moment I first told you about Owen every day since you left. I'm sorry, Parker."

Parker nodded, then stepped into the chest and descended the staircase, her mother shutting the chest's lid behind her. At the bottom was a door, and she took a deep breath before opening it and walking into a room decorated similarly to where she'd learned Owen was alive, including a simple bed with a bright bedspread, a chest, and a dresser. Parker's eyes adjusted to the dark room as sconces flickered.

Owen was seated on the bed.

"What are you doing here?" he asked.

"I had to come to see you. Lady Julie said yours is *The Story of Will*. She said you would have a choice. I want to make sure you have everything you need to make it."

Parker pulled out the inkwell and her journal, placing them on the bed between them. The inkwell began to glow.

"This is the Apportionment we told you about, where you find out your order. I know it's supposed to be this big, crazy ceremony or something, but since the rest of the Plumes got their orders, I figure you need yours too."

"The rest of the Plumes? Does that mean—"

"Yep," Parker said, smiling. "It's official now."

"So, what do I do now?"

"Well, you take this quill, put it in the inkwell, and you see what happens." She handed him the quill and slid the inkwell toward him.

Owen smiled and bit his lip, and then he dipped the quill into the glowing inkwell. The room went pitch black, then the ink glowed, the rainbow of colors spinning until it glowed purple and sparks burst to the ceiling. The glowing purple dust formed into a raven that flew through the air, diving and dipping before perching itself on the far wall.

"Owen Wickerland," a voice came from the inkwell. "You will have stories of joy and tragedy, stories that will bring happiness and sadness to others. You will have a choice. You are the Order of Enigma."

He removed the quill from the inkwell, and the candlelight lit the room again. "She said Dagamar was an Enigma. Is that what she meant by I have a choice?" he asked.

"Maybe. I—I don't know," Parker replied. "She said we all have choices. All of us write our stories."

"I'm scared, Parker."

"Me too, but you're safe here. We'll be careful."

Parker returned the inkwell into the hidden pocket of her dress. Then she picked up the journal and placed it in his lap.

"This is my journal," she continued. "Open it."

It was clear he'd never held a book. His eyes moved from the book to her, and she gave him a kind, reassuring nod to urge him on. Then, he slowly opened it, delicately feeling the edges of the paper with his fingers and looking intently at the words she'd written inside. She watched as he studied the words as if he were looking at a piece of art, his hands and fingers pointing to letters and words as he flipped. Then he came to a blank page.

"I want you to write your name."

He turned quickly to meet her eyes.

"I want to see what happens. Just write your name. Have you ever written your name?"

Owen shook his head.

She studied his face, imagining his name, not only the sound but what the connected grooves and sticks of lettering would look like on a page, scribed in ink. "Here, let me show you. Hold it like this," Parker instructed as she picked up the quill in her hand. She didn't have any fresh ink, but some damp droplets remained on the tip.

"We are going to draw a circle—O." Parker gently guided his hand to hold the quill on the page, beginning the stroke of the O. "O is how we write Owen, your name."

He sank the tip of the quill to the paper. A single spot of ink soaked into the page. Then, following Parker's instructions, he swung the quill into a tight circle, creating the first letter of his name.

The quill glowed. Owen continued circling around and around, purple dust rising from the page, enveloping the boy and illuminating the room, the raven circling above them.

He didn't notice, focused on the circle and his motions.

Parker removed her hand from his. He was still tracing the circle with her quill. She reached inside her dress, removed the *Book of the Seven Ancient Stories* from her hidden pouch, and handed it to him, taking her journal back.

"You can have this book and that quill. Quinn picked it out for you," she said, smiling at the boy as he admired the striped feather he was holding. "This journal is mine, but you're the first person besides me ever to write in it. Now, I'll always remember this moment with you. We wouldn't be here without you."

He smiled at her. "Guess that means you're team Owen then. Huh?" he said, his fingers touching the edges of the book now in his lap.

"You know you don't have to do this, right?"

Owen looked at her, the seriousness of the moment visible on his face. "I know, but for the first time in my life, I finally feel like I'm right where I belong," Owen replied. "And I wouldn't be here without you. So no, I don't have to do this. I want to do this."

Parker stood up to go and returned her journal to her dress.

"Just be careful tonight," Parker said. "I'm planning to stay on team Owen for a long, long time."

Chapter Twenty-Nine

The Illiterate Boy

"Parker! Parker! You have got to see this, it's the cutest thing you're ever going to see," Aven said, joining the others assembled in the Hall of Resplendence.

The full moon and clear sky created a warm, inviting feeling as flowering vines filled with white flowers in full bloom climbed the massive columns in the hall all the way to the glass ceiling. The scent of flowers and food blended in near-perfect harmony as musicians greeted the guests as they arrived for the festivities.

Quinn, Monty, Tatiana, and Lady Mary smiled as the sisters reunited with their signature fist bump. Parker smiled at them and put her arm around her younger sister, happy to see Aven again and have all of them together.

Aven took the enchanted leather pouch and opened it for her older sister to peer inside where a three-inch-tall goat, dwarf, and man with gray hair all waved back at her. It looked like a bag full of living dolls with the full-sized oven mitt, measuring cup, and the tea ball next to them.

"It's so nice to be back in Everly," came the squeaky, whispered voice of Beau from the bag. Parker looked to be sure no one heard, then winked back at the goat.

Aven wasn't kidding. They are adorable.

"Who's the man in there?" Parker whispered to her sister. "The tall one with the gray hair."

"Oh, so that's Dante."

"Wait, what?" Parker said as she peered back inside the bag.

"I know, right?" Aven said. "Were. Wolf. For real, he's a real werewolf. The whole full waning moon thing, and this shrinking cup... yeah, so Dante is a werewolf. But, like, the nicest werewolf ever. He said he'll come for dinner. Who knew? Oh, and don't tell the other wolves in the pack because... they don't even know yet. Kinda our secret."

Parker glanced around to ensure no one else was looking and then waved the group inside. They'd all decided it was best to keep the magical creatures hidden for the evening, but they should attend in the event things didn't go according to plan.

"We are grateful you decided to come," Parker said to Mary, Lady Julie's sister who had served as Riley and Aven's de facto guardian for the trek. Mary had also brought the blue lotus, the fourth item on their quest.

"Thank you, all of you. I was angry and afraid, but I couldn't let that cloud stop what I can do for you, for all of us," Mary offered. "We've warned our kingdoms. They all know if for any reason we fail, Dagamar will come looking for them next. For the first time in a century, Zuma has ordered the chain of mice to stop to avoid anyone from discovering their hidden kingdom."

"And Bralwynn was able to talk to the brothers of Bask," Quinn added. "I suppose it was funny, but Riley was right. Once the brothers had someone else to direct their anger toward, they began talking again. One hundred and eighty years of silence, and all it took was our invisible brother taking their things to bring them together."

"And they let Bralwynn leave?" Parker asked. "They didn't send the army after us?"

"She told them of Dagamar's plot," Quinn answered, "and our plans to stop him. The dwarven army is building fortifications in Baskerville and beyond. Only in the event they are needed. They are at war with the elves and know that loyalties are stretched, but Bralwynn promised you'd return the halos."

Parker looked into the pouch again at the group inside, and the flowers on Bralwynn's hat began to dance seeing Parker again. Monty nudged Tatiana as they looked inside the bag and stared at the dancing, high-fiving flowers.

"And Riley?" Parker asked.

"He's where we told him to be," Quinn answered. "I positioned him near the food to keep him occupied. He keeps asking for rotten bark and lima bean shakes, and I don't have the heart to tell him those aren't on the castle's menu. Let's hope no one notices a floating dinner roll or two."

"I said I'd try and babysit," Tatiana said. "But wow, it's a whole lot harder to keep an eye on an invisible kid, P. Like, impossible. I also went to the storarium like you asked and invited all the storytellers and the curator. I thought they'd laugh me out of the place when I invited them, but they all agreed to come—even the super-duper old history storyteller showed."

Parker looked around the room. Nearly all the storytellers had gathered in the Hall. Even her short-lived tutor Frau Dagogus and her mentor from the Storarium had joined.

"And the rest of the Plumes got in," Aven added.

"But how did you get them all inside past the guards?" Parker asked. "They would have gotten suspicious if three dozen kids from our school showed up at the front gate."

"My skills of invention came in handy once again," Quinn said with a wry smile. "We promised all the Plumes a one-of-a-kind ride on an underground roller coaster. That let us sneak every one of the Plumes into the castle under their noses, so no one even noticed. Who could pass up that opportunity? Our cask carriage came in very handy once again."

"I guess the only one who is going to notice is the chef who is probably just figuring out he didn't make nearly enough food for tonight," Aven said, pointing to a few of the Plumes wolfing down the appetizers served throughout the hall.

"The Plumes, they're ready," Monty added, "for whatever tonight brings. Since your inkwell and everything at Drain Day, they all seem like different people—ready to do whatever it takes for one another and Everly. We got our army."

"Quinn and I showed Monty how to use the cask-carriage to get from the castle back to Everly," Aven said, smiling at Monty. "He got a little bit sick on the first ride, but I'm sure you'll be fine if you need to take Riley and escape—if it comes to it. Just don't puke in Quinn's carriage, okay?"

"It won't come to that," Parker replied. "It won't, Aven."

Tatiana said, "We've got the chronicles on hallway duty, the legends on window duty, the scribes on every entrance and exit, the poets are watching your parents, and the enigmas are keeping their eyes on Lazlo. Even though they don't know what their order means, they all feel like they have a superpower or something. It's amazing; you did something special for us all, Parker. Plus, you can see we are all color-coordinated. Legends are all legendary, as you'd expect." She gestured to her outfit.

"We told the Plumes to find Matteus or Marcus at the first sign of trouble," Monty said. "Those two are a head taller than anyone else in the Plumes, so they should be easy to spot."

Parker picked out the twins standing in the crowd, who both spotted her and gave her a small salute in unison.

"And the rest of the Plumes are looking for anything out of place," Monty continued. "I just wish there were a guest list or something, so we knew who was coming or who wasn't supposed to be here. But otherwise, we've got the whole place covered."

"Uh, what do I do?" Aven asked. "Last time, no one told me about the Plumes hand thing. I turned around, and everyone was doing it, so do I get to do the cool birdwatching hand sign thing again? What do I do to help?"

"Just stay out of trouble. Okay?" Parker said. "We got this. We'll protect you."

A frustrated frown appeared on Aven's face, but she nodded as if accepting the instructions.

"We're going to check in with the rest of the Plumes," Monty said, motioning for Tatiana to join him.

Aven nudged Parker. "I was kinda expecting you to show up tonight in those black pajamas with your monogrammed towel as a cape."

Parker smiled, remembering how ridiculous it had been when they'd broken into the library. "You think the cape was too much?"

"So, now we wait," Quinn said, surveying the scene in front of them. "I've got all the items here," she said, tapping the pouch she was wearing around her neck that held the four artifacts. "Aven's got our friends if needed." She gestured to the purse she held. Quinn leaned closer to Parker. "What happens if I can't do it—like what happened on the bridge or the river? What happens if I can't remember the words or do the script, and then everything falls apart? And Riley—"

"Just think of us," Parker said with a gentle smile. "In Serpentine, when we first saw Lady Julie, you were amazing. And then, when we first saw the fire, you kept us safe. You are brave, and you just take charge because you protect us like you always do. Just think of us, okay? That's why I know you'll be amazing. And then afterward, do you think you can help me get my streak in my hair like you? I'm thinking red or maybe orange or maybe both."

Parker nudged her with her elbow, and Quinn smiled back. Quinn mouthed, "*It's going to be okay.*"

The Hall of Resplendence was vibrant, filled with many important people wearing their finest robes, expensive jewelry, and enjoying the celebration. As the food and drink flowed freely, Parker kept her eyes on Lazlo, who stood alone, bandages covering the scratches on his face and arms.

"I've been wondering something," Parker asked out loud. "What do you think she meant when Lady Julie left the inscription 'Truth Inside'? I always assumed it meant my journal and quill, but what if that wasn't the truth she's talking about?"

"I imagine it's what you've been telling us all along," Quinn suggested. "There's a story. And I think Lady Julie wanted us to find it."

"You're right," Parker said. "I think it's something bigger than all of us."

"Bigger?" Quinn continued. "What's a bigger truth than the Ravagers and evil magic writing returning?"

"Well, what if it's not *outside* the room? But what's the biggest thing in the room?"

Quinn raised her shoulder and turned up her palms, shaking her head.

"What if it's Boots?" Parker asked.

"Huh? What does your runaway cat have to do with anything?" Aven said, joining the conversation.

"Lady Julie told us a magical enchantment protects the last item. Right?" Parker continued. "And, we can all see that big Boots is magical. She also said it was more than just an enchantment. She said something Dagamar couldn't break was protecting the item."

"She said protected by love," Quinn said, nodding. "Something impossible for Dagamar but something the four of us could solve, and only the four of us."

"Not many things are unique to only the four of us," Parker said, "except Boots."

"You think Boots is protecting the real fourth item? It is protected by more than magic, so what else could it be? Maybe Lazlo is trying to find whatever Boots is guarding."

"Yeah, he did have pretty bad scratches, and Boots was pretty protective of whatever is in the bindery," Parker said. She remembered the sweet stray kitten who'd often slept in her lap while she practiced her letters and how the cat had become an enchanted lion, tiger, *and* a bear who'd been stung by a million bees all rolled into one.

"I suppose it makes sense," Quinn said.

"My sister is most certainly clever, but I must say we have never spoken of this. As I'm sure she didn't want anyone else to know where she'd hidden the fourth ancient item," Mary said.

"What does it matter?" Quinn wondered. "All three of us are here right now, and Riley is hiding, plus Mary and Julie are both here and are powerful magic writers who can protect us. Even if Lazlo figured it out, Boots isn't going to let that wizard rub her ears."

"I guess you're right," Parker agreed. "Lazlo must have tried to figure out what's in the bindery, and Boots was never a mean cat—unless provoked. I'd guess big Boots gave him a couple of swipes to stop him from trying again."

Trumpets.

The doors to the Hall of Resplendence opened, and the king and queen entered the room dressed in the same royal attire they'd worn to the Drain Day festivities. The Pennymore sisters couldn't quite place four individuals following close behind.

"Who are they?" Mary asked.

This can't be. Who would invite them?

"What are they doing here?" Parker sneered.

"This isn't good," Quinn whispered.

Her parents' guests of honor were Mr. and Mrs. Waddle and their daughter Cassandra. The entire family had the same white-blond hair illuminated by cool, icy tones as if a chill followed them. With Cassandra was Muddle, the blue-eyed boy who called Parker a liar in Avenir.

Parker leaned over to Quinn. "Our father invited leaders of the Illiterates *into* the castle," she whispered. "The same people who had booed him days earlier are now his guests."

"They thought it was over when I gave them the broken quill, remember?" Quinn said. "Nothing changes. We stick to your plan."

Cassandra smiled and nudged Muddle as she made eye contact with Parker.

Parker muttered, "Sure. Nothing changes," as she kept her eyes fixed on the Waddles. Cassandra's father followed behind the two children carrying a metal cane. Parker could see a look of disdain on Cassandra's father's face, probably because her father was never the true king of Everly to old families like the Waddles, given his parentage. Cassandra's father lifted the rod and put it under her chin, prompting her to stand straighter and taller, her smile vanishing as he did. *Maybe her dad can keep her in line tonight.*

"Honored guests," bellowed their father to the room as the conversation fell silent. "Tonight is a celebration—in honor of the return of our daughters, who captured a woman who had forced us to live in fear. Tonight, we celebrate them."

Parker couldn't stop watching Cassandra and Muddle whisper to one another. Applause rolled through the crowd when their father pointed to his daughters. The siblings nodded politely, acknowledging the recognition.

"Because of the witch's capture, I have invited the Waddles as honored guests," their father continued. "We welcome them as we begin to work with them and the concerned citizens of Everly to return our kingdom to the way it once was, making it stronger and safer for all families."

Why can't he just stop trying to fix everything?

Parker's face burned. Her parents had no idea what they'd done. They were welcoming their enemies in. Quinn motioned to the Gazette twins, instructing them to keep their eyes on Cassandra and Muddle.

"A word?" Lazlo stood behind them, his downtrodden, green eyes framed by the bandage on the side of his face. "Your father has asked me to bring the witch here to the hall for confrontation," he said. "He wants this done tonight while the guests are here."

"Why would he want that?" Parker demanded, already angry from her father's decision to bring the Waddles here.

"He believes she'll confess and reveal where Riley is," Lazlo answered. "And I agree. She has strong feelings for you children."

Parker shook her head.

"Do you have your book, Parker?" Lazlo asked.

"My book?"

"The journal. Hidden in your dress, yes," he said, looking at the subtle outline of a book inside her dress.

Parker looked at Quinn, who shrugged. "Why?" she replied, but he said nothing. Then Parker nodded. "Yes, I have it here."

"Keep it there," he instructed. "Always on you."

"Fine," she said. "I will."

"And you've brought the ancient items?" Lazlo continued, turning to Quinn.

"We have," Quinn said, holding out her satchel containing the four items for Lazlo to take.

He cringed. "No, no. You must keep them safe," he stammered. "I simply need to know you have them to save your brother before the waning moon tonight if she reveals his whereabouts."

Quinn returned the pouch around her neck. "You think you can save our brother?"

"Yes, I suspect your brother is near," he said. "And when she reveals his whereabouts, her magic was strong, but you've snapped her quill, so yes, I do."

Parker studied him, trying to understand him. She saw sadness in him. She remembered the boy who she met the night they'd shared stories and she'd learned of his powers. Parker desperately wanted to trust Lazlo, recalling from the stories Lady Julie once read to her, the most wicked of people, those willing to hurt others, turned out to be deeply hurt themselves.

"When the time comes," Lazlo continued as he turned to depart. "I'll call on you."

Our plan is still on track. We knew our father would want to confront Lady Julie publicly to get her to tell him where Riley was. His pride would not let him miss this moment to show his power and reunite his family, whatever the cost.

"We're ready," Quinn said to Parker, patting the satchel.

Parker looked for her friends, quickly spotting Monty and Tatiana engaging with other guests. There were other Plumes wearing reds, blues, greens, yellows, and purples.

But where are the Gazette twins? I should be able to see them.

"Guys, I don't see Cassandra anywhere," Parker blurted out.

"Or the twins," Quinn said.

"She's gone," Parker said, her pace quickening. "Maybe the twins followed her. We can't have the Illiterates snooping around the castle. This could ruin our plan, ruin everything."

"It's okay," Mary said. "She couldn't have gotten far. We'll find her."

"This can't be happening," Parker said, and she looked at Quinn. "Who knows what Cassandra could be doing. This is exactly what I was worried about. She wasn't supposed to be here."

"Let's split up," Quinn said. "It'll be okay. It will. We just need to find her before Lazlo returns with Lady Julie."

They nodded, and the three siblings and Mary moved in opposite directions. Parker felt the familiar tingle in her fingertips. *Just breathe.* She headed into the hallway leading from the Hall of Resplendence.

No one else was in the hallway. As she surveyed for any sign of the twins or Cassandra, her gaze caught on a small, broken shard of wood under the solitary, maroon and gold tapestry still hung in the center of the hall.

Someone found the enchanted library.

Wasting no time, Parker wedged herself through the broken boards. The quills were frantic, diving and dipping, and the leapfrog flames hid in the lanterns. The bookshelves no longer moved, and the books flew in erratic patterns, emitting angry noises. Even the writing desk papers shivered as if they'd seen a ghost.

Parker made her way to the back of the room.

"Help! Parker!"

Owen Wickerland hung by his shirt from one of the torches, struggling to escape.

"Ah, you decided to join us," Muddle called to her from the entrance to the bindery.

"You were right, Parker. I followed her here," Owen said, his voice shaking. "They were trying to get in here, and I followed them both to stop them."

"Silence, boy!" Muddle called out.

A twisting piece of paper from one of the writing desks flew through the air and wrapped itself over Owen's mouth, muffling any sound.

"That's much better," Muddle said with a smile. "A silent *tongue*. So much nicer. Now we can talk without annoying interruptions. The boy who drowned... well, he didn't, I see. Your parents let us believe he did. You Pennymores like to lie. You lied to us. Remember, Owen, how I tried to save you? I tried, and you wouldn't take my hand. Like you wanted to be pulled under the water."

Owen shook his head, trying to move.

"What are the two of you doing here?"

Boots no longer obscured the entrance to the bindery. The massive cat lay on her side and panted in heavy, sporadic breaths as if in a trance, her eyes open, scanning wildly but unable to move. The angry, voracious beast who lunged at her was physically still the same, but now she reminded Parker of the scared stray she'd first coaxed out of the stacks. Boots's strained purr reverberated throughout the room.

Cassandra gently rubbed the tips of the massive cat's ears, the same way she'd first helped Parker relax the stray kitten and eventually make

Boots fall asleep. The tears in Cassandra's eyes and the concern in her face exposed the same worry Parker had for her cat.

"What did you do to Boots?" Parker demanded Cassandra as the cat's calls became more pained and labored.

"I—"

"Shut up," Muddle said, cutting off Cassandra.

It was odd, watching Cassandra care for the cat while the boy who'd followed her around hurled insults at them.

"Why are you here?" Parker continued. "You can't tell the other Illiterates—"

"Oh, can't I?" the boy replied.

"What do you want?" Parker asked.

Muddle laughed, then looked at Parker.

"Parker, I—" Cassandra said.

Muddle reached into his cloak and removed a black quill with an eye above the tip. He pointed his palm at Cassandra and quickly scripted on his fingers. A cloud of eerie magic dust floated to the girl, and she slumped over.

"Her incessant talking was annoying me," Muddle said. "She did what I needed, so I am finished with her. And what about the boy who drowned? What shall we do with him?"

Muddle pointed his palm at the bookshelves and smiled at Parker as his quill glided across his fingers. "Maybe he should drown for real... in *books*?"

The shelves levitated, their wood creaking. Muddle flung his palm toward Owen. Owen's eyes were wide with fear as shelves crashed all around him, breaking and cracking, books piled higher and higher until there was no trace of him.

"Stop!" Parker called out. "He hasn't done anything to hurt you. Why are you doing this? Why did the two of you come in here?"

"Silly girl," Muddle said, as the remaining shelves crashed down around the room. He paced back and forth across the entrance of the bindery. "Cassandra was a pawn in our game. Her movements are my whispers. And all thanks to you."

"Me?"

"Do you think she was smart enough to arrange that little scene at the Drain Day amphitheater? It was easy once Lazlo realized the cat couldn't be defeated with magic alone. You were weak and told him about losing your best friend, Cassandra. Lady Julie didn't realize you had a weakness, but you told Lazlo everything that first night. How your cat loved the four of you, and she told us of the poor animal you'd found, how you'd calmed it down, and how it grew to love you. And her. She knew how to get the cat to do what I wanted."

"Did you kill Owen?" Parker asked, fear beginning to permeate her words. "Did you kill Cassandra?"

"Not *yet*. I'm sure if you listen, you can hear the boy's breath. And Cassandra is sleeping like this cat she loved so much… for now."

Parker reached into her dress and grabbed her quill, holding it in front of her outstretched palm now pointed at Muddle. "Stop or I'll—"

"Or you'll what? You don't know what you're doing with that."

Parker touched the quill to her pinky nail where Quinn had written the synchronous spell, but nothing happened. Then she tried to touch each of her other nails as she'd seen her sister do.

"Put it down," he said, chuckling to himself. "You're pitiful—a magic writer who can't even write."

Muddle smirked as he ran his quill over his hand. A jet of air flew at her hand, ripping the quill from her fingers, letting it float harmlessly to the ground.

"I told you," he said, turning to admire the mass of books and shelves covering Owen, "you're nothing. It's quite hilarious."

Muddle could write magic. Parker knew there were other magic writers, but why would he help Cassandra and the Illiterates if he could write magic? They'd kill him if they learned he could.

"No one is going to save you now," Muddle said, laughing.

Parker froze, trying to understand why Muddle was doing this. Then she reached into her dress and retrieved the small knife she still had in one of the hidden pockets, running toward him with it. Muddle's arm reached out, his palm extended, like an invisible shield formed around him, the pocketknife bouncing away.

"Ah, Parker Pennymore. So confused, I see. Your grandmother gave me that same sad look too," he continued.

"What did you say?" Parker looked around, trying to find anything to help her fight back. "What did you do to her?" Pain raced through her chest.

"Nothing she didn't deserve."

Her head ached, and her heart raced, its beats pulsing to her fingertips.

"Cat got your tongue?" he asked, motioning to her still-panting cat.

Muddle's gaze darted over her shoulder.

A glowing quill whizzed across the library as if it had been tossed at the boy. The first glowing quill arched through the air and hit Muddle in the middle of his chest, a brightly colored blue ink spot covering him.

Another arching quill hit his shoulder, this time red-orange, followed by another and another.

"Haberdash!" Aven called out.

The red, green, and blue colored inks poured over the boy, creating a slippery, sticky mess.

Aven was using Beau's Haberdash bobbin to shoot color splatter quills.

"What is this?" Muddle asked, shaking the ink off his arms.

Sheets of paper folded into swans, birds, dragonflies, and bats, and other flying paper creatures were hurtling toward Muddle. He swatted at them as more and more of it headed toward him, sticking to the ink, pounding him, and pushing him to the ground.

"What did you do?"

Parker smiled and shrugged, even though she didn't know.

"It's a *sub*-plot!" Aven yelled from behind the remaining library shelves. "Now write! Write! Write!"

As the paper animals landed on Muddle, swarms of quills of all colors and shapes excitedly buzzed toward the paper.

"Ouch!" he snapped when the first sharp quill struck him. "What's going on?"

More quills anxiously buzzed to the boy, sticking him with their sharp points as he yelped in pain. He thrashed at them, but as more of the paper airplanes obscured his view, the quills diving in and out toward the paper made multiple strikes. Piles of paper covered the boy, quills sticking him and drawing blood.

Dozens of small, red books threw themselves at Muddle as he struggled under the piles of writing paper.

A red-orange dust cardinal guided the books. It was *her* cardinal.

Her eyes saw the massive mirror. The Scott family mirror wasn't reflecting her image; it revealed how Aven had been orchestrating her attacks.

Parker called out, "You're doing it, Aven!"

Huge brown dictionaries raced over to snap at the spinning red books as if they were trying to catch them, causing more chaos around the boy.

Parker heard a low groan from the pile. Suddenly a terrifying roar boomed out of the growing pile of wriggling paper, attacking quills, and snapping books. "Enough!" Muddle screamed, much louder and more frightening than she'd ever heard from the boy.

A flash and papers, books, and quills exploded across the room. Muddle stood with his palm pointed up, and his black quill was touching his fingernails, his eyes scanning the library.

"Where is *she*?" the boy demanded of Parker, his palm looking for any movement in the library. Muddle snapped his fingers, and his black quill floated from his hand, its tip glowing purple. "Sepitus, find the girl. Now!"

"Run, Aven!" Parker called.

The quill raced to the ceiling and streaked around the room, running right into one of the flying books. The book shuttered, the quill's purple tip searing a hole right through the book, which fluttered and fell to the floor.

Aven scampered toward the exit as Sepitus raced to catch her before she escaped. Muddle rubbed his hands together, then snapped his fingers, calling his quill back to him.

"You think these silly tricks can stop me?" Muddle said, Sepitus now floating next to him. "Me? All you Pennymores think I'm weak, a fool." He turned his back to Parker.

"I don't get it," Parker said. "What do you and Cassandra want?"

The boy laughed. "You can't possibly think I want anything to do with this girl." He pushed at her sleeping friend with his boot.

"But you're a Serif. You write magic," Parker said, staring at the boy's glowing quill. "Then why would you be a part of the Illiterates?"

The boy held up his fist, revealing the four dots she'd seen him wearing before.

"You think I'm an Illiterate?" The dots began to move, spinning around until they vanished from his hand. "The Illiterates were the perfect way to force your father to do what I wanted. His fear and thirst for power made it easy for me to convince him to bring Lazlo inside your home and reintroduce magic writing. Once your father had done as I wanted, the Illiterates emerged from the shadows into the light, exactly when I needed."

"Who are you?" Parker demanded, energy pulsing through her.

"You *know* who I am," he hissed.

The boy narrowed his eyes, pulling off his cloak. His small body began to expand and transform from Muddle the boy into an adult, the larger body inside the boy crawling out.

"The Pennymores have been a scourge on Fonde for far too long," Muddle said as his body transformed. "Your mother and father, Lady Julie, your grandmother, your entire family must pay for that day. They must all face punishment for what they did. The Incendio will return."

Horrified, Parker watched purple dust whirl around the hulking figure.

"I am the one you've gathered the ancient items for. I am the one you've led to the answers. I am the one you've helped return to power to make them pay," came a new adult voice. "We've always had this connection since before you were born, you and I. Now your undoing will allow for my rise again, never to bow to a Motsan *again*!"

The deep scars and burns on the entire left side of his body illuminated under the room's lights.

"Yes, child, you did as I asked. Now *your* story comes to its end as we step from out of the shadows and into the light. The silent darkness is nearly upon us."

Dagamar had returned.

Chapter Thirty

The Unwriting

"A single word from you," Dagamar instructed, "and I'll kill Cassandra."

The three of them slowly walked back to the Hall of Resplendence. Parker transfixed as Dagamar, under the sleeve of his cloak, pointed his quill at Cassandra's back. Cassandra walked in a daze, unaware as Dagamar morphed back into the form of the blue-eyed, Illiterate Muddle.

Parker's heart pounded as she opened the door, entering the Hall of Resplendence with Cassandra and the disguised Dagamar behind her. She hoped Aven escaped to tell Quinn and the Plumes to be ready.

Standing at the front of the room, shackled in chains, was their caretaker, their teacher, their friend.

Lady Julie. Parker froze, afraid of what Dagamar might do to her, to Cassandra, or to the others.

Julie stood across from their father and Lazlo stood nearby, behind a table he'd placed several items upon.

Their father stepped forward. "While no mercy is required, we seek an understanding with you, witch. We brought you into our home, and you took our son. What do you say?"

Parker cringed at the way he spoke to her. She wanted to save Lady Julie from this ridicule but knew she wouldn't want her to. Quinn flinched. She scanned the room for Aven but couldn't see her through the dense crowd.

"I am the witch's sister," Mary called from the back of the hall. "I have come to offer my condemnation for the pain she has caused our family."

Whispers and chatter came from the crowd. "A sister?" voices said.

The crowd began to chant: "Burn the witch! Burn the witch."

"Silence," their father commanded. The room went silent. "While we shall not show mercy, we shall offer her a choice. Where is the child?" their father asked.

Julie kept her eyes down.

"I repeat, where is my son?"

Dagamar yelled from behind Parker, in his Muddle voice, "She *knows*!"

Voices chanted: "She knows! She knows! Burn the witch! Burn the witch!"

"Where is my son?" their father asked again, more resolve in his voice.

Lady Julie focused on the floor.

Lazlo twitched, seemingly aware he only had a few minutes left to harness the power of the unwriting for his master.

"She will be made to speak!" Lazlo boomed, his voice filling the room. He had transformed from the shy, obedient boy into an angry force sucking the energy from the room upon seeing that Muddle had returned to the room.

Lady Julie stalled with silence.

"Where is the boy?" he demanded. "Where is he?" Lazlo slammed his hands on the table.

Her father curiously eyed the boy, having never seen such anger from him.

"Why would you leave us?" Lazlo yelled out.

Lady Julie flinched and cringed at his accusation.

Us?

"Why, witch?" Lazlo shouted again. He knelt and reached behind the table. "You leave me no choice! Tell us where the boy is." A menacing grin spread across his face as he hoisted something onto the table.

A wave of panic rushed over Parker.

A terrified girl looked everywhere for help, her hands and feet tightly tied with rope as she lay on the table.

"Now, you will speak for these children!"

"Aven!" shouted Quinn. "No, let her go!"

"No, Lazlo!" the king called out.

"I will *make* the witch speak, sire," he said to the king, less of a sign of obedience than a sinister threat. "She is weak of mind and cannot bear to see children suffer. Like this one."

The wizard grabbed his quill from the table, placing its glowing tip to Aven's throat.

"Lazlo!" her father said.

"This isn't part of the plan," Parker gasped, turning to see Dagamar smiling. *We've got to protect her.*

Lazlo shook Aven. The crowd gasped and wept.

A green flash burst in the room, blinding everyone for a second.

What is that? "Enough!" the king said, holding out a hand to the young wizard.

"Child!" Lazlo called out, ignoring their father. He stared at Quinn standing in the back. "Bring me the bag, Quinndaline Pennymore. Bring me the ancient items. Now, child!"

"I said enough!" the king shouted again. "Guards! Arrest him."

A dozen men raced at Lazlo from every corner of the room, their swords drawn. Their father drew his weapon and stepped forward.

"Sire," Lazlo replied with a sick grin, "you'll not be issuing orders anymore."

He wrote a series of letters on his forearm, burning his skin as he did. Blue fire encircled his fist. Opening his palm, Lazlo revealed a flaming blue ball.

"Be gone!" Lazlo yelled and threw fireball after fireball at the advancing guards. They exploded with each hit, engulfing them in a magical blue cord before a soldier collapsed to the ground. The remaining guards dropped their weapons.

"You'd be wise to do the same," Lazlo said to Domnall. "Perhaps your children listen to your commands, but I am *not* a child. This is no place for you."

"This is our home!" Domnall yelled. "You *will* listen, boy."

Then the king rushed at Lazlo with his sword raised. Lazlo touched his fingertips, an invisible shield stopping their father's sword in midair. Lazlo's quill moved across his forearm again, and a burst of air flung their father across the room, his body hitting the wall with a thud.

"I said this is no place for you. Now, where is the boy?" Lazlo demanded from Lady Julie.

"Stop!" Queen Pip called out. "Stop this madness, Lazlo."

"Bring me the items, child," Lazlo yelled at Quinn. "I said now!"

Quinn looked at Lady Julie and Mary, uncertain what she should do. Lazlo twitched as she slowly approached him with the bag, placing it on the table and removing the four items inside.

Parker turned to look at Dagamar, the eerie purple tip of his quill pressed into Cassandra's back.

He mouthed to Parker, "She. Dies," shaking Cassandra as he did.

"Wait," Parker called out, "I have one of the ancient items you seek."

Quinn turned to her sister, wide-eyed at hearing Parker's confession.

Parker stepped forward, joining her sister at Lazlo's side. She opened her hand and placed the ancient leather sewing awl from the bindery—that had looked like the small knife in the orb—on the table.

Now Lazlo had everything, except for the boy.

"You think your silence will save them?" Lazlo asked, his words to Julie sharp and angry.

Lazlo moved his hand in the air, moonbeams illuminating as if a spider's web stretched from the moon to every corner and surface of the hall.

"We don't need the boy," Lazlo said through gritted teeth. "We will still harness the power of the waning moon. You, too, can be unwritten," he said to Aven as he waved his glowing quill in front of her face. Hundreds of the bright blue moonbeams affixed themselves to every inch of her body.

"Somebody, anybody, help her!" Mother called out.

"Let *her* go," Parker said to Lazlo in a calm, direct voice. Dagamar tightened his grip on Cassandra.

"You children and this family deserve this," Lazlo said, waving his arm again. Rays of silver-blue moonbeams flickered into the hall, connecting to Aven.

"It's the waning moon," Quinn shouted as the threads pulsed and glowed. "We don't have much time!"

Lazlo laughed as a breeze blew his robes. "Your sister has *no* time!"

Touching the leather bag where each of the ancient items now glowed and pulsed in time with the moonbeams, he screamed, his hand burning from the enchantment on the objects. His face contorted in pain, but he refused to remove his hand.

"Tenebris umbra," he commanded, scripting the letters with the quill onto the stone table as the moonbeams glowed and pulsed faster, concentrating their light on Aven. He raised his glowing quill above his head.

"Farewell, my child!" he called out.

Lazlo brought his quill down hard on Aven's chest.

Parker heard a gasp and shrill cry from her mother.

The quill stopped, hanging in the air inches above Aven's heart.

Confusion rushed over Lazlo's face. He lifted the glowing quill again, yelling as he brought it down harder this time, veins pulsing on his neck, but his quill again stopped just inches from her, unable to pierce the invisible, protective layer around her.

Aven smiled, wiggling the oven mitt on her hand.

"Now!" Parker shouted.

Quinn and Mary pulled quills from their cloaks. The tips pulsed and danced across their fingers as Mary raised her palm at Lazlo, glowing green dust encircling his arm and quill, freezing them in place. Quinn aimed her palm at Lady Julie, and the teal flecks raced to unlock the chains and shackles, freeing her.

Tatiana reached into her pocket and tossed Lady Julie her unbroken quill they'd duplicated and snapped, hidden for this moment.

"Hurry," Parker called to Lady Julie as the waning moonbeams pulled away from Aven and the bright glow faded.

Smoke billowed from Lazlo's hand as the enchanted items continued to burn him.

"*Bolt!*" the three magic Serif writers shouted in unison, letting their quills dot their fingernails as teal, green, and red-orange electricity twisted together, racing from their quills and striking Lazlo in his chest.

The wizard lurched back, his limp body slamming against the wall.

"Watch out! There's more of them!" Tatiana called out as six more of the guests in the hall had removed their quills with black etchings and raised their palms at Julie, Mary, and Quinn.

Quinn wheeled around, sliding perfectly to the left to avoid a bolt that flew toward her, her quill racing across her fingers. Teal dust poured from her palm in the shape of a fox. The dust whirled around one of the Ravagers like a tornado before it knocked him to the ground.

"That's *my* special, little invention," Quinn said with a grin, moving toward the other Ravagers.

"You're up," Parker shouted. Dante let out an ear-shattering howl from the back of the room, Bralwynn and Beau by his side. Dante was twice as large as when they'd first met him. The enchanted purse that had kept this trio hidden and the measuring cup that had grown the wolf to this massive size floated behind the trio. Parker knew her mischievous and invisible brother was carrying them. Dante howled again and chased two of the Ravagers into one of the wings of the hall, pouncing on the terrified men, while Beau and Bralwynn cornered another, knocking the quill from his fingers.

The two remaining attackers crept toward the sisters, palms outstretched and lips moving. Lady Julie and Mary stood back-to-back. Lady Julie raised her left foot and gently tapped her sister's calf. A smile crept across Mary's face, and the sisters each stretched out their arms, forming a back-to-back T. Then they twisted their hands and began to write on the *other* sister's nails.

The pair moved their arms as if they were flapping.

Boom! Boom! Boom!

A sonic wave burst out from their arms and knocked the two Ravagers to the ground.

Storytellers from the storarium pulled their hidden, glowing quills and raced to the fallen Ravagers. These Serifs knelt on each of the Ravager's arms, gathering the dark quills from their hands, while Parker's mentor ran to the side of the hall to check on her father. The Plumes joined them, moving people away from the Ravagers and the unfolding chaos.

"Go," yelled the storarium curator to the Windhorn sisters. "We've got them!"

Julie and Mary turned and ran to Lazlo's table.

Aven sat up on the table, a familiar smile on her face. "It's our plot twist!" she called out, waving the oven mitt covering her hand to her mother. "Turns out this *was* a pretty great gift. You were right. Grandma gives the *best* gifts."

Mary quickly untied Aven, who bent to lift Riley onto the table. The moonbeams disconnected from her and reattached to Riley.

Lady Julie arranged the four ancient items, including the key.

"Rest, my child," she said as she gently laid the invisible boy down on the table, cupping his head in her arm much like she'd done the day she'd first taken him away from the castle to protect him and the kingdom. Julie placed the glowing fabric from Zuma over Riley, slid the halo bracelets onto each of his arms, and squeezed the enchanted key in his left hand. Then Mary took out the blue lotus flower and placed it on his forehead.

"The moon!" shouted Aven as the weblike beams started to pull away from Riley's body.

Mary and Julie held hands and touched their quills into the last strand of the waning moonbeams: "Levis umbra!" they called together, writing the words onto the boy.

A flash of light filled the room, and everyone covered their eyes.

Riley appeared, levitating as if suspended by the moonbeams that shimmered through the glass ceiling. His wide eyes scanned the room as those gathered began to whisper and gasp. The vanished boy had returned.

"Riley!" Mother called, running forward. "Riley's alive."

Everyone stared at the glowing boy suspended by moonbeams. Smiles crept across the faces of the storytellers and curators. The Plumes and the others gathered hugged, cheered, celebrated, and gasped at the power and spectacle of the scene before them. They'd done it.

Parker saw a flash of red as the orange-red cardinal hovered and glided near the doors to the Hall of Resplendence. She felt the warmth of the stone on her chest and reached up to touch it.

Everything slowed, each second a minute. The beautiful bird flew above the doors to enchant her and call her to look.

What are you trying to tell me?

Parker turned to see Dagamar throw Cassandra to the ground, his glowing dark quill in hand and his face filled with rage. His body shook as he again transformed into an adult, the scars on the left arm pulsing as the whirl of purple dust enveloped him, his bright blue eyes fixed on Riley. His lips moved. Dagamar was summoning his own incantation. She watched as he pushed past those staring at her levitating brother. Then, Dagamar raised his palm toward Riley, his dark-eyed quill now moving from finger to finger, scripting his powerful enchantment.

As his quill touched his thumb, a magnificent flash exploded from his palm.

Parker felt a perfect calm wash over her mind and body. Then she rushed forward, throwing herself between Dagamar and Riley.

Everything went black.

Chapter Thirty-One

The Etching

"I think she's waking up," a muffled voice said. "That's it… open up those eyes…"

Parker opened her eyes to a circle of people around her but unable to make out their faces. Her throat was dry, and her body throbbed and ached from head to toe.

"How're you feeling?" Quinn asked.

"She's awake now. Is it howling time?" Aven asked. "Can I please celebrate with a howl now that she's awake?"

As Parker's eyes refocused, she saw her mother beside her, gently stroking her cheek. Her siblings, parents, and Mary and Lady Julie filled the room. They were all here, safe.

"You gave us quite the scare, child," Lady Julie said.

"Wha-what happened?" she said weakly.

"Rest your voice," Lady Julie said. "You've been out for the last two days. We've all been very worried."

"Is Riley okay?" Parker asked.

"Ask him yourself," Lady Julie said as he moved into her view.

Parker smiled at the sight of her brother. Tiny freckles still dotted his cheeks. His mischievous grin was something she'd missed over the last year. "Hiya, Parker," he said, his rolled R's filling her with happiness.

Parker looked at Julie. "You stopped it? The unwriting?"

"Yes," she replied with a warm smile. "Your brother is safe from the unwriting—it skipped him. We are not done with the forces of the unwriting, but you children are all safe for now."

Quinn moved in front of Riley. "You are the coolest sister in the world. You know that. Right?"

Parker nodded. "Good role model," she said.

Quinn wiped the tears forming in the corner of her eyes. "When you stepped in front of Dagamar, you probably had no idea."

Quinn ducked out of view for a moment and returned holding Parker's purple journal with its eight-pointed compass on the front, much like what had guided them to obtain the ancient items.

"When Dagamar scripted his powerful spell," Quinn said, waving the journal in front of her, "it hit you. And this blocked it—*your* book. His spell rebounded and threw him against the wall. Suppose you didn't have your journal hidden in your dress. Who knows what would have happened. Look."

Quinn flipped the book over where the plain purple back had been replaced with an ornate gold and silver etching like on Quinn's fingernails. When Quinn tilted it, she saw the distinctive crown of the red cardinal. Tiny threads moved as if the journal was alive with the twinkles of a million stars.

"It's remarkable," Lady Julie said. "The words, your words, saved you. They saved us all."

"But I didn't write magic," Parker said.

"Yes, what you had written in this book is not magical but was still powerful enough to stop the magic of the strongest Serif in Fonde. Your words protected your family and stopped him."

Parker studied the etchings on the book, wanting to run her fingers over the tiny lines, patterns, and marks without corners or ends. She thought back to the moment when she'd seen the dark wizard lunge forward, the anger in his eyes and the dim purple glow from his quill.

"But wait," Parker said. "What happened to Dagamar?"

The whole room exchanged looks, shaking their heads. "He got away, Parker," Riley said.

Her father leaned forward and put one of his hands on hers. "It all happened too fast," he said. Parker saw his other arm must have been injured from Lazlo's blast and was now in a sling. "We were unable to capture him or Lazlo or the other Ravagers. They all escaped in the chaos. But we're safe. We're all safe."

Her heart sank. She desperately wanted this to be over.

"I know now I let Lazlo into the kingdom and Dagamar with him, and that was a mistake. I didn't realize what I'd done trying to keep the kingdom safe," their father continued. "There are consequences to my decision, and I know that."

"Father sent soldiers back to Serpentine," Quinn added. "They were never supposed to burn it. That wasn't the order. So they've found everyone, they've gathered all the people who lived in the castle and brought them back here. To be safe."

"Yes," Father continued. "We had no idea at the time, but Ravagers infiltrated our guards. They scripted a powerful spell over the soldiers trying to find you. The Ravagers were looking to find you, too, but once they knew you weren't there in Serpentine, they knew destroying it would force you to return to Everly. It was their plan all along, and I'm so, so sorry."

Parker nodded; his hand grabbed hers and squeezed.

Over his shoulder, Quinn mouthed, "He's trying," and Parker nodded to her and smiled at her father. She knew this all couldn't be easy on him, either.

"But everyone saw the magic writing," Parker said weakly. "Cassandra, her parents, the Illiterates, all of them. They saw the magic. They saw all of you and the others write."

Mary placed her hand on Parker's.

"Only the Serifs in the room saw," Mary offered. "The bright green flash before Lazlo drew his quill was me. The flash made sure only those who could write magic saw what happened. Most only saw the flash and then nothing until Dagamar was gone."

"Anyone who saw it," Quinn said, putting her hand on Parker's shoulder, "now will know they are a magic writer. A few people might be surprised when they realize it too."

"There are many here now with us in Everly protecting the kingdom," Mary added. "They've come because you helped reveal his aims. Whereas before, you might have missed the signs that magic writers were amongst us. I'm certain you'll see we are not alone in this fight anymore."

Parker knew she wouldn't ever see the animals in the barn quite the same. "What about Owen and the rest of my friends?" Parker asked. "Dagamar and the shelves in the library. I—I couldn't help him."

"You know a shelf is no match for me, right?" Owen said, stepping into her view from behind her father.

"You saved Owen's life," Lady Julie said. "Arcus led us to Owen."

"Arcus?" Parker asked.

"Yes, your quill with the red tip on the feather," Lady Julie said, giving Parker a confused look. "Your quill... Has no one told you your quill has a name? Well, in that case, I'll tell you your quill is called Arcus. She'll be with you for quite some time—keeps you safe and keeps an eye on you..."

"For your overbearing parents," her mother added with a smile.

Parker smiled.

Arcus. Arcus is a good name for a quill. A perfect name.

"When Lady Julie came to you after Dagamar had hit you," her mother continued, "she found your quill, and it led us back to the library, and then Arcus wouldn't let us leave until we'd rescued Owen. Who knows what would have happened if you hadn't found Dagamar first."

"See, I always knew you were team Owen," the boy replied with a wry smile. "Arcus too."

"This is Trinket," Quinn said. She gave a soft whistle, and Arcus and Trinket, Quinn's quill with its flecks of gray and white and a blue circle at the top, burst out of one of Quinn's pockets and excitedly raced around Parker. "I think they'll get along well."

"Hi, Trinket," Parker said as the quill gently glided past her before they both whizzed out of view to hide again in one of Quinn's pockets.

"I'll keep her safe for you," Quinn said with a smile. "And the rest of your friends are all outside. They haven't left your side once. We had to put Monty in talking time out. That guy just will *not* shut up. But it's okay. They were pretty worried about you."

Aven craned her head for Parker to see her and formed a circle with her thumb and forefinger, spreading her other fingers out as if they were feathers. "The twins said I'm an official Plume now," Aven said. Parker smiled, mimicking the sign with her hand resting beside her.

"Even Beau, Bralwynn, and Dante stayed to keep an eye on you," Aven added as she leaned over and opened the enchanted purse where they'd been during the attacks. "We didn't want to freak the doctors and everyone else out. I mean, a talking goat, a wolf, and a dwarf are a lot to take in. So, they went back to small size again and got to ride with me."

Parker peered into the bag and waved down to them.

Beau motioned to her, and a squeaky voice rose out of the bag. "It's wonderful to be back again with you in Everly, Madam Pennymore," he called up. "Although I must say your sister is a far *less* hospitable host than you were."

Aven quickly closed the bag. "Beau is just mad because I beat him at Haberdash again. He's been teaching me everything about Haberdash—he says I'm a natural with a bobbin. There are a few ink spots in our room... and on your bed. Sorry."

Parker smiled at her. "Thank you for everything," she whispered to the bag.

"Oh, I almost forgot. Uh, how amazing was my plot twist, right?" Aven asked.

"That was the best plot twist, Aven. The absolute best," Parker said nodding, grateful her idea had kept everyone safe.

"Without your plan, we don't believe Dagamar would have revealed himself to us as he isn't fully healed and hasn't truly regained all his power," Julie said. "Your idea, your twist as you called it, finally brought him out of the shadows. And now that he's out, we can be vigilant to keep him far away from here."

"Now we are not alone in this fight," Mary added.

Quinn squeezed Parker's shoulder. "Your Plumes are pretty anxious to get their leader back. Monty has some big ideas. But not all of the Plumes saw what happened because of Mary's inscription, including Monty. Remember, he's not a Serif, so he and some of the other Plumes don't remember much of anything. You'll probably have some explaining to do. But we've told those who saw everything what this means for them. All of them will be glad to know you're all right. We got an army now." Quinn leaned down to her sister and whispered, "We are the they."

"Okay, okay. Let's give Parker a little space," Lady Julie said. "Plenty of time to talk. We'll have your friends come to see you once you've had a bit more time to rest."

Everyone moved away, their voices and laughter lifting her spirits as they left the room. Even Aven got to howl, a softer, less ear-piercing one than usual.

Her mother lingered in the room, waiting for them to exit before closing the door. "How's my girl?" Mother said.

Parker smiled back at her. "I'm okay. Pretty sore."

"You know, you probably saved Owen and Cassandra's lives in the library," she continued. "That was brave, going into the library alone. Your courage and commitment to him told me *I* needed to be braver myself."

Her mother took Parker's hand and squeezed it three times.

"We brought Owen's parents here to see him, and I told them the truth."

"You told them everything?" Parker asked, aware of what that meant.

"Everything. We suspected part of the reason Owen survived the drain is that he was a Serif, but you sensed it before anyone else. We didn't have proof, but the boy had a brush with magic, which scares anyone, especially if your family members are Illiterates. After you stopped Dagamar, we showed Owen's parents their son's powers, we gave him a quill, and they saw he's a magic writer. They were terrified of him. But they were incredibly grateful for you, Parker, for keeping him safe. And they didn't want him to be hurt. Being a writer and a magic writer is... well, it's still perilous. They decided it was best to send Owen away."

"Away?" Parker asked with sadness in her voice.

"Yes, he won't go home with them. We are taking him to live at a literati library in the Northern Pass. They'll keep him safe and help him to learn to harness his writing powers."

Parker nodded, her smile matching her mother's. "So, a literati library does exist beyond the Northern Pass."

"It does. And we are sending *you* away too," her mother said. "We are sending you and Owen to live with your aunt, my sister."

"That's the aunt you were talking about," Parker said. "Your younger sister is a Serif, huh?"

"She is, and she's heard a lot about you and is pretty excited to meet you. *Only* if you want to go, though. We are hoping you'll go with Owen to keep him company. To learn how to harness your power. You'll write again and learn magic writing too. And you'll finally get a chance to meet your cousin, who is quite the character, you'll see. I suspect the two of you will have some interesting times."

It sounds like I won't be locked in some drafty dungeon with a straw bed and singing squirrels after all.

Parker felt a lump in her throat, realizing what this all meant for her, their family, and Everly.

Ring-ring. Ring-ring.

Parker looked to her feet, and she saw a small collar with a bell floating in front of her. *A floating collar with a bell?* The bell jingled again, and she saw her cat Boots suddenly become visible as she turned around and around to find a comfortable spot to lie down.

"She's back to Boots size," Parker said, smiling at the cat.

"Yes, and she's not nearly as angry as she was in the library when she was *big* Boots," her mother added. "As you just saw, she needs to wear that bell now because she now has this very odd ability to make herself visible or invisible. You have no idea what it's like to have an invisible cat jump on your lap when you can't see her. It scared the dickens out of me."

"I'm just glad she's back," Parker added, gently jostling the cat nestling between her feet.

"And we know what you did for Cassandra too," Mother continued. "Dagamar used her and her family. Cassandra doesn't remember any of it. She doesn't know what you sacrificed for her."

Her mother paused, holding Parker's hand.

"I know she was your friend, but the Illiterates have not changed their minds. When your father broke the sacred law against magic writing, he became a ruler they may never trust. Dagamar is no worse than any other writer or magic writer in their eyes. We're not sure if Everly will ever return to the way it was. I'm sorry you lost your friend. I wish she knew what she'd lost too."

Parker nodded. She still had questions and wondered when her parents would tell her about their past and the secrets they'd refused to share.

"Thank you," Parker said to her mother. "Did they find Grandmother? Where is she?"

Her mother let out a worried sigh. "No, and I'm torn up about it. But I'm sure she's safe. Scotts know how to take care of themselves, and she's as feisty as they come. As Lady Julie said, you've got a lot of your Grandmother in you. I know this: your grandmother would be extremely proud of you."

"I miss her. We—we have to keep trying to find her."

"I know. And we will. I know you must have so so many questions about what happened, our family, and your story," Mother replied as she patted her daughter's wrist. "That's your destiny, Parker Pennymore, my storyteller. All that's for another day. First, you should get some rest."

Parker almost pressed her, but she knew this story was still to be written. It was her destiny to discover the truth. And she would.

"Oh, we found this in your journal," her mother said, handing Parker a small, folded piece of paper, still wrapped in string. "I didn't open it, but it looked like you meant to save it."

Her mother patted Parker's hand and left.

She held the small piece of paper given to her by the storyteller at the storarium, her mentor, before she'd left. She'd never had time to open it and read it.

She carefully untied and unfolded the paper, read it, and then placed it on her heart.

It read:

All Writing Is Magic

THE END.

This map of Fonde was hand drawn using a quill and inkwell by Chaim Holtjer

Acknowledgments

Writing the Pennymores was exponentially more rewarding than I could have ever imagined.

On New Years Day 2021, we started creating our story. At first, this was a simple bedtime story that Quinn, Parker, and I imagined and built together. But after feeling the energy in the room that very first night, I knew needed to capture what was transpiring and began recording the audio from these nightly conversations. Night after night, we built on the story and after a month of bedtime conversations, the three of us had imagined characters, a world, a conflict, and an adventure that would become the Pennymores. Those recordings became the early foundation of this book.

I have to start by thanking my awesome wife, Allison. She first encouraged the idea of imagining our own stories and then let the three of us stay up far later than normal so we could finish discussing "just a few more details." Allison always encouraged us to imagine, to laugh, to discuss, and to continue. She is as important to this book getting done as anyone. Thank you so much!

Quinn, Parker, and Aven are the stars of the Pennymores, and it was your imaginations, ideas, sparks, and encouragement that kept us putting words on the page, making this book become more than just our bedtime story. Quinn's "what about...", Parker's "oh, this would be a good idea..." and Aven's ear-splitting howls made the process of creating the book just as rewarding as the final product. This book will always be something that encapsulates what was special about the extra time the pandemic brought us with the three of you.

I'm grateful for Brian Bies who encouraged me to see this book as a learning and growth opportunity. It might have been easy to push me to stay in my lane and to write another nonfiction book. Instead his belief in me and this project, plus his support, have made it possible.

Telling a bedtime story was far easier than turning that story into a book. I am in awe of authors like J.R.R. Tolkien, CS Lewis, JK Rowling, Rick Riorden, Neil Gaiman, Victoria Schwab, Daniel Handler and many many more who bring childlike wonder onto the page. Writing this story for my first novel wouldn't have been possible without my writing coaches and editors, ChandaElaine Spurlock and Haley Newlin. I've been fortunate to know both of you through our shared work helping and coaching other authors. I was already sure you were both were magnificent, but when you were teaching, supporting, urging, and helping us with the Pennymores I realized what it feels like to have someone else love these characters and this story as much as we did. I learned so much, am a better teacher and writer for it. The Pennymores wouldn't be what it is with you both.

We were fortunate to have incredible artists help this book. Nurkaydar Tomiris was our character and sketch artist who patiently turned words and imagination into the character art and sketches you see throughout the book. As an art student from Kazakhstan, we were grateful for her commitment to this project. Gjorgji Pejkovski and Bojana Gigovska designed our incredible cover art.

To produce a book, you need a group of people who believe in the story far beyond just the editorial help, beautiful artistic support, keen insight, and ongoing support in bringing our story to life. Amanda Brown, Leah Picket, Ethan Turer, Brian Bies, Grzegorz Laszczyk, Mateusz Cichosz and others from the New Degree Press publishing team were amazing partners. It is because of your effort and encouragement that others will get to experience this magical world that simply didn't exist before.

Finally, we are particularly grateful for an extra special group — our real world Plumes. You were kind and gracious enough to read this story when it was still incomplete and messy, share thoughts on the ideas, sketches, and covers, or offer kind words of encouragement for the concept. You helped make this book a true community. For many, many of you, I reached out and asked for a small favor (little did you realize I was going to be asking you to not only read it but help us make the book better.) So many of you saw the magical potential in moments and helped us to find where our quill still needed a bit more magic (and we know the early versions some of you read sure did!) It was special for me to bring together people from my past including family members, elementary school, high school, college and graduate school friends, and various colleagues from stops along the way. Plus, I was incredibly fortunate to have the help and support from many authors and writers I've come to meet through their own books. The coolest part was me and my girls getting to meet children, nieces, nephews, grandchildren, neighbors and classmates of people from my own past (especially with people all over the world).

You are our Plumes and we forever will give you our Plume sign for your help!

We are eternally grateful for each of you as early readers and supporters. Know that without your input, the Pennymores wouldn't be what it is today:

Gabriela & Walter Afable, Mohammed Ali, Nifemi Aluko, Brian Anderson, Sean Armstrong, Jennifer Rose Asher, Jaime Atilano, Emily & Jodie Austin, Helena Backus, John Backus, Keriann Baker, Mary & Brock Banks, Cora & Brooks Thompson, Jennifer Barnes, Shoshi & Jason Barnwell, Hadley, Mila, Mia & Michelle Basilio, Adam Basma, Nico & Connie Bateson, Miles & Asher Bearman, Buster Benson, Nolan Beran, Molly Biedermann, Kristi Bigos, Alex, Gracie & Barbara Bijelic, Brooke & Lindsey Binstock, Kristie, Jacquilynn & Aji Fung Blase, Brenna Blaylock, Ben Bolte, Landry, Fuller, Bennett & Trey Bowles, Jessica, Katelyn & Dan Bradach, Kelsey & Scott Bragg, Nolan Braman, Kate Riles & Maria Brendel, Adam Brock, Jeremy Brown, Brandon Bruno, Evan Burfield, Michael Buse, Brian, Lilah & Joon Byun, DeDee Cai, Ashley & Spencer Calhoon, Kerri Bongle, Jennifer Ruege, & Maryn Camacho, Michael Caprio, Elizabeth Cardone, Meg, Quinn & Joel Carney, Juvencio Castro, Victoria Charters, Andrew & Steve Chiagorus, Grace Chowdhry, Kamilyn & El Ciammaichella, Lila & Caleb Clark, Sophia & Christina Conroy, Pasqualina Coppola, Ava & Susan Corke, Kent & Benjamin Corley, Connor & Matt Crespin, Mary Crocker, Finn & Brendan Cronin, Michaela Cullan Altenhofen, Jeff Curry, Caroline & Calista Edwards, Tracy Deutmeyer, Ava, Will, Olivia & Matt Devlin, Casey Dexter, Lauren DiTullio, Warren Dotson, Andrew & Jodi Drake, Gina Droegkamp, Alain & Ava Eav, Maddie, Thomas & Katie Ebert Enos, Alki Economou, MaryBeth Edmundson, Spencer & Laura Edwards, William Ehrlich, Carl & Dominic Esposito, Katy Everett, Alexa, Ryan, Patricia & Mike Fasciotti, Janine & Dave Fell, Noah Fenstermacher, Joe Fernandez, Rhys & Desmond Fernando, Sophia Warren & Rachel Fleishman, Mike Folden, Shepard & Courtney Foster, Clinton Foy, Cory Frankiel, Charlie, Andy & Cara Frasco Lai, Jack & Nicole Fuentes, Will Fuentes, Lexi & Ben Fuller, Ceci, Oakley & Arianna Gallo, Jacob Gardner, Dave Gartlan, Teddy, Liz & Gavin Gaukroger, Jennifer & Parker Gaynor,

Sarah Gerin, Isadora, Spencer & Jane Ginns, Cranston Gittens, Sean Glass, Audrey & Joseph Gnorski, Michelle Goñi, Matias Gonzalez, Bella, Abby & Michael Grace, Julie, Miley & Braydin Grady, Sophie, Charlie & Lisa Johnson Graziano, Gaby Grebski, Amelia & Adele Green, Anika Gupta, Arya Gupta, David Hain, Jennifer Hale, Bassil Hamideh, Chaetan, Kavia, Praveen Misra & Dana Harrar, Justin Heather, Lauren Heidbrink, Aaron & Joe Heitzeberg, Josephine & Maria Hench, Steve Hennessy, Ollie, Mabel, & Christine Henningsen, Logan & Bruce Henry, Allyson Hernandez, Jenny Herritz, Shayla Herron, Madison & Nicole Herter, HanhLinh Ho, Evie, Hannah & Greg Hosé, Josh & Amanda Huetinck, Jeanne Hull, Trey Humphreys, Olivia Hussey, Elizabeth Ivanecky, Dustin Jackson, Bibiana Jakubianska, Sam Jammal, Julie & Steve Jones, April Jones Rector, Kenneth Joyner, Kekanumaikawaiake'anae & Kelii Kaneshiro, Nancy Kantor, Arabella & Isabella Kapuschansky-Rivera, Alessandra Kariotis, the Keefners, Jonathan, Isabella & Harper Kennedy, Saad Khan, Taylor Kickbush, Julia Kim, Sierra & Rob Kimmer, Carrie Kingston, Donte Kirby, David Kirchofer, Andrew Klein, Nickey Knighton, Annie Fahrenkrug, Pei-Ru Ko, Jack, Evie & Ben Koch, Darren Kochansky, Kathy & Larry Koester, Mark Koester, Miles, Titus, Drew & Amanda Koester, Linda Kolterman, Shannon, Jamie & Henry Konn, Matthew Kopf, Francis Koykar, Jeffrey, Quinn, Ella, Penny & Layla Krajicek, Lauren Krasnodembski, Esme, Oliver & Laura Kravet, Joe Krebs, Nile Kurashige, CeCe & Brad Kwiatek, Chris Kyle, Charles E Lagerbom, Jill Laing, Ava, Niko & Mike Lamberson, Clare, Conor, Nora, Angela & Jason Langenfeld, Eleanor & Courtney Larkin, Iman Lavery, Kelly & David Lawler, Kate Lehman & Anna Brokaw, Belinda Lei, Anna Lenaker, Mason, Josie & Matthew Ley, Charlie & Tyson Leyendecker, Mika & Jeremy Lightsmith, Lisa Liljegrun, Julie Little, John Locke, Leah Umezaki & Jamie Long, Evan, Owen & James LoPiccolo, Lizzie, Frankie & Riley Lorenz, Corwin Lothlorien, Rebecca Lovell, Shane Mac, Jennifer MacPhail, Emma & Sara Magnussen, Luke, Connor, & Jasmine Marchant, Meredith Margolis, Kate, Joshua & Rachel Markell, Paul Marsnik, Chrissy Martin, Paula Gutiérrez Martínez, Jim Massey, Scott Mathews, Steven Matos, Gabby, Ben & Andrea Mausbach, Jill McCall, Rebecca McDermott, Kellan, Toran, & Erin Byrne McElroy, Alexandra, Meaghan & Lisa McManus, Brianna & Brandy McMillion, Aidan, Cavan, Kat & Christian McMurray, Greg & Annie McRobbie, Kelly, Charlie, Mae, David, & Teddy Meiners, Courtney Mellinkoff, Izzy Mendoza, Kaia, Shannon & Sean Miglini, Ashlyn & Pete Miller, Erin & Harrison Mickel, Alexa, Aaron & Dan Mindus, Derrick & Billie Minor, Malu Mirones, Shawn

Mirza, Praveen Misra, Evie & Megan Mocho, Olivia Monteleone, Dave Morin, Ella & Heather Morrison, Jon Myalls, Daryn Nakhuda, Sonz Nath, Maggie & Colleen Naughton, Finn & April Neale, Kit & Jason Nellis, Shayleah Neth, Hanna Newlin, Scott Newman, Victoria Ogunniyi, Danielle Galiette Orchard, Aidan & Josh Orosco, Isabella, Frankie & Cris Otepka, Kerry & Ella Pace, Amanda Page, Kimberly Page, Elaine Pan, Alisa Parenti, Kiran, Mihir & Jigna Patel, David Pierce, Stacey Pierre, Alexis & Jenna Pietropola, Charu & Khelan Pillai, Jake & Vadim Polikov, Ava, Jennifer & Ryan Pollard, Daniel Post, Joseph & Alexis Post, Audrey, Lindsay & Jake Punzenberger, Susan Puska, Christina Qi, Bridget & Kelly Quigley, Wan Rahardja, Jivika Rajani, Ellis & Jeremy Reding, Christopher & Carrie Reed, Ryan Reed, Henry, Charlotte, & Kevin Reiner, Josh Rickel, Pilar Rivera, Parker & Nicole Roberts, McKenzie & Jason Roberts, Daniel Rossi, Chris Rotella, Caroline, Cienna & Callia Sabo, Linda Saether, Mary Ann Saiyed, John Saunders, Aria, Elsa & Raegan Sawyer, Gianna & Bill Schindler, Joseph Schmidt, Sarah Schott, Jack & Megan Schulte, Oliver & Heather Schwartz, Meredith Schwartz, Courtney Hoke Schwenk, Andy & Aurora Sedlacek, Dolimami & Mansi Shah, Audrey & Jeff Showalter, Srushti & Skanda Shyamsundar, Nicole & Christopher Sievers, Shannon Simmons, Melissa Skelton, Alyssa Skites, Jeff Slobotski, Kay Smeal, Lily Smith, Mary Smith, Allison Soled, Allie Soucie, Andrew, Natalie & Audrey Sousa, Sammy Spector, Laurie Spector, Bill Speros, Kat & Shannon Stabbert, Maddi & Christina Stange, Jason Steele, Lily & Shelly Steffen, Becky Steinbach, Bailey & Cristy Stewart-Harfmann, Claire, Natalie, Jack, Lydia & Al Stonich, Jeremy Streich, Nicaury Suarez, Maria Fernanda Suarez, Ileana Sung, Timmy Tamisea, Caroline Tan, Michelle Tanney, Avery Tarp, Alan Tauber, Hillary & Corwin Taylor-Hartle, Brooke Timmer, Timothy Ting, Lola, Jack & Ben Travers, Julia Tvardovskaya, Henry & Molly Twellinger, Heather Underhill, Kiki Van Son, Kimi Vander Ploeg, Liam & Adam Vaughan, Kailey Walters, Robb Warren, Shannon Watson, Evi & Jessica Webster, Ruby Wei, Dave Weinberg, Corrie Westmoreland-Vairo, JJ & Justin Williams, James Wilson, Anthony Wong, Dustin Woodard, Yerusalem Work, Khadijah Wynter, Flora Yang, Christina Yao, Cathan, Tina & Allen Yap, Carol Yee, Mandy & Mary Yount, Mohammed Yousuf, Gabrielle Zora.

Made in United States
North Haven, CT
06 March 2023

33662807R00207